Dracula's Guest

Dracula's Guest

A Connoisseur's Collection of Victorian Vampire Stories

Edited by Michael Sims

Walker & Company

NEW YORK

Published by Walker Publishing Company, Inc., New York

All papers used by Walker & Company are natural, recyclable products
made from wood grown in well-managed forests. The manufacturing pro-
cesses conform to the environmental regulations of the country of origin.

Library of Congress Cataloging-in-Publication Data

Dracula's guest a connoisseur's collection of
Victorian vampire stories / edited by Michael Sims. — 1st U.S. ed.
p. cm.
Includes bibliographical references.
ISBN 978-0-8027-1971-3
1. Vampires—Fiction.   2. Horror tales, English.   I. Sims, Michael, 1958–
PR1309.H6D73 2010
823'.0873808—dc22
2010004449

Visit Walker & Company's Web site at www.walkerbooks.com

First U.S. edition 2010

1 3 5 7 9 10 8 6 4 2

Typeset by Westchester Book Group
Printed in the United States of America by Worldcolor Fairfield

I felt in my heart a wicked, burning desire
that they would kiss me with those red lips.

—Jonathan Harker
in *Dracula*, by Bram Stoker

Contents

Part III: *The Fruit*

❋

Introduction: The Cost of Living

I DON'T REMEMBER WHEN the nightmares began. Looking back now, I'm inclined to assign my vampire dreams a start date of early adolescence, but perhaps I'm influenced by pseudo-Freudian mis-information and the urge for a tidy narrative. Did the dreams be-gin earlier? I don't know. But they had become common by the time I reached my midteens.

I was experiencing the usual hormone-fueled typhoon of ado-lescent angst—shyness, arrogance, lethargy, ambition, energy, re-sentment, fear. But I had also lost my father at a very young age and found that his death's legacy was my own anxiety, distrust of life, and conviction that I too would die young. Not surprisingly, vampires weren't the only recurring theme in my nightmare play-list. For a couple of years, I was one of those teenage boys who can't resist the horrific. I read about ax murderers, the Holocaust, bubonic plague, werewolves, nuclear war, vampires. Thanks to TV, I dreamed a panoply of vaudevillian overkill—gunshot, stab-bing, explosion, a push from a high building, a runaway car with crippled brakes. Books fueled the fires of anxiety. Poe contributed such charming scenarios as being buried alive or starving while trapped inside a walled-up room. During my childhood in rural eastern Tennessee, one night when I was inspired by W. W. Jacobs's brilliant ghost story "The Monkey's Paw," I dreamed that my dead

1

grandfather limped up the gravel road from our family cemetery and tapped on my bedroom window. He wanted me to join him. Of course he did; the dead always want us to join them. They frighten us because we know that someday we will.

What I recall about my vampire dreams is not the kind of cinematic adventures that amuse my mostly peaceful sleep nowadays, but instead a sense of darkness and attack, betrayal and violation, the terrifying moment at which a dream swirled out of control and the vampire lunged toward my neck. At this instant I would awake, gasping. Because of these teenage dreams, I have always associated vampires with the essence of nightmare—the dead coming back for the living, or breaking their contract with life by never dying at all, and the wild-animal savagery in an attack by biting. What could be more terrifying than the poisoning and eventual theft of such an intimate and essential part of yourself—your own sacred blood? Well, perhaps one scenario is even more frightening: the thought of finding *yourself* doomed to become a vampire, to eternally prey upon your fellow human beings.

Despite my nightmares, I never woke up anemic. Eventually the dreams stopped and I grew up and worried about job security and health insurance instead of monsters. Eventually I found myself in the happy daylight job of nature and science writing. My childhood spooks and goblins became extinct, I assumed, because science's rational spotlight erodes their natural habitat—darkness. But I must have missed the dark shadows, because I can't resist the shameless melodrama of the best vampire stories of the Victorian era, and I seldom tire of either misty moors or cobblestone streets. This is the loony period in which medical first aid—even for vampire attacks—usually begins with a cry of "Brandy! For God's sake, bring her some brandy!"

Soon I found myself back among the old stories that used to terrify me, plus many I had never read before. No, my nightmares didn't return—but about halfway through one of the tales in this volume, I suddenly glimpsed myself as a sleepless teenager, instinctively tapping into the venerable and potent unease that character-izes this kind of story. In this book, you will encounter memorably chilling moments such as these: a literal race against death in which a man on horseback tries to escape from a terrifying child vampire and the rest of its family; a young bride who fears that she has in-herited the family bloodthirst; and a man who abandons his wife because he has brought her sister's corpse back to some semblance of life. If you think of the Victorians as waistcoated prudes with BBC accents, you're in for a shock.

CERTAIN THEMES AND IMAGES recur often in Victorian vampire stories, from the magical power of blood to the Christian sym-bolism of the crucifix. The natural history of vampires is also fascinating—the fear of dead bodies that emerged out of crowded eighteenth-century cemeteries and plague-ridden corpses, as well as the real-death circumstances that kept corpses from behaving in the grave as people believed they ought to. After all, the fear that ghoulish revenants can come back for the living did not emerge out of thin air.

Should you already be a fan of the early writing in the vampire genre, you know what to expect in the pages ahead. If you're new to it—arriving only with a mental image of *Buffy* or *Twilight* or of Christopher Lee waking in his coffin with sudden chest pain—you will soon observe some commonalities among these tales. "Vampire stories" wouldn't be its own species of supernatural fiction without certain taxonomic peculiarities that a reader learns to expect. Surely we return to a genre, be it Gothic romance or film noir, because we seek a predictable emotional or aesthetic satisfaction. When I pick up a good Victorian vampire story, I know it will provide a few tonic goose bumps, a comfortably brief holiday jaunt to my favorite historical turf, and a bracing frisson of my own mortality.

So what can we generalize about Victorian vampires? They are already dead, yet not exactly dead, and clammy-handed. They can be magnetically repelled by crucifixes and they don't show up in mirrors. No one is safe; vampires prey upon strangers, family, and lovers. Unlike zombies, vampires are individualists, seldom traveling in packs and never en masse. Many suffer from mortuary halitosis despite our reasonable expectation that they would no longer breathe.

But our vampires herein also differ in interesting ways. Some fear sunlight; others do not. Many are bound by a supernatural edict that forbids them to enter a home without some kind of invitation, no matter how innocently mistaken. Dracula, for example, greets Jonathan Harker with this creepy exclamation that underlines another recurring theme, the betrayal of innocence (and also explains why I chose Stoker's story "Dracula's Guest" as the title of this anthology): "Welcome to my house! Enter freely and of your own will." Yet other vampires seem immune to this hospitality prohibition.

One common bit of folklore was that you ought never to refer to a suspected vampire by name, yet in some tales people do so without consequence. Contrary to their later presentation in movies and television, not all Victorian vampires are charming or handsome or beautiful. Some are gruesome. Some are fiends wallowing in satanic bacchanal and others merely contagious victims of fate, à la Typhoid Mary. A few, in fact, are almost sympathetic figures, like the hero of a Greek epic who suffers the anger of the gods.

Curious bits of other similar folklore pop up in scattered places. Vampires in many cultures, for example, are said to be allergic to garlic. Over the centuries, this aromatic herb has become associated with sorcerers and even with the devil himself. It protected Odysseus from Circe's spells. In Islamic folklore, garlic springs up from Satan's first step outside the Garden of Eden and onion from his second. Garlic has become as important in vampire defense as it is in Italian cooking. If, after refilling your necklace sachet and outlining your window frames, you have some left over, you can even use garlic to guard your pets or livestock—although animals luxuriate in soullessness and thus appeal less to the undead.

The vampire story as we know it was born in the early nineteenth century. As the wicked love child of rural folklore and urban decadence, however, it showed a marked resemblance to both parents and their long family histories. As the chronological selections in this anthology unfold, the genealogy of Victorian vampires' forebears and heirs will be revealed, demonstrating what made the vampire mythos of the time so compelling, evocative, and influential.

But what *is* a vampire? How might we define a cultural icon so familiar that you need only a set of plastic fangs to get into a costume party? "A dead person," runs the definition in *The New Penguin English Dictionary*, "believed to come from the grave at night and suck the blood of sleeping people." Actually not all of vampires' victims are sleeping when attacked, but the key points we're all familiar with are here: vampires are already dead; they're coming back from the grave despite this considerable handicap; and they're out for blood. Yet vampires and zombies, both risen from the dead, differ in interesting ways. Zombies seem motivated largely by other concerns than the perpetuation of their own foul existence. Vampires' incentive is not necessarily bloodlust so much as the thirst to prolong life—or at least life's dark doppelgänger, the state of being undead, trapped in the agonizing limbo between life and death and clinging desperately to it because even undeath seems better than oblivion. Vampires nourish themselves on the living not merely out of revenge but in seeking renewal, and in doing so they slowly drain the victim of life force.

This distinction is why vampires have become such a potent metaphor over the last couple of centuries. They played a well-established role in the public imagination long before *Dracula* was published in 1897. Thirty years earlier, Karl Marx described capitalism as "dead labor, which, vampire-like, lives only by sucking living labor, and lives the more, the more labor it sucks." Six years before *Dracula*, John Tenniel, the popular cartoonist and illustrator of Lewis Carroll's *Alice* books, portrayed the Irish National League's opposition to British rule as a vampire bat hovering over a swooning woman. Perhaps the most striking Victorian analogy with vampires appeared in 1888, the year of Jack the Ripper's rampage, when the *East London Advertiser* summoned the undead to explain the monster who prowled their streets at night:

> It is so impossible to account, on any ordinary hypothesis, for these revolting acts of blood that the mind turns as it were instinctively to some theory of occult force, and myths of the Dark Ages arise before the imagination. Ghouls, vampires, blood-suckers . . . take form and seize control of the excited fancy.

Most of us have known someone we thought of as a psychic vampire, one of those negative souls who feed off others' energy, who take endlessly without giving. Such bloodless vampires are common in fiction, and they raise an important question: Is it the presence of blood or—as the metaphors mentioned above indicate— the act of depriving others of their life's energy that identifies a vampire in our minds? For *Dracula's Guest*, I have mostly chosen stories from within the ranks of the truly bloodthirsty, but I couldn't resist including a couple of chilling adventures from the borderlands of this definition. These outside-the-fence tales only emphasize the potent myth that animates the others.

FOR VAMPIRES, THE COST of staying alive, or at least of staying not quite dead, is the price of lives other than their own—as if, when they have exhausted their own allotted wealth, they can steal someone else's to keep the creditor at bay. We can see a less religious version of the same idea in the legend of Elizabeth Báthory, Hungary's infamous sixteenth-century "Blood Countess." A historical figure who was accused of torturing and murdering dozens if not hundreds of girls and young women, the countess was protected from a death sentence by her aristocratic position, but several of her co-conspirators were themselves tortured and executed. Her legend, however, has eclipsed even her official rap sheet. The most common scenario, invoked in both horrific entertainment and sermons on vanity, claims that she bathed in the blood of virgins to prolong her youth—sort of a Botox vampire.

In mythology and religion, the practice of drinking human blood is frowned upon because blood always represents far more than nutrients. Sacred strictures from the Talmud to the Koran forbid the consumption of blood of any kind, equating it with the soul. In Leviticus, Yahweh warns that he will set his face against anyone in the house of Israel who eats blood. The admonition shows up elsewhere in the Bible, too, including Genesis and this verse from Deuteronomy: "Only be sure that thou eat not the blood: for the blood is the life; and thou mayest not eat the life with the flesh."

Like most of public Victorian Europe, vampire stories take place against a Christian worldview, so vampires respond to a crucifix as Superman does to kryptonite. This image of the repelled fiend backing away from the symbol of Christianity is so prevalent that the Lutheran Church once ran a magazine ad showing Bela Lugosi's Dracula approaching a victim with a cruciform shadow behind them and this caption underneath: "Are your kids learning about the power of the cross from the late, late show?" The crucifix symbolizes the magical value of blood sacrifice, the core tenet of Christianity. Many commentators have pointed out that the Catholic doctrine of transubstantiation, the belief that during a Communion mass the wine and wafer literally become the blood and flesh of Christ ("Drink ye all of this, for this is my blood"), makes Communion a form of cannibalism if not vampirism.

"In this writer's own informal but extensive observation," writes horror scholar David J. Skal, "the vampire myth resonates with a particular strength with lapsed and ex-Catholics—scratch a vampire buff, and it's more than a little likely you'll find a Catholic school uniform bunched beneath the cape." Joyce Carol Oates wrote an essay that examines Bela Lugosi's Dracula as a dark priest in black vestments, the evil twin of the priests of her childhood. Needless to say, there are countless vampire fans who did not grow up Catholic, including myself, but the Church's influence remains throughout the genre.

AS IS REVEALED IN Part I, especially from the supposedly non-fictional accounts of eighteenth-century vampires, the predecessors of the Victorian stories emerged from all over the map of Europe—urban France, rural Russia, the islands of Greece, the mountains of Romania. Many sources inspired these ideas. Nowadays, for example, most of us never see a dead body; in the industrialized world, death is sanitized and hidden offstage. But during the Middle Ages and the Renaissance, dead bodies were a common sight. Plague and countless other illnesses ravaged every community. Corpses of the executed and tortured were publicly displayed. Once buried, few bodies seemed to rest peacefully in the ground. With a frequency that we would find unbelievable, people in the eighteenth century had an opportunity not only to see corpses but also to glimpse them again *after* they had been buried. Cemeteries in urban areas were densely overcrowded, with the dead stacked several graves deep in some places. More corpses than the ground could assimilate resulted in the stench of decay and the ever-present risk of disease.

Desecration of graves was common for many reasons, including the growing need for illicit cadavers in medical dissection, but primarily inspired by religious rivalry. For example, after Louis XIV abolished the monastery at Port-Royal des Champs as a hotbed of Jansenist heresy, drunken locals were caught disinterring nuns' bodies from the cemetery and permitting dogs to devour them. Bodies of executed heretics were dragged through the streets, then reburied in too-small graves by breaking the body into small pieces. French Protestants were not legally assured of a consecrated burial until the revolution in 1789.

In his 1746 compendium, *The Phantom World*, excerpts of which appear in Part I, Dom Augustin Calmet writes at length about "the vampires or ghosts of Hungary, Moravia, and Poland; of the vrou-colacas of Greece." In a section headed "Do the excommunicated rot in the earth?" he explores the common fear that the body of a heretic does not decompose but instead lingers in the earth, pro-faning the laws of God in death as it did in life, polluting the ground with its sinfulness and disease. Unlikely comrades, such as Academy scientists and village priests, found themselves allied in the antipollution movement, fighting for the segregation of ceme-teries to rural areas beyond dense centers of population—where their decomposing inhabitants could inflict less harm on the living. Scholar Marie-Hélène Huet sums up the subtext of many early vam-pire accounts: "All the dead are vampires, poisoning the air, the blood, the life of the living, contaminating their body and their soul, robbing them of their sanity."

Not surprisingly, decay within a subterranean chamber was little understood at the time; no forensic Body Farm to graph a corpse's fade from stink to bones to a mere stain in the dirt. Any variation from a presumed norm in decay provoked fear. Yet what people were unable to comprehend within their limited frame of reference is that there are innumerable ways a body may change after death. Graves in different climes and latitudes vary enormously, depending upon air temperature and humidity, soil composition, insects and other subterranean animals, and the microscopic sanita-tion workers who turn us all back into the dust from which we came. (About these latter creatures, of course, the vampire-fearing were completely ignorant.) Lime helps preserve a body, as do clay soils and low humidity. Some coffins defend their inhabitant better than others.

Yet all sorts of natural bodily changes were revealed to posthu-mously convict someone of vampirism. Fingernails, of course, don't actually continue to grow after death, any more than hair does, but as fingers decompose, the skin shrinks, making the nails look ab-normally long and clawlike. After sloughing off its top layer, skin appears flushed as if with fresh blood. Damp soil's chemicals can produce in the skin a waxy secretion, sometimes brownish or even white, from fat and protein—adipocere, "grave wax." In one eye-witness account from the eighteenth century, a vampire is even found—further proof of his vile nature—to have an erection. Yet the genitals often inflate during decomposition.

And what about the blood reported around the mouths of resurrected corpses? This phenomenon, too, has a surprisingly natural explanation. Without the heart's pump to keep it moving, blood, like other liquids, follows the path of least resistance and pools at the lowest point available. Many bodies were buried face-down, resulting in pooled blood in the face. Blood also gets lifted up toward the mouth by the gases of decomposition. Life is messy, but death is messier, even without invoking the supernatural undead.

We can learn even more about the origins of vampire stories by looking at the reasons why someone might turn into a vampire after death. Much of the original folklore does not include our familiar theme nowadays, that the undead recruit their own next generation by infecting victims when they drink their blood. Peasant superstitions were saturated with the fear that a corpse might spontaneously transform into a monster even without its having made any unwilling blood donation during life. Suicides were considered a high risk for posthumous transformation, as were murderers, their victims, felons of every stripe, the battlefield dead, stroke victims, the drowned, the first person to fall in an epidemic, heretics, wizards, redheads, curmudgeons, women of ill repute, and people who talk to themselves. Alcoholics were considered especially likely to return as vampires.

With these signals of potential unease in the grave to warn them, grieving survivors tended to emphasize prophylactic strictures in the hours and days following death to reduce the likelihood of such a tragedy. In fact, as Paul Barber and other commentators have pointed out, one reason that suicides, murder victims, and those slain in war made it onto this list of vampire nominees may be that, dying unattended, they were not properly escorted from this world into the next. Every culture has its venerable funerary procedures, comprised half of primordial custom and half of imaginative response to natural history. With communicable disease rampant, for example, it was a sound idea to dispose of the deceased's belongings in the grave alongside the corpse—a habit for which archaeologists are always grateful. Other notions seem less reasonable to us now, such as keeping mirrors away from the dead, so that doubling the corpse's image won't result either in its living on after death or in the death of another.

The risk of trouble at the end of life might even be signaled at its beginning. Some children were thought to arrive in this world marked with a warning that they would have trouble leaving it. Those at risk included babies born tailed, furry, split-lipped, with an extra nipple, out of wedlock, or with a red birthmark. Anything blood-red is a helpful badge of vampirism. Those born with a red caul, instead of the normal grayish white, were prime candidates. The amniotic sac that protects a fetus in the womb remains intact through only about one tenth of 1 percent of births, or even fewer now with prenatal medical interference. Throughout history this rarity has contributed to the idea that such a birth betokens good luck in childhood and the rest of life; this belief, too, is medically sound, because the sac protects the infant from infection. (David Copperfield is born with a caul, which is later, to his discomfiture, raffled off.) But a red sac, resulting from prenatal bleeding, naturally wound up on the list of warning signs for vampirism. Worried parents tackled this risk head-on by preserving a red caul, drying it, and sprinkling it into the child's food as a form of inoculation. In myth and superstition, the line between natural and supernatural has always been blurry.

ONE REASON TO KEEP a corpse indoors until burial was that outdoors it ran the risk of a bat flying over it. Such proximity alone might communicate vampirism. Any animate creature passing over the corpse however, might have the same effect. Bats—despite their crepuscular habits and their refusal to fit snugly into a single category with either birds or beasts—were not considered particularly important in early vampire folklore. Europe has no indigenous blood-imbibing bats, so these animals could not join vampire folklore until after Europeans learned of their existence elsewhere in the world. This meeting of myth and reality took place in the eighteenth century, just in time for the Romantic revolution, with the discovery of the bloodsucking Central and South American bats that the legendary taxonomist Georges-Louis Leclerc, Comte de Buffon, soon dubbed "vampire" bats. Blood is a distilled, nutrient-rich fluid. Many creatures—including lampreys, leeches, one species of catfish and one finch, as well as vampire bats—have evolved clever methods to tap into its stored nourishment, a survival mechanism that scientists call hematophagy. Even the imagination of horror writers rarely surpasses nature's reckless creativity.

The discovery that bloodsucking is not an imaginary form of predation added new cachet to vampire stories, but in turn such fiction seemed to taint real-life exploration. Many naturalists faced incredulity as they returned from foreign lands with exotic animals or their remains. When Charles Waterton, the nineteenth-century English naturalist and explorer, described his experiences with vampire bats, his account sounded to many like peasant folklore:

At the close of the day, the vampires leave the hollow trees, whither they fled at the morning's dawn, and scour along the river's banks in quest of prey. On waking from sleep, the astonished traveler finds his hammock all stained with blood. It is the vampire that hath sucked him. Not man alone, but every unprotected animal, is exposed to his depredations: and so gently does this nocturnal surgeon draw the blood, that instead of being roused, the patient is lulled into a still profounder sleep.

It didn't help Waterton's reputation that he did indeed perpetrate a hoax or two, employing his extraordinary skill at taxidermy, but his account of the vampire bat was accurate. The three known species—*white-legged, hairy-winged*, and the more common one cleverly dubbed *common*—are all native to Central and South America. (These three are the only known blood-feeding bats among eleven hundred species; most are highly beneficial to humans, feeding on countless millions of insects every night.) Two of these species feed primarily on birds or small mammals, but the common vampire bat finds human blood the tastiest of meals. It facilitates its bloodthirst with heat-seeking thermoreceptors worthy of the Pentagon. While dining, the bats inject their victims with an anticoagulant enzyme to keep the nutrients flowing smoothly. And what might this glycoprotein be called? Draculin, of course. You may consume it yourself one day. Draculin's four-hundred-plus amino acids are many times stronger than any other known anticoagulant; as a consequence, a drug derived from it, desmoteplase, has been approved for victims of stroke or heart attack.

A vampire bat's saliva even produces a compound that prevents the edges of its victim's wound from constricting. Lacking fat in their diet to bind protein, the vampire bats possess a curious trait familiar to fans of their human counterparts: they must feed every single night to quench their steady thirst for blood. As a further example of Bram Stoker's outrageous legacy in the modern world, scientists have also identified fossils of a prehistoric giant vampire bat, which they inevitably named *Desmodus draculae*.

LIKE MOST PEOPLE I know who aren't historians, I tend to casually say "the Victorian era" as if referring to a brief period characterized by definite commonalities. Yet Victoria ruled Britain and its empire from 1837 to 1901—and besides, this book includes authors from several other countries. So I use Victoria's reign as the time span of Part II, with Part I devoted to Victorian authors' recent ancestors and Part III to their immediate descendants, leading up through World War I, or roughly a generation after Victoria's death. The borders of a time period are as porous as those of a nation, and the calendar itself is arbitrary.

In this book you will find authors not only from Britain but also from the United States, France, Germany, and Russia. As we all know from the books and movies of the twentieth century and of our science fictional new millennium, vampires have a global appeal, but it's interesting to see that the earliest stories about them are equally widespread. Long before the media whirlwind surrounding new books and movies about them, vampires had been established as international celebrities.

Their star power also attracted some fine writers. The roster of brilliant authors within includes, for example, Lord Byron, Aleksei Tolstoy, and Fitz-James O'Brien. A new anthology in any genre must decide upon a policy toward the usual suspects: How many of the acknowledged classics ought to be included and how many can be omitted to make room for equally deserving but lesser known gems? In *Dracula's Guest*, you will find a compelling blend of the finest stories in both categories. We can't explore the great original vampire tales without Byron's and Polidori's groundbreaking contributions. But I omit their contemporaries' early vampire poetry, to make room for less famous but even more powerful works, such as Johann Ludwig Tieck's and Theophile Gautier's stories. Sheridan Le Fanu's novella "Carmilla" is brilliant and influential, but its length would be out of proportion to the other stories here—and besides, it has already been endlessly reprinted. Some stories that show up often in vampire anthologies aren't truly vampire stories (such as Eliza Lynn Linton's "The Fate of Madame Cabanel") or just barely sneak in under that definition (such as Guy de Maupassant's "The Horla"). So I omit these and make room for some of the fascinating nonfictional accounts from over the centuries, including eye-witness reports of seventeenth-century exhumations and on-sight exposure to nineteenth-century superstitions.

I have assigned titles to excerpts by choosing a phrase from within the text.

In a number of places throughout this book, you will glimpse the role of dreams in the making of these fictions. As I began writing this introduction, my own teenage nightmares came to mind in part because recently I had been reminded that a number of horror stories have resulted from or been influenced by nightmares. Even Horace Walpole credited a dream with sowing the seed of his melodramatic novel *The Castle of Otranto*—the book generally considered to have launched the Gothic revival of the late eighteenth century. All he could remember of his 1764 dream "was that I had thought myself in an ancient castle . . . and that on the upper-most banister of a great staircase I saw a gigantic hand in armour." It was enough. "In the evening I sat down to write." Walpole's contemporaries, such as the English novelist Ann Radcliffe and the Swiss painter Henry Fuseli, deliberately consumed raw meat and other troublesome foods in the hope of provoking interesting nightmares. Byron and Coleridge turned to opium. Shelley liked laudanum. During the famously stormy summer at the Villa Diodati in 1816, with Shelley and Byron, Mary Wollstonecraft—not yet Mary Shelley—woke from a nightmare to begin writing *Frankenstein*.

This tradition continues today. One June morning in 2003, a twenty-nine-year-old named Stephenie Meyer, who had never written a book before, woke up to vivid memories of a dream. She dreamed that a young woman and a young man were carrying on an intense conversation in a woodland glade. The woman, really more of a girl, was an ordinary human being. "The other person," Meyer later recalled, "was fantastically beautiful, sparkly, and a vampire." He wasn't attacking her, but he was talking about his *desire* to attack her, his attraction to the scent of her blood, and his determination to resist because he was in love with her. After feeding and dressing her three children, Meyer postponed as many household tasks as possible in order to type up the dream before it began to fade. The result grew into *Twilight* and its sequels, some

of the bestselling fiction of recent memory and the inspiration for
the series of blockbuster films. It seems appropriate that the most
popular characters in contemporary vampire lore—the latest heirs
to Lord Ruthven and Varney and Dracula—appeared in a vision
while Stephenie Meyer was asleep. For centuries, the restless undead have crept in and out of our dreams.

"You begin in a very Victorian manner," I said;
"is this to continue?"

"Remember, if you please," said my friend, looking at me over
his spectacles, *"that I am a Victorian by birth and education,
and that the Victorian tree may not unreasonably
be expected to bear Victorian fruit."*

—M. R. James

I

The Roots

Jean-Baptiste de Boyer, Marquis d'Argens

(1703–1771)

BEFORE WE BRING OUR Victorians onstage, we need a glimpse of certain real-world attitudes toward the undead that were well established before even Byron put quill to paper. These are the stories that were circulating among both peasantry and gentry in the century before the one that mostly concerns us in this anthology; they formed the raw ore from which the Victorian era would refine an entire vampire mythology. The Renaissance rediscovery of classical learning and art had resulted in the period to which historians have since pinned such labels as the Enlightenment and the Age of Reason. The German philosopher Immanuel Kant invoked a line from the Latin poet Horace as the motto of the entire period—*Sapere aude*, "dare to know," meaning to think for yourself instead of merely trusting authority. But the era doesn't look enlightened or reasonable in these eyewitness accounts of vampire frenzy.

Jean-Baptiste de Boyer, the Marquis d'Argens, was a French Enlightenment philosopher and writer—a *philosophe*, a public intellectual engaged with the issues of his time. His youth seems to have been one wild carouse even after he joined the military in his midteens, and eventually his father disowned him. As an adult, however, Argens became well-known for his many writings, helping disseminate the ideas of Voltaire and of Pierre Bayle, the advocate of rational religious tolerance, and of Bernard de Fontenelle, who is often considered the first popular-science writer. The thirty-eight volumes of writings Argens left behind include the *Correspondance philosophique* (*Chinese Letters, Jewish Letters, Cabalistic Letters*, and others) and an earlier work that was revised and expanded into fourteen volumes of a *History of the Human Spirit*. Argens spent a quarter of a century in the court of Frederick the Great at Potsdam, beginning when his patron was merely Prince Frederick. While in Berlin, he married a French actress.

His account of "a scene of vampirism" comes from Letter 137 of *Jewish Letters*, first published anonymously between 1738 and 1742. Augustin Calmet, whose work follows this selection, included this excerpt from *Jewish Letters* in his own *Phantom World*, which is why the two have the same translator, an industrious Victorian named Henry Christmas.

They Opened the Graves

WE HAVE JUST HAD in this part of Hungary a scene of vampirism, which is duly attested by two officers of the tribunal of
Belgrade, who went down to the places specified; and by an officer
of the emperor's troops at Graditz, who was an ocular witness of
the proceedings.

In the beginning of September there died in the village of Kivsi-
loa, three leagues from Graditz, an old man who was sixty-two
years of age. Three days after he had been buried, he appeared in
the night to his son, and asked him for something to eat; the son
having given him something, he ate and disappeared. The next day
the son recounted to his neighbors what had happened. That night
the father did not appear; but the following night he showed himself, and asked for something to eat. They know not whether the
son gave him anything or not; but the next day he was found dead
in his bed. On the same day, five or six persons fell suddenly ill in
the village, and died one after the other in a few days.

The officer or bailiff of the place, when informed of what had
happened, sent an account of it to the tribunal of Belgrade, which
dispatched to the village two of these officers and an executioner to
examine into this affair. The imperial officer from whom we have
this account repaired thither from Graditz, to be witness of a circumstance which he had so often heard spoken of.

They opened the graves of those who had been dead six weeks. When they came to that of the old man, they found him with his eyes open, having a fine color, with natural respiration, nevertheless motionless as the dead; whence they concluded that he was most evidently a vampire. The executioner drove a stake into his heart; they then raised a pile and reduced the corpse to ashes. No mark of vampirism was found either on the corpse of the son or on the others.

Thanks be to God, we are by no means credulous. We avow that all the light which physics can throw on this fact discovers none of the causes of it. Nevertheless, we cannot refuse to believe that to be true which is juridically attested, and by persons of probity.

Antoine Augustin Calmet

(1672–1757)

BORN IN 1672, THE French monk Antoine Augustin Calmet had the scholarly good fortune to live during the frenzy of vampire encounters reported during the early part of the eighteenth century. What we now read as quaint folklore was breaking news to him. Educated by Benedictines in Breuil, he joined their order in 1689 and was ordained a few years later, after which he taught theology and philosophy. Slowly he assembled a massive two-part, forty-nine-volume study of the Bible.

Although that popular anthology's characters include resurrected corpses, a talking donkey, and demon-haunted pigs, apparently these wonders were not enough to satisfy Dom Augustin's appetite. He enters our story because, late in life, he wrote a different kind of book that became something of a surprise bestseller when published in 1746. Originally burdened with the exhausting title *Dissertations sur les apparitions des anges, des démons et des esprits, et sur les revenants et vampires de Hongrie, de Bohme, de Moravie, et de Silesie*, it was translated into English in 1850 by the British scholar Henry Christmas, under the evocative title *The Phantom World*.

This fascinating and outrageous volume—basically a compilation of ghost stories and theological commentary upon them—asks such questions as "Can a man really dead appear in his own body?" Calmet ranges from vampires in Moravia to ghosts in Peru. One moment he is cheerfully citing the eyewitness accounts of learned Christians and the next skeptically analyzing the words of peasant or pagan. Calmet solemnly recounts stories of bodies being ejected during the night from their consecrated graves, coughed up by the earth itself, because during life the individuals had been excommunicated. He also narrates in detail several alleged accounts of vampire attacks. Calmet speculated that perhaps a belief in vampires resulted from a lack of nutrition, leading to blood poisoning that prompts the imagination to turn morbid.

Some of Calmet's accounts appear here, following excerpts from his preface and his introduction to Part Two, "Dissertation on the Ghosts Who Return to Earth Bodily, the Excommunicated, the Oupires or Vampires, Vroucolacas, Etc." (The latter word is the Greek name for vampires and related to the Russian word *vourdalak*, both of which we will encounter later.)

In the following montage of excerpts, line spaces indicate more sizable deletions than those noted by the standard ellipsis.

Dead Persons in Hungary

Preface

My AIM IS NOT to foment superstition, nor to feed the vain curiosity of visionaries, and those who believe without examination everything that is related to them as soon as they find therein anything marvelous and supernatural. I write only for reasonable and unprejudiced minds, which examine things seriously and coolly; I speak only for those who assent even to known truth but after mature reflection, who know how to doubt of what is uncertain, to suspend their judgment on what is doubtful, and to deny what is manifestly false.

I HAVE ALWAYS BEEN much struck with what was related of the vampires or ghosts of Hungary, Moravia, and Poland; of the vroucolacas of Greece; and of the excommunicated, who are said not to rot. I thought I ought to bestow on it all the attention in my power; and I have deemed it right to treat on this subject in a particular dissertation . . . The subject of the return of vampires is worthy the attention of the curious and the learned, and deserves to be seriously studied, to have the facts related of it examined, and the causes, circumstances, and means sounded deeply . . . I have been reproached for having related several false histories, several doubt-ful facts, and several fabulous events. This is true; but I give them for what they are.

Dissertation on the Ghosts Who Return to Earth Bodily, the Excommunicated, the Oupires or Vampires, Vroucolacas, Etc.

EVERY AGE, EVERY NATION, every country has its prejudices, its maladies, its customs, its inclinations, which characterize them, and which pass away, and succeed to one another; often that which has appeared admirable at one time, becomes pitiful and ridiculous at another . . . Towards the end of the sixteenth and at the beginning of the seventeenth century, nothing was talked of in Lorraine but wiz-ards and witches. For a long time we have heard nothing of them. When the philosophy of M. Descartes appeared, what a vogue it had! The ancient philosophy was despised; nothing was talked of but ex-periments in physics, new systems, new discoveries. M. Newton ap-pears; all minds turn to him. The system of M. Law, bank notes, the rage of the Rue Quinquampoix, what movements did they not cause in the kingdom? A sort of convulsion had seized on the French.

In this age, a new scene presents itself to our eyes, and has done for about sixty years in Hungary, Moravia, Silesia, and Poland: they see, it is said, men who have been dead for several months, come back to earth, talk, walk, infest villages, ill use both men and beasts, suck the blood of their near relations, make them ill, and finally cause their death; so that people can only save themselves from their dangerous visits and their hauntings by exhuming them, impaling them, cutting off their heads, tearing out the heart, or burning them. These *revenans* are called by the name of oupires or vampires, that is to say, leeches; and such particulars are related of them, so singular, so detailed, and invested with such probable circumstances and such judicial informa-tion, that one can hardly refuse to credit the belief which is held in those countries, that these *revenans* come out of their tombs and produce those effects which are proclaimed of them.

IT IS TRUE THAT we remark in history, though rarely, that certain persons after having been some time in their tombs and considered as dead, have returned to life. We shall see even that the ancients believed that magic could cause death and evoke the souls of the dead. Several passages are cited, which prove that at certain times they fancied that sorcerers sucked the blood of men and children, and caused their death. They saw also in the twelfth century in England and Denmark, some *revenans* similar to those of Hungary. But in no history do we read anything so usual or so pronounced, as what is related to us of the vampires of Poland, Hungary, and Moravia.

THE VROUCOLACAS OF GREECE and the Archipelago are again *revenans* of a new kind. We can hardly persuade ourselves that a nation so witty as the Greeks could fall into so extraordinary an opinion. Ignorance or prejudice, must be extreme among them since neither an ecclesiastic nor any other writer has undertaken to undeceive them.

THE IMAGINATION OF THOSE who believe that the dead chew in their graves, with a noise similar to that made by hogs when they eat, is so ridiculous that it does not deserve to be seriously refuted.

Let Us Now Examine the Fact of the *Revenans* or Vampires of Moravia

I HAVE BEEN TOLD . . . that it was common enough in that country to see men who had died some time before, present themselves in a party, and sit down to table with persons of their acquaintance without saying anything; but that nodding to one of the party, he would infallibly die some days afterwards. This fact was confirmed by several persons, and amongst others by an old curé, who said he had seen more than one instance of it.

[CHARLES FERDINAND DE SCHERTZ, author of *Magia Posthuma*, tells the story] of a shepherd of the village of Blow, near the town of Kadam, in Bohemia, who appeared during some time, and called certain persons, who never failed to die within eight days after. The peasants of Blow took up the body of this shepherd, and fixed it in the ground with a stake which they drove through it.

This man, when in that condition, derided them for what they made him suffer, and told them they were very good to give him thus a stick to defend himself from the dogs. The same night he got up again, and by his presence alarmed several persons, and strangled more amongst them than he had hitherto done. Afterwards, they delivered him into the hands of the executioner, who put him in a cart to carry him beyond the village and there burn him. This corpse howled like a madman, and moved his feet and hands as if alive. And when they again pierced him through with stakes he uttered very loud cries, and a great quantity of bright vermilion blood flowed from him. At last he was consumed, and this execution put an end to the appearance and hauntings of this spectre.

Dead Persons in Hungary
Who Suck the Blood of the Living

About fifteen years ago, a soldier who was billeted at the house of a Haidamaque peasant, on the frontiers of Hungary, as he was one day sitting at table near his host, the master of the house saw a person he did not know come in and sit down to table also with them. The master of the house was strangely frightened at this, as were the rest of the company. The soldier knew not what to think of it, being ignorant of the matter in question. But the master of the house being dead the very next day, the soldier inquired what it meant. They told him that it was the body of the father of his host, who had been dead and buried for ten years, which had thus come to sit down next to him, and had announced and caused his death.

The soldier informed the regiment of it in the first place, and the regiment gave notice of it to the general officers, who commissioned the Count de Cabreras, captain of the regiment of Alandetti infantry, to make information concerning this circumstance. Having gone to the place, with some other officers, a surgeon and an auditor, they heard the depositions of all the people belonging to the house, who attested unanimously that the ghost was the father of the master of the house, and that all the soldier had said and reported was the exact truth, which was confirmed by all the inhabitants of the village.

In consequence of this, the corpse of this spectre was exhumed, and found to be like that of a man who has just expired, and his blood like that of a living man. The Count de Cabreras had his head cut off, and caused him to be laid again in his tomb. He also took information concerning other similar ghosts, amongst others, of a man dead more than thirty years, who had come back three times to his house at meal time. The first time he had sucked the blood from the neck of his own brother, the second time from one of his sons, and the third from one of the servants in the house; and all three died of it instantly and on the spot. Upon this deposition the commissary had this man taken out of his grave, and finding that, like the first, his blood was in a fluid state, like that of a living person, he ordered them to run a large nail into his temple, and then to lay him again in the grave.

He caused a third to be burnt, who had been buried more than sixteen years, and had sucked the blood and caused the death of two of his sons. The commissary having made his report to the general officers, was deputed to the court of the emperor, who commanded that some officers, both of war and justice, some physicians and surgeons, and some learned men, should be sent to examine the causes of these extraordinary events. The person who related these

particulars to us had heard them from Monsieur the Count de Cabreras, at Fribourg en Brigau, in 1730.

*Here is a letter which has been written to one of my friends, to be commu-
nicated to me.*

In reply to the questions of the Abbé dom Calmet concerning
vampires, the undersigned has the honor to assure him that nothing is more true or more certain than what he will doubtless have
read about it in the deeds or attestations which have been made
public, and printed in all the Gazettes in Europe. But amongst all
these public attestations which have appeared, the Abbé must fix
his attention as a true and notorious fact on that of the deputation
from Belgrade, ordered by his late Majesty Charles VI, of glorious
memory, and executed by his Serene Highness the late Duke
Charles Alexander of Wirtemberg, then Viceroy or Governor of the
kingdom of Servia; but I cannot at present cite the year or the day,
for want of papers which I have not now by me.

That prince sent off a deputation from Belgrade, half consisting
of military officers and half of civil, with the auditor-general of the
kingdom, to go to a village where a famous vampire, several years
deceased, was making great havoc amongst his kin; for note well,
that it is only in their family and amongst their own relations
that these blood-suckers delight in destroying our species. This
deputation was composed of men and persons well-known for their
morality and even their information, of irreproachable character;
and there were even some learned men amongst the two orders:
they were put to the oath, and accompanied by a lieutenant of the
grenadiers of the regiment of Prince Alexander of Wirtemberg,
and by twenty-four grenadiers of the said regiment.

All that were most respectable, and the duke himself, who was
then at Belgrade, joined this deputation in order to be ocular spectators of the veracious proof about to be made.

When they arrived at the place, they found that in the space of a fortnight the vampire, uncle of five persons, nephews and nieces, had already dispatched three of them and one of his own brothers. He had begun with his fifth victim, the beautiful young daughter of his niece, and had already sucked her twice, when a stop was put to this sad tragedy by the following operations.

They repaired with the deputed commissaries to a village not far from Belgrade, and that publicly, at night-fall, and went to the vampire's grave. The gentleman could not tell me the time when those who had died had been sucked, nor the particulars of the subject. The persons whose blood had been sucked found themselves in a pitiable state of languor, weakness, and lassitude, so violent is the torment. He had been interred three years, and they saw on this grave a light resembling that of a lamp, but not so bright.

They opened the grave, and found there a man as whole and apparently as sound as any of us who were present; his hair, and the hairs on his body, the nails, teeth, and eyes as firmly fast as they now are in ourselves who exist, and his heart palpitating.

Next they proceeded to draw him out of his grave, the body in truth not being flexible, but wanting neither flesh nor bone; then they pierced his heart with a sort of round, pointed, iron lance; there came out a whitish and fluid matter mixed with blood, but the blood prevailing more than the matter, and all without any bad smell. After that they cut off his head with a hatchet, like what is used in England at executions; there came out also a matter and blood like what I have just described, but more abundantly in proportion to what had flowed from the heart.

And after all this they threw him back again into his grave, with quick-lime to consume him promptly; and thenceforth his niece, who had been twice sucked, grew better. At the place where these persons are sucked a very blue spot is formed; the part whence the blood is drawn is not determinate, sometimes it is in one place and sometimes in another. It is a notorious fact, attested by the most authentic documents, and passed or executed in sight of more than 1,300 persons, all worthy of belief.

But I reserve, to satisfy more fully the curiosity of the learned Abbé dom Calmet, the pleasure of detailing to him more at length what I have seen with my own eyes on this subject.

Singular Instance of a Hungarian Ghost

THE MOST REMARKABLE INSTANCE cited by Rauff is that of one Peter Plogojovitz, who had been buried ten weeks in a village of Hungary, called Kisolova. This man appeared by night to some of the inhabitants of the village while they were asleep, and grasped their throat so tightly that in four-and-twenty hours it caused their death. Nine persons, young and old, perished thus in the course of eight days.

The widow of the same Plogojovitz declared that her husband since his death had come and asked her for his shoes, which frightened her so much that she left Kisolova to retire to some other spot.

From these circumstances the inhabitants of the village determined upon disinterring the body of Plogojovitz and burning it, to deliver themselves from these visitations. They applied to the emperor's officer, who commanded in the territory of Gradiska, in Hungary, and even to the curé of the same place, for permission to exhume the body of Peter Plogojovitz. The officer and the curé made much demur in granting this permission, but the peasants declared that if they were refused permission to disinter the body of this man, whom they had no doubt was a true vampire (for so they called these revived corpses), they should be obliged to forsake the village, and go where they could.

The emperor's officer, who wrote this account, seeing he could hinder them neither by threats nor promises, went with the curé of Gradiska to the village of Kisolova, and having caused Peter Plogojovitz to be exhumed, they found that his body exhaled no bad smell; that he looked as when alive, except the tip of the nose; that his hair and beard had grown, and instead of his nails, which had fallen off, new ones had come; that under his upper skin, which appeared whitish, there appeared a new one, which looked healthy, and of a natural color; his feet and hands were as whole as could be desired in a living man. They remarked also in his mouth some fresh blood, which these people believed that this vampire had sucked from the men whose death he had occasioned.

The emperor's officer and the curé having diligently examined all these things, and the people who were present feeling their indignation awakened anew, and being more fully persuaded that he was the true cause of the death of their compatriots, ran directly for a sharp-pointed stake, which they thrust into his breast, whence there issued a quantity of fresh and crimson blood, and also from the nose and mouth; something also proceeded from that part of his body which decency does not allow us to mention. After this the peasants placed the body on a pile of wood and saw it reduced to ashes.

George Gordon, Lord Byron

(1788–1824)

DESPITE THE SUPERSTITIOUS MANIA recorded in Augustin Calmet's *Phantom World*, Europe in the seventeenth century had slowly changed. Philosophers such as Francis Bacon and René Descartes formulated a new approach to what would come to be called science; the Royal Society encouraged attention to the world beyond illuminated manuscripts; Hobbes and Locke and company lay the groundwork for vast political change. In an influential swing of the Western cultural pendulum—the Romantic backlash against the Enlightenment—many people objected to evidence-based thinking as arid and godless, and worried that science was fumigating all the fun out of the world. Not that Romanticism was by any means a rejection of all things scientific; the schoolboy Shelley was notorious for his reckless experiments with electricity and magnetism. But the Romantics definitely tried to restore wonder and mystery to their world, and they enthusiastically welcomed vampire folklore into their moody writings.

In 1815, a volcano called Tambora erupted on the Indonesian island of Sumbawa. Its crown exploded in the largest and most dramatic eruption in history, flinging countless tons of volcanic ash and dust into the air. The particles reached a high enough altitude to travel around the world for months, contributing to dramatic sunsets and stormy weather in places far distant from the site of their origin. "It will ever be remembered by the present generation," proclaimed one English newspaper, "that the year 1816 was a year in which there was no summer." Bad weather prevailed over Europe, North America, and other northern regions.

During the rainy summer of 1816, the poet George Gordon, Lord Byron, rented the Villa Diodati on Lake Geneva in Switzerland. His physician and hanger-on, John Polidori, was with him. Staying nearby were poet Percy Bysshe Shelley, Shelley's not-yet-wife Mary Wollstonecraft Godwin, their illegitimate baby daughter, and Mary's stepsister Claire. Byron and Polidori soon met the others, who visited the villa often. The party planned to sail the lake and explore the history-rich region (the villa was named after a former owner, whose friend John Milton had visited him there), but the awful weather kept them off the water and mostly trapped indoors. So they sat before the fire and read ghost stories aloud, especially the supernatural collection *Phantasmagoriana*, which they read in a new French translation.

Finally, as Mary Shelley later told it, "We shall each write a ghost story," said Byron. It was a historic evening. Percy Shelley made little attempt to meet the challenge, although he was fascinated by ghosts and thought he had encountered them, but Godwin began what grew into *Frankenstein*. Byron wrote a brief tale that he never developed further, which follows. Probably everyone present had read Robert Southey's long poem *Thalaba* and its extensive notes about vampires, and Byron had already mentioned vampires in his 1816 poem "The Giaour," so it isn't surprising that they occurred to him again as a topic. Polidori's late but powerful contribution was in response to Byron's and follows immediately after it.

The End of My Journey

J UNE 17, 1816 IN the year 17—, having for some time determined on a journey through countries not hitherto much frequented by travellers, I set out, accompanied by a friend, whom I shall designate by the name of Augustus Darvell. He was a few years my elder, and a man of considerable fortune and ancient family: advantages which an extensive capacity prevented him alike from undervaluing or overrating. Some peculiar circumstances in his private history had rendered him to me an object of attention, of interest, and even of regard, which neither the reserve of his manners, nor occasional indications of an inquietude at times nearly approaching to alienation of mind, could extinguish.

I was yet young in life, which I had begun early; but my intimacy with him was of a recent date: we had been educated at the same schools and university; but his progress through these had preceded mine, and he had been deeply initiated into what is called the world, while I was yet in my novitiate. While thus engaged, I heard much both of his past and present life; and, although in these accounts there were many and irreconcilable contradictions, I could still gather from the whole that he was a being of no common order, and one who, whatever pains he might take to avoid remark, would still be remarkable. I had cultivated his acquaintance subsequently, and endeavoured to obtain his friendship, but this last appeared to be unattainable; whatever affections he might have possessed seemed now, some to have been extinguished, and others to be concentered: that his feelings were acute, I had sufficient opportunities of observing; for, although he could control, he could not altogether disguise them: still he had a power of giving to one passion the appearance of another, in such a manner that it was difficult to define the nature of what was working within him; and the expressions of his features would vary so rapidly, though slightly, that it was useless to trace them to their sources. It was evident that he was a prey to some cureless disquiet; but whether it arose from ambition, love, remorse, grief, from one or all of these, or merely from a morbid temperament akin to disease, I could not discover: there were circumstances alleged which might have justified the application to each of these causes; but, as I have before said, these were so contradictory and contradicted, that none could be fixed upon with accuracy. Where there is mystery, it is generally supposed that there must also be evil: I know not how this may be, but in him there certainly was the one, though I could not ascertain the extent of the other—and felt loath, as far as regarded himself, to believe in its existence. My advances were received with sufficient coldness: but I was young, and not easily discouraged, and at length succeeded in obtaining, to a certain degree, that common-place intercourse and moderate confidence of common and every-day concerns, created and cemented by similarity of pursuit and frequency of meeting, which is called intimacy, or friendship, according to the ideas of him who uses those words to express them.

Darvell had already travelled extensively; and to him I had applied for information with regard to the conduct of my intended journey. It was my secret wish that he might be prevailed on to accompany me; it was also a probable hope, founded upon the shadowy restlessness which I observed in him, and to which the animation which he appeared to feel on such subjects, and his apparent indifference to all by which he was more immediately surrounded, gave fresh strength. This wish I first hinted, and then expressed: his answer, though I had partly expected it, gave me all the pleasure of surprise—he consented; and, after the requisite arrangement, we commenced our voyages. After journeying through various countries of the south of Europe, our attention was turned towards the East, according to our original destination; and it was in my progress through these regions that the incident occurred upon which will turn what I may have to relate.

The constitution of Darvell, which must from his appearance have been in early life more than usually robust, had been for some time gradually giving away, without the intervention of any apparent disease: he had neither cough nor hectic, yet he became daily more enfeebled; his habits were temperate, and he neither declined nor complained of fatigue; yet he was evidently wasting away: he became more and more silent and sleepless, and at length so seriously altered, that my alarm grew proportionate to what I conceived to be his danger.

We had determined, on our arrival at Smyrna, on an excursion to the ruins of Ephesus and Sardis, from which I endeavoured to dissuade him in his present state of indisposition—but in vain: there appeared to be an oppression on his mind, and a solemnity in his manner, which ill corresponded with his eagerness to proceed on what I regarded as a mere party of pleasure little suited to a valetudinarian; but I opposed him no longer—and in a few days we set off together, accompanied only by a serrugee and a single janissary.

We had passed halfway towards the remains of Ephesus, leaving behind us the more fertile environs of Smyrna, and were entering upon that wild and tenantless tract through the marshes and defiles which lead to the few huts yet lingering over the broken columns of Diana—the roofless walls of expelled Christianity, and the still more recent but complete desolation of abandoned mosques—when the sudden and rapid illness of my companion obliged us to halt at a Turkish cemetery, the turbaned tombstones of which were the sole indication that human life had ever been a sojourner in this wilderness. The only caravanserai we had seen was left some hours behind us, not a vestige of a town or even cottage was within sight or hope, and this "city of the dead" appeared to be the sole refuge of my unfortunate friend, who seemed on the verge of becoming the last of its inhabitants.

In this situation, I looked round for a place where he might most conveniently repose: contrary to the usual aspect of Mahometan burial-grounds, the cypresses were in this few in number, and these thinly scattered over its extent; the tombstones were mostly fallen, and worn with age: upon one of the most considerable of these, and beneath one of the most spreading trees, Darvell supported himself, in a half-reclining posture, with great difficulty. He asked for water. I had some doubts of our being able to find any, and prepared to go in search of it with hesitating despondency: but he desired me to remain; and turning to Suleiman, our janissary, who stood by us smoking with great tranquillity he said, "Suleiman, verbana su" (i.e., "bring some water"), and went on describing the spot where it was to be found with great minuteness, at a small well for camels, a few hundred yards to the right: the janissary obeyed. I said to Darvell, "How did you know this?" He replied, "From our situation; you must perceive that this place was once inhabited, and could not have been so without springs: I have also been here before."

"You have been here before! How came you never to mention this to me? and what could you be doing in a place where no one would remain a moment longer than they could help it?"

To this question I received no answer. In the meantime Suleiman returned with the water, leaving the serrugee and the horses at the fountain. The quenching of his thirst had the appearance of reviving him for a moment; and I conceived hopes of his being able to proceed, or at least to return, and I urged the attempt. He was silent—and appeared to be collecting his spirits for an effort to speak. He began—

"This is the end of my journey, and of my life; I came here to die; but I have a request to make, a command—for such my last words must be.—You will observe it?"

"Most certainly; but I have better hopes."

"I have no hopes, nor wishes, but this—conceal my death from every human being."

"I hope there will be no occasion; that you will recover, and—"

"Peace! It must be so: promise this."

"I do."

"Swear it, by all that—" He here dictated an oath of great solemnity.

"There is no occasion for this. I will observe your request; and to doubt me is—"

"It cannot be helped, you must swear."

I took the oath, it appeared to relieve him. He removed a seal ring from his finger, on which were some Arabic characters, and presented it to me. He proceeded—

"On the ninth day of the month, at noon precisely (what month you please, but this must be the day), you must fling this ring into the salt springs which run into the Bay of Eleusis; the day after, at the same hour, you must repair to the ruins of the temple of Ceres, and wait one hour."

"Why?"

"You will see."

"The ninth day of the month, you say?"

"The ninth."

As I observed that the present was the ninth day of the month, his countenance changed, and he paused. As he sat, evidently becoming more feeble, a stork, with a snake in her beak, perched upon a tombstone near us; and, without devouring her prey, appeared to be steadfastly regarding us. I know not what impelled me to drive it away, but the attempt was useless; she made a few circles in the air, and returned exactly to the same spot. Darvell pointed to it, and smiled—he spoke—I know not whether to himself or to me—but the words were only " 'Tis well!"

"What is well? What do you mean?"

"No matter, you must bury me here this evening, and exactly

where that bird is now perched. You know the rest of my injunctions."

He then proceeded to give me several directions as to the manner in which his death might be best concealed. After these were finished, he exclaimed, "You perceive that bird?"

"Certainly."

"And the serpent writhing in her beak?"

"Doubtless: there is nothing uncommon in it; it is her natural prey. But it is odd that she does not devour it."

He smiled in a ghastly manner, and said faintly, "It is not yet time!" As he spoke, the stork flew away. My eyes followed it for a moment—it could hardly be longer than ten might be counted. I felt Darvell's weight, as it were, increase upon my shoulder, and, turning to look upon his face, perceived that he was dead!

I was shocked with the sudden certainty which could not be mistaken—his countenance in a few minutes became nearly black. I should have attributed so rapid a change to poison, had I not been aware that he had no opportunity of receiving it unperceived. The day was declining, the body was rapidly altering, and nothing remained but to fulfill his request. With the aid of Suleiman's yataghan and my own sabre, we scooped a shallow grave upon the spot which Darvell had indicated: the earth easily gave way, having already received some Mahometan tenant. We dug as deeply as the time permitted us, and throwing the dry earth upon all that remained of the singular being so lately departed, we cut a few sods of greener turf from the less withered soil around us, and laid them upon his sepulchre.

Between astonishment and grief, I was tearless.

※

John Polidori

(1795–1821)

BYRON'S 1816 FICTION REMAINED a fragment; he never developed the idea. But its potent imagery inspired John Polidori, Byron's former physician and acolyte. Polidori had long been drawn to such topics; in true Romantic style, his Edinburgh dissertation concerned nightmares, somnambulism, and mesmerism. He took Byron's narrative germ and grew it into a full story, expanding the tale and patterning the main character on his own observations of Byron as well as on the dark public persona that Byron had been acquiring through his irreverent writings and scandalous affairs. In case any reader missed the similarity, Polidori even named his vampire after a character in Caroline Lamb's 1816 Gothic novel *Glenarvon*. One of Byron's many disgruntled conquests, Lamb published the novel only two years after their affair ended, basing her predatory antihero, Ruthven, on her former lover. Lamb famously described Byron as "mad, bad, and dangerous to know." Polidori's notes indicate that he first called his vampire Lord Strongmore, which sounds like something in a Bad Dickens contest, but ultimately he named him Lord Ruthven instead.

Although Polidori said that he did not authorize publication, later claiming that he considered "The Vampyre" unfinished, in April 1819 the story appeared in London's *New Monthly Magazine*.

If Polidori's account is true, it must have been the editor who shamelessly attributed the piece to Byron himself, apparently knowing that such a move would attract the British public far more than a weird tale by an anonymous nobody. The ploy worked. Readers scooped up thousands of copies and its fame spread to other countries. Soon Goethe—to the bafflement of critics ever since—pronounced "The Vampyre" some of Byron's best work.

In the magazine's next issue, Polidori emerged from anonymity to rebut the speculation:

> I beg leave to state, that your correspondent has been mistaken in attributing that tale, *in its present form*, to Lord Byron. The fact is, that though *the groundwork* is certainly Lord Byron's, its development is mine, produced at the request of a lady, who denied the possibility of any thing being drawn from the materials which Lord Byron had said he intended to have employed in the formation of his Ghost story.

In 1819 Polidori also published his only other work of fiction, the novella *Ernestus Berchtold*. Two years later he was dead at the age of twenty-six. But his influence survives in this brief story, the first major prose fiction in English about vampires. Quirky as his writing can be, Polidori nonetheless linked ruthless manipulation and vampiric predation in the public mind. After Ruthven, vampires were no longer peasant folklore; they had become handsome aristocratic metaphors. You will perceive Ruthven's heritage in other characters throughout this volume, all the way to Dracula and beyond, and certainly in twentieth- and twenty-first-century representations from Anne Rice to the *Twilight* series.

Byron possessed many qualities that Polidori lacked, including wit. He disclaimed authorship of "The Vampyre" with these words: "I have a personal dislike to Vampires, and the little acquaintance I have with them would by no means induce me to reveal their secrets." How apt that in 1995 Tom Holland published a novel, *Vampyre*, in which both Byron and Polidori are literal bloodsucking nightstalkers. Byron would have been pleased to find that, long after he ought to have been moldering in his grave, he still walks among us.

The Vampyre

IT HAPPENED THAT IN the midst of the dissipations attendant upon a London winter, there appeared at the various parties of the leaders of the *ton* a nobleman, more remarkable for his singularities, than his rank. He gazed upon the mirth around him, as if he could not participate therein. Apparently, the light laughter of the fair only attracted his attention, that he might by a look quell it, and throw fear into those breasts where thoughtlessness reigned. Those who felt this sensation of awe, could not explain whence it arose: some attributed it to the dead grey eye, which, fixing upon the object's face, did not seem to penetrate, and at one glance to pierce through to the inward workings of the heart; but fell upon the cheek with a leaden ray that weighed upon the skin it could not pass. His peculiarities caused him to be invited to every house; all wished to see him, and those who had been accustomed to violent excitement, and now felt the weight of *ennui*, were pleased at having something in their presence capable of engaging their attention. In spite of the deadly hue of his face, which never gained a warmer tint, either from the blush of modesty, or from the strong emotion of passion, though its form and outline were beautiful, many of the female hunters after notoriety attempted to win his attentions, and gain, at least, some marks of what they might term affection: Lady Mercer, who had been the mockery of every monster shewn in drawing-rooms since

her marriage, threw herself in his way, and did all but put on the dress
of a mountebank, to attract his notice—though in vain;—when she
stood before him, though his eyes were apparently fixed upon hers,
still it seemed as if they were unperceived;—even her unappalled im-
pudence was baffled, and she left the field. But though the common
adultress could not influence even the guidance of his eyes, it was
not that the female sex was indifferent to him: yet such was the apparent caution with which he spoke to the virtuous wife and innocent daughter, that few knew he ever addressed himself to females.
He had, however, the reputation of a winning tongue; and whether it
was that it even overcame the dread of his singular character, or that
they were moved by his apparent hatred of vice, he was as often
among those females who form the boast of their sex from their
domestic virtues, as among those who sully it by their vices.

About the same time, there came to London a young gentleman
of the name of Aubrey: he was an orphan left with an only sister in
the possession of great wealth, by parents who died while he was
yet in childhood. Left also to himself by guardians, who thought
it their duty merely to take care of his fortune, while they relinquished the more important charge of his mind to the care of
mercenary subalterns, he cultivated more his imagination than his
judgment. He had, hence, that high romantic feeling of honour
and candour, which daily ruins so many milliners' apprentices. He
believed all to sympathise with virtue, and thought that vice was
thrown in by Providence merely for the picturesque effect of the
scene, as we see in romances: he thought that the misery of a cottage
merely consisted in the vesting of clothes, which were as warm,
but which were better adapted to the painter's eye by their irregular folds and various coloured patches. He thought, in fine, that the
dreams of poets were the realities of life. He was handsome, frank,
and rich: for these reasons, upon his entering into the gay circles,
many mothers surrounded him, striving which should describe
with least truth their languishing or romping favourites: the daugh-
ters at the same time, by their brightening countenances when he

approached, and by their sparkling eyes, when he opened his lips, soon led him into false notions of his talents and his merit. Attached as he was to the romance of his solitary hours, he was startled at finding, that, except in the tallow and wax candles that flickered, not from the presence of a ghost, but from want of snuffing, there was no foundation in real life for any of that congeries of pleasing pictures and descriptions contained in those volumes, from which he had formed his study. Finding, however, some compensation in his gratified vanity, he was about to relinquish his dreams, when the extraordinary being we have above described, crossed him in his career.

He watched him; and the very impossibility of forming an idea of the character of a man entirely absorbed in himself, who gave few other signs of his observation of external objects, than the tacit assent to their existence, implied by the avoidance of their contact: allowing his imagination to picture every thing that flattered its propensity to extravagant ideas, he soon formed this object into the hero of a romance, and determined to observe the offspring of his fancy, rather than the person before him. He became acquainted with him, paid him attentions, and so far advanced upon his notice, that his presence was always recognised. He gradually learnt that Lord Ruthven's affairs were embarrassed, and soon found, from the notes of preparation in——Street, that he was about to travel. Desirous of gaining some information respecting this singular character, who, till now, had only whetted his curiosity, he hinted to his guardians, that it was time for him to perform the tour, which for many generations has been thought necessary to enable the young to take some rapid steps in the career of vice towards putting themselves upon an equality with the aged, and not allowing them to appear as if fallen from the skies, whenever scandalous intrigues are mentioned as the subjects of pleasantry or of praise, according to the degree of skill shewn in carrying them on. They consented: and Aubrey immediately mentioning his intentions to Lord Ruthven, was surprised to receive from him a proposal to join him. Flattered by such a mark of esteem from him, who, apparently, had nothing in common with other men, he gladly accepted it, and in a few days they had passed the circling waters.

Hitherto, Aubrey had had no opportunity of studying Lord Ruthven's character, and now he found, that, though many more of his actions were exposed to his view, the results offered different conclusions from the apparent motives to his conduct. His companion was profuse in his liberality;—the idle, the vagabond, and the beggar, received from his hand more than enough to relieve their immediate wants. But Aubrey could not avoid remarking, that it was not upon the virtuous, reduced to indigence by the misfortunes attendant even upon virtue, that he bestowed his alms;—these were sent from the door with hardly suppressed sneers; but when the profligate came to ask something, not to relieve his wants, but to allow him to wallow in his lust, or to sink him still deeper in his iniquity, he was sent away with rich charity. This was, however, attributed by him to the greater importunity of the vicious, which generally prevails over the retiring bashfulness of the virtuous indigent. There was one circumstance about the charity of his Lordship, which was still more impressed upon his mind: all those upon whom it was bestowed, inevitably found that there was a curse upon it, for they were all either led to the scaffold, or sunk to the lowest and the most abject misery. At Brussels and other towns through which they passed, Aubrey was surprized at the apparent eagerness with which his companion sought for the centres of all fashionable vice; there he entered into all the spirit of the faro table: he betted, and always gambled with success, except where the known sharper was his antagonist, and then he lost even more than he gained; but it was always with the same unchanging face, with which he generally watched the society around: it was not, however, so when he encountered the rash youthful novice, or the luckless father of a numerous family; then his very wish seemed fortune's law—this apparent abstractedness of mind was laid aside, and his eyes sparkled with more fire than that of the cat whilst dallying with the half-dead mouse. In every town, he left the formerly affluent youth, torn from the circle he adorned, cursing, in the solitude of a dungeon, the fate that had drawn him within the reach of this fiend; whilst many a father sat frantic, amidst the speaking looks of mute hungry children, without a single farthing of his late immense wealth, wherewith to buy even sufficient to satisfy their present craving. Yet he took no money from the gambling table; but immediately lost, to the ruiner of many, the last gilder he had just snatched from the convulsive grasp of the innocent: this might but be the result of a certain degree of knowledge, which was not, however, capable of combating the cunning of the more experienced. Aubrey often wished to represent this to his friend, and beg him to resign that charity and pleasure which proved the ruin of all, and did not tend to his own profit; but he delayed it—for each day he hoped his friend would give him some opportunity of speaking frankly and openly to him; however, this never occurred. Lord Ruthven in his carriage, and amidst the various wild and rich scenes of nature, was always the same: his eye spoke less than his lip; and though Aubrey was near the object of his curiosity, he obtained no greater gratification from it than the constant excitement of vainly wishing to break that mystery, which to his exalted imagination began to assume the appearance of something supernatural.

They soon arrived at Rome, and Aubrey for a time lost sight of his companion; he left him in daily attendance upon the morning circle of an Italian countess, whilst he went in search of the memorials of another almost deserted city. Whilst he was thus engaged, letters arrived from England, which he opened with eager impatience; the first was from his sister, breathing nothing but affection; the others were from his guardians, the latter astonished him; if it had before entered into his imagination that there was an evil power resident in his companion, these seemed to give him almost sufficient reason for the belief. His guardians insisted upon his immediately leaving his friend, and urged, that his character was dreadfully vicious, for that the possession of irresistible powers of seduction, rendered his licentious habits more dangerous to society. It had been discovered, that his contempt for the adultress had not originated in hatred of her character; but that he had required, to enhance his gratification, that his victim, the partner of his guilt, should be hurled from the pinnacle of unsullied virtue, down to the lowest abyss of infamy and degradation: in fine, that all those females whom he had sought, apparently on account of their virtue, had, since his departure, thrown even the mask aside, and had not scrupled to expose the whole deformity of their vices to the public gaze.

Aubrey determined upon leaving one, whose character had not yet shown a single bright point on which to rest the eye. He resolved to invent some plausible pretext for abandoning him altogether, purposing, in the mean while, to watch him more closely, and to let no slight circumstances pass by unnoticed. He entered into the same circle, and soon perceived, that his Lordship was endeavouring to work upon the inexperience of the daughter of the lady whose house he chiefly frequented. In Italy, it is seldom that an unmarried female is met with in society; he was therefore obliged to carry on his plans in secret; but Aubrey's eye followed him in all his windings, and soon discovered that an assignation had been appointed, which would most likely end in the ruin of an innocent, though thoughtless girl. Losing no time, he entered the apartment of Lord Ruthven, and abruptly asked him his intentions with respect to the lady, informing him at the same time that he was aware of his being about to meet her that very night. Lord Ruthven answered, that his intentions were such as he supposed all would have upon such an occasion; and upon being pressed whether he intended to marry her, merely laughed. Aubrey retired; and, immediately writing a note, to say, that from that moment he must decline accompanying his Lordship in the remainder of their proposed tour, he ordered his servant to seek other apartments, and calling upon the mother of the lady, informed her of all he knew, not only with regard to her daughter, but also concerning the character of his Lordship. The assignation was prevented. Lord Ruthven next day merely sent his servant to notify his complete assent to a separation; but did not hint any suspicion of his plans having been foiled by Aubrey's interposition.

Having left Rome, Aubrey directed his steps towards Greece, and crossing the Peninsula, soon found himself at Athens. He then fixed his residence in the house of a Greek; and soon occupied himself in tracing the faded records of ancient glory upon monuments that apparently, ashamed of chronicling the deeds of freemen only before slaves, had hidden themselves beneath the sheltering soil or many coloured lichen. Under the same roof as himself, existed a being, so beautiful and delicate, that she might have formed the model for a painter, wishing to pourtray on canvass the promised hope of the faithful in Mahomet's paradise, save that her eyes spoke too much mind for any one to think she could belong to those who had no souls. As she danced upon the plain, or tripped along the mountain's side, one would have thought the gazelle a poor type of her beauties; for who would have exchanged her eye, apparently the eye of animated nature, for that sleepy luxurious look of the animal suited but to the taste of an epicure. The light step of Ianthe often accompanied Aubrey in his search after antiquities, and often would the unconscious girl, engaged in the pursuit of a Kashmere butterfly, show the whole beauty of her form, floating as it were upon the wind, to the eager gaze of him, who forgot the letters he had just decyphered upon an almost effaced tablet, in the contemplation of her sylph-like figure. Often would her tresses falling, as she flitted around, exhibit in the sun's ray such delicately brilliant and swiftly fading hues, as might well excuse the forgetfulness of the antiquary, who let escape from his mind the very object he had before thought of vital importance to the proper interpretation of a passage in Pausanias. But why attempt to describe charms which all feel, but none can appreciate?—It was innocence, youth, and beauty, unaffected by crowded drawing-rooms and stifling balls. Whilst he drew those remains of which he wished to preserve a memorial for his future hours, she would stand by, and watch the magic effects of his pencil, in tracing the scenes of her native place; she would then describe to him the circling dance upon the open plain, would paint to him in all the glowing colours of youthful memory, the marriage pomp she remembered viewing in her infancy; and then, turning to subjects that had evidently made a greater impression upon her mind, would tell him all the super-natural tales of her nurse. Her earnestness and apparent belief of what she narrated, excited the interest even of Aubrey; and often as she told him the tale of the living vampyre, who had passed years amidst his friends, and dearest ties, forced every year, by feeding upon the life of a lovely female to prolong his existence for the ensu-ing months, his blood would run cold, whilst he attempted to laugh her out of such idle and horrible fantasies; but Ianthe cited to him the names of old men, who had at last detected one living among them-selves, after several of their near relatives and children had been found marked with the stamp of the fiend's appetite; and when she found him so incredulous, she begged of him to believe her, for it had been remarked, that those who had dared to question their exis-tence, always had some proof given, which obliged them, with grief and heartbreaking, to confess it was true. She detailed to him the traditional appearance of these monsters, and his horror was in-creased, by hearing a pretty accurate description of Lord Ruthven; he, however, still persisted in persuading her, that there could be no truth in her fears, though at the same time he wondered at the many coincidences which had all tended to excite a belief in the super-natural power of Lord Ruthven.

Aubrey began to attach himself more and more to Ianthe; her innocence, so contrasted with all the affected virtues of the women among whom he had sought for his vision of romance, won his heart; and while he ridiculed the idea of a young man of English habits, marrying an uneducated Greek girl, still he found himself more and more attached to the almost fairy form before him. He would tear himself at times from her, and, forming a plan for some antiquarian research, he would depart, determined not to return until his object was attained; but he always found it impossible to fix his attention upon the ruins around him, whilst in his mind he retained an image that seemed alone the rightful possessor of his thoughts. Ianthe was unconscious of his love, and was ever the same frank infantile being he had first known. She always seemed to part from him with reluctance; but it was because she had no longer anyone with whom she could visit her favourite haunts, whilst her guardian was occupied in sketching or uncovering some fragment which had yet escaped the destructive hand of time. She had appealed to her parents on the subject of Vampyres, and they both, with several present, affirmed their existence, pale with horror at the very name. Soon after, Aubrey determined to proceed upon one of his excursions, which was to detain him for a few hours; when they heard the name of the place, they all at once begged of him not to return at night, as he must necessarily pass through a wood, where no Greek would ever remain, after the day had closed, upon any consideration. They described it as the resort of the vampyres in their nocturnal orgies, and denounced the most heavy evils as impending upon him who dared to cross their path. Aubrey made light of their representations, and tried to laugh them out of the idea; but when he saw them shudder at his daring thus to mock a superior, infernal power, the very name of which apparently made their blood freeze, he was silent.

Next morning Aubrey set off upon his excursion unattended; he was surprised to observe the melancholy face of his host, and was concerned to find that his words, mocking the belief of those horrible fiends, had inspired them with such terror. When he was about to depart, Ianthe came to the side of his horse, and earnestly begged of him to return, ere night allowed the power of these beings to be put in action;—he promised. He was, however, so occupied in his research, that he did not perceive that day-light would soon end, and that in the horizon there was one of those specks which, in the warmer climates, so rapidly gather into a tremendous mass, and pour all their rage upon the devoted country.—He at last, however, mounted his horse, determined to make up by speed for his delay: but it was too late. Twilight, in these southern climates, is almost unknown; immediately the sun sets, night begins: and ere he had advanced far, the power of the storm was above—its echoing thunders had scarcely an interval of rest;—its thick heavy rain forced its way through the canopying foliage, whilst the blue forked lightning seemed to fall and radiate at his very feet. Suddenly his horse took fright, and he was carried with dreadful rapidity through the entangled forest. The animal at last, through fatigue, stopped, and he found, by the glare of lightning, that he was in the neighbourhood of a hovel that hardly lifted itself up from the masses of dead leaves and brushwood which surrounded it. Dismounting, he approached, hoping to find some one to guide him to the town, or at least trusting to obtain shelter from the pelting of the storm. As he approached, the thunders, for a moment silent, allowed him to hear the dreadful shrieks of a woman mingling with the stifled, exultant mockery of a laugh, continued in one almost unbroken sound;—he was startled: but, roused by the thunder which again rolled over his head, he, with a sudden effort, forced open the door of the hut. He found himself in utter darkness: the sound, however, guided him. He was apparently unperceived; for, though he called, still the sounds continued, and no notice was taken of him. He found himself in contact with some one, whom he immediately seized; when a voice cried, "Again baffled!" to which a loud laugh succeeded; and he felt himself grappled by one whose strength seemed superhuman: determined to sell his life as dearly as he could, he struggled; but it was in vain: he was lifted from his feet and hurled with enormous force against the ground:— his enemy threw himself upon him, and kneeling upon his breast, had placed his hands upon his throat—when the glare of many torches penetrating through the hole that gave light in the day, disturbed him;—he instantly rose, and, leaving his prey, rushed through the door, and in a moment the crashing of the branches, as he broke through the wood, was no longer heard. The storm was now still; and Aubrey, incapable of moving, was soon heard by those without.

They entered; the light of their torches fell upon the mud walls, and the thatch loaded on every individual straw with heavy flakes of soot. At the desire of Aubrey they searched for her who had attracted him by her cries; he was again left in darkness; but what was his horror, when the light of the torches once more burst upon him, to perceive the airy form of his fair conductress brought in a lifeless corpse. He shut his eyes, hoping that it was but a vision arising from his disturbed imagination; but he again saw the same form, when he unclosed them, stretched by his side. There was no colour upon her cheek, not even upon her lip; yet there was a stillness about her face that seemed almost as attaching as the life that once dwelt there:— upon her neck and breast was blood, and upon her throat were the marks of teeth having opened the vein:—to this the men pointed, crying, simultaneously struck with horror, "A Vampyre! a Vampyre!" A litter was quickly formed, and Aubrey was laid by the side of her who had lately been to him the object of so many bright and fairy visions, now fallen with the flower of life that had died within her. He knew not what his thoughts were—his mind was benumbed and seemed to shun reflection, and take refuge in vacancy;—he held almost unconsciously in his hand a naked dagger of a particular construction, which had been found in the hut. They were soon met by different parties who had been engaged in the search of her whom a mother had missed. Their lamentable cries, as they approached the city, forewarned the parents of some dreadful catastrophe.—To describe their grief would be impossible; but when they ascertained the cause of their child's death, they looked at Aubrey, and pointed to the corpse. They were inconsolable; both died brokenhearted.

Aubrey being put to bed was seized with a most violent fever, and was often delirious; in these intervals he would call upon Lord Ruthven and upon Ianthe—by some unaccountable combination he seemed to beg of his former companion to spare the being he loved. At other times he would imprecate maledictions upon his head, and curse him as her destroyer. Lord Ruthven chanced at this

time to arrive at Athens, and, from whatever motive, upon hearing
of the state of Aubrey, immediately placed himself in the same
house, and became his constant attendant. When the latter recovered from his delirium, he was horrified and startled at the sight of
him whose image he had now combined with that of a Vampyre;
but Lord Ruthven, by his kind words, implying almost repentance
for the fault that had caused their separation, and still more by the
attention, anxiety, and care which he showed, soon reconciled him
to his presence. His lordship seemed quite changed; he no longer
appeared that apathetic being who had so astonished Aubrey; but
as soon as his convalescence began to be rapid, he again gradually
retired into the same state of mind, and Aubrey perceived no difference from the former man, except that at times he was surprised
to meet his gaze fixed intently upon him, with a smile of malicious
exultation playing upon his lips: he knew not why, but this smile
haunted him. During the last stage of the invalid's recovery, Lord
Ruthven was apparently engaged in watching the tideless waves
raised by the cooling breeze, or in marking the progress of those
orbs, circling, like our world, the moveless sun;—indeed, he appeared to wish to avoid the eyes of all.

Aubrey's mind, by this shock, was much weakened, and that
elasticity of spirit which had once so distinguished him now seemed
to have fled for ever. He was now as much a lover of solitude and
silence as Lord Ruthven; but much as he wished for solitude, his
mind could not find it in the neighbourhood of Athens; if he
sought it amidst the ruins he had formerly frequented, Ianthe's
form stood by his side;—if he sought it in the woods, her light step
would appear wandering amidst the underwood, in quest of the
modest violet; then suddenly turning round, would show, to his
wild imagination, her pale face and wounded throat, with a meek
smile upon her lips. He determined to fly scenes, every feature of
which created such bitter associations in his mind. He proposed to
Lord Ruthven, to whom he held himself bound by the tender care
he had taken of him during his illness, that they should visit those

parts of Greece neither had yet seen. They travelled in every direction, and sought every spot to which a recollection could be attached: but though they thus hastened from place to place, yet they seemed not to heed what they gazed upon. They heard much of robbers, but they gradually began to slight these reports, which they imagined were only the invention of individuals, whose interest it was to excite the generosity of those whom they defended from pretended dangers. In consequence of thus neglecting the advice of the inhabitants, on one occasion they travelled with only a few guards, more to serve as guides than as a defence. Upon entering, however, a narrow defile, at the bottom of which was the bed of a torrent, with large masses of rock brought down from the neighbouring precipices, they had reason to repent their negligence; for scarcely were the whole of the party engaged in the narrow pass, when they were startled by the whistling of bullets close to their heads, and by the echoed report of several guns. In an instant their guards had left them, and, placing themselves behind rocks, had begun to fire in the direction whence the report came. Lord Ruthven and Aubrey, imitating their example, retired for a moment behind the sheltering turn of the defile: but ashamed of being thus detained by a foe, who with insulting shouts bade them advance, and being exposed to unresisting slaughter, if any of the robbers should climb above and take them in the rear, they determined at once to rush forward in search of the enemy. Hardly had they lost the shelter of the rock, when Lord Ruthven received a shot in the shoulder, which brought him to the ground. Aubrey hastened to his assistance; and, no longer heeding the contest or his own peril, was soon surprised by seeing the robbers' faces around him—his guards having, upon Lord Ruthven's being wounded, immediately thrown up their arms and surrendered.

By promises of great reward, Aubrey soon induced them to convey his wounded friend to a neighbouring cabin; and having agreed upon a ransom, he was no more disturbed by their presence—they being content merely to guard the entrance till their comrade should return with the promised sum, for which he had an order. Lord Ruthven's strength rapidly decreased; in two days mortification ensued, and death seemed advancing with hasty steps. His conduct and appearance had not changed; he seemed as unconscious of pain as he had been of the objects about him: but towards the close of the last evening, his mind became apparently uneasy, and his eye often fixed upon Aubrey, who was induced to offer his assistance with more than usual earnestness—"Assist me! You may save me—you may do more than that—I mean not my life, I heed the death of my existence as little as that of the passing day; but you may save my honour, your friend's honour."—"How? tell me how? I would do any thing," replied Aubrey.—"I need but little—my life ebbs apace—I cannot explain the whole—but if you would conceal all you know of me, my honour were free from stain in the world's mouth—and if my death were unknown for some time in England—I—I—but life."— "It shall not be known."—"Swear!" cried the dying man, raising himself with exultant violence. "Swear by all your soul reveres, by all your nature fears, swear that for a year and a day you will not impart your knowledge of my crimes or death to any living being in any way, whatever may happen, or whatever you may see."—His eyes seemed bursting from their sockets: "I swear!" said Aubrey; he sunk laughing upon his pillow, and breathed no more.

Aubrey retired to rest, but did not sleep; the many circumstances attending his acquaintance with this man rose upon his mind, and he knew not why; when he remembered his oath a cold shivering came over him, as if from the presentiment of something horrible awaiting him. Rising early in the morning, he was about to enter the hovel in which he had left the corpse, when a robber met him, and informed him that it was no longer there, having been conveyed by himself and comrades, upon his retiring, to the pinnacle of a neighbouring mount, according to a promise they had given his lordship, that it should be exposed to the first cold ray of the moon that rose after his death. Aubrey astonished, and taking several of the men, determined to go and bury it upon the spot where it lay. But, when he had mounted to the summit he found no trace of either the corpse or the clothes, though the robbers swore they pointed out the identical rock on which they had laid the body. For a time his mind was bewildered in conjectures, but he at last returned, convinced that they had buried the corpse for the sake of the clothes.

Weary of a country in which he had met with such terrible misfortunes, and in which all apparently conspired to heighten that superstitious melancholy that had seized upon his mind, he resolved to leave it, and soon arrived at Smyrna. While waiting for a vessel to convey him to Otranto, or to Naples, he occupied himself in arranging those effects he had with him belonging to Lord Ruthven. Amongst other things there was a case containing several weapons of offence, more or less adapted to ensure the death of the victim. There were several daggers and yataghans. Whilst turning them over, and examining their curious forms, what was his surprise at finding a sheath apparently ornamented in the same style as the dagger discovered in the fatal hut;—he shuddered;—hastening to gain further proof, he found the weapon, and his horror may be imagined when he discovered that it fitted, though peculiarly shaped, the sheath he held in his hand. His eyes seemed to need no further certainty—they seemed gazing to be bound to the dagger; yet still he wished to disbelieve; but the particular form, the same varying tints upon the haft and sheath were alike in splendour on both, and left no room for doubt; there were also drops of blood on each.

He left Smyrna, and on his way home, at Rome, his first inquiries were concerning the lady he had attempted to snatch from Lord Ruthven's seductive arts. Her parents were in distress, their fortune ruined, and she had not been heard of since the departure of his lordship. Aubrey's mind became almost broken under so many repeated horrors; he was afraid that this lady had fallen a victim to the destroyer of Ianthe. He became morose and silent; and his only occupation consisted in urging the speed of the postilions, as if he were going to save the life of some one he held dear. He arrived at

Calais; a breeze, which seemed obedient to his will, soon wafted him to the English shores; and he hastened to the mansion of his fathers, and there, for a moment, appeared to lose, in the embraces and caresses of his sister, all memory of the past. If she before, by her infantine caresses, had gained his affection, now that the woman began to appear, she was still more attaching as a companion.

Miss Aubrey had not that winning grace which gains the gaze and applause of the drawing-room assemblies. There was none of that light brilliancy which only exists in the heated atmosphere of a crowded apartment. Her blue eye was never lit up by the levity of the mind beneath. There was a melancholy charm about it which did not seem to arise from misfortune, but from some feeling within, that appeared to indicate a soul conscious of a brighter realm. Her step was not that light footing, which strays where'er a butterfly or a colour may attract—it was sedate and pensive. When alone, her face was never brightened by the smile of joy; but when her brother breathed to her his affection, and would in her presence forget those griefs she knew destroyed his rest, who would have exchanged her smile for that of the voluptuary? It seemed as if those eyes, that face were then playing in the light of their own native sphere. She was yet only eighteen, and had not been presented to the world, it having been thought by her guardians more fit that her presentation should be delayed until her brother's return from the Continent, when he might be her protector. It was now, therefore, resolved that the next drawing-room, which was fast approaching, should be the epoch of her entry into the "busy scene." Aubrey would rather have remained in the mansion of his fathers, and fed upon the melancholy which overpowered him. He could not feel interest about the frivolities of fashionable strangers, when his mind had been so torn by the events he had witnessed; but he determined to sacrifice his own comfort to the protection of his sister. They soon arrived in town, and prepared for the next day, which had been announced as a drawing-room.

The crowd was excessive—a drawing-room had not been held for a long time, and all who were anxious to bask in the smile of royalty, hastened thither. Aubrey was there with his sister. While he was standing in a corner by himself, heedless of all around him, engaged in the remembrance that the first time he had seen Lord Ruthven was in that very place—he felt himself suddenly seized by the arm, and a voice he recognized too well, sounded in his ear— "Remember your oath." He had hardly courage to turn, fearful of seeing a spectre that would blast him, when he perceived, at a little distance, the same figure which had attracted his notice on this spot upon his first entry into society. He gazed till his limbs almost refusing to bear their weight, he was obliged to take the arm of a friend, and forcing a passage through the crowd, he threw himself into his carriage, and was driven home. He paced the room with hurried steps, and fixed his hands upon his head, as if he were afraid his thoughts were bursting from his brain. Lord Ruthven again before him—circumstances started up in dreadful array—the dagger—his oath.—He roused himself, he could not believe it possible—the dead rise again!—He thought his imagination had conjured up the image his mind was resting upon. It was impossible that it could be real—he determined, therefore, to go again into society; for though he attempted to ask concerning Lord Ruthven, the name hung upon his lips, and he could not succeed in gaining information. He went a few nights after with his sister to the assembly of a near relation. Leaving her under the protection of a matron, he retired into a recess, and there gave himself up to his own devouring thoughts. Perceiving, at last, that many were leaving, he roused himself, and entering another room, found his sister surrounded by several, apparently in earnest conversation; he attempted to pass and get near her, when one, whom he requested to move, turned round, and revealed to him those features he most abhorred. He sprang forward, seized his sister's arm, and, with hurried step, forced her towards the street: at the door he found himself impeded by the crowd of servants who were waiting for their lords; and while he was engaged in

passing them, he again heard that voice whisper close to him—
"Remember your oath!"—He did not dare to turn, but, hurrying
his sister, soon reached home.

Aubrey became almost distracted. If before his mind had been
absorbed by one subject, how much more completely was it engrossed, now that the certainty of the monster's living again pressed
upon his thoughts. His sister's attentions were now unheeded, and
it was in vain that she entreated him to explain to her what had
caused his abrupt conduct. He only uttered a few words, and those
terrified her. The more he thought, the more he was bewildered.
His oath startled him;—was he then to allow this monster to roam,
bearing ruin upon his breath, amidst all he held dear, and not avert
its progress? His very sister might have been touched by him. But
even if he were to break his oath, and disclose his suspicions, who
would believe him? He thought of employing his own hand to free
the world from such a wretch; but death, he remembered, had been
already mocked. For days he remained in this state; shut up in his
room, he saw no one, and ate only when his sister came, who, with
eyes streaming with tears, besought him, for her sake, to support
nature. At last, no longer capable of bearing stillness and solitude,
he left his house, roamed from street to street, anxious to fly that
image which haunted him. His dress became neglected, and he
wandered, as often exposed to the noon-day sun as to the mid-night
damps. He was no longer to be recognized; at first he returned with
the evening to the house; but at last he laid him down to rest wherever fatigue overtook him. His sister, anxious for his safety, employed people to follow him; but they were soon distanced by him
who fled from a pursuer swifter than any—from thought. His conduct, however, suddenly changed. Struck with the idea that he left
by his absence the whole of his friends, with a fiend amongst them,
of whose presence they were unconscious, be determined to enter
again into society, and watch him closely, anxious to forewarn, in
spite of his oath, all whom Lord Ruthven approached with intimacy. But when he entered into a room, his haggard and suspicious

looks were so striking, his inward shudderings so visible, that his sister was at last obliged to beg of him to abstain from seeking, for her sake, a society which affected him so strongly. When, however, remonstrance proved unavailing, the guardians thought proper to interpose, and, fearing that his mind was becoming alienated, they thought it high time to resume again that trust which had been before imposed upon them by Aubrey's parents.

Desirous of saving him from the injuries and sufferings he had daily encountered in his wanderings, and of preventing him from exposing to the general eye those marks of what they considered folly, they engaged a physician to reside in the house, and take constant care of him. He hardly appeared to notice it, so completely was his mind absorbed by one terrible subject. His incoherence became at last so great, that he was confined to his chamber. There he would often lie for days, incapable of being roused. He had become emaciated, his eyes had attained a glassy lustre;—the only sign of affection and recollection remaining displayed itself upon the entry of his sister; then he would sometimes start, and, seizing her hands, with looks that severely afflicted her, he would desire her not to touch him. "Oh, do not touch him—if your love for me is aught, do not go near him!" When, however, she inquired to whom he referred, his only answer was "True! True!" and again he sank into a state, whence not even she could rouse him. This lasted many months: gradually, however, as the year was passing, his incoherences became less frequent, and his mind threw off a portion of its gloom, whilst his guardians observed, that several times in the day he would count upon his fingers a definite number, and then smile.

The time had nearly elapsed, when, upon the last day of the year, one of his guardians entering his room, began to converse with his physician upon the melancholy circumstance of Aubrey's being in so awful a situation, when his sister was going next day to be married. Instantly Aubrey's attention was attracted; he asked anxiously to whom. Glad of this mark of returning intellect, of which they feared he had been deprived, they mentioned the name of the Earl of Marsden. Thinking this was a young Earl whom he had met with in society, Aubrey seemed pleased, and astonished them still more by his expressing his intention to be present at the nuptials, and desiring to see his sister. They answered not, but in a few minutes his sister was with him. He was apparently again capable of being affected by the influence of her lovely smile; for he pressed her to his breast, and kissed her cheek, wet with tears, flowing at the thought of her brother's being once more alive to the feelings of affection. He began to speak with all his wonted warmth, and to congratulate her upon her marriage with a person so distinguished for rank and every accomplishment; when he suddenly perceived a locket upon her breast; opening it, what was his surprise at beholding the features of the monster who had so long influenced his life. He seized the portrait in a paroxysm of rage, and trampled it underfoot. Upon her asking him why he thus destroyed the resemblance of her future husband, he looked as if he did not understand her;—then seizing her hands, and gazing on her with a frantic expression of countenance, he bade her swear that she would never wed this monster, for he—But he could not advance—it seemed as if that voice again bade him remember his oath—he turned suddenly round, thinking Lord Ruthven was near him but saw no one. In the meantime the guardians and physician, who had heard the whole, and thought this was but a return of his disorder, entered, and forcing him from Miss Aubrey, desired her to leave him. He fell upon his knees to them, he implored, he begged of them to delay but for one day. They, attributing this to the insanity they imagined had taken possession of his mind, endeavoured to pacify him, and retired.

Lord Ruthven had called the morning after the drawing-room, and had been refused with every one else. When he heard of Aubrey's ill health, he readily understood himself to be the cause of it; but when he learned that he was deemed insane, his exultation and pleasure could hardly be concealed from those among whom

he had gained this information. He hastened to the house of his
former companion, and, by constant attendance, and the pretence
of great affection for the brother and interest in his fate, he gradually won the ear of Miss Aubrey. Who could resist his power? His
tongue had dangers and toils to recount—could speak of himself as
of an individual having no sympathy with any being on the crowded
earth, save with her to whom he addressed himself;—could tell
how, since he knew her, his existence had begun to seem worthy
of preservation, if it were merely that he might listen to her soothing accents;—in fine, he knew so well how to use the serpent's art,
or such was the will of fate, that he gained her affections. The title
of the elder branch falling at length to him, he obtained an important embassy, which served as an excuse for hastening the marriage
(in spite of her brother's deranged state), which was to take place
the very day before his departure for the continent.

Aubrey, when he was left by the physician and his guardians,
attempted to bribe the servants, but in vain. He asked for pen and
paper; it was given him; he wrote a letter to his sister, conjuring
her, as she valued her own happiness, her own honour, and the
honour of those now in the grave, who once held her in their arms
as their hope and the hope of their house, to delay but for a few
hours that marriage, on which he denounced the most heavy curses.
The servants promised they would deliver it; but giving it to the
physician, he thought it better not to harass any more the mind of
Miss Aubrey by, what he considered, the ravings of a maniac. Night
passed on without rest to the busy inmates of the house; and Aubrey heard, with a horror that may more easily be conceived than
described, the notes of busy preparation. Morning came, and the
sound of carriages broke upon his ear. Aubrey grew almost frantic.
The curiosity of the servants at last overcame their vigilance; they
gradually stole away, leaving him in the custody of an helpless old
woman. He seized the opportunity, with one bound was out of the
room, and in a moment found himself in the apartment where all
were nearly assembled. Lord Ruthven was the first to perceive

him: he immediately approached, and, taking his arm by force, hurried him from the room, speechless with rage. When on the staircase, Lord Ruthven whispered in his ear—"Remember your oath, and know, if not my bride to day, your sister is dishonoured. Women are frail!" So saying, he pushed him towards his attendants, who, roused by the old woman, had come in search of him. Aubrey could no longer support himself; his rage not finding vent, had broken a blood-vessel, and he was conveyed to bed. This was not mentioned to his sister, who was not present when he entered, as the physician was afraid of agitating her. The marriage was solemnized, and the bride and bridegroom left London.

Aubrey's weakness increased; the effusion of blood produced symptoms of the near approach of death. He desired his sister's guardians might be called, and when the midnight hour had struck, he related composedly what the reader has perused—he died immediately after.

The guardians hastened to protect Miss Aubrey; but when they arrived, it was too late. Lord Ruthven had disappeared, and Aubrey's sister had glutted the thirst of a VAMPYRE!

Attributed to *Johann Ludwig Tieck*

(1773–1853)

IN 1823, A THREE-VOLUME anthology of translations was published in London under the title *Popular Tales and Romances of the Northern Nations*. The preface mentions that only two of the tales had previously been translated, then adds:

> The English reader of these volumes must not expect to find in them the style of romance, which is now so popular, and justly popular, in his own country. These tales do not pretend to be a picture of human nature or human manners; they are either imitations of early traditions, or the traditions themselves, amplified by some modern writer, and must be judged of in reference to such origin . . . Though supernatural agency forms the basis of all, the superstructures vary with the varying characters of the authors.

With fierce Romantic disdain, the editor complains that "fiction is banished from the nursery" and that "the reign of reason is speedily about to commence, when we shall believe nothing but what can be proved to be, and shall attain a happy exemption from those vulgar prejudices, which have hitherto held society together."

Although the stories were unsigned, "Wake Not the Dead" has long been attributed to Johann Ludwig Tieck, an important early force in German Romanticism. Like many of the contributors to this anthology, Tieck was a poet, dramatist, and novelist as well as a critic and translator. Along with Novalis and other contemporaries, he fanned the Romantic flames with both scholarship and original creative fictions. In the introduction to *Popular Tales*, the editor remarks, when discussing various authors, "Lebrecht and Tieck are the authors of many beautiful legends, but they have generally trusted to their own fancy instead of building themselves on antient traditions." The story "Wake Not the Dead" is self-consciously archaic in style, but in its morass of death and sexuality reads like a Romantic-era saga, not a recycled fable.

The story opens with these lines, which usually have been omitted in reprintings:

> Wake not the Dead:—they bring but gloomy night
> And cheerless desolation into day
> For in the grave who mouldering lay,
> No more can feel the influence of light,
> Or yield them to the sun's prolific might;
> Let them repose within their house of clay—
> Corruption, wilt thou vainly e'er essay
> To quicken:—it sends forth a pest'lent blight;
> And neither fiery sun, nor bathing dew,
> Nor breath of spring the dead can e'er renew.
> That which from life is pluck'd, becomes the foe
> Of life, and whoso wakes it waketh woe.
> Seek not the dead to waken from that sleep
> In which from mortal eye they lie enshrouded deep.

Wake Not the Dead

WILT THOU FOR EVER sleep? Wilt thou never more awake, my beloved, but henceforth repose for ever from thy short pilgrimage on earth? O yet once again return! and bring back with thee the vivifying dawn of hope to one whose existence hath, since thy departure, been obscured by the dunnest shades. What! dumb? forever dumb? Thy friend lamenteth, and thou heedest him not? He sheds bitter, scalding tears, and thou reposest unregarding his affliction? He is in despair, and thou no longer openest thy arms to him as an asylum from his grief? Say then, doth the paly shroud become thee better than the bridal veil? Is the chamber of the grave a warmer bed than the couch of love? Is the spectre death more welcome to thy arms than thy enamoured consort? Oh! return, my beloved, return once again to this anxious disconsolate bosom." Such were the lamentations which Walter poured forth for his Brunhilda, the partner of his youthful passionate love: thus did he bewail over her grave at the midnight hour, what time the spirit that presides in the troublous atmosphere, sends his legions of monsters through mid-air; so that their shadows, as they flit beneath the moon and across the earth, dart as wild, agitating thoughts that chase each other o'er the sinner's bosom: thus did he lament under the tall linden trees by her grave, while his head reclined on the cold stone.

Walter was a powerful lord in Burgundy, who, in his earliest youth, had been smitten with the charms of the fair Brunhilda, a beauty far surpassing in loveliness all her rivals; for her tresses, dark as the raven face of night, streaming over her shoulders, set off to the utmost advantage the beaming lustre of her slender form, and the rich dye of a cheek whose tint was deep and brilliant as that of the western heaven: her eyes did not resemble those burning orbs whose pale glow gems the vault of night, and whose immeasurable distance fills the soul with deep thoughts of eternity, but rather as the sober beams which cheer this nether world, and which, while they enlighten, kindle the sons of earth to joy and love. Brunhilda became the wife of Walter, and both being equally enamoured and devoted, they abandoned themselves to the enjoyment of a passion that rendered them reckless of aught besides, while it lulled them in a fascinating dream. Their sole apprehension was lest aught should awaken them from a delirium which they prayed might continue for ever. Yet how vain is the wish that would arrest the decrees of destiny! as well might it seek to divert the circling planets from their eternal course. Short was the duration of this phrenzied passion; not that it gradually decayed and subsided into apathy, but death snatched away his blooming victim, and left Walter to a widowed couch. Impetuous, however, as was his first burst of grief, he was not inconsolable, for ere long another bride became the partner of the youthful nobleman.

Swanhilda also was beautiful; although nature had formed her charms on a very different model from those of Brunhilda. Her golden locks waved bright as the beams of morn: only when excited by some emotion of her soul did a rosy hue tinge the lily paleness of her cheek: her limbs were proportioned in the nicest symmetry, yet did they not possess that luxuriant fullness of animal life: her eye beamed eloquently, but it was with the milder radiance of a star, tranquillizing to tenderness rather than exciting to warmth. Thus formed, it was not possible that she should steep him in his former delirium, although she rendered happy his waking hours—tranquil

and serious, yet cheerful, studying in all things her husband's pleasure, she restored order and comfort in his family, where her presence shed a general influence all around. Her mild benevolence
tended to restrain the fiery, impetuous disposition of Walter: while
at the same time her prudence recalled him in some degree from his
vain, turbulent wishes, and his aspirings after unattainable enjoyments, to the duties and pleasures of actual life. Swanhilda bore her
husband two children, a son and a daughter; the latter was mild
and patient as her mother, well contented with her solitary sports,
and even in these recreations displayed the serious turn of her character. The boy possessed his father's fiery, restless disposition, tempered, however, with the solidity of his mother. Attached by his
offspring more tenderly towards their mother, Walter now lived for
several years very happily: his thoughts would frequently, indeed,
recur to Brunhilda, but without their former violence, merely as we
dwell upon the memory of a friend of our earlier days, borne from
us on the rapid current of time to a region where we know that he
is happy.

But clouds dissolve into air, flowers fade, the sands of the hour-
glass run imperceptibly away, and even so, do human feelings dissolve, fade, and pass away, and with them too, human happiness.
Walter's inconstant breast again sighed for the ecstatic dreams of
those days which he had spent with his equally romantic, enamoured Brunhilda—again did she present herself to his ardent fancy
in all the glow of her bridal charms, and he began to draw a parallel between the past and the present; nor did imagination, as it is
wont, fail to array the former in her brightest hues, while it pro-
portionably obscured the latter; so that he pictured to himself, the
one much more rich in enjoyments, and the other, much less so
than they really were. This change in her husband did not escape
Swanhilda; whereupon, redoubling her attentions towards him,
and her cares towards their children, she expected, by this means,
to re-unite the knot that was slackened; yet the more she endeavoured to regain his affections, the colder did he grow—the more

intolerable did her caresses seem, and the more continually did the image of Brunhilda haunt his thoughts. The children, whose endearments were now become indispensable to him, alone stood between the parents as genii eager to affect a reconciliation; and, beloved by them both, formed a uniting link between them. Yet, as evil can be plucked from the heart of man, only ere its root has yet struck deep, its fangs being afterwards too firm to be eradicated; so was Walter's diseased fancy too far affected to have its disorder stopped, for, in a short time, it completely tyrannized over him. Frequently of a night, instead of retiring to his consort's chamber, he repaired to Brunhilda's grave, where he murmured forth his discontent, saying: "Wilt thou sleep forever?"

One night as he was reclining on the turf, indulging in his wonted sorrow, a sorcerer from the neighbouring mountains entered into this field of death for the purpose of gathering, for his mystic spells, such herbs as grow only from the earth wherein the dead repose, and which, as if the last production of mortality, are gifted with a powerful and supernatural influence. The sorcerer perceived the mourner, and approached the spot where he was lying.

"Wherefore, fond wretch, dost thou grieve thus, for what is now a hideous mass of mortality—mere bones, and nerves, and veins? Nations have fallen unlamented; even worlds themselves, long ere this globe of ours was created, have mouldered into nothing; nor hath any one wept over them; why then should'st thou indulge this vain affliction for a child of the dust—a being as frail as thyself, and like thee the creature but of a moment?"

Walter raised himself up:—"Let yon worlds that shine in the firmament," replied he, "lament for each other as they perish. It is true, that I who am myself clay, lament for my fellow-clay: yet is this clay impregnated with a fire,—with an essence, that none of the elements of creation possess—with love: and this divine passion, I felt for her who now sleepeth beneath this sod."

"Will thy complaints awaken her: or could they do so, would

she not soon upbraid thee for having disturbed that repose in which she is now hushed?"

"Avaunt, cold-hearted being: thou knowest not what is love. Oh! that my tears could wash away the earthy covering that conceals her from these eyes; that my groan of anguish could rouse her from her slumber of death! No, she would not again seek her earthy couch."

"Insensate that thou art, and couldst thou endure to gaze without shuddering on one disgorged from the jaws of the grave? Art thou too thyself the same from whom she parted; or hath time passed o'er thy brow and left no traces there? Would not thy love rather be converted into hate and disgust?"

"Say rather that the stars would leave yon firmament, that the sun will henceforth refuse to shed his beams through the heavens. Oh! that she stood once more before me; that once again she reposed on this bosom!—how quickly should we then forget that death or time had ever stepped between us."

"Delusion! mere delusion of the brain, from heated blood, like to that which arises from the fumes of wine. It is not my wish to tempt thee; to restore to thee thy dead; else wouldst thou soon feel that I have spoken truth."

"How! restore her to me," exclaimed Walter casting himself at the sorcerer's feet. "Oh! if thou art indeed able to effect that, grant it to my earnest supplication; if one throb of human feeling vibrates in thy bosom, let my tears prevail with thee: restore to me my beloved; so shalt thou hereafter bless the deed, and see that it was a good work."

"A good work! a blessed deed!"—returned the sorcerer with a smile of scorn; "for me there exists nor good nor evil; since my will is always the same. Ye alone know evil, who will that which ye would not. It is indeed in my power to restore her to thee: yet, bethink thee well, whether it will prove thy weal. Consider too, how deep the abyss between life and death; across this, my power can build a bridge, but it can never fill up the frightful chasm."

Walter would have spoken, and have sought to prevail on this powerful being by fresh entreaties, but the latter prevented him, saying: "Peace! bethink thee well! and return hither to me tomorrow at midnight. Yet once more do I warn thee, 'Wake not the dead.'"

Having uttered these words, the mysterious being disappeared. Intoxicated with fresh hope, Walter found no sleep on his couch; for fancy, prodigal of her richest stores, expanded before him the glittering web of futurity; and his eye, moistened with the dew of rapture, glanced from one vision of happiness to another. During the next day he wandered through the woods, lest wonted objects by recalling the memory of later and less happier times, might disturb the blissful idea, that he should again behold her—again fold her in his arms, gaze on her beaming brow by day, repose on her bosom at night: and, as this sole idea filled his imagination, how was it possible that the least doubt should arise: or that the warning of the mysterious old man should recur to his thoughts.

No sooner did the midnight hour approach, than he hastened before the grave-field where the sorcerer was already standing by that of Brunhilda. "Hast thou maturely considered!" inquired he.

"Oh! restore to me the object of my ardent passion," exclaimed Walter with impetuous eagerness. "Delay not thy generous action, lest I die even this night, consumed with disappointed desire; and behold her face no more."

"Well then," answered the old man, "return hither again tomorrow at the same hour. But once more do I give thee this friendly warning, 'Wake not the dead.'"

All in the despair of impatience, Walter would have prostrated himself at his feet, and supplicated him to fulfill at once a desire now increased to agony; but the sorcerer had already disappeared. Pouring forth his lamentations more wildly and impetuously than ever, he lay upon the grave of his adored one, until the grey dawn streaked the east. During the day, which seemed to him longer than any he had ever experienced, he wandered to and fro, restless and impatient, seemingly without any object, and deeply buried in his own reflections, unquiet as the murderer who meditates his first deed of blood: and the stars of evening found him once more at the appointed spot. At midnight the sorcerer was there also.

"Hast thou yet maturely deliberated?" inquired he, as on the preceding night.

"Oh what should I deliberate?" returned Walter impatiently. "I need not to deliberate: what I demand of thee, is that which thou hast promised me—that which will prove my bliss. Or dost thou but mock me? If so, hence from my sight, lest I be tempted to lay my hands on thee."

"Once more do I warn thee," answered the old man with undisturbed composure. " 'Wake not the dead'—let her rest."

"Aye, but not in the cold grave: she shall rather rest on this bosom which burns with eagerness to clasp her."

"Reflect, thou mayst not quit her until death, even though aversion and horror should seize thy heart. There would then remain only one horrible means."

"Dotard!" cried Walter, interrupting him. "How may I hate that which I love with such intensity of passion? How should I abhor that for which my every drop of blood is boiling?"

"Then be it even as thou wishest," answered the sorcerer; "step back."

The old man now drew a circle round the grave, all the while muttering words of enchantment. Immediately the storm began to bowl among the tops of the trees; owls flapped their wings, and uttered their low voice of omen; the stars hid their mild, beaming aspect, that they might not behold so unholy and impious a spectacle; the stone then rolled from the grave with a hollow sound, leaving a free passage for the inhabitant of that dreadful tenement. The sorcerer scattered into the yawning earth, roots and herbs of most magic power, and of most penetrating odour, so that the worms crawling forth from the earth congregated together, and raised themselves in a fiery column over the grave: while rushing wind burst from the earth, scattering the mould before it, until at length the coffin lay uncovered. The moonbeams fell on it, and the lid burst open with a tremendous sound. Upon this the sorcerer poured upon it some blood from out of a human skull, exclaiming at the same time: "Drink, sleeper, of this warm stream, that thy heart may again beat within thy bosom." And, after a short pause, shedding on her some other mystic liquid, he cried aloud with the voice of one inspired: "Yes, thy heart beats once more with the flood of life: thine eye is again opened to sight. Arise, therefore, from the tomb."

As an island suddenly springs forth from the dark waves of the ocean, raised upwards from the deep by the force of subterraneous fires, so did Brunhilda start from her earthy couch, borne forward by some invisible power. Taking her by the hand, the sorcerer led her towards Walter, who stood at some little distance, rooted to the ground with amazement.

"Receive again," said he, "the object of thy passionate sighs: mayest thou never more require my aid; should that, however, happen, so wilt thou find me, during the full of the moon, upon the mountains in that spot and where the three roads meet."

Instantly did Walter recognize in the form that stood before him, her whom he so ardently loved; and a sudden glow shot through his frame at finding her thus restored to him: yet the night-frost had chilled his limbs and palsied his tongue. For a while he gazed upon her without either motion or speech, and during his pause, all was again become hushed and serene; and the stars shone brightly in the clear heavens.

"Walter!" exclaimed the figure; and at once the well-known sound, thrilling to his heart, broke the spell by which he was bound.

"Is it reality? Is it truth?" cried he, "or a cheating delusion?"

"No, it is no imposture: I am really living:—conduct me quickly to thy castle in the mountains."

Walter looked around: the old man had disappeared, but he perceived close by his side, a coal-black steed of fiery eye, ready equipped to conduct him thence; and on his back lay all proper attire for

Brunhilda, who lost no time in arraying herself. This being done, she cried, "Haste, let us away ere the dawn breaks, for my eye is yet too weak to endure the light of day." Fully recovered from his stupor, Walter leaped into his saddle, and catching up, with a mingled feeling of delight and awe, the beloved being thus mysteriously restored from the power of the grave, he spurred on across the wild, towards the mountains, as furiously as if pursued by the shadows of the dead, hastening to recover from him their sister.

The castle to which Walter conducted his Brunhilda, was situated on a rock between other rocks rising up above it. Here they arrived, unseen by any save one aged domestic, on whom Walter imposed secrecy by the severest threats.

"Here will we tarry," said Brunhilda, "until I can endure the light, and until thou canst look upon me without trembling: as if struck with a cold chill." They accordingly continued to make that place their abode: yet no one knew that Brunhilda existed, save only that aged attendant, who provided their meals. During seven entire days they had no light except that of tapers; during the next seven, the light was admitted through the lofty casements only while the rising or setting-sun faintly illumined the mountain-tops, the valley being still enveloped in shade.

Seldom did Walter quit Brunhilda's side: a nameless spell seemed to attach him to her; even the shudder which he felt in her presence, and which would not permit him to touch her, was not unmixed with pleasure, like that thrilling awful emotion felt when strains of sacred music float under the vault of some temple; he rather sought, therefore, than avoided this feeling. Often too as he had indulged in calling to mind the beauties of Brunhilda, she had never appeared so fair, so fascinating, so admirable when depicted by his imagination, as when now beheld in reality. Never till now had her voice sounded with such tones of sweetness; never before did her language possess such eloquence as it now did, when she conversed with him on the subject of the past. And this was the magic fairy-land towards which her words constantly conducted him. Ever did she dwell upon the days of their first love, those hours of delight which they had participated together when the one derived all enjoyment from the other: and so rapturous, so enchanting, so full of life did she recall to his imagination that blissful season, that he even doubted whether he had ever experienced with her so much felicity, or had been so truly happy. And, while she thus vividly portrayed their hours of past delight, she delineated in still more glowing, more enchanting colours, those hours of approaching bliss which now awaited them, richer in enjoyment than any preceding ones. In this manner did she charm her attentive auditor with enrapturing hopes for the future, and lull him into dreams of more than mortal ecstacy; so that while he listened to her siren strain, he entirely forgot how little blissful was the latter period of their union, when he had often sighed at her imperiousness, and at her harshness both to himself and all his household. Yet even had he recalled this to mind would it have disturbed him in his present delirious trance? Had she not now left behind in the grave all the frailty of mortality? Was not her whole being refined and purified by that long sleep in which neither passion nor sin had approached her even in dreams? How different now was the subject of her discourse! Only when speaking of her affection for him, did she betray anything of earthly feeling: at other times, she uniformly dwelt upon themes relating to the invisible and future world; when in descanting and declaring the mysteries of eternity, a stream of prophetic eloquence would burst from her lips.

In this manner had twice seven days elapsed, and, for the first time, Walter beheld the being now dearer to him than ever, in the full light of day. Every trace of the grave had disappeared from her countenance; a roseate tinge like the ruddy streaks of dawn again beamed on her pallid cheek; the faint, mouldering taint of the grave was changed into a delightful violet scent; the only sign of earth that never disappeared. He no longer felt either apprehension or awe, as he gazed upon her in the sunny light of day: it is not until now, that he seemed to have recovered her completely; and, glowing with all his former passion towards her, he would have pressed her to his bosom, but she gently repulsed him, saying?—"Not yet—spare your caresses until the moon has again filled her horn."

Spite of his impatience, Walter was obliged to await the lapse of another period of seven days: but, on the night when the moon was arrived at the full, he hastened to Brunhilda, whom he found more lovely than she had ever appeared before. Fearing no obstacles to his transports, he embraced her with all the fervour of a deeply enamoured and successful lover. Brunhilda, however, still refused to yield to his passion. "What!" exclaimed she, "is it fitting that I who have been purified by death from the frailty of mortality, should become thy concubine, while a mere daughter of the earth bears the tide of thy wife: never shall it be. No, it must be within the walls of thy palace, within that chamber where I once reigned as queen, that thou obtainest the end of thy wishes—and of mine also," added she, imprinting a glowing kiss on the lips, and immediately disappeared.

Heated with passion, and determined to sacrifice everything to the accomplishment of his desires, Walter hastily quitted the apartment, and shortly after the castle itself. He travelled over mountain and across heath, with the rapidity of a storm, so that the turf was flung up by his horse's hoofs; nor once stopped until he arrived home.

Here, however, neither the affectionate caresses of Swanhilda, or those of his children could touch his heart, or induce him to restrain his furious desires. Alas! is the impetuous torrent to be checked in its devastating course by the beauteous flowers over which it rushes, when they exclaim:—"Destroyer, commiserate our helpless innocence and beauty, nor lay us waste?"—the stream sweeps over them unregarding, and a single moment annihilates the pride of a whole summer.

Shortly afterwards, did Walter begin to hint to Swanhilda, that they were ill-suited to each other; that he was anxious to taste that wild, tumultuous life, so well according with the spirit of his sex, while she, on the contrary, was satisfied with the monotonous circle of household enjoyments:—that he was eager for whatever promised novelty, while she felt most attached to what was familiarized to her by habit: and lastly, that her cold disposition, bordering upon indifference, but ill assorted with his ardent temperament: it was therefore more prudent that they should seek apart from each other, that happiness which they could not find together. A sigh, and a brief acquiescence in his wishes was all the reply that Swanhilda made: and, on the following morning, upon his presenting her with a paper of separation, informing her that she was at liberty to return home to her father, she received it most submissively: yet, ere she departed, she gave him the following warning: "Too well do I conjecture to whom I am indebted for this our separation. Often have I seen thee at Brunhilda's grave, and beheld thee there even on that night when the face of the heavens was suddenly enveloped in a veil of clouds. Hast thou rashly dared to tear aside the awful veil that separates the mortality that dreams, from that which dreameth not? Oh! then woe to thee, thou wretched man, for thou has attached to thyself that which will prove thy destruction." She ceased nor did Walter attempt any reply, for the similar admonition uttered by the sorcerer flashed upon his mind, all obscured as it was by passion, just as the lightning glares momentarily through the gloom of night without dispersing the obscurity.

Swanhilda then departed, in order to pronounce to her children, a bitter farewell, for they, according to national custom, belonged to the father; and, having bathed them in her tears, and consecrated them with the holy water of maternal love, she quitted her husband's residence, and departed to the home of her father's.

Thus was the kind and benevolent Swanhilda, driven an exile from those halls, where she had presided with such graces—from halls which were now newly decorated to receive another mistress. The day at length arrived, on which Walter, for the second time, conducted Brunhilda home, as a newly made bride. And he caused it to be reported amongst his domestics, that his new consort had gained his affections by her extraordinary likeness to Brunhilda, their former mistress. How ineffably happy did he deem himself, as he conducted his beloved once more into the chamber which had often witnessed their former joys, and which was now newly gilded and adorned in a most costly style: among the other decorations were figures of angels scattering roses, which served to support the purple draperies, whose ample folds o'ershadowed the nuptial couch. With what impatience did he await the hour that was to put him in possession of those beauties, for which he had already paid so high a price, but, whose enjoyment was to cost him most dearly yet! Unfortunate Walter! revelling in bliss, thou beholdest not the abyss that yawns beneath thy feet, intoxicated with the luscious perfume of the flower thou hast plucked, thou little deemest how deadly is the venom with which it is fraught, although, for a short season, its potent fragrance bestows new energy on all thy feelings.

Happy, however, as Walter now was, his household were far from being equally so. The strange resemblance between their new lady and the deceased Brunhilda, filled them with a secret dismay—an undefinable horror; for there was not a single difference of feature, of tone of voice, or of gesture. To add too to these mysterious circumstances, her female attendants discovered a particular mark on her back, exactly like one which Brunhilda had. A report was now soon circulated, that their lady was no other than Brunhilda herself, who had been recalled to life by the power of necromancy. How truly horrible was the idea of living under the same roof with one who had been an inhabitant of the tomb, and of being obliged to attend upon her, and acknowledge her as mistress! There was also in Brunhilda, much to increase this aversion, and favour their superstition: no ornaments of gold ever decked her person; all that others were wont to wear of this metal, she had formed of silver: no richly coloured and sparkling jewels glittered upon her; pearls alone, lent their pale lustre to adorn her bosom. Most carefully did she always avoid the cheerful light of the sun, and was wont to spend the brightest days in the most retired and gloomy apartments: only during the twilight of the commencing, or declining day did she ever walk abroad, but her favourite hour was, when the phantom light of the moon bestowed on all objects a shadowy appearance, and a sombre hue; always too at the crowing of the cock, an involuntary shudder was observed to seize her limbs. Imperious as before her death, she quickly imposed her iron yoke on every one around her, while she seemed even far more terrible than ever, since a dread of some supernatural power attached to her, and appalled all who approached her. A malignant withering glance seemed to shoot from her eye on the unhappy object of her wrath, as if it would annihilate its victim. In short, those halls which, in the time of Swanhilda were the residence of cheerfulness and mirth, now resembled an extensive desert tomb. With fear imprinted on their pale countenances, the domestics glided through the apartments of the castle; and, in this abode of terror, the crowing of the cock caused the living to tremble, as if they were the spirits of the departed; for the sound always reminded them of their mysterious mistress. There was no one but who shuddered at meeting her in a lonely place, in the dusk of evening, or by the light of the moon, a circumstance that was deemed to be ominous of some evil: so great was the apprehension of her female attendants, they pined in continual disquietude, and, by degrees, all quitted her. In the course of time even others of the domestics fled, for an insupportble horror had seized them.

The art of the sorcerer had indeed bestowed upon Brunhilda an artificial life, and due nourishment had continued to support the restored body; yet, this body was not able of itself to keep up the genial glow of vitality, and to nourish the flame whence springs all the affections and passions, whether of love or hate; for death had for ever destroyed and withered it: all that Brunhilda now possessed was a chilled existence, colder than that of the snake. It was nevertheless necessary that she should love, and return with equal ardour the warm caresses of her spell-enthralled husband, to whose passion alone she was indebted for her renewed existence. It was necessary that a magic draught should animate the dull current in her veins, and awaken her to the glow of life and the flame of love—a potion of abomination—one not even to be named without a curse—human blood, imbibed whilst yet warm, from the veins of youth. This was the hellish drink for which she thirsted: possessing no sympathy with the purer feelings of humanity; deriving no enjoyment from aught that interests in life, and occupies its varied hours; her existence was a mere blank, unless when in the arms of her paramour husband, and therefore was it that she craved incessantly after the horrible draught. It was even with the utmost effort that she could forbear sucking even the blood of Walter himself, as he reclined beside her. Whenever she beheld some innocent child, whose lovely face denoted the exuberance of infantine health and vigour, she would entice it by soothing words and fond caresses into her most secret apartment, where, lulling it to sleep in her arms, she would suck from its bosom the warm, purple tide of life. Nor were youths of either sex safe from her horrid attack: having first breathed upon her unhappy victim, who never failed immediately to sink into a lengthened sleep, she would then in a similar manner drain his veins of the vital juice. Thus children, youths, and maidens quickly faded away, as flowers gnawn by the cankering worm: the fullness of their limbs disappeared; a sallow line succeeded to the rosy freshness of their cheeks, the liquid lustre of the eye was deadened, even as the sparkling stream when arrested by the touch of frost; and their locks became thin and grey, as if already ravaged by the storm of life. Parents beheld with horror this desolating pestilence, devouring their offspring; nor could simple charm, potion, or amulet avail aught against it. The grave swallowed up one after the other; or did the miserable victim survive, he became cadaverous and wrinkled even in the very morn of existence. Parents observed with horror, this devastating pestilence snatch away their offspring—a pestilence which, nor herb however potent, nor charm, nor holy taper, nor exorcism could avert. They either beheld their children sink one after the other into the grave, or their youthful forms, withered by the unholy, vampire embrace of Brunhilda, assume the decrepitude of sudden age.

At length strange surmises and reports began to prevail; it was whispered that Brunhilda herself was the cause of all these horrors; although no one could pretend to tell in what manner she destroyed her victims, since no marks of violence were discernible. Yet when young children confessed that she had frequently lulled them asleep in her arms, and elder ones said that a sudden slumber had come upon them whenever she began to converse with them, suspicion became converted into certainty, and those whose offspring had hitherto escaped unharmed, quitted their hearths and home—all their little possessions—the dwellings of their fathers and the inheritance of their children, in order to rescue from so horrible a fate those who were dearer to their simple affections than aught else the world could give.

Thus daily did the castle assume a more desolate appearance; daily did its environs become more deserted; none but a few aged decrepit old women and grey-headed menials were to be seen remaining of the once numerous retinue. Such will in the latter days of the earth, be the last generation of mortals, when child-bearing shall have ceased, when youth shall no more be seen, nor any arise to replace those who shall await their fate in silence.

Walter alone noticed not, or heeded not, the desolation around him; he apprehended not death, lapped as he was in a glowing Elysium of love. Far more happy than formerly did he now seem in the possession of Brunhilda. All those caprices and frowns which had been wont to overcloud their former union had now entirely disappeared. She even seemed to dote on him with a warmth of passion that she had never exhibited even during the happy season of bridal love; for the flame of that youthful blood, of which she drained the veins of others, rioted in her own. At night, as soon as he closed his eyes, she would breathe on him till he sank into delicious dreams, from which he awoke only to experience more rapturous enjoyments. By day she would continually discourse with him on the bliss experienced by happy spirits beyond the grave, assuring him that, as his affection had recalled her from the tomb, they were now irrevocably united. Thus fascinated by a continual spell, it was not possible that he should perceive what was taking place around him. Brunhilda, however, foresaw with savage grief that the source of her youthful ardour was daily decreasing, for, in a short time, there remained nothing gifted with youth, save Walter and his children, and these latter she resolved should be her next victims.

On her first return to the castle, she had felt an aversion towards the off-spring of another, and therefore abandoned them entirely to the attendants appointed by Swanhilda. Now, however, she began to pay considerable attention to them, and caused them to be frequently admitted into her presence. The aged nurses were filled with dread at perceiving these marks of regard from her towards their young charges, yet dared they not to oppose the will of their terrible and imperious mistress. Soon did Brunhilda gain the affection of the children, who were too unsuspecting of guile to apprehend any danger from her; on the contrary, her caresses won them completely to her. Instead of ever checking their mirthful gambols, she would rather instruct them in new sports; often too did she recite to them tales of such strange and wild interests as to exceed all the stories of their nurses. Were they wearied either with play or with listening to her narratives, she would take them on her knees and lull them to slumber. Then did visions of the most surpassing magnificence attend their dreams: they would fancy themselves in some garden where flowers of every hue rose in rows one above the other, from the humble violet to the tall sun-flower, forming a party-coloured broidery of every hue, sloping upwards towards the golden clouds, where little angels, whose wings sparkled with azure and gold, descended to bring them delicious foods, or splendid jewels; or sung to them soothing melodious hymns. So delightful did these dreams in short time become to the children, that they longed for nothing so eagerly as to slumber on Brunhilda's lap, for never did they else enjoy such visions of heavenly forms. Thus were they most anxious for that which was to prove their destruction:—yet do we not all aspire after that which conducts us to the grave—after the enjoyment of life? These innocents stretched out their arms to approaching death, because it assumed the mask of pleasure; for, while they were lapped in these ecstatic slumbers, Brunhilda sucked the life-stream from their bosoms. On waking, indeed, they felt themselves faint and exhausted, yet did no pain, nor any mark betray the cause. Shortly, however, did their strength entirely fail, even as the summer brook is gradually dried up; their sports became less and less noisy; their loud, frolicsome laughter was converted into a faint smile; the full tones of their voices died away into a mere whisper. Their attendants were filled with horror and despair, too well did they conjecture the horrible truth, yet dared not to impart their suspicions to Walter, who was so devotedly attached to his horrible partner. Death had already smote his prey: the children were but the mere shadows of their former selves, and even this shadow quickly disappeared.

The anguished father deeply bemoaned their loss, for, notwithstanding his apparent neglect, he was strongly attached to them, nor until he had experienced their loss was he aware that his love was so great. His affliction could not fail to excite the displeasure of Brunhilda. "Why dost thou lament so fondly," said she, "for these little ones? What satisfaction could such unformed beings yield to thee, unless thou wert still attached to their mother? Thy heart then is still hers? Or dost thou now regret her and them, because thou art satiated with my fondness, and weary of my endearments? Had these young ones grown up, would they not have attached thee, thy spirit and thy affections more closely to this earth of clay—to this dust, and have alienated thee from that sphere to which I, who have already passed the grave, endeavour to raise thee? Say is thy spirit so heavy, or thy love so weak, or thy faith so hollow, that the hope of being mine for ever is unable to touch thee?" Thus did Brunhilda express her indignation at her consort's grief, and forbade him her presence. The fear of offending her beyond forgiveness, and his anxiety to appease her soon dried up his tears; and he again abandoned himself to his fatal passion, until approaching destruction at length awakened him from his delusion.

Neither maiden, nor youth, was any longer to be seen, either within the dreary walls of the castle, or the adjoining territory:—all had disappeared; for those whom the grave had not swallowed up, had fled from the region of death. Who, therefore, now remained to quench the horrible thirst of the female vampire, save Walter himself? and his death she dared to contemplate unmoved; for that divine sentiment that unites two beings in one joy and one sorrow was unknown to her bosom. Was he in his tomb, so was she free to search out other victims, and glut herself with destruction, until she herself should, at the last day, be consumed with the earth itself, such is the fatal law, to which the dead are subject, when awoke by the arts of necromancy from the sleep of the grave.

She now began to fix her blood-thirsty lips on Walter's breast, when cast into a profound sleep by the odour of her violet breath, he reclined beside her quite unconscious of his impending fate: yet soon did his vital powers begin to decay; and many a grey hair peeped through his raven locks. With his strength, his passion also declined; and he now frequently left her in order to pass the whole day in the sports of the chase, hoping thereby, to regain his wonted vigour. As he was reposing one day in a wood beneath the shade of an oak, he perceived, on the summit of a tree, a bird of strange appearance, and quite unknown to him; but, before he could take aim at it with his bow, it flew away into the clouds; at the same time, letting fall a rose-coloured root which dropped at Walter's feet, who immediately took it up, and, although he was well acquainted with almost every plant, he could not remember to have seen any at all resembling this. Its delightfully odoriferous scent induced him to try its flavour, but ten times more bitter than

wormwood, it was even as gall in his mouth; upon which, impatient of the disappointment, he flung it away with violence. Had
he, however, been aware of its miraculous quality, and that it acted
as a counter charm against the opiate perfume of Brunhilda's breath,
he would have blessed it in spite of its bitterness: thus do mortals
often blindly cast away in displeasure, the unsavoury remedy that
would otherwise work their weal.

When Walter returned home in the evening and laid him down
to repose as usual by Brunhilda's side, the magic power of her
breath produced no effect upon him; and for the first time during
many months did he close his eyes in a natural slumber. Yet hardly
had he fallen asleep, ere a pungent smarting pain disturbed him
from his dreams; and, opening his eyes, he discerned, by the gloomy
rays of a lamp, that glimmered in the apartment, what for some
moments transfixed him quite aghast, for it was Brunhilda, drawing with her lips, the warm blood from his bosom. The wild cry of
horror which at length escaped him, terrified Brunhilda, whose
mouth was besmeared with the warm blood. "Monster!" exclaimed
he, springing from the couch, "is it thus that you love me?"

"Aye, even as the dead love," replied she, with a malignant
coldness.

"Creature of blood!" continued Walter, "the delusion which has
so long blinded me is at an end: thou art the fiend who hast destroyed my children—who hast murdered the offspring of my vas-
sals." Raising herself upwards and, at the same time, casting on
him a glance that froze him to the spot with dread, she replied, "It
is not I who have murdered them;—I was obliged to pamper myself with warm youthful blood, in order that I might satisfy thy
furious desires—thou art the murderer!"—These dreadful words
summoned, before Walter's terrified conscience, the threatening
shades of all those who had thus perished; while despair choked his
voice. "Why," continued she, in a tone that increased his horror,
"why dost thou make mouths at me like a puppet? Thou who hadst
the courage to love the dead—to take into thy bed, one who had

been sleeping in the grave, the bed-fellow of the worm—who hast clasped in thy lustful arms, the corruption of the tomb—dost thou, unhallowed as thou art, now raise this hideous cry for the sacrifice of a few lives?—They are but leaves swept from their branches by a storm.—Come, chase these idiot fancies, and taste the bliss thou hast so dearly purchased." So saying, she extended her arms to-wards him; but this motion served only to increase his terror, and exclaiming: "Accursed Being,"—he rushed out of the apartment.

All the horrors of a guilty, upbraiding conscience became his companions, now that he was awakened from the delirium of his unholy pleasures. Frequently did he curse his own obstinate blind-ness, for having given no heed to the hints and admonitions of his children's nurses, but treating them as vile calumnies. But his sor-row was now too late, for, although repentance may gain pardon for the sinner, it cannot alter the immutable decrees of fate—it cannot recall the murdered from the tomb. No sooner did the first break of dawn appear, than he set out for his lonely castle in the mountains, determined no longer to abide under the same roof with so terrific a being; yet vain was his flight, for, on waking the following morning, he perceived himself in Brunhilda's arms, and quite entangled in her long raven tresses, which seemed to involve him, and bind him in the fetters of his fate; the powerful fascina-tion of her breath held him still more captivated, so that, forgetting all that had passed, he returned her caresses, until awakening as if from a dream he recoiled in unmixed horror from her embrace. During the day he wandered through the solitary wilds of the mountains, as a culprit seeking an asylum from his pursuers; and, at night, retired to the shelter of a cave; fearing less to couch himself within such a dreary place, than to expose himself to the horror of again meeting Brunhilda; but alas! it was in vain that he endeav-oured to flee her. Again, when he awoke, he found her the partner of his miserable bed. Nay, had he sought the centre of the earth as his hiding place; had he even imbedded himself beneath rocks, or formed his chamber in the recesses of the ocean, still had he found

her his constant companion; for, by calling her again into existence, he had rendered himself inseparably hers; so fatal were the
links that united them.

Struggling with the madness that was beginning to seize him,
and brooding incessantly on the ghastly visions that presented themselves to his horror-stricken mind, he lay motionless in the gloom-
iest recesses of the woods, even from the rise of sun till the shades
of eve. But, no sooner was the light of day extinguished in the
west, and the woods buried in impenetrable darkness, than the apprehension of resigning himself to sleep drove him forth among
the mountains. The storm played wildly with the fantastic clouds,
and with the rattling leaves, as they were caught up into the air, as
if some dread spirit was sporting with these images of transitoriness
and decay: it roared among the summits of the oaks as if uttering a
voice of fury, while its hollow sound rebounding among the distant hills, seemed as the moans of a departing sinner, or as the faint
cry of some wretch expiring under the murderer's hand: the owl
too, uttered its ghastly cry as if foreboding the wreck of nature.
Walter's hair flew disorderly in the wind, like black snakes wreath-
ing around his temples and shoulders; while each sense was awake
to catch fresh horror. In the clouds he seemed to behold the form
of the murdered; in the howling wind to hear their laments and
groans; in the chilling blast itself he felt the dire kiss of Brunhilda;
in the cry of the screeching bird he heard her voice; in the moldering leaves he scented the charnel-bed out of which he had awakened her. "Murder of thy own off-spring," exclaimed he in a voice
making night, and the conflict of the elements still more hideous,
"paramour of a blood-thirsty vampire, reveller with the corruption
of the tomb!" while in his despair he rent the wild locks from his
head. Just then the full moon darted from beneath the bursting
clouds; and the sight recalled to his remembrance the advice of the
sorcerer, when he trembled at the first apparition of Brunhilda rising from her sleep of death;—namely, to seek him, at the season of
the full moon, in the mountains, where three roads met. Scarcely

had this gleam of hope broke in on his bewildered mind, than he flew to the appointed spot.

On his arrival, Walter found the old man seated there upon a stone, as calmly as though it had been a bright sunny day, and completely regardless of the uproar around. "Art thou come then?" exclaimed he to the breathless wretch, who, flinging himself at his feet, cried in a tone of anguish:—"Oh save me—succour me—rescue me from the monster that scattereth death and desolation around her."

"And wherefore a mysterious warning? why didst thou not perceive how wholesome was the advice—'Wake not the dead'?"

"And wherefore a mysterious warning? why didst thou not rather disclose to me, at once, all the horrors that awaited my sacrilegious profanation of the grave?"

"Wert thou able to listen to any other voice than that of thy impetuous passions? Did not thy eager impatience shut my mouth at the very moment I would have cautioned thee?"

"True, true:—thy reproof is just: but what does it avail now;—I need the promptest aid."

"Well," replied the old man, "there remains even yet a means of rescuing thyself, but it is fraught with horror, and demands all thy resolution."

"Utter it then, utter it; for what can be more appalling, more hideous than the misery I now endure?"

"Know then," continued the sorcerer, "that only on the night of the new moon, does she sleep the sleep of mortals; and then all the supernatural power which she inherits from the grave totally fails her. 'Tis then that thou must murder her."

"How! murder her!" echoed Walter.

"Aye," returned the old man calmly, "pierce her bosom with a sharpened dagger, which I will furnish thee with; at the same time renounce her memory for ever, swearing never to think of her intentionally, and that, if thou dost involuntarily, thou wilt repeat the curse."

"Most horrible! yet what can be more horrible than she herself is?—I'll do it."

"Keep then this resolution until the next new moon."

"What, must I wait until then?" cried Walter, "alas ere then, either her savage thirst for blood will have forced me into the night of the tomb, or horror will have driven me into the night of madness."

"Nay," replied the sorcerer, "that I can prevent"; and, so saying he conducted him to a cavern further among the mountains. "Abide here twice seven days," said he; "so long can I protect thee against her deadly caresses. Here wilt thou find all due provision for thy wants; but take heed that nothing tempt thee to quit this place. Farewell, when the moon renews itself, then do I repair hither again." So saying, the sorcerer drew a magic circle around the cave, and then immediately disappeared.

Twice seven days did Walter continue in this solitude, where his companions were his own terrifying thoughts, and his bitter repentance. The present was all desolation and dread; the future presented the image of a horrible deed, which he must perforce commit; while the past was empoisoned by the memory of his guilt. Did he think on his former happy union with Brunhilda, her horrible image presented itself to his imagination with her lips defiled with dripping blood: or, did he call to mind the peaceful days he had passed with Swanhilda, he beheld her sorrowful spirit, with the shadows of her murdered children. Such were the horrors that attended him by day: those of night were still more dreadful, for then he beheld Brunhilda herself, who, wandering round the magic circle which she could not pass, called upon his name, till the cavern re-echoed the horrible sound. "Walter, my beloved," cried she, "wherefore dost thou avoid me? art thou not mine? forever mine—mine here, and mine hereafter? And dost thou seek to murder me?—ah! commit not a deed which hurls us both to perdition—thyself as well as me." In this manner did the horrible visitant torment him each night, and, even when she departed, robbed him of all repose.

The night of the new moon at length arrived, dark as the deed it was doomed to bring forth. The sorcerer entered the cavern; "Come," said he to Walter, "let us depart hence, the hour is now arrived"; and he forthwith conducted him in silence from the cave to a coal-black steed, the sight of which recalled to Walter's remembrance the fatal night. He then related to the old man Brunhilda's noctural visits, and anxiously inquired whether her apprehensions of eternal perdition would be fulfilled or not. "Mortal eye," exclaimed the sorcerer, "may not pierce the dark secrets of another world, or penetrate the deep abyss that separates earth from heaven." Walter hesitated to mount the steed. "Be resolute," exclaimed his companion, "but this once is it granted to thee to make the trial, and, should thou fail now, nought can rescue thee from her power."

"What can be more horrible than she herself?—I am determined"; and he leaped on the horse, the sorcerer mounting also behind him.

Carried with a rapidity equal to that of the storm that sweeps across the plain, they in brief space arrived at Walter's castle. All the doors flew open at the bidding of his companion, and they speedily reached Brunhilda's chamber, and stood beside her couch. Reclining in a tranquil slumber; she reposed in all her native loveliness, every trace of horror had disappeared from her countenance; she looked so pure, meek, and innocent that all the sweet hours of their endearments rushed to Walter's memory, like interceding angels pleading in her behalf. His unnerved hand could not take the dagger which the sorcerer presented to him. "The blow must be struck even now"; said the latter, "shouldst thou delay but an hour, she will lie at day-break on thy bosom, sucking the warm life drops from thy heart."

"Horrible! most horrible!" faltered the trembling Walter, and turning away his face, he thrust the dagger into her bosom, exclaiming—"I curse thee for ever!"—and the cold blood gushed upon his hand. Opening her eyes once more, she cast a look of ghastly horror on her husband, and, in a hollow dying accent said— "Thou too art doomed to perdition."

"Lay now thy hand upon her corse," said the sorcerer, "and swear the oath."—Walter did as commanded, saying—"Never will I think of her with love, never recall her to mind intentionally, and, should her image recur to my mind involuntarily, so will I exclaim to it: be thou accursed."

"Thou has now done everything," returned the sorcerer; "restore her therefore to the earth, from which thou didst so foolishly recall her; and be sure to recollect thy oath: for, shouldst thou forget it but once, she would return, and thou wouldst be inevitably lost. Adieu—we see each other no more." Having uttered these words he quitted the apartment, and Walter also fled from this abode of horror, having first given direction that the corse should be speedily interred.

Again did the terrific Brunhilda repose within her grave; but her image continually haunted Walter's imagination, so that his existence was one continued martyrdom, in which he continually struggled, to dismiss from his recollection the hideous phantoms of the past; yet, the stronger his effort to banish them, so much the more frequently and the more vividly did they return; as the night-wanderer, who is enticed by a fire-wisp into quagmire or bog, sinks the deeper into his damp grave the more he struggles to escape. His imagination seemed incapable of admitting any other image than that of Brunhilda: now he fancied he beheld her expiring, the blood streaming from her beautiful bosom: at others he saw the lovely bride of his youth, who reproached him with having disturbed the slumbers of the tomb: and to both he was compelled to utter the dreadful words, "I curse thee for ever." The terrible imprecation was constantly passing his lips; yet was he in incessant terror lest he should forget it, or dream of her without being able to repeat it, and then, on awakening, find himself in her arms. Else would he recall her expiring words, and, appalled at their terrific import, imagine that the doom of his perdition was irrecoverably passed. Whence should he fly from himself? or how erase from his brain these images and forms of horror? In the din of combat, in the tumult of war and its incessant pour of victory to defeat; from the cry of anguish to the exultation of victory—in these he hoped to find at least relief of distraction: but here too he was disappointed. The giant fang of apprehension now seized him who had never before known fear; each drop of blood that sprayed upon him seemed the cold blood that had gushed from Brunhilda's wound; each dying wretch that fell beside him looked like her, when expiring, she exclaimed:—"Thou too art doomed to perdition"; so that the aspect of death seemed more full of dread to him than aught beside, and this unconquerable terror compelled him to abandon the battlefield. At length, after many a weary and fruitless wandering, he returned to his castle. Here all was deserted and silent, as if the sword, or a still more deadly pestilence had laid everything waste: for the few inhabitants that still remained, and even those servants who had once shewn themselves the most attached, now fled from him, as though he had been branded with the mark of Cain. With horror he perceived that, by uniting himself as he had done with the dead, he had cut himself off from the living, who refused to hold any intercourse with him. Often, when he stood on the battlements of his castle, and looked down upon desolate fields, he compared their present solitude with the lively activity they were wont to exhibit, under the strict but benevolent discipline of Swanhilda. He now felt that she alone could reconcile him to life, but durst he hope that one, whom he so deeply aggrieved, could pardon him, and receive him again? Impatience at length got the better of fear; he sought Swanhilda, and, with the deepest contrition, acknowledged his complicated guilt; embracing her knees he beseeched her to pardon him, and to return to his desolate castle, in order that it might again become the abode of contentment and peace. The pale form which she beheld at her feet, the shadow of the lately blooming youth, touched Swanhilda. "The folly," said she gently, "though it has caused me much sorrow, has never excited my resentment or my anger. But say, where are my children?" To this dreadful interrogation the agonized father could for a while frame no reply: at length he was obliged to confess the dreadful truth. "Then we are sundered for ever," returned Swanhilda; nor could all his tears or supplications prevail upon her to revoke the sentence she had given.

Stripped of his last earthly hope, bereft of his last consolation, and thereby rendered as poor as mortal can possibly be on this side of the grave, Walter returned homewards; when, as he was riding through the forest in the neighbourhood of his castle, absorbed in his gloomy meditations, the sudden sound of a horn roused him from his reverie. Shortly after he saw appear a female figure clad in black, and mounted on a steed of the same colour: her attire was like that of a huntress, but, instead of a falcon, she bore a raven in her hand; and she was attended by a gay troop of cavaliers and dames. The first salutations being passed, he found that she was proceeding the same road as himself; and, when she found that Walter's castle was close at hand, she requested that he would lodge her for that night, the evening being far advanced. Most willingly did he comply with this request, since the appearance of the beautiful stranger had struck him greatly; so wonderfully did she resemble Swanhilda, except that her locks were brown, and her eye dark and full of fire. With a sumptuous banquet did he entertain his guests, whose mirth and songs enlivened the lately silent halls. Three days did this revelry continue, and so exhilarating did it prove to Walter, that he seemed to have forgotten his sorrows and his fears; nor could he prevail upon himself to dismiss his visitors, dreading lest, on their departure, the castle would seem a hundred times more desolate than before, and his grief be proportionately increased. At his earnest request, the stranger consented to stay seven days, and again another seven days. Without being requested, she took upon herself the superintendence of the household, which she regulated as discreetly and cheerfully as Swanhilda had been wont to do, so that the castle, which had so lately been the abode of melancholy and horror, became the residence of pleasure and festivity, and Walter's grief disappeared altogether in the midst of so much gaiety. Daily did his attachment to the fair unknown increase; he even made her his confidant; and, one evening as they were walking together apart from any of her train, he related to her his melancholy and frightful history. "My dear friend," returned she, as soon as he had finished his tale, "it ill beseems a man of thy discretion to afflict thyself, on account of all this. Thou hast awakened the dead from the sleep of the grave, and afterwards found—what might have been anticipated, that the dead possess no sympathy with life. What then? thou wilt not commit this error a second time. Thou hast however murdered the being whom thou hadst thus recalled again to existence—but it was only in appearance, for thou couldst not deprive that of life, which properly had none. Thou hast, too, lost a wife and two children: but, at thy years, such a loss is most easily repaired. There are beauties who will gladly share thy couch, and make thee again a father. But thou dreadst the reckoning of hereafter:—go, open the graves and ask the sleepers there whether that hereafter disturbs them." In such manner would she frequently exhort and cheer him, so that, in a short time, his melancholy entirely disappeared. He now ventured to declare to the unknown the passion with which she had inspired him, nor did she refuse him her hand. Within seven days afterwards the nuptials were celebrated, and the very foundations of the castle seemed to rock from the wild tumultuous uproar of unrestrained riot. The wine streamed in abundance; the goblets circled incessantly: intemperance reached its utmost bounds, while shouts of laughter, almost resembling madness, burst from the numerous train belonging to the unknown. At length Walter, heated with wine and love, conducted his bride into the nuptial chamber: but, oh horror! scarcely had he clasped her in his arms, ere she transformed herself into a monstrous serpent, which entwining him in its horrid folds, crushed him to death. Flames crackled on every side of the apartment; in a few minutes after, the whole castle was enveloped in a blaze that consumed it entirely: while, as the walls fell in with a tremendous crash, a voice exclaimed aloud—"Wake not the dead!"

❊

Théophile Gautier

(1811–1872)

A MAN ADMIRED BY writers as diverse as Oscar Wilde and the brothers Goncourt, Théophile Gautier was, in the words of fellow critic Albert de La Fizelière, "the most authoritative and popular writer in the field of art criticism." He knew everyone from Balzac to Ingres; Baudelaire dedicated *Les Fleurs du Mal* to him. Friendly but opinionated, an enemy of bourgeois thinking in every category, Gautier was larger-than-life. He wore flowing capes with hats that were worthy of them and once notoriously wore a shocking red vest to the premiere of a drama by his friend Victor Hugo.

Lucky Parisian artists might find themselves invited to Gautier's Thursday-night soirees, where he lounged on cushions, stroked his purring cats, and smoked a hookah. One of his portraits by the now legendary photographer Nadar shows a bearded, long-haired Gautier leaning against a bureau, managing to radiate insouciant authority even while gazing off into space in a studied artsy pose. He supported himself with journalism, writing especially as a theater critic for *La Presse* and *Le Figaro* and other periodicals, and only gradually developed his influential career as an art critic. He was one of the first critics to recognize talent in Édouard Manet and became an important promoter of the Impressionists. Nowadays, when his books are read at all, commentators seem to admire his stylish, cultured travel memoirs as much as anything else.

Gautier's own fiction, influenced especially by E. T. A. Hoff-mann, the German master of the grotesque, often leaned toward the aberrant and supernatural. He published "La morte amoureuse" in 1843, early in his career. When the French critic F. C. de Sumichrast published his translation of the story in 1900, as part of his ongoing translation of Gautier's collected works, he chose simply to title it "The Vampire." Such a title wouldn't narrow it down much within these pages, so here it has one closer to the original. Gautier has a great deal of irreverent fun with his narrator, who fears women more than he fears vampires.

The Deathly Lover

YOU ASK ME, BROTHER, if I have ever loved. I have. It is a strange story, and though I am sixty, I scarce venture to stir the ashes of that remembrance. I mean to refuse you nothing, but to no soul less tried than yours would I tell the story. The events are so strange that I can hardly believe they did happen. I was for more than three years the plaything of a singular and diabolical illusion. I, a poor priest, I led in my dreams every night—God grant they were dreams only!—the life of the damned, the life of the worldly, the life of Sardanapalus. A single glance, too full of approval, cast upon a woman, nearly cost me the loss of my soul. But at last, by the help of God and of my holy patron, I was able to drive away the evil spirit which had possessed me. My life was complicated by an entirely different nocturnal life. During the day I was a priest of God, chaste, busied with prayers and holy things; at night, as soon as I had closed my eyes, I became a young nobleman, a connoisseur of women, of horses and dogs, gambling, drinking, and cursing, and when at dawn I awoke, it seemed to me rather that I was going to sleep and dreaming of being a priest. Of that somnambulistic life there have remained in my remembrance things and words I cannot put away, and although I have never left the walls of my presbytery, you will be apt to think, on hearing me, that I am a man who, having worn out everything and having given up the world and entered religion, means to end in the bosom of God days too greatly agitated, rather than a humble student in a seminary, who has grown old in a forgotten parish in the depths of a forest, and who has never had anything to do with the things of the day.

Yes, I have loved, as no one on earth ever loved, with an insensate and furious love, so violent that I wonder it did not break my heart. Ah! what nights what nights I have had! From my youngest childhood I felt the vocation to the priesthood and all my studies were therefore bent in that direction. My life until the age of twenty-four was nothing but one long novitiate. Having finished my theological studies, I passed successfully through the minor orders, and my superiors considered me worthy, in spite of my youth, of crossing the last dread limit. The day of my ordination was fixed for Easter week. I had never gone into the world. The world, to me, lay within the walls of the college and of the seminary. I knew vaguely that there was something called a woman, but my thoughts never dwelt upon it; I was utterly innocent. I saw my old, infirm mother but twice a year; she was the only connection I had with the outer world. I regretted nothing; I felt not the least hesitation in the presence of the irrevocable engagement I was about to enter into; nay, I was joyous and full of impatience. Never did a young bridegroom count the hours with more feverish ardour. I could not sleep; I dreamed that I was saying Mass; I saw nothing more glorious in the world than to be a priest. I would have refused, had I been offered a kingdom, to be a king or a poet instead, for my ambition conceived nothing finer.

What I am telling you is to show you that what happened to me ought not to have happened, and that I was the victim of the most inexplicable fascination.

The great day having come, I walked to the church with so light a step that it seemed to me that I was borne in the air, or that I had wings on my shoulders; I thought myself an angel, and I was amazed at the sombre and preoccupied expression of my companions,—for there were several of us. I had spent the night in prayer, and was in a

state bordering on ecstasy. The bishop, a venerable old man, seemed
to me like God the Father bending from eternity, and I beheld the
heavens through the vault of the dome.

You are acquainted with the details of the ceremony: the bene-
diction, the Communion in both kinds, the anointing of the palms
of the hands with the oil of the catechumens, and finally the sacred
sacrifice offered in conjunction with the bishop. I will not dwell on
these things. Oh! how right was Job, "Imprudent is he who has not
made a covenant with his eyes"! I happened to raise my head, which
until then I had kept bent down, and I saw before me, so close that I
might have touched her, although in reality she was a long way off,
on the other side of the railing, a young woman of wondrous beauty
dressed with regal magnificence. It was as though scales had fallen
from my eyes. I felt like a blind man suddenly recovering his sight.
The bishop, so radiant but now, was suddenly dimmed, the flame of
the tapers on their golden candlesticks turned pale like stars in the
morning light, and the whole church was shrouded in deep obscurity. The lovely creature stood out against this shadow like an angelic revelation. She seemed illumined from within, and to give
forth light rather than to receive it. I cast down my eyes, determined
not to look up again, so as to avoid the influence of external objects,
for I was becoming more and more inattentive and I scarcely knew
what I was about. Yet a moment later I opened my eyes again, for
through my eyelids I saw her dazzling with the prismatic colours in
a radiant penumbra, just as when one has gazed upon the sun.

Oh, how beautiful she was! The greatest painters had never approached this fabulous reality, even when, pursuing ideal beauty in
the heavens, they brought back to earth the divine portrait of the
Madonna. Neither the verse of the poet nor the palette of the painter
can give you an idea of her. She was rather tall, with the figure and
the port of a goddess. Her hair, of a pale gold, was parted on her
brow and flowed down her temples like two golden streams; she
looked like a crowned queen. Her forehead, of a bluish whiteness,
spread out broad and serene over the almost brown eyebrows, a sin-

gularity which added to the effect of the sea-green eyes, the brilliancy and fire of which were unbearable. Oh, what eyes! With one
flash they settled a man's fate. They were filled with a life, a limpid-
ity, an ardour, a moist glow, which I have never seen in any other
human eyes. From them flashed glances like arrows, which I distinctly saw striking my heart. I know not whether the flame that
illumined them came from heaven or hell, but undoubtedly it came
from one or the other place. That woman was an angel or a demon,
perhaps both. She certainly did not come from the womb of Eve,
our common mother. Teeth of the loveliest pearl sparkled through
her rosy smile, and little dimples marked each inflection of her
mouth in the rosy satin of her adorable cheeks. As to her nose, it was
of regal delicacy and pride, and betrayed the noblest origin. An
agate polish played upon the smooth, lustrous skin of her half-
uncovered shoulders, and strings of great fair pearls, almost similar
in tone to her neck, fell upon her bosom. From time to time she
drew up her head with the undulating movement of an adder or of
a peacock, and made the tall embroidered ruff that surrounded her
like a silver trellis tremble slightly. She wore a dress of orange-red
velvet, and out of the broad, ermine-lined sleeves issued wondrously
delicate patrician hands, with long, plump fingers, so ideally transparent that the light passed through them as through the fingers of
Dawn.

All these details are still as vivid to me as if I had seen her but
yesterday, and although I was a prey to the greatest agitation, nothing escaped me; the faintest tint, the smallest dark spot on the corner of the chin, the scarcely perceptible down at the corners of the
lips, the velvety brow, the trembling shadow of the eyelashes on
her cheeks,—I noted all with astonishing lucidity.

As I gazed at her, I felt open within me doors hitherto fast-closed;
passages obstructed until now were cleared away in every direction
and revealed unsuspected prospects; life appeared in a new guise; I
had just been born into a new order of ideas. Frightful anguish
clutched my heart, and every minute that passed seemed to me a

second and an age. Yet the ceremony was proceeding, and I was being carried farther from the world, the entrance to which was fiercely besieged by my nascent desires. I said "Yes," however, when I meant to say "no," when everything in me was revolting and protesting against the violence my vow was doing to my will. An occult force dragged the words from my mouth in spite of myself.

It is perhaps just what so many young girls do when they go to the altar with a firm resolve to boldly refuse the husband forced upon them. Not one carries out her intention. It is no doubt the same thing which makes so many poor novices take the veil, although they are quite determined to tear it to pieces at the moment of speaking their vows. No one dares to cause such a scandal before everybody, nor to deceive the expectations of so many present. The numerous wills, the numerous glances, seem to weigh down on one like a leaden cloak. And then, every precaution is so carefully taken, everything is so well settled beforehand in a fashion so evidently irrevocable that thought yields to the weight of fact and completely gives way.

The expression of the fair unknown changed as the ceremony progressed. Her glance, tender and caressing at first, became disdainful and dissatisfied as if to reproach me with dullness of perception. I made an effort, mighty enough to have overthrown a mountain, to cry out that I would not be a priest, but I could not manage it; my tongue clove to the roof of my mouth and it was impossible for me to express my will by the smallest negative sign. I was, although wide-awake, in a state similar to that of nightmare, when one seeks to call out a word on which one's life depends, and yet is unable to do so.

She seemed to understand the martyrdom I was suffering, and as if to encourage me, she cast upon me a look full of divine promise. Her eyes were a poem, her every glance was a canto; she was saying to me, "If you will come with me, I will make you more happy than God Himself in Paradise. The angels will be jealous of you. Tear away the funeral shroud in which you are about to wrap

yourself. I am beauty and youth and love; come to me, and together we shall be Love. What can Jehovah offer you in compensation? Our life shall pass like a dream, and will be but one eternal
kiss. Pour out the wine in that cup and you are free. We will go
away to unknown isles and you shall sleep on my bosom on a bed
of massive gold under a pavilion of silver. For I love you and mean
to take you from your God, before whom so many youthful hearts
pour out floods of love that never reach Him."

It seemed to me that I heard these words on a rhythm of infinite sweetness, for her glance was almost sonorous, and the phrases
her eyes sent me sounded within my heart as if invisible lips had
breathed them. I felt myself ready to renounce God, but my hand
was mechanically accomplishing the formalities of the ceremony.
The beauty cast upon me a second glance so beseeching, so despairing that sharp blades pierced my heart, and I felt more swords
enter my breast than did the Mother of Sorrows.

Never did any human face exhibit more poignant anguish. The
maiden who sees her betrothed fall suddenly dead by her side, the
mother by the empty cradle of her child, Eve seated on the threshold of the gate of Paradise, the miser who finds a stone in place of
his treasure, the poet who has accidentally dropped into the fire
the only manuscript of his favourite work,—not one of them could
look more inconsolable, more stricken to the heart. The blood left
her lovely face and she turned pale as marble. Her beautiful arms
hung limp by her body as if the muscles had been unknotted, and
she leaned against a pillar, for her limbs were giving way under her.
As for me, livid, my brow covered with a sweat more bloody than
that of Calvary, I staggered towards the church door. I was stifling;
the vaulting seemed to press down on me and my hand to upbear
alone the weight of the cupola.

As I was about to cross the threshold, a woman's hand suddenly
touched mine. I had never touched one before. It was cold like the
skin of a serpent, yet it burned me like the print of a red-hot iron.

It was she. "Oh, unfortunate man! Unfortunate man! What have you done?" she whispered; then disappeared in the crowd.

The old bishop passed by. He looked severely at me. My appearance was startlingly strange. I turned pale, blushed red, and flames passed before my eyes. One of my comrades took pity on me and led me away; I was incapable of finding alone the road to the seminary. At the corner of a street, while the young priest happened to look in another direction, a quaintly dressed negro page approached me and without staying his steps handed me a small pocket-book with chased gold corners, signing to me to conceal it. I slipped it into my sleeve and kept it there until I was alone in my cell. I opened it. It contained but two leaves with these words: "Clarimonda, at the Palazzo Concini." I was then so ignorant of life that I did not know of Clarimonda, in spite of her fame, and I was absolutely ignorant where the Palazzo Concini was situated. I made innumerable conjectures of the most extravagant kind, but the truth is that, provided I could see her again, I cared little what she might be, whether a great lady or a courtesan.

This new-born love of mine was hopelessly rooted within me. I did not even attempt to expel it from my heart, for I felt that that was an impossibility. The woman had wholly seized upon me; a single glance of hers had been sufficient to change me; she had breathed her soul into me, and I no longer lived but in her and through her. I indulged in countless extravagant fancies; I kissed on my hand the spot she had touched, and I repeated her name for hours at a time. All I needed to do to see her as plainly as if she had been actually present was to close my eyes; I repeated the words which she had spoken to me, "Unfortunate man! Unfortunate man! What have you done?" I grasped the full horror of my situation, and the dread, sombre aspects of the state which I had embraced were plainly revealed to me. To be a priest; that is, to remain chaste, never to love, never to notice sex or age; to turn aside from beauty, to voluntarily blind myself, to crawl in the icy shadows of a cloister or a church, to see none but the dying, to watch by strangers' beds, to wear mourning for myself in the form of the black cassock, a robe that may readily be used to line your coffin.

Meanwhile I felt life rising within me like an internal lake, swelling and overflowing; my blood surged in my veins; my youth, so long suppressed, burst out suddenly like the aloe that blooms but once in a hundred years, and then like a thunder-clap. How could I manage to see Clarimonda again? I could find no pretext to leave the seminary, for I knew no one in town. Indeed, my stay in it was to be very short, for I was merely waiting to be appointed to a parish. I tried to loosen the bars of the window, but it was at a terrific height from the ground, and having no ladder, I had to give up that plan. Besides, I could go out at night only, and how should I ever find my way through the labyrinth of streets? All these difficulties, which would have been slight to other men, were tremendous for me, a poor seminarist, in love since yesterday, without experience, without money, and without clothes.

"Ah, if only I had not been a priest, I might have seen her every day; I might have been her lover, her husband," I said to myself in my blindness. Instead of being wrapped in my gloomy shroud, I should have worn silk and velvet, chains of gold, a sword and a plume, like handsome young cavaliers. My hair, instead of being dishonoured by a broad tonsure, would have fallen in ringlets around my neck; I should have worn a handsome waxed moustache; I should have been a valiant man. A single hour spent before an altar, a few words scarcely breathed, had cut me off forever from the living; I had myself sealed the stone of my tomb; I had pushed with my own hand the bolts of my prison door.

I looked out of the window. The heavens were wondrously blue, the trees had assumed their springtime livery, nature exhibited ironical joy. The square was full of people coming and going. Young dandies and young beauties in couples were going towards the gardens and the arbours; workmen passed by, singing drinking songs; there was an animation, a life, a rush, a gaiety, which contrasted all the more painfully with my mourning and my solitude. A young mother was playing with her child on the threshold of a door. She kissed its little rosy lips still pearly with drops of milk, and indulged, as she teased it, in those many divine puerilities which mothers alone can invent. The father, who stood a little way off, was smiling gently at the charming group, and his crossed arms pressed his joy to his heart. I could not bear the sight. I closed the window and threw myself on my bed, my heart filled with frightful hatred and jealousy, and I bit my fingers and my coverlet as if I had been a tiger starving for three days.

I know not how long I remained in this condition, but in turning over in a furious spasm, I perceived Father Serapion standing in the middle of the room gazing attentively at me. I was ashamed of myself, and letting fall my head upon my breast, I covered my face with my hands.

"Romualdo, my friend, something extraordinary is taking place in you," said Serapion after a few moments' silence. "Your conduct is absolutely inexplicable. You, so pious, so calm, and so gentle, you have been raging in your cell like a wild beast. Beware, my brother, and do not listen to the suggestions of the devil. The evil spirit, angered at your having devoted yourself to the Lord, prowls around you like a ravening wolf, and is making a last effort to draw you to himself. Instead of allowing yourself to be cast down, dear Romualdo, put on the breastplate of prayer, take up the shield of mortification, and valiantly fight the enemy. You will overcome him. Trial is indispensable to virtue, and gold emerges finer from the crucible. Be not dismayed nor discouraged; the best guarded and the strongest souls have passed through just such moments. Pray, fast, meditate, and the evil one will flee from you."

The father's discourse brought me back to myself, and I became somewhat calmer. "I was coming," he said, "to inform you that you are appointed to the parish of C—. The priest who occupied it has just died, and his lordship the Bishop has charged me to install you there. Be ready to-morrow."

I signed that I would be ready, and the father withdrew.

I opened my breviary and began to read my prayers, but the lines soon became confused; I lost the thread of my thoughts, and the book slipped from my hands without my noticing it.

To leave to-morrow without having seen her again.

To add one more impossibility to all those that already existed between us! To lose forever the hope of meeting her unless a miracle occurred! Even if I were to write to her, how could I send my letter? Considering the sacred functions which I had assumed, to whom could I confide, in whom could I trust? I felt terrible anxiety. Then what Father Serapion had just said to me of the wiles of the devil recurred to my memory. The strangeness of the adventure, the supernatural beauty of Clarimonda, the phosphorescent gleam of her glance, the burning touch of her hand, the trouble into which she had thrown me, the sudden change which had occurred in me, my piety vanished in an instant,—everything went to prove plainly the presence of the devil, and that satin-like hand could only be the glove that covered his claws. These thoughts caused me much terror. I picked up the breviary that had fallen to the ground from my knees, and I again began to pray.

The next day Serapion came for me. Two mules were waiting for us at the door, carrying our small valises. He got on one and I on the other as well as I could. While traversing the streets of the town, I looked at every window and every balcony in the hope of seeing Clarimonda, but it was too early; and the town was not yet awake. My glance tried to pierce through the blinds and curtains of all the palaces in front of which we were passing. No doubt Serapion thought my curiosity was due to the admiration caused in me by the beauty of the architecture, for he slackened his mule's speed to give me time to look. Finally we reached the city gate and began to ascend the hill. When we reached the top, I turned around once again to gaze at the spot where lived Clarimonda. The shadow of a cloud covered the whole town; the blue and red roofs were harmonized in one uniform half-tint, over which showed, like flecks of foam, the morning smoke. By a singular optical effect there stood out bright under a single beam of light a building that rose far above the neighbouring houses, wholly lost in the mist. Although it was certainly three miles away, it seemed quite close; the smallest detail could be made out,—the turrets, the platforms, the windows, even the swallow-tailed vanes.

"What is that palace yonder lighted by a sunbeam?" I asked Serapion.

He shaded his eyes with his hand, and after having looked, answered: "That is the old palazzo which Prince Concini gave to Clarimonda the courtesan. Fearful things take place there."

At that moment,—I have never known whether it was a reality or an illusion,—I thought I saw on the terrace a slender white form that gleamed for a second and vanished. It was Clarimonda. Oh! Did she know that at that very moment, from the top of the rough road which was taking me away from her, ardent and restless, I was watching the palace she dwelt in, and which a derisive effect of light seemed to draw near to me as if to invite me to enter it as its master? No doubt she knew it, for her soul was too much in sympathy with mine not to have felt its every emotion, and it was that feeling which had urged her, still wearing her night-dress, to ascend to the terrace in the icy-cold dew of morning.

The shadow reached the palace, and all turned into a motionless ocean of roofs and attics in which nothing was to be distinguished save swelling undulations. Serapion urged on his mule; mine immediately started too, and a turn in the road concealed forever from me the town of S, for I was never to return there. After three days' travelling through a monotonous country, we saw rising above the trees the weathercock of the steeple of the church to which I had been appointed; and after having traversed some tortuous streets bordered by huts and small gardens, we arrived before the facade, which was not very magnificent. A porch adorned with a few mouldings and two or three sandstone pillars roughly cut, a tiled roof, and buttresses of the same sandstone as the pillars,—that

was all. On the left, the cemetery overgrown with grass, with a tall
iron cross in the centres to the right, in the shadow of the church,
the presbytery, a very plain, poor, but clean house. We entered. A
few hens were picking up scattered grain. Accustomed, apparently,
to the black dress of ecclesiastics, they were not frightened by our
presence, and scarcely moved out of the way. A hoarse bark was
heard, and an old dog ran up to us; it was my predecessor's dog. Its
eye was dim, its coat was gray, and it exhibited every symptom of
the greatest age a dog can reach. I patted it gently with my hand,
and it immediately walked beside me with an air of inexpressible
satisfaction. An old woman, who had been housekeeper to the former priest, also came to meet us, and after having shown us into
the lower room, asked me if I intended to keep her. I told her that
I should do so, and the dog and the hens also, and whatever furniture her master had left her at his death, which caused her a trans-
port of joy, Father Serapion having at once paid her the price she
had set upon it.

Having thus installed me, Father Serapion returned to the seminary. I therefore remained alone and without any other help than
my own. The thought of Clarimonda again began to haunt me,
and in spite of the efforts I made to drive it away, I was not always
successful. One evening as I was walking through the box-edged
walks of my little garden, I thought I saw through the shrubbery a
female form watching my movements, and two sea-green eyes flashing amid the foliage, but it was merely an illusion. Having passed
on the other side of the walk, I found only the imprint of a foot on
the sand, so small that it looked like a child's foot. The garden was
shut in by very high walls. I visited every nook and corner of it,
but found no one. I have never been able to explain the fact,
which, for the matter of that, was nothing by comparison with the
strange things that were to happen to me.

I had been living in this way for a year, carefully fulfilling all
the duties of my profession, praying, fasting, exhorting, and suc-
couring the sick, giving alms even to the extent of depriving

myself of the most indispensable necessaries; but I felt within me
extreme aridity, and the sources of grace were closed to me. I did
not enjoy the happiness which comes of fulfilling a holy mission;
my thoughts were elsewhere, and Clarimonda's words often recurred to me. O my brother, ponder this carefully. Because I had
a single time looked at a woman, because I had committed a fault
apparently so slight, I suffered for several years the most dreadful
agitation and my life was troubled forever.

I shall not dwell longer upon these inward defeats and victories
which were always followed by greater falls, but I shall pass at once
to a decisive circumstance. One night there was a violent ringing at
my door. The housekeeper went to open it, and a dark complex-
ioned man, richly dressed in a foreign fashion, wearing a long dagger, showed under the rays of Barbara's lantern. Her first movement
was one of terror, but the man reassured her, and told her that he
must see me at once on a matter concerning my ministry. Barbara
brought him upstairs. I was just about to go to bed. The man told
me that his mistress, a very great lady, was dying and asking for a
priest. I replied that I was ready to follow him, took what was
needed for extreme unction, and descended quickly. At the door
were impatiently pawing and stamping two horses black as night,
breathing out long jets of smoke. He held the stirrup for me and
helped me to mount one, then sprang on the other, merely resting
his hand upon the pommel of the saddle. He pressed in his knees
and gave his horse its head, when it went off like an arrow. My
own, of which he held the bridle, also started at a gallop and kept up
easily with the other. We rushed over the ground, which flashed by
us gray and streaked, and the black silhouettes of the trees fled like
the rout of an army. We traversed a forest, the darkness of which
was so dense and icy that I felt a shudder of superstitious terror. The
sparks which our horses' hoofs struck from the stones formed a trail
of fire, and if any one had seen us at that time of night, he would
have taken us for two spectres bestriding nightmares. From time to
time will-o'-the-wisps flashed across the road, and the jackdaws

croaked sadly in the thickness of the wood, in which shone here and there the phosphorescent eyes of wildcats. Our horses' manes streamed out wildly, sweat poured down their sides, and their breath came short and quick through their nostrils; but when the equerry saw them slackening speed, he excited them by a guttural cry which had nothing of human in it, and the race began again madder than ever. At last our whirlwind stopped. A black mass dotted with brilliant points suddenly rose before us. The steps of our steeds sounded louder upon the ironbound flooring, and we entered under an archway the sombre mouth of which yawned between two huge towers. Great excitement reigned in the château. Servants with torches in their hands were traversing the courts in every direction, and lights were ascending and descending from story to story. I caught a confused glimpse of vast architecture,—columns, arcades, steps, stairs, a perfectly regal and fairylike splendour of construction. A negro page, the same who had handed me Clarimonda's tablets, and whom I at once recognised, helped me to descend, and a majordomo, dressed in black velvet, with a gold chain around his neck and an ivory cane, advanced towards me. Great tears fell from his eyes and flowed down his cheeks upon his white beard. "Too late," he said, shaking his head. "Too late, my lord priest. But if you have not been able to save the soul, come and pray for the poor body." He took me by the arm and led me to the room of death. I wept as bitterly as he did, for I had understood that the dead woman was none else than Clarimonda, whom I had loved so deeply and madly. A *prie-dieu* was placed by the bedside; a bluish flame rising from a bronze cup cast through the room a faint, vague light, and here and there brought out of the shadow the corner of a piece of furniture or of a cornice. On a table, in a chased urn, was a faded white rose, the petals of which, with a single exception, had all fallen at the foot of the vase like perfumed tears. A broken black mask, a fan, and disguises of all kinds lay about on the armchairs, showing that death had entered this sumptuous dwelling unexpectedly and without warning. I knelt, not daring to cast my eyes on the bed, and began to recite the psalms with great fervour, thanking God for having put the tomb between the thought of that woman and myself, so that I might add to my prayers her name, henceforth sanctified. Little by little, however, my fervour diminished, and I fell into a reverie. The room had in no wise the aspect of a chamber of death. Instead of the fetid and cadaverous air which I was accustomed to breathe during my funeral watches, a languorous vapour of Oriental incense, a strange, amorous odour of woman, floated softly in the warm air. The pale light resembled less the yellow flame of the night-light that flickers by the side of the dead than the soft illumination of voluptuousness. I thought of the strange chance which made me meet Clarimonda at the very moment when I had lost her forever, and a sigh of regret escaped from my breast. I thought I heard some one sigh behind me, and I turned involuntarily. It was the echo. As I turned, my eyes fell upon the state-bed which until then I had avoided looking at. The red damask curtains with great flowered pattern, held back by golden cords, allowed the dead woman to be seen, lying full length, her hands crossed on her breast. She was covered with a linen veil of dazzling whiteness, made still more brilliant by the dark purple of the hangings; it was so tenuous that it concealed nothing of the charming form of her body, and allowed me to note the lovely lines, undulating like the neck of a swan, which even death itself had been unable to stiffen. She looked like an alabaster statue, the work of some clever sculptor, intended to be placed on a queen's tomb, or a young sleeping girl on whom snow had fallen.

I was losing my self-mastery. The sensuous air intoxicated me, the feverish scent of the half-faded rose went to my brain, and I strode up and down the room, stopping every time before the dais to gaze at the lovely dead woman through her transparent shroud. Strange thoughts came into my mind; I imagined that she was not really dead, that this was but a feint she had employed to draw me to her château and to tell me of her love. Once indeed I thought I saw her foot move under the white veil, disarranging the straight folds of the shroud.

Then I said to myself, "But is it Clarimonda? How do I know? The black page may have passed into some other woman's service. I am mad to grieve and worry as I am doing." But my heart replied, as it beat loud, "It is she,—it is none but she." I drew nearer the bed and gazed with increased attention at the object of my uncertainty. Shall I confess it? The perfection of her form, though refined and sanctified by the shadow of death, troubled me more voluptuously than was right, and her repose was so like sleep that any one might have been deceived by it. I forgot that I had come there to perform the funeral offices, and I imagined that I was a young husband entering the room of his bride who hides her face through modesty and will not allow herself to be seen. Sunk in grief, mad with joy, shivering with fear and pleasure, I bent towards her and took up the corner of the shroud; I raised it slowly, holding in my breath for fear of waking her. My arteries palpitated with such force that I felt the blood surging in my temples and my brow was covered with sweat as if I had been lifting a marble slab. It was indeed Clarimonda, such as I had seen her in the church on the day of my ordination. She was as lovely as then, and death seemed to be but a new coquetry of hers. The pallor of her cheeks, the paler rose of her lips, the long-closed eyelashes showing their brown fringes against the whiteness, gave her an inexpressibly seductive expression of melancholy chastity and of pensive suffering. Her long hair, undone, in which were still a few little blue flowers, formed a pillow for her head and protected with its curls the nudity of her shoulders. Her lovely hands, purer and more diaphanous than the Host, were crossed in an attitude of pious repose and of silent prayer that softened the too great seduction, even in death, of the exquisite roundness and the ivory polish of her bare arms from which the pearl bracelets had not been removed. I remained long absorbed in mute contemplation. The longer I looked at her, the less I could believe that life had forever forsaken that lovely frame. I know not whether it was an illusion or a reflection of the lamp, but it seemed to me that the blood was beginning to course again under the mat pallor; yet she still remained perfectly motionless. I gently touched her arm; it was cold, yet no colder than her hand on the day it touched me under the porch of the church. I resumed my position, bending my face over hers, and let fall upon her cheeks the warm dew of my tears. Oh, what a bitter despair and powerlessness I felt! Oh, what agony I underwent during that watch! I wished I could take my whole life in order to give it to her, and breathe upon her icy remains the flame that devoured me. Night was passing, and feeling the moment of eternal separation approaching, I was unable to refuse myself the sad and supreme sweetness of putting one kiss upon the dead lips of her who had had all my love. But, oh, wonder! A faint breath mingled with mine, and Clarimonda's lips answered to the pressure of mine. Her eyes opened, became somewhat brighter, she sighed, and moving her arms, placed them around my neck with an air of ineffable delight. "Oh, it is you, Romualdo!" she said in a voice as languishing and soft as the last faint vibrations of a harp. "I waited for you so long that I am dead. But now we are betrothed; I shall be able to see you and to come to you. Farewell, Romualdo, farewell! I love you; that is all I wish to say to you, and I give you back the life which you have recalled to me for one moment with your kiss. Good-bye, but not for long."

Her head fell back, but her arms were still around me as if to hold me. A wild gust of wind burst in the window and rushed into the room; the last leaf of the white rose fluttered for a moment like a wing at the top of the stem, then broke away and flew out of the casement, bearing Clarimonda's soul. The lamp went out and I swooned away on the bosom of the lovely dead.

When I recovered my senses, I was lying on my bed in my little room in my house, and the old dog of the former priest was licking my hand that was hanging out from under the blanket. Barbara, shaky with old age, was busy opening and closing drawers and mixing powders in glasses. On seeing me open my eyes, the old woman uttered a cry of joy, while the dog yelped and wagged his tail; but I was so weak that I could neither move nor speak. I learned later that I had remained for three days in that condition, giving no other sign of life than faint breathing. These three days are cut out of my life. I do not know where my mind was during that time, having absolutely no remembrance of it. Barbara told me that the same copper-complexioned man who had come to fetch me during the night, had brought me back the next morning in a closed litter and had immediately departed. As soon as I could collect my thoughts, I went over in my own mind all the circumstances of that fatal night. At first I thought I had been the dupe of some magical illusion, but real and palpable circumstances soon shattered that supposition. I could not believe I had been dreaming, since Barbara had seen, just as I had, the man with two black horses, and described his dress and appearance accurately. Yet no one knew of any château in the neighbourhood answering to the description of that in which I had again met Clarimonda.

One morning I saw Father Serapion enter. Barbara had sent him word that I was ill, and he had hastened to come to me. Although this eagerness proved affection for and interest in me, his visit did not give me the pleasure I should have felt. The penetration and the inquisitiveness of his glance troubled me; I felt embarrassed and guilty in his presence. He had been the first to notice my inward trouble, and I was annoyed by his clear-sightedness. While asking news of my health in a hypocritically honeyed tone he fixed upon me his two yellow, lion-like eyes, and plunged his glance into my soul like a sounding-rod. Then he asked me a few questions as to the way in which I was working my parish, if I enjoyed my position, how I spent the time which my duties left me, if I had made any acquaintances among the inhabitants of the place, what was my favourite reading, and many other details of the same kind. I answered as briefly as possible, and he himself, without waiting for me to finish, passed on to something else. The conversation evidently had nothing to do with what he meant to say to me. Then, without any preparation, as if it were a piece of news which he had just recollected and which he was afraid to again forget, he said, in a clear, vibrant voice that sounded in my ear like the trump of the Last Judgment:—

"The great courtesan Clarimonda died recently, after an orgy that lasted eight days and nights. It was infernally splendid. They renewed the abominations of the feasts of Belshazzar and Cleopatra. What an age we are living in! The guests were served by dark slaves speaking an unknown language, who, I think, must have been fiends; the livery of the meanest of them might have served for the gala dress of an emperor. There have always been very strange stories about this Clarimonda; all her lovers have died a wretched and violent death. It is said that she was a ghoul, a female vampire, but I am of opinion that she was Beelzebub in person."

He was silent and watched me more attentively than ever to see the effect his words produced upon me. I had been unable to repress a start on hearing the name of Clarimonda, and the news of her death, besides the grief it caused me, through the strange coincidence with the nocturnal scene of which I had been a witness, filled me with a trouble and terror that showed in my face in spite of the efforts I made to master myself. Serapion looked at me anxiously and severely; then he said, "My son, I am bound to warn you that you have one foot over the abyss. Beware lest you fall in. Satan has a long arm, and tombs are not always faithful. The stone over Clarimonda should be sealed with a triple seal, for it is not, I am told, the first time that she has died. May God watch over you, Romualdo!"

With these words he walked slowly towards the door, and I did not see him again, for he left for S almost immediately.

I had at last entirely recovered, and had resumed my usual duties. The remembrance of Clarimonda and the words of the old priest were ever present to my mind; yet no extraordinary event had confirmed Serapion's gloomy predictions. I therefore began to believe that his fears and my terrors were exaggerated; but one night I dreamed a dream. I had scarcely fallen asleep when I heard the curtains of my bed open and the rings sliding over the bars with a rattling sound. I sat up abruptly, leaning on my elbow, and saw the shadow of a woman standing before me. I at once recognised Clarimonda. In her hand she bore a small lamp, of the shape of those put into tombs, the light of which gave to her slender fingers a rosy transparency that melted by insensible gradations into the opaque milky whiteness of her bare arm. Her sole vestment was the linen shroud that had covered her upon her state bed, and the folds of which she drew over her bosom as if she were ashamed of being so little clothed, but her small hand could not manage it. It was so white that the colour of the drapery was confounded with that of the flesh under the pale light of the lamp. Enveloped in the delicate tissue which revealed all the contours of her body, she resembled an antique marble statue of a bather rather than a woman filled with life. Dead or living, statue or woman, shadow or body, her beauty was still the same; only the green gleam of her eyes was somewhat dulled, and her mouth, so purple of yore, had now only a pale, tender rose-tint almost like that of her cheeks. The little blue flowers which I had noticed in her hair were dried up and had lost most of their leaves. And yet she was charming, so charming that in spite of the strangeness of the adventure and the inexplicable manner in which she had entered the room, I did not experience a single thrill of terror.

She placed the lamp on the table and sat down on the foot of my bed. Then bending towards me, she said in the silvery, velvety voice which I had heard from no one but her:—

"I have made you wait a long time, dear Romualdo, and you must have thought I had forgotten you. But I have come from a very long distance, from a bourne whence no traveller has yet returned. There is neither moon nor sun in the country whence I have come; neither road nor path; naught but space and shadow; no ground for the foot, no air for the wing; and yet I am here, for love is stronger than death and overcomes it. Ah, what worn faces, what terrible things I have seen on my way! What difficulty my soul, which returned to this world by the power of will, experienced before it could find its own body and re-enter it! What efforts I had to make before I could push up the tombstone with which they had covered me! See! The palms of my poor hands are all bruised. Kiss them and cure them, my dear love." And one after the other, she put the cold palms of her hands upon my lips. I did kiss them many a time, and she watched me with a smile of ineffable satisfaction.

I confess it to my shame,—I had wholly forgotten the counsels of Father Serapion and my own profession; I had fallen without resisting and at the first blow; I had not even endeavoured to drive away the tempter. The freshness of Clarimonda's skin penetrated mine, and I felt voluptuous thrills running through my body. Poor child! In spite of all that I have seen of her, I find it difficult to believe that she was a demon; she certainly did not look like one, and never did Satan better conceal his claws and horns. She had pulled her feet up under her, and was curled up on the edge of my bed in an attitude full of nonchalant coquetry. From time to time she passed her little hand through my hair and rolled it into ringlets as if to try how different ways of dressing it would suit my face. I allowed her to go on with the most guilty complaisance, and while she toyed with me she chatted brightly. The remarkable thing is that I experienced no astonishment at so extraordinary an adventure, and with the facility we enjoy in dreams of admitting as quite simple the most amazing events, it seemed to me that everything that was happening was quite natural.

"I loved you long before I had seen you, dear Romualdo, and I had looked for you everywhere. You were my dream, and when I saw you in church at that fatal moment, I at once said, 'It is he!' I cast on you a glance in which I put all the love which I had had, which I had, and which I was to have for you; a glance that would have damned a cardinal and made a king kneel before my feet in the presence of his whole court. But you remained impassible; you preferred your God to me. Oh, I am jealous of God, whom you loved, and whom you still love more than me! Unfortunate that I am,—oh, most unfortunate! Your heart will never be wholly mine, though you brought me back to life with a kiss, though I am Clarimonda, who was dead and who for your sake burst the cerements of the tomb, and has come to devote to you a life which she has resumed only to make you happy!"

With these words she mingled intoxicating caresses which penetrated my senses and my reason to such a degree that I did not hesitate, in order to console her, to utter frightful blasphemies and to tell her that I loved her as much as I did God.

Her eyes brightened and shone like chrysoprase. "True? Quite true? As much as God?" she said, clasping me in her lovely arms. "Since that is so, you will go with me, you will follow me where I will. You shall cast off your ugly black clothes, you shall be the proudest and most envied of men, you shall be my lover. Oh, the lovely, happy life we shall lead! When shall we start?"

"To-morrow! To-morrow!" I cried in my delirium.

"To-morrow be it," she replied. "I shall have time to change my dress, for this one is rather scanty and not of much use for travelling. Then I must also warn my people, who think me really dead, and who are mourning as hard as they can. Money, clothes, and carriage,—everything shall be ready, and I shall call for you at this same hour. Good-bye, dear heart," and she touched my brow with her lips.

The lamp went out, the windows were closed, and I saw no more. A leaden, dreamless sleep overcame me and held me fast until the next morning. I awoke later than usual, and the remembrance of the strange vision agitated me the livelong day. At last I managed to persuade myself that it was a mere fever of my heated brain. Yet the sensation had been so intense that it was difficult to believe it was not real, and it was not without some apprehension of what might happen that I went to bed, after having prayed God to drive away from me evil thoughts and to protect the chastity of my sleep.

I soon fell fast asleep and my dream continued. The curtains were opened, and I saw Clarimonda, not as the first time, wan in her pale shroud, and the violets of death upon her cheeks, but gay, bright, and dainty, in a splendid travelling-dress of green velvet with gold braid, caught up on the side and showing a satin under-skirt. Her fair hair escaped in great curls from below her broad black felt hat with capriciously twisted white feathers. She held in her hand a small riding-whip ending in a golden whistle. She touched me lightly with it and said: "Well, handsome sleeper, is that the way you get ready? I expected to find you up. Rise quickly, we have no time to lose."

I sprang from my bed.

"Come, put on your clothes and let us go," she said, pointing to a small parcel which she had brought. "The horses are impatiently champing their bits at the door. We ought to be thirty miles away by now."

I dressed hastily, and she herself passed me the clothes, laughing at my awkwardness and telling me what they were when I made a mistake. She arranged my hair for me, and when it was done, she held out a small pocket-mirror of Venice crystal framed with silver filigree and said to me, "What do you think of yourself? Will you take me as your valet?"

I was no longer the same man and did not recognise myself. I was no more like myself than a finished statue is like a block of stone. My former face seemed to me but a coarse sketch of the one reflected in the mirror. I was handsome, and my vanity was sensibly tickled by the metamorphosis. The elegant clothes, the rich embroidered jacket, made me quite a different person, and I admired the power of transformation possessed by a few yards of stuff cut in a certain way. The spirit of my costume entered into me, and in ten minutes I was passably conceited. I walked up and down the room a few times to feel more at my ease in my new garments. Clarimonda looked at me with an air of maternal complaisance and appeared well satisfied with her work.

"Now, that is childishness enough. Let us be off, dear Romualdo;

we are going a long way and we shall never get there." As she touched the doors they opened, and we passed by the dog without waking it.

At the door we found Margheritone, the equerry who had already conducted me. He held three horses, black like the first, one for me, one for himself, and one for Clarimonda. The horses must have been Spanish jennets, sired by the gale, for they went as fast as the wind, and the moon, which had risen to light us at our departure, rolled in the heavens like a wheel detached from its car. We saw it on our right spring from tree to tree, breathlessly trying to keep up with us. We soon reached a plain where by a clump of trees waited a carriage drawn by four horses. We got into it and the horses started off at a mad gallop. I had one arm around Clarimonda's waist and one of her hands in mine; she leaned her head on my shoulder, and I felt her half-bare bosom against my arm. I had never enjoyed such lively happiness. I forgot everything at that moment. I no more remembered having been a priest, so great was the fascination which the evil spirit exercised over me. From that night my nature became in some sort double. There were in me two men unknown to each other. Sometimes I fancied myself a priest who dreamed every night he was a nobleman; sometimes I fancied I was a nobleman who dreamed he was a priest. I was unable to distinguish between the vision and the waking, and I knew not where reality began and illusion ended. The conceited libertine rallied the priest; the priest hated the excesses of the young nobleman. Two spirals, twisted one within the other and confounded without ever touching, very aptly represent this bicephalous life of mine. Yet, in spite of the strangeness of this position, I do not think that for one instant I was mad. I always preserved very clearly the perception of my double life. Only there was an absurd fact which I could not explain: it was that the feeling of the same self should exist in two men so utterly different. That was an anomaly which I did not understand, whether I believed myself to be the parish priest of the little village of——or il Signor Romualdo, the declared lover of Clarimonda.

What is certain is that I was, or at least believed that I was, in Venice. I have never yet been able to make out what was true and what was imaginary in that strange adventure. We dwelt in a great marble palace on the Canaleio, full of frescoes and statues, with two paintings in Titian's best manner in Clarimonda's bedroom. It was a palace worthy of a king. Each of us had his own gondola and gondoliers, his own livery, music-room, and poet. Clarimonda liked to live in great style, and she had something of Cleopatra in her nature. As for me, I lived like a prince's son, and acted as if I belonged to the family of the twelve Apostles or the four Evangelists of the Most Serene Republic; I would not have got out of my way to let the Doge pass, and I do not think that since Satan fell from heaven there was any one so proud and so insolent as I. I used to go to the Ridotto and gamble fearfully. I met the best society in the world, ruined eldest sons, swindlers, parasites, and swashbucklers, yet in spite of this dissipated life, I remained faithful to Clarimonda. I loved her madly. She would have awakened satiety itself and fixed inconstancy. I should have been perfectly happy but for the accursed nightmare which returned every night, and in which I thought myself a parish priest living an ascetic life and doing penance for his excesses of the daytime. Reassured by the habit of being with her, I scarcely ever thought of the strange manner in which I had made her acquaintance. However, what Father Serapion had told me about her occasionally occurred to my mind and caused me some uneasiness.

For some time past Clarimonda's health had been failing. Her complexion was becoming paler and paler every day. The doctors, when called in, failed to understand her disease and knew not how to treat it. They prescribed insignificant remedies, and did not return. Meanwhile she became plainly paler, and colder and colder. She was almost as white and as dead as on that famous night in the unknown château. I was bitterly grieved to see her thus slowly pining away. She, touched by my sorrow, smiled gently and sadly at me with the smile of one who knows she is dying.

One morning I was seated by her bed breakfasting at a small table, in order not to leave her a minute. As I pared a fruit I happened to cut my finger rather deeply. The blood immediately flowed in a purple stream, and a few drops fell upon Clarimonda. Her eyes lighted up, her face assumed an expression of fierce and savage joy which I had never before beheld. She sprang from her bed with the agility of an animal, of a monkey or of a cat, and sprang at my wound, which she began to suck with an air of inexpressible delight. She sipped the blood slowly and carefully like a gourmand who enjoys a glass of sherry or Syracuse wine; she winked her eyes, the green pupils of which had become oblong instead of round. From time to time she broke off to kiss my hand, then she again pressed the wound with her lips so as to draw out a few more red drops. When she saw that the blood had ceased to flow, she rose up, rosier than a May morn, her face full, her eyes moist and shining, her hand soft and warm; in a word, more beautiful than ever and in a perfect state of health.

"I shall not die! I shall not die!" she said, half mad with joy, as she hung around my neck. "I shall be able to love you a long time yet. My life is in yours, and all that I am comes from you. A few drops of your rich, noble blood, more precious and more efficacious than all the elixirs in the world, have restored my life."

The scene preoccupied me a long time and filled me with strange doubts concerning Clarimonda. That very evening, when sleep took me back to the presbytery, I saw Father Serapion, graver and more care-worn than ever. He looked at me attentively, and said to me: "Not satisfied with losing your soul, you want to lose your body also. Unfortunate youth, what a trap you have fallen into!" The tone in which he said these few words struck me greatly, but in spite of its vivacity, the impression was soon dispelled and numerous other thoughts effaced it from my mind. However, one evening I saw in my mirror, the perfidious position of which she had not taken into account, Clarimonda pouring a powder into the cup of spiced wine she was accustomed to prepare for me after the meal. I took the cup, feigned to carry it to my lips, and put it away as if to finish it later at leisure, but I profited by a moment when my beauty had turned her back, to throw the contents under the table, after which I withdrew to my room and went to bed, thoroughly determined not to sleep, and to see what she would do. I had not long to wait. Clarimonda entered in her night-dress, and having thrown it off, stretched herself in the bed by me. When she was quite certain that I was asleep, she bared my arm, drew a golden pin from her hair, and whispered, "One drop, nothing but a little red drop, a ruby at the end of my needle! Since you still love me, I must not die. Oh, my dear love! I shall drink your beautiful, brilliant, purple blood. Sleep, my sole treasure, my god and my child. I shall not hurt you, I shall only take as much of your life as I need not to lose my own. If I did not love you so much, I might make up my mind to have other lovers whose veins I would drain; but since I have known you, I have a horror of every one else. Oh, what a lovely arm, how round and white it is! I shall never dare to prick that pretty blue vein." And as she spoke, she wept, and I felt her tears upon my arm which she held in her hands. At last she made up her mind, pricked me with the needle, and began to suck the blood that flowed. Though she had scarcely imbibed a few drops, she feared to exhaust me. She tied my arm with a narrow band, after having rubbed my wound with an unguent which healed it immediately.

I could no longer doubt; Father Serapion was right. However, in spite of the certainty, I could not help loving Clarimonda, and I would willingly have given her all the blood she needed in order to support her factitious existence. Besides, I was not much afraid, for the woman guarded me against the vampire; what I had heard and seen completely reassured me. At that time I had full-blooded veins which would not be very speedily exhausted, and I did not care whether my life went drop by drop. I would have opened my arm myself and said to her, "Drink, and let my life enter your body with my blood." I avoided alluding in the least to the narcotic which she had poured out for me and the scene of the pin,—and we lived in the most perfect harmony.

Yet my priestly scruples tormented me more than ever, and I knew not what new penance to invent to tame and mortify my flesh. Although all these visions were involuntary and I in no wise took part in them, I dared not touch the crucifix with hands so impure and a mind so soiled by such debauch, whether real or imaginary. After falling into these fatiguing hallucinations, I tried to keep from sleeping. I kept my eyes open with my fingers, and remained standing by the wall struggling against slumber with all my strength; but soon it would force itself into my eyes, and seeing that the struggle was useless, I let fall my arms with discouragement and weariness, while the current carried me again to the perfidious shores. Serapion exhorted me most vehemently, and harshly reproached me with weakness and lack of fervour. One day, when he had been more agitated than usual, he said to me:—

"There is but one way of ridding you of this obsession, and although it is extreme, we must make use of it. Great evils require great remedies. I know where Clarimonda is buried. We must dig her up, and you shall see in what a pitiful condition is the object of your love. You will no longer be tempted to lose your soul for a loathsome body devoured by worms and about to fall into dust. It will assuredly bring you back to your senses."

For myself, I was so wearied of my double life that I accepted, wishing to know once for all whether it was the priest or the nobleman who was the dupe of an illusion. I was determined to kill, for the benefit of the one or the other, one of the two men who were in me, or to kill them both, for such a life as I had been leading was unendurable. Father Serapion provided a pick, a crowbar, and a lantern, and at midnight we repaired to the cemetery of the place of which he knew accurately, as well as the disposition of the graves. Having cast the light of our lantern upon the inscriptions on several tombs, we at last reached a stone half hidden by tall grass and covered with moss and parasitical plants, on which we made out this partial inscription: "Here lies Clarimonda, who in her lifetime was the most beautiful woman in the world . . ."

"This is the spot," said Serapion, and putting down the lantern, he introduced the crowbar in the joints of the stone and began to raise it. The stone yielded, and he set to work with the pick. I watched him, darker and more silent than the night itself. As for him, bending over this funereal work, he perspired heavily and his quick breath sounded like the rattle in a dying man's throat. It was a strange spectacle, and any one who might have seen us would have taken us rather for men profaning the tomb and robbing the shrouds than for priests of God. Serapion's zeal had something harsh and savage which made him resemble a demon rather than an apostle or an angel, and his face, with its austere features sharply brought out by the light of the lantern, was in no wise reassuring. I felt an icy sweat break out on my limbs, my hair rose upon my head. Within myself I considered the action of the severe Serapion an abominable sacrilege, and I wished that from the sombre clouds that passed heavily over our heads might flash a bolt that would reduce him to powder. The owls, perched on the cypresses, troubled by the light of the lantern, struck the glass with their dusty wings and uttered plaintive cries. The foxes yelped in the distance, and innumerable sinister noises rose in the silence.

At last Serapion's pick struck the coffin, which gave out the dull, sonorous sound which nothingness gives out when it is touched. He pulled off the cover, and I saw Clarimonda, pale as marble, her hands clasped, her white shroud forming but one line from her head to her feet. A little red drop shone like a rose at the corner of her discoloured lips. Serapion at the sight of it became furious.

"Ah! There you are, you demon, you shameless courtesan! You who drink blood and gold!" and he cast on the body and the coffin quantities of holy water, tracing with the sprinkler a cross upon the coffin.

The holy dew no sooner touched poor Clarimonda than her

lovely body fell into dust and became only a hideous mass of ashes and half-calcined bones.

"There is your mistress, my lord Romualdo," said the inexorable priest, as he pointed to the remains. "Are you now still tempted to go to the Lido and Fusino with your beauty?"

I bowed my head. Something had been shattered within me. I returned to my presbytery, and lord Romualdo, the lover of Clarimonda, left the poor priest with whom he had so long kept such strange company. Only the next night I saw Clarimonda. She said to me, as the first time under the porch of the church, "Unfortunate man! Unfortunate man! What have you done? Why did you listen to that foolish priest? Were you not happy? What have I done to you, that you should go and violate my poor tomb and lay bare the wretchedness of my nothingness? All communion between our souls and bodies is henceforth broken. Farewell; you will regret me."

She vanished in air like a vapour, and I never saw her again. Alas! She spoke the truth. I have regretted her more than once, and I still regret her. I purchased the peace of my soul very dearly. The love of God was not too much to replace her love.

Such, brother, is the story of my youth. Never look upon a woman, and walk always with your eyes cast on the ground, for chaste and calm though you may be, a single minute may make you lose eternity.

II

The Tree

❄

Aleksei Tolstoy

(1817–1875)

ALTHOUGH HE PALES IN significance beside his distant cousin Leo, Aleksei Konstantinovich Tolstoy was a prominent writer in his time. Born in St. Petersburg barely a century after its founding, he grew up in a city already growing rich in literary traditions. Walking beside the Neva, gazing out at the Baltic, he formed grand ambitions for his writing career—and achieved most of them. "I was born," he declaimed in adulthood, "not to serve but to sing." In contrast with writers such as Chekhov or Gogol, he had an easy life—at least in material terms. He was born into the Tolstoy family, which had already distinguished itself in the Napoleonic Wars, and spent most of his adulthood as a courtier before retiring to write full-time. He was also able to travel often to Western Europe. Yet money and social connections didn't solve all his problems. He took an overdose of morphine and died penniless at the age of fifty-eight.

Under the collective pseudonym Kozma Prutkov—who was presented as a real author, with a history—Tolstoy and three cousins published epigrams, verse, and political satire in the literary and political magazine *Sovremennik* (The Contemporary). Founded by Pushkin, this influential periodical published everyone from Gogol to Turgenev and was the first journal to translate the works of Dickens and other foreign writers. But Tolstoy was best known in his lifetime for lyrical poetry about nature and romance, and for plays such as the blank-verse drama *The Death of Ivan the Terrible*, which launched a trilogy that he modeled after *Boris Godunov*, by the patron saint of Russian literature, Alexander Pushkin. But he also wrote the popular historical novel *The Silver Knight* and a series of ghostly stories, including "Upir" and "The Family of the Vourdalak." The latter has had a curious publication history. Like most educated Russians in the nineteenth century, Tolstoy was fluent in French, in which language he originally wrote the story in 1839, under the pseudonym Krasnorogsky (after Krasny Rog, the Tolstoy estate). But the story wasn't published in Russian until 1884, nine years after Tolstoy's death; Tolstoy's peers in the Russian literary community disdained such Gothic folklore. The French manuscript was lost until after World War II. The following translation is by scholar Christopher Frayling, who remarked of it, "Tolstoy succeeded in fusing the sexual allegory of vampirism . . . with the folklore of peasants." In fact, Tolstoy explicitly cites Calmet's accounts of Bosnian and Hungarian Vourdalaks who returned from their graves to prey upon their own families.

The Family of the Vourdalak

VIENNA. 1815. WHILE THE Congress had been in session, the city had attracted all the most distinguished European intellectuals, the fashion leaders of the day, and, of course, members of the highest diplomatic elite. But the Congress of Vienna was no longer in session.

Royalist émigrés were preparing to return to their country châteaux (hoping to stay there this time); Russian soldiers were anxiously awaiting the time when they could return to their abandoned homes; and discontented Poles—still dreaming of liberty—were wondering whether their dreams would come true, back in Cracow, under the protection of the precarious "independence" that had been arranged for them by the trio of Prince Metternich, Prince Hardenberg, and Count Nesselrode.

It was as if a masked ball were coming to an end. Of the assembled "guests," only a select few had stayed behind and delayed packing their bags in the hope of still finding some amusement, preferably in the company of the charming and glamorous Austrian ladies.

This delightful group of people (of which I was a member) met twice a week in a château belonging to Madame the dowager Princess of Schwarzenberg. It was a few miles from the city centre, just beyond a little hamlet called Hitzing. The splendid hospitality of our hostess, as well as her amiability and intellectual brilliance, made any stay at her château extremely agreeable.

Our mornings were spent *á la promenade*; we lunched all together either at the château or somewhere in the grounds; and in the evenings, seated around a welcoming fireside, we amused ourselves by gossiping and telling each other stories. A rule of the house was that we should not talk about anything to do with politics. Everyone had had enough of *that* subject. So our tales were based either on legends from our own countries or else on our own experiences.

One evening, when each of us had told a tale and when our spirits were in that tense state which darkness and silence usually create, the Marquis d'Urfé, an elderly émigré we all loved dearly for his childish gaiety and for the piquant way in which he reminisced about his past life and good fortunes, broke the ominous silence by saying, "Your stories, gentlemen, are all out of the ordinary, of course, but it seems to me that each one lacks an essential ingredient—I mean *authenticity*; for I am pretty sure that none of you has seen with his own eyes the fantastic incidents that he has just narrated, nor can he vouch for the truth of his story on his word of honour as a gentleman."

We all had to agree with this, so the elderly gentleman continued, after smoothing down his jabot: "As for me, gentlemen, I know only one story of this kind, but it is at once so strange, so horrible, and so *authentic* that it will suffice to strike even the most jaded of imaginations with terror. Having unhappily been both a witness to these strange events and a participant in them, I do not, as a rule, like to remind myself of them—but just this once I will tell the tale, provided, of course, the ladies present will permit me."

Everyone agreed instantly. I must admit that a few of us glanced furtively at the long shadows which the moonlight was beginning to sketch out on the parquet floor. But soon our little circle huddled closer together and each of us kept silent to hear the Marquis's story. M. d'Urfé took a pinch of snuff, slowly inhaled it, and began as follows:

Before I start, mesdames (said d'Urfé), I ask you to forgive me if, in the course of my story, I should find occasion to talk of my *affaires de coeur* more often than might be deemed appropriate for a man of my advanced years. But I assure that they must be mentioned if you are to make full sense of my story. In any case, one can forgive an elderly man for certain lapses of this kind—surrounded as I am by such attractive young ladies, it is no fault of mine that I am tempted to imagine myself a young man again. So, without further apology, I will commence by telling you that in the year 1759 I was madly in love with the beautiful Duchesse de Gramont. This passion, which I then believed was deep and lasting, gave me no respite either by day or by night, and the Duchesse, as young girls often do, enjoyed adding to my torment by her *coquetterie*. So much so that in a moment of spite I determined to solicit and be granted a diplomatic mission to the hospodar of Moldavia, who was then involved in negotiations with Versailles over matters that it would be as tedious as it would be pointless to tell you about.

The day before my departure I called in on the Duchesse. She received me with less mockery than usual and could not hide her emotions as she said, "D'Urfé, you are behaving like a madman, but I know you well enough to be sure that you will never go back on a decision, once taken. So I will only ask one thing of you. Accept this little cross as a token of my affection and wear it until you return. It is a family relic which we treasure a great deal."

With *galanterie* that was perhaps misplaced at such a moment I kissed not the relic but the delightful hand which proffered it to me, and I fastened the cross around my neck—you can see it now. Since then, I have never been parted from it.

I will not bore you, mesdames, with the details of my journey nor with the observations that I made on the Hungarians and the Serbians, those poor and ignorant people who, enslaved as they were by the Turks, were brave and honest enough not to have forgotten either their dignity or their time-honoured independence. It's enough for me to tell you that having learned to speak a little

Polish during my stay in Warsaw, I soon had a working knowledge
of Serbian as well—for these two languages, like Russian and
Bohemian, are, as you no doubt know very well, only branches of
one and the same root, which is known as Slavonian.

Anyway, I knew enough to make myself understood. One day I
arrived in a small village. The name would not interest you very
much. I found those who lived in the house where I intended to
stay in a state of confusion, which seemed to me all the more
strange because it was a Sunday, a day when the Serbian people
customarily devote themselves to different pleasures, such as dancing, arquebus shooting, wrestling and so on. I attributed the confusion of my hosts to some very recent misfortune and was about
to withdraw when a man of about thirty, tall and impressive to
look at, came up to me and shook me by the hand.

"Come in, come in, stranger," he said. "Don't let yourself be put
off by our sadness; you will understand it well enough when you
know the cause."

He then told me about how his old father (whose name was
Gorcha), a man of wild and unmanageable temperament, had got
up one morning and had taken down his long Turkish arquebus
from a rack on a wall.

"My children," he had said to his two sons, Georges and Pierre,
"I am going to the mountains to join a band of brave fellows who
are hunting that dog Ali Bek." (That was the name of a Turkish
brigand who had been ravaging the countryside for some time.)
"Wait for me patiently for ten days and if I do not return on the
tenth, arrange for a funeral mass to be said—for by then I will have
been killed. But," old Gorcha had added, looking very serious indeed, "if, may God protect you, I should return after the ten days
have passed, do not under any circumstances let me come in. I
command you, if this should happen, to forget that I was once your
father and to pierce me through the heart with an aspen stake,
whatever I might say or do, for then I would no longer be human.
I would be a cursed *vourdalak*, come to suck your blood."

It is important at this stage to tell you, mesdames, that the *vourdal-aks* (the name given to vampires by Slavic peoples) are, according to local folklore, dead bodies who rise from their graves to suck the blood of the living. In this respect they behave like all types of vampire, but they have one other characteristic which makes them even more terrifying. The *vourdalaks*, mesdames, prefer to suck the blood of their closest relatives and their most intimate friends; once dead, the victims become vampires themselves. People have claimed that entire villages in Bosnia and Hungary have been transformed into *vourdalaks* in this way. The Abbé Augustin Calmet in his strange book on apparitions cites many horrible examples.

Apparently, commissions have been appointed many times by German emperors to study alleged epidemics of vampirism. These commissions collected many eyewitness accounts. They exhumed bodies, which they found to be sated with blood, and ordered them to be burned in the public square after staking them through the heart. Magistrates who witnessed these executions have stated on oath that they heard blood-curdling shrieks coming from these corpses at the moment the executioner hammered his sharpened stake into their hearts. They have formal depositions to this effect and have corroborated them with signatures and with oaths on the Holy Book.

With this information as background, it should be easier for you to understand, mesdames, the effect that old Gorcha's words had on his sons. Both of them went down on their bended knees and begged him to let them go in his place. But instead of replying, he had turned his back on them and had set out for the mountains, singing the refrain of an old ballad. The day I arrived in the village was the very day that Gorcha had fixed for his return, so I had no difficulty understanding why his children were so anxious.

This was a good and honest family. Georges, the older of the two sons, was rugged and weather-beaten. He seemed to me a serious and decisive man. He was married with two children. His brother Pierre, a handsome youth of about eighteen, looked rather less tough and appeared to be the favourite of a younger sister called Sdenka, who was a genuine Slavic beauty. In addition to the striking beauty of her features, a distant resemblance to the Duchesse de Gramont struck me especially. She had a distinctive line on her forehead which in all my experience I have found only on these two people. This line did not seem particularly attractive at first glance, but became irresistible when you had seen it a few times.

Perhaps I was still very naïve. Perhaps this resemblance, combined with a lively and charmingly simple disposition, was really irresistible. I do not know. But I had not been talking with Sdenka for more than two minutes when I already felt for her an affection so tender that it threatened to become something deeper still if I stayed in the village much longer.

We were all sitting together in front of the house, around a table laden with cheeses and dishes of milk. Sdenka was sewing; her sister-in-law was preparing supper for her children, who were playing in the sand; Pierre, who was doing his best to appear at ease, was whistling as he cleaned a yataghan, or long Turkish knife. Georges was leaning on the table with his head in his hands and looking for signs of movement on the great highway. He was silent.

For my part, I was profoundly affected by the general atmosphere of sadness and, in a fit of melancholy, looked up at the evening clouds which shrouded the dying sun and at the silhouette of a monastery, which was half hidden from my view by a black pine forest.

This monastery, as I subsequently discovered, had been very famous in former times on account of a miraculous icon of the Virgin Mary which, according to legend, had been carried away by the angels and set down on an old oak tree. But at the beginning of the previous century the Turks had invaded this part of the country; they had butchered the monks and pillaged the monastery. Only the walls and a small chapel had survived; an old hermit continued to say Mass there. This hermit showed travellers around the ruins and gave hospitality to pilgrims who, as they walked from one place of devotion to another, liked to rest a while at the Monastery of Our Lady of the Oak. As I have said, I didn't learn all this until much later, for on this particular evening my thoughts were very far from the archaeology of Serbia. As often happens when one allows one's imagination free rein, I was musing on past times—on the good old days of my childhood; on the beauties of France that I had left for a wild and faraway country. I was thinking about the Duchesse de Gramont and—why not admit it?—I was also thinking about several other ladies who lived at the same time as your grandmothers, the memory of whose beauty had quietly entered my thoughts in the train of the beautiful Duchesse. I had soon forgotten all about my hosts and their terrible anxiety.

Suddenly Georges broke the silence. "Wife," he said, "at exactly what time did the old man set out?"

"At eight o'clock. I can clearly remember hearing the monastery bell."

"Well, that's all right then," said Georges. "It cannot be more than half past seven." And he again looked for signs of movement on the great highway which led to the dark forest.

I have forgotten to tell you, mesdames, that when the Serbians suspect that someone has become a vampire, they avoid mentioning him by name or speaking of him directly, for they think that this would be an invitation for him to leave his tomb. So Georges, when he spoke of his father, now referred to him simply as "the old man."

There was a brief silence. Suddenly one of the children started tugging at Sdenka's apron and crying, "Auntie, when will grandpapa be coming back?"

The only reply he got to this untimely question was a hard slap from Georges. The child began to cry, but his little brother, who by now was surprised and frightened, wanted to know more. "Father, why are we not allowed to talk about grandpapa?"

Another slap shut him up firmly. Both children now began to howl and the whole family made a sign of the cross. Just at that moment, I heard the sound of the monastery bell. As the first chime of eight was ringing in our ears, we saw a human figure coming out of the darkness of the forest and approaching us.

"It is he, God be praised," cried Sdenka, her sister-in-law, and Pierre all at once.

"May the good God protect us," said Georges solemnly. "How are we to know if the ten days have passed or not?"

Everyone looked at him, terror-struck. But the human form came closer and closer. It was a tall old man with a silver moustache and a pale, stern face; he was dragging himself along with the aid of a stick. The closer he got, the more shocked Georges looked. When the new arrival was a short distance from us, he stopped and stared at his family with eyes that seemed not to see—they were dull, glazed, deep sunk in their sockets.

"Well, well," he said in a dead voice, "will no one get up to welcome me? What is the meaning of this silence, can't you see I am wounded?"

I saw that the old man's left side was dripping with blood.

"Go and help your father," I said to Georges. "And you, Sdenka, offer him some refreshment. Look at him—he is almost collapsing from exhaustion!"

"Father," said Georges, going up to Gorcha, "show me your wound. I know all about such things and I can take care of it . . ."

He was just about to take off the old man's coat when Gorcha pushed his son aside roughly and clutched at his body with both hands. "You are too clumsy," he said, "leave me alone . . . Now you have hurt me."

"You must be wounded in the heart," cried Georges, turning pale. "Take off your coat, take it off. You must, I insist."

The old man pulled himself up to his full height. "Take care," he said in a sepulchral voice. "If you so much as touch me, I shall curse you."

Pierre rushed between Georges and his father. "Leave him alone," he said. "Can't you see that he's suffering?"

"Do not cross him," Georges's wife added. "You know he has never tolerated that."

At that precise moment we saw a flock of sheep returning from pasture raising a cloud of dust as it made its way towards the house. Whether the dog which was escorting the flock did not recognize its own master, or whether it had some other reason for acting as it did, as soon as it caught sight of Gorcha it stopped dead, hackles raised, and began to howl as if it had seen a ghost.

"What is wrong with that dog?" said the old man, looking more and more furious. "What is going on here? Have I become a stranger in my own house? Have ten days spent in the mountains changed me so much that even my own dogs do not recognize me?"

"Did you hear that?" said Georges to his wife.

"What of it?"

"He admits that the ten days *have been spent*."

"Surely not, for he has come back to us within the appointed time."

"I know what has to be done."

The dog continued to howl. "I want that dog destroyed!" cried Gorcha. "Well, did you hear me?"

Georges made no move, but Pierre got up with tears in his eyes, and grabbed his father's arquebus; he aimed at the dog, fired, and the creature rolled over in the dust.

"That was my favourite dog," he said sulkily. "I don't know why father wanted it to be destroyed."

"Because it deserved to be," bellowed Gorcha. "Come on now, it's cold and I want to go inside."

While all this was going on outside, Sdenka had been preparing a cordial for the old man consisting of pears, honey, and raisins, laced with eau-de-vie, but her father pushed it aside with disgust. He seemed equally disgusted by the plate of mutton with rice that Georges offered him. Gorcha shuffled over to the fireplace, muttering gibberish from behind clenched teeth.

A pine-log fire crackled in the grate and its flickering light seemed to give life to the pale, emaciated features of the old man. Without the fire's glow, his features could have been taken for those of a corpse.

Sdenka sat down beside him. "Father," she said, "you do not wish to eat anything, you do not wish to rest; perhaps you feel up to telling us about your adventures in the mountains."

By suggesting that, the young girl knew that she was touching her father's most sensitive spot, for the old man loved to talk of wars and adventures. The trace of a smile creased his colourless lips, although his eyes showed no animation, and as he began to stroke his daughter's beautiful blonde hair, he said: 'Yes, my daughter, yes, Sdenka, I would like to tell you all about my adventures in the mountains—but that must wait for another time, for I am too tired today. I can tell you, though, that Ali Bek is dead and that he perished by my hand. If anyone doubts my word," continued the old man, looking hard at his two sons, "here is the proof."

He undid a kind of sack which was slung behind his back, and pulled out a foul, bloody head which looked about as pale as his own! We all recoiled in horror, but Gorcha gave it to Pierre.

"Take it," he said, "and nail it above the door, to show all who pass by that Ali Bek is dead and that the roads are free of brigands—except, of course, for the Sultan's janissaries!"

Pierre was disgusted. But he obeyed. "Now I understand why that poor dog was howling," he said. "He could smell dead flesh!"

"Yes, he could smell dead flesh," murmured Georges; he had gone out of the room without anyone noticing him and had returned at that moment with something in his hand which he placed carefully against a wall. It looked to me like a sharpened stake.

"Georges," said his wife, almost in a whisper, "I hope you do not intend to . . ."

"My brother," Sdenka added anxiously, "what do you mean to do? No, no—surely you're not going to . . ."

"Leave me alone," replied Georges, "I know what I have to do and I will only do what is absolutely necessary."

While all this had been going on, night had fallen, and the family went to bed in a part of the house which was separated from my room only by a narrow partition. I must admit that what I had seen that evening had made an impression on my imagination. My candle was out; the moonlight shone through a little window near my bed and cast blurred shadows on the floor and walls, rather like those we see now, mesdames, in this room. I wanted to go to sleep but I could not. I thought this was because the moonlight was so clear; but when I looked for something to curtain the window, I could find nothing suitable. Then I overheard confused voices from the other side of the partition. I tried to make out what was being said.

"Go to sleep, wife," said Georges. "And you, Pierre, and you, Sdenka. Do not worry, I will watch over you."

"But, Georges," replied his wife, "it is I who should keep watch over you—you worked all last night and you must be tired. In any case, I ought to be staying awake to watch over our eldest boy. You know he has not been well since yesterday!"

"Be quiet and go to sleep," said Georges. "I will keep watch for both of us."

"Brother," put in Sdenka in her sweetest voice, "there is no need to keep watch at all. Father is already asleep—he seems calm and peaceful enough."

"Neither of you understands what is going on," said Georges in a voice which allowed for no argument. "Go to sleep, I tell you, and let me keep watch."

There followed a long silence. Soon my eyelids grew heavy and sleep began to take possession of my senses.

I THOUGHT I SAW the door of my room opening slowly, and old Gorcha standing in the doorway. Actually, I did not so much see as *feel* his presence, as there was only darkness behind him. I felt his dead eyes trying to penetrate my deepest thoughts as they watched the movement of my breathing. One step forward, then another. Then, with extreme care, he began to walk towards me, with a wolf-like motion. Finally he leapt forward. Now he was right beside my bed. I was absolutely terrified, but somehow managed not to move. The old man leaned over me and his waxen face was so close to mine that I could feel his corpse-like breath. Then, with a superhuman effort, I managed to wake up, soaked in perspiration.

There was nobody in my room, but as I looked towards the window I could distinctly see old Gorcha's face pressed against the glass from outside, staring at me with his sunken eyes. By sheer willpower I stopped myself from crying out and I had the presence of mind to stay lying down, just as if I had seen nothing out of the ordinary. Luckily, the old man was only making sure that I was asleep, for he made no attempt to come in, and after staring at me long enough to satisfy himself, he moved away from the window and I could hear his footsteps in the neighbouring room. Georges was sound asleep and snoring loudly enough to wake the dead.

At that moment the child coughed, and I could make out Gorcha's voice. "You are not asleep little one?"

"No, grandpapa," replied the child, "and I would so like to talk with you."

"So, you would like to talk with me, would you? And what would we talk about?"

"We would talk about how you fought the Turks. I would love to fight the Turks!"

"I thought you might, child, and I brought back a little yataghan for you. I'll give it to you tomorrow."

"Grandpapa, grandpapa, give it to me now."

"But, little one, why didn't you talk to me about this when it was daytime?"

"Because papa would not let me."

"He is careful, your papa . . . So you really would like to have your little yataghan?"

"Oh yes, I would love that, but not here, for papa might wake up."

"Where then?"

"If we go outside, I promise to be good and not to make any noise at all."

I thought I could hear Gorcha chuckle as the child got out of bed. I didn't believe in vampires, but the nightmare had preyed on my nerves, and just in case I should have to reproach myself in the morning I got up and banged my fist against the partition. It was enough to wake up the "seven sleepers," but there was no sign of life from the family. I threw myself against the door, determined to save the child—but it was locked from the outside and I couldn't shift the bolts. While I was trying to force it open, I saw the old man pass by my window with the little child in his arms.

"Wake up! Wake up!" I cried at the top of my voice, as I shook the partition. Even then only Georges showed any sign of movement.

"Where is the old man?" he murmured blearily.

"Quick," I yelled, "he's just taken away your child."

With one kick, Georges broke down the door of his room—which like mine had been locked from the outside—and he sprinted in the direction of the dark forest. At last I succeeded in waking Pierre, his sister-in-law, and Sdenka. We all assembled in front of the house and after a few minutes of anxious waiting we saw Georges return from the dark forest with his son. The child had apparently passed out on the highway, but he was soon revived and didn't seem to be any more ill than before. After questioning him we discovered that his grandpapa had not, in fact, done him any harm; they had apparently gone out together to talk undisturbed, but once outside the child had lost consciousness without remembering why. Gorcha himself had disappeared.

As you can imagine, no one could sleep for the rest of that night. The next day, I learned that the river Danube, which cut across the highway about a quarter of a league from the village, had begun to freeze over; drift ice now blocked my route. This often happens in these parts some time between the end of autumn and the beginning of spring. Since the highway was expected to be blocked for some days, I could not think of leaving. In any case, even if I could have left, curiosity—as well as a more powerful emotion—would have held me back. The more I saw Sdenka, the more I felt I was falling in love with her.

I am not among those, mesdames, who believe in love at first sight of the kind which novelists so often write about; but I do believe that there are occasions when love develops more quickly than is usual. Sdenka's strange beauty, her singular resemblance to the Duchesse de Gramont—the lady from whom I had fled in Paris, and who I saw again in this remote setting, dressed in a rustic costume and speaking in a musical foreign tongue—the fascinating line on her forehead, like that for which I had been prepared to kill myself at least twenty times in France: all this, combined with the incredible, mysterious situation in which I found myself . . . everything helped to nurture in me a passion which, in other circumstances, would perhaps have proved itself to be more vague and passing.

During the course of the day I overheard Sdenka talking to her younger brother. "What do you think of all this?" she asked. "Do you also suspect our father?"

"I dare not suspect him," replied Pierre, "especially since the child insists that he came to no harm. And as for father's disappearance, you know that he never used to explain his comings and goings."

"I know," said Sdenka. "All the more reason why we must think about saving him, for you know that Georges . . ."

"Yes, yes, I know. It would be useless to talk him out of it. We can at least hide the stake. He certainly won't go out looking for another one, since there is not a single aspen tree this side of the mountains."

"Yes, let's hide the stake—but don't mention it to the children, for they might chatter about it with Georges listening."

"We must take care not to let that happen," said Pierre. And they went their separate ways.

At nightfall we had still discovered nothing about old Gorcha. As on the previous night I was lying on my bed, and the moonlight again stopped me from going to sleep. When at last sleep began to confuse my thoughts, I again felt, as if by instinct, that the old man was coming towards me. I opened my eyes and saw his waxen face pressed against my window.

This time I wanted to get up but could not. All my limbs seemed to be paralysed. After taking a good long look at me, the old man disappeared. I heard him wandering around the house and tapping gently on the window of Georges's room. The child turned over on his bed and moaned as he dreamed. After several minutes' silence the tapping on the window resumed. Then the child groaned once again and woke up. "Is that you, grandpapa?" he asked.

"It is me," replied a dead voice, "and I have brought you your little yataghan."

"But I dare not go outside. Papa has forbidden it."

"There is no need to go outside; just open the window and embrace me!"

The child got up and I could hear him opening the window. Then somehow finding the strength, I leaped to the foot of my bed and ran over to the partition. I struck it hard with my fist. In a few seconds Georges was on his feet. I heard him mutter an oath. His wife screamed. In no time at all the whole household had gathered around the lifeless child. Just as on the previous occasion, there was no sign of Gorcha. We tried carefully to revive the child, but he was very weak and breathed with difficulty. The poor little chap had no idea why he had passed out. His mother and Sdenka thought it was because of the shock of being caught talking with his grandpapa. I said nothing. However, by now the child seemed to be more calm and everybody except Georges went back to bed.

At daybreak, I overheard Georges waking his wife and whispering

with her. Sdenka joined them and I could hear both the women sob-
bing. The child was dead.

Of the family's despair, the less said the better. Strangely enough
no one blamed the child's death on old Gorcha—at least, not openly.
Georges sat in silence, but his expression, always gloomy, now became terrible to behold. Two days passed and there was still no sign
of the old man. On the night of the third day (the day of the child's
burial) I thought I heard footsteps all around the house and an old
man's voice which called out the name of the dead child's brother.
For a split second I also thought I saw Gorcha's face pressed against
my window, but I couldn't be sure if I was imagining it or not, for
the moon was veiled by cloud that night. Nevertheless I considered
it my duty to mention this apparition to Georges. He questioned
the child, who replied that he *had* in fact heard grandpapa calling
and had also seen him looking in through the window. Georges
strictly charged his son to wake him up if the old man should appear again.

All these happenings did not prevent my passion for Sdenka from
developing more and more each day. In the daytime, I couldn't talk
to her alone. At night, the mere thought that I would shortly have
to leave broke my heart. Sdenka's room was separated from mine
only by a kind of corridor which led to the road on one side and a
courtyard on the other. When the whole family had gone to bed, I
decided to go for a short walk in the fields to ease my mind. As
I walked along the corridor I saw that Sdenka's door was slightly
open. Instinctively, I stopped and listened. The rustling of her dress,
a sound I knew well, made my heart pound against my chest. Then
I heard her singing softly. She was singing about a Serbian king who
was saying farewell to his lady before going to war.

"Oh my young Poplar," said the old king, "I am going to the
war and you will forget me.

"The trees which grow beneath the mountain are slender and
pliant, but they are nothing beside your young body!

"The berries of the rowan tree which sway in the wind are red, but your lips are more red than the berries of the rowan tree!

"And I am like an old oak stripped of leaves, and my beard is whiter than the foam of the Danube!

"And you will forget me, oh my soul, and I will die of grief, for the enemy will not dare to kill the old King!"

The beautiful lady replied: "I swear to be faithful to you and never to forget you. If I should break my oath, come to me after your death and drink all my heart's blood!"

And the old king said: "So be it!"

And he set off for the war. Soon the beautiful lady forgot him . . . !

At this point Sdenka paused, as if she was frightened to finish the ballad. I could restrain myself no longer. That voice—so sweet, so expressive—was the voice of the Duchesse de Gramont . . . Without pausing to think, I pushed open the door and went in. Sdenka had just taken off her knitted jacket (of a kind often worn by women in those regions). All she was wearing was a nightgown of red silk, embroidered with gold, held tight against her body by a simple, brightly coloured belt. Her fine blonde hair hung loose over her shoulders. She looked more beautiful than ever. She did not seem upset by my sudden entry, but she was confused and blushed slightly.

"Oh," she said, "why have you come? What will the family think of me if we are discovered?"

"Sdenka, my soul, do not be frightened! Everyone is asleep. Only the cricket in the grass and the mayfly in the air can hear what I have to say to you."

"Oh, my friend, leave me, leave me! If my brother should discover us I am lost!"

"Sdenka, I will not leave you until you have promised to love me for ever, as the beautiful lady promised the king in your ballad. Soon I will have to leave . . . Who knows when we will see each other again? Sdenka, I love you more than my soul, more than my salvation . . . my life's blood is yours . . . may I not be granted one hour with you in return?"

"Many things can happen in an hour," said Sdenka calmly. But she did let her hand slip into mine.

"You do not know my brother," she continued, beginning to tremble. "I fear he will discover us."

"Calm yourself, my darling Sdenka. Your brother is exhausted from watching late into the night; he has been lulled to sleep by the wind rustling in the trees; heavy is his sleep, long is the night, and I only ask to be granted one hour—then, farewell, perhaps for ever!"

"Oh no, no, not for ever!" cried Sdenka; then she recoiled, as if frightened by the sound of her own voice.

"Oh, Sdenka, I see only you, I hear only you; I am no longer master of my own destiny; a superior strength commands my obedience. Forgive me, Sdenka!" Like a madman I clutched her to my heart.

"You are no friend to me," she cried, tearing herself from my embrace and rushing to another part of the room. I do not know what I said to her then, for I was as alarmed as she was by my own forwardness, not because such boldness had failed me in the past—far from it—but because in spite of my passion, I could not help having a sincere respect for Sdenka's innocence. It is true that I had used the language of *galanterie* with this girl at first (a language which did not seem to displease the society ladies of the time), but I was now ashamed of these empty phrases and renounced them when I saw that the young girl was too naïve to comprehend fully what I meant by them—what you, mesdames, to judge by your suggestive smiles, have understood immediately. I stood before her, at a loss as to what to say, when suddenly she began to tremble and look towards the window, terror-struck. I followed her gaze and clearly saw the corpse-like face of Gorcha, staring at us from outside.

At precisely that moment, I felt a heavy hand on my shoulder.

I froze. It was Georges. "What are you doing here!" he snapped.

Embarrassed by his tone of voice, I simply pointed towards his father, who was still staring at us through the window—but he disappeared the moment Georges turned to look at him.

"I heard the old man and came to warn your sister," I stammered.

Georges looked me straight in the eye, as if trying to read my innermost thoughts. Then he took me by the arm, led me to my room, and left, without a single word.

THE NEXT DAY THE family had gathered in front of the house, around a table laden with jugs of milk and cakes.

"Where is the child?" said Georges.

"In the courtyard," replied his wife. "He is playing his favourite game, imagining that he is fighting the Turks single-handed."

No sooner had she said these words, than to our amazement we saw the tall figure of Gorcha walking slowly towards us from out of the dark forest. He sat at the table just as he had done the day I arrived.

"Father, we welcome you," murmured Georges's wife in a hoarse voice.

"We welcome you, father," whispered Sdenka and Pierre in unison.

"My father," said Georges firmly, turning pale, "we are waiting for you to say Grace!"

The old man glared at him and turned away.

"Yes . . . Grace—say it now!" repeated Georges, crossing himself. "Say it this instant, or by St. George . . ."

Sdenka and her sister-in-law threw themselves at the old man's feet and begged him to say Grace.

"No, no, no," said the old man. "He has no right to speak to me in that way, and if he continues, I will curse him!"

Georges got up and rushed into the house. He returned almost immediately, looking furious. "Where is that stake?" he yelled. "Where have you hidden it?"

Sdenka and Pierre looked at each other.

"Corpse!" Georges shouted at the old man. "What have you done with my elder boy? Why have you killed my little child? Give me back my son, you creature of the grave!"

As he said this, he became more and more pale and his eyes began to burn with fury. The old man simply glared at him.

"The stake, the stake," yelled Georges. "Whoever has hidden it must answer for all the evils which will befall us!"

At this moment we heard the excited laughter of the younger child. We saw him galloping towards us on a wooden horse, or rather on a long aspen stake, shrieking the Serbian battle cry at the top of his voice. Georges's eyes lit up as he realized what was happening. He grabbed the stake from the child and threw himself at his father. The old man let out a fearful groan and began to sprint towards the dark forest as if possessed by demons. Georges raced after him across the fields, and soon they were both out of sight.

It was after sunset when Georges returned to the house. He was as pale as death; his hair stood on end. He sat down by the fireside, and I could hear his teeth chattering. No one could pluck up the courage to question him. By about the time the family normally went to bed he seemed to be more his usual self and, taking me to one side, said to me quite calmly: "My dear guest, I have been to the river. The ice has gone, the road is clear—nothing now prevents you from leaving. There is no need," he added, glancing at Sdenka, "to take your leave of my family. Through me, the family wishes you all the happiness you could desire and I hope that you will have some happy memories of the time you have spent with us. Tomorrow at daybreak, you will find your horse saddled and your guide ready to escort you. Farewell. Think about your host from time to time, and forgive him if your stay here has not been as carefree as he would have liked."

As he said this, even Georges's rough features looked almost friendly. He led me to my room and shook my hand for one last time. Then he began to tremble and his teeth chattered as if he were suffering from the cold.

Now I was alone, I had no thoughts of going to sleep—as you can imagine. Other things were on my mind. I had loved many times in my life, and had experienced the whole range of passions— tenderness, jealousy, fury—but never, not even when I left the Duchesse de Gramont, had I felt anything like the sadness that I felt in my heart at that moment. Before sunrise, I changed into my travelling clothes, hoping to have a few words with Sdenka before I departed. But Georges was waiting for me in the hall. There was no chance of my seeing her again.

I leaped into the saddle and spurred on my horse. I made a reso- lution to return from Jassy via this village, and although that might be some time hence, the thought made me feel easier in my mind. It was some consolation for me to imagine in advance all the details of my return. But this pleasant reverie was soon shattered. My horse shied away from something and nearly had me out of the saddle. The animal stopped dead, dug in its forelegs and began to snort wildly, as if some danger was nearby. I looked around anxiously and saw something moving about a hundred paces away. It was a wolf digging in the ground. Sensing my presence, the wolf ran away; digging my spurs into the horse's flanks, I managed with difficulty to get him to move forward. It was then that I realized that on the spot where the wolf had been standing, there was a freshly dug grave. I seem to remember also that the end of a stake protruded a few inches out of the ground where the wolf had been digging. However, I do not swear to this, for I rode away from that place as fast as I could.

AT THIS POINT THE Marquis paused and took a pinch of snuff.

"Is that the end of the story?" the ladies asked.

"I'm afraid not," replied M. d'Urfé. "What remains to be told is a very unhappy memory for me, and I would give much to cast it from my mind."

MY REASONS FOR GOING to Jassy (he continued) kept me there for much longer than I had expected—well over six months, in fact. What can I say to justify my conduct during that time? It is a sad fact, but a fact nonetheless, that there are very few emotions in this life which can stand the test of time. The success of my negotiations, which were very well received in Versailles—politics, in a word, vile politics, a subject which has become so boring to us in recent times—preoccupied my thoughts and dimmed the memory of Sdenka. In addition, from the moment I arrived, the wife of the hospodar, a very beautiful lady who spoke fluent French, did me the honour of receiving my attentions, singling me out from among all the other young foreigners who were staying in Jassy. Like me, she had been brought up to believe in the principles of French *galanterie*; the mere thought that I should rebuff the advances of such a beautiful lady stirred up my Gallic blood. So I received her advances with courtesy, and since I was there to represent the interests and rights of France, I made a start by representing those of her husband the hospodar as well.

When I was recalled home, I left by the same road I had ridden to Jassy. I no longer even thought about Sdenka or her family, but one evening when I was riding in the countryside, I heard a bell ringing the eight o'clock chime. I seemed to recognize that sound and my guide told me that it came from a nearby monastery. I asked him the name: it was the monastery of Our Lady of the Oak. I galloped ahead and in no time at all we had reached the monastery gate. The old hermit welcomed us and led us to his hostel.

The number of pilgrims staying there put me off the idea of spending the night at the hostel, and I asked if there was any accommodation available in the village.

"You can stay where you like in the village," replied the old hermit with a gloomy sigh. "Thanks to that devil Gorcha, there are plenty of empty houses!"

"What on earth do you mean?" I asked. "Is old Gorcha still alive?"

"Oh no, he's well and truly buried with a stake through his heart! But he rose from the grave to suck the blood of Georges's little son. The child returned one night and knocked on the door, crying that he was cold and wanted to come home. His foolish mother, although she herself had been present at his burial, did not have the strength of mind to send him back to the cemetery, so she opened the door. He threw himself at her throat and sucked away her life's blood. After she had been buried, she in turn rose from the grave to suck the blood of her second son, then the blood of her husband, then the blood of her brother-in-law. They all went the same way."

"And Sdenka?"

"Oh, she went mad with grief; poor, poor child, do not speak to me of her!"

The old hermit had not really answered my question, but I did not have the heart to repeat it. He crossed himself. "Vampirism is contagious," he said after a pause. "Many families in the village have been afflicted by it, many families have been completely destroyed, and if you take my advice you will stay in my hostel tonight; for even if the *vourdalaks* of the village do not attack you, they will terrify you so much that your hair will have turned white before I ring the bells for morning mass.

"I am only a poor and simple monk," he continued, "but the generosity of passing travellers gives me enough to provide for their needs. I can offer you fresh country cheese and sweet plums which will make your mouth water; I also have some flagons of Tokay wine which are every bit as good as those which grace the cellars of His Holiness the Patriarch!"

The old hermit seemed to be behaving more like an inn-keeper than a poor and simple monk. I reckoned he had told me some old wives' tales about the village in order to make me feel grateful enough for his hospitality to show my appreciation in the usual way, by giving the holy man enough to provide for the needs of passing travellers. In any case, the word *terror* has always had the effect on me that a battle cry has on a war horse. I would have been thoroughly ashamed of myself if I had not set out immediately to see for myself. But my guide, who was less enthusiastic about the idea, asked my permission to stay in the hostel. This I willingly granted.

It took me about half an hour to reach the village. Deserted. No lights shone through the windows, no songs were being sung. I rode past many houses that I knew, all as silent as the grave. Finally I reached Georges's. Whether I was being sentimental or just rash, I don't know, but it was there I decided to spend the night. I got off my horse, and banged on the gate. Still no sign of life. I pushed the gate and the hinges creaked eerily as it slowly opened. Then I crept into the courtyard. In one of the outhouses I found enough oats to last the night, so I left my horse tethered there, still saddled, and strode towards the main house. Although all the rooms were deserted, no doors were locked. Sdenka's room had been occupied only a few hours before. Some of her clothes were draped carelessly over the bed. A few pieces of jewellery that I had given her, including a small enamel cross from Budapest, lay on her table sparkling in the moonlight. Even though my love for her was a thing of the past, I must admit that my heart was heavy. Nevertheless, I wrapped myself up in my cloak and stretched out on her bed. Soon I was asleep. I cannot recall everything, but I do remember that I dreamed of Sdenka, as beautiful, as simple, and as loving as she had been when first I met her. I remember also feeling ashamed of my selfishness and my inconstancy. How could I have abandoned that poor child who loved me; how could I have forgotten her? Then her image became confused with that of the Duchesse de Gramont and I saw only one person. I threw myself at Sdenka's feet and begged her forgiveness. From the depths of my being, from the depths of my soul came an indescribable feeling of melancholy and of joy.

I lay there dreaming, until I was almost awakened by a gentle musical sound, like the rustling of a cornfield in a light breeze. I heard the sweet rustling of the corn and the music of singing birds, the rushing of a waterfall and the whispering of trees. Then I realized that all these sounds were merely the swishing of a woman's dress and I opened my eyes. There was Sdenka standing beside my bed. The moon was shining so brightly that I could distinguish every single feature which had been so dear to me and which my dream made me love again as if for the first time. Sdenka seemed more beautiful, and somehow more mature. She was dressed as she had been when last I saw her alone: a simple nightgown of red silk, gold embroidered, and a coloured belt, clinging tightly above her hips.

"Sdenka!" I cried, sitting up. "Is it really you, Sdenka?"

"Yes, it is me," she replied in a sweet, sad voice. "It is that same Sdenka you have forgotten. Why did you not return sooner? Everything is finished now; you must leave; a moment longer and you are lost! Farewell my friend, farewell for ever!"

"Sdenka, you have seen so much unhappiness they say! Come, let us talk, let us ease your pain!"

"Oh, my friend, you must not believe everything they say about us; but leave me, leave me now, for if you stay a moment longer you are doomed."

"Sdenka, what are you afraid of? Can you not grant me an hour, just one hour to talk with you?"

Sdenka began to tremble and her whole being seemed to undergo a strange transformation. "Yes," she said, "one hour, just one hour, the same hour you begged of me when you came into this room and heard me singing the ballad of the old king. Is that what you mean? So be it, I will grant you one hour! But no, no!" she cried, as if fighting her inclinations. "Leave me, go away!—leave now, I tell you, fly! Fly, while you still have the chance!"

Her features were possessed with a savage strength. I could not understand why she should be saying these things, but she was so beautiful that I determined to stay, whatever she said. At last she surrendered, sat down beside me, and spoke to me of the past; she blushed as she admitted that she had fallen in love with me the moment she set eyes on me. But little by little I began to notice that Sdenka was not as I had remembered her. Her former timidity had given way to a strange wantonness of manner. She seemed more forward, more knowing. It dawned on me that her behaviour was no longer that of the naïve young girl I recalled in my dream. Is it possible, I mused, that Sdenka was never the pure and innocent maiden that I imagined her to be? Did she simply put on an act to please her brother? Was I gulled by an affected virtue? If so, why insist that I leave? Was this perhaps a refinement of *coquetterie*? And I thought I knew her! What did it matter? If Sdenka was not a Diana, as I thought, she began to resemble another goddess at least as attractive—perhaps more so. By God! I preferred the role of Adonis to that of Actaeon.

If this classical style that I adopted seems a little out of place, mesdames, remember that I have the honour to be telling you of incidents which occurred in the year of grace 1758. At that time mythology was *very* fashionable, and I am trying to keep my story in period. Things have changed a lot since then, and it was not so long ago that the Revolution, having overthrown both the traces of paganism and the Christian religion, erected the goddess Reason in their place. This goddess, mesdames, has never been my patron saint, least of all when I am in the presence of other goddesses, and, at the time I am referring to, I was less disposed than ever to worship at her shrine.

I abandoned myself passionately to Sdenka, and willingly outdid even her in the provocative game she was playing. Some time passed in sweet intimacy, until, as Sdenka was amusing me by trying on various pieces of jewellery, I thought it would be a good idea to place the little enamel cross around her neck. But as I tried to do this, Sdenka recoiled sharply.

"Enough of these childish games, my dearest," she said. "Let us talk about you and what is on your mind!"

This sudden change in Sdenka's behaviour made me pause a moment and think. Looking at her more closely I noticed that she no longer wore around her neck the cluster of tiny icons, holy relics, and charms filled with incense which Serbians are usually given as children, to wear for the rest of their lives.

"Sdenka," I asked, "where are those things you used to wear around your neck?"

"I have lost them," she replied impatiently, and hastily changed the subject.

I do not know exactly why, but at that moment I began to feel a strong sense of foreboding. I wanted to leave, but Sdenka held me back. "What is this?" she said. "You asked to be granted an hour, and here you are trying to leave after only a few minutes!"

"Sdenka, you were right when you tried to persuade me to leave; I think I hear a noise and I fear we will be discovered!"

"Calm yourself, my love, everyone is asleep; only the cricket in the grass and the mayfly in the air can hear what I have to say!"

"No, no, Sdenka, I must leave now . . . !"

"Stay, stay," she implored, "I love you more than my soul, more than my salvation. You once told me that your life's blood belonged to me . . . !"

"But your brother—your brother, Sdenka—I have a feeling he will discover us!"

"Calm yourself, my soul; my brother has been lulled to sleep by the wind rustling in the trees; heavy is his sleep, long is the night, and I ask only to be granted one hour!"

As she said this, Sdenka looked so ravishing that my vague sense of foreboding turned into a strong desire to remain near her. A strange, almost sensual feeling, part fear, part excitement, filled my whole being. As I began to weaken, Sdenka became more tender, and I resolved to surrender, hoping to keep up my guard. However, as I told you at the beginning, I have always overestimated my own strength of mind, and when Sdenka, who had noticed that I was holding back, suggested that we chase away the chill of the night by drinking a few glasses of the good hermit's full-blooded wine, I agreed with a readiness which made her smile. The wine had its desired effect. By the second glass, I had forgotten all about the incident of the cross and the holy relics; Sdenka, with her beautiful blonde hair falling loose over her shoulders, with her jewels sparkling in the moonlight, was quite irresistible. Abandoning all restraint, I held her tight in my arms.

Then, mesdames, a strange thing happened. One of those mysterious revelations that I can never hope to explain. If you had asked me then, I would have denied such things could happen, but now I know better. As I held Sdenka tightly against my body, one of the points of the cross which the Duchesse de Gramont gave me before I left stuck sharply into my chest. The stab of pain that I felt affected me like a ray of light passing right through my body. Looking up at Sdenka I saw for the first time that her features, though still beautiful, were those of a corpse; that her eyes did not see; and that her smile was the distorted grimace of a decaying skull. At the same time, I sensed in that room the putrid smell of the charnel-house. The fearful truth was revealed to me in all its ugliness, and I remembered too late what the old hermit had said to me. I realized what a fearsome predicament I was in. Everything depended on my courage and my self-control.

I turned away from Sdenka to hide the horror which was written on my face. It is then that I looked out of the window and saw the satanic figure of Gorcha, leaning on a bloody stake and staring at me with the eyes of a hyena. Pressed against the other window were the waxen features of Georges, who at that moment looked as terrifying as his father. Both were watching my every movement, and I knew that they would pounce on me the moment I tried to escape. So I pretended not to know they were there, and, with incredible self-control, continued—yes, mesdames, I actually continued—passionately to embrace Sdenka, just as I had done before my horrifying discovery. Meanwhile, I desperately racked my brains for some means of escape. I noticed that Gorcha and Georges were exchanging knowing glances with Sdenka and that they were showing signs of losing patience. Then, from somewhere outside, I heard a woman's shriek and the sound of children crying, like the howling of wild cats; these noises set my nerves on edge.

Time to make for home, I said to myself, *and the sooner the better!*

Turning to Sdenka, I raised my voice so that her hideous family would be sure to hear me: "I am tired, my dear child; I must go to bed and sleep for a few hours. But first I must go and see whether my horse needs feeding. I beg you to stay where you are and to wait for me to come back." I then pressed my mouth against her cold, dead lips and left the room.

I found my horse in a panic, covered with lather and crashing his hooves against the outhouse wall. He had not touched the oats, and the fearful noise he made when he saw me coming gave me gooseflesh, for I feared he would give the game away. But the vampires, who had almost certainly overheard my conversation with Sdenka, did not appear to think that anything suspicious was happening. After making sure that the main gate was open, I vaulted into the saddle and dug my spurs into the horse's flanks.

As I rode out of the gates I just had time to glimpse a whole crowd gathered around the house, many of them with their faces pressed against the windows. I think it was my sudden departure which first confused them, but I cannot be sure: the only sound I could hear at that moment was the regular beat of my horse's hooves which echoed in the night. I was just about to congratulate myself on my cunning, when all of a sudden I heard a fearful noise behind me, like the sound of a hurricane roaring through the mountains. A thousand discordant voices shrieked, moaned, and contended with one another. Then complete silence, as if by common assent. And I heard a rhythmic stamping, like a troop of foot soldiers advancing in double-quick time.

I spurred on my horse until I tore into his flanks. A burning fever coursed through my veins. I was making one last effort to preserve my sanity, when I heard a voice behind me which cried out: "Stop, don't leave me, my dearest! I love you more than my soul, I love you more than my salvation! Turn back, turn back, your life's blood is mine!"

A cold breath brushed my ear and I sensed that Sdenka had leaped on to my horse from behind. "My heart, my soul!" she cried. "I see only you, hear only you! I am not mistress of my own destiny—a superior force commands my obedience. Forgive me, my dearest, forgive me!"

Twisting her arms around me she tried to sink her teeth into my neck and to wrench me from my horse. There was a terrible struggle. For some time I had difficulty even defending myself, but eventually I managed to grab hold of Sdenka by curling one arm around her waist and knotting the other hand in her hair. Standing bolt upright in my stirrups, I threw her to the ground!

Then my strength gave out completely and I became delirious. Frenzied shapes pursued me—mad, grimacing faces. Georges and his brother, Pierre, ran beside the road and tried to block my way. They did not succeed, but just as I was about to give thanks, I looked over my shoulder and caught sight of old Gorcha, who was using his stake to propel himself forward as the Tyrolean mountain men do when they leap over Alpine chasms. But Gorcha did not manage to catch up with me. Then his daughter-in-law, dragging her children behind her, threw one of them to him; he caught the child on the sharpened point of his stake. Using the stake as a catapult, he slung the creature towards me with all his might. I fended off the blow, but with the true terrier instinct the little brat sunk his teeth into my horse's neck, and I had some difficulty tearing him away. The other child was propelled towards me in the same way, but he landed beyond the horse and was crushed to pulp. I do not know what happened after that, but when I regained consciousness it was daylight, and I found myself lying near the road next to my dying horse.

So ended, mesdames, a love affair which should perhaps have cured me for ever of the desire to become involved in any others. Some contemporaries of your grandmothers could tell you whether I had learned my lesson or not. But, joking aside, I still shudder at the thought that if I had given in to my enemies, I would myself have become a vampire. As it was, Heaven did not allow things to come to that, and so far from wishing to suck your blood, mesdames, I only ask—old as I am—to be granted the privilege of shedding my own blood in your service!

James Malcolm Rymer

(1814–1884)

FOR DECADES, SCHOLARS THOUGHT *Varney the Vampire* had been written by a tireless Victorian hack named Thomas Peckett Prest, author of the penny dreadful *A String of Pearls*, which featured a bloodthirsty barber who is still a popular character today— Sweeney Todd. But apparently Prest had nothing to do with *Varney*. Scholars have now determined that the actual author was a *different* tireless Victorian hack, James Malcolm Rymer. The confusion is understandable. Both even worked for a thriller factory, the English publisher Edward Lloyd, who made a living in part by shamelessly copying Charles Dickens. Prest even used the pen name Bos, too close for comfort to Dickens's own first pen name, Boz. Rymer also published under anagrams of his name, including Malcolm J. Merry, and under house names such as Bertha Thorne Bishop and Septimus R. Urban.

Vampire fans cherish Rymer, in an Ed Wood sort of way, as the author of a pioneer vampire novel that was influential but, at least by our standards, unintentionally hilarious—*Varney the Vampyre, or, The Feast of Blood.* This seemingly endless novel appeared in breathless weekly installments—109 of them—between 1845 and 1847. In his shameless Sturm und Drang, his screaming blond and slurping monster, Rymer makes Bram Stoker look demure. *Varney* was hugely popular and equally influential. Elements of this story show up everywhere from "Carmilla" to *Dracula*. The following selection comprises chapter 1, the first week's installment.

Varney the Vampyre

Or, The Feast of Blood

Chapter I

"How graves give up their dead,
And how the night air hideous grows
With shrieks!"

MIDNIGHT.—THE HAIL-STORM.— THE DREADFUL VISITOR.— THE VAMPYRE.

THE SOLEMN TONES OF an old cathedral clock have announced midnight—the air is thick and heavy—a strange, death-like stillness pervades all nature. Like the ominous calm which precedes some more than usually terrific outbreak of the elements, they seem to have paused even in their ordinary fluctuations, to gather a terrific strength for the great effort. A faint peal of thunder now comes from far off. Like a signal gun for the battle of the winds to begin, it appeared to awaken them from their lethargy, and one awful, warring hurricane swept over a whole city, producing more devastation in the four or five minutes it lasted, than would a half century of ordinary phenomena.

It was as if some giant had blown upon some toy town, and

scattered many of the buildings before the hot blast of his terrific breath; for as suddenly as that blast of wind had come did it cease, and all was as still and calm as before.

Sleepers awakened, and thought that what they had heard must be the confused chimera of a dream. They trembled and turned to sleep again.

All is still—still as the very grave. Not a sound breaks the magic of repose. What is that—a strange pattering noise, as of a million fairy feet? It is hail—yes, a hailstorm has burst over the city. Leaves are dashed from the trees, mingled with small boughs; windows that lie most opposed to the direct fury of the pelting particles of ice are broken, and the rapt repose that before was so remarkable in its intensity, is exchanged for a noise which, in its accumulation, drowns every cry of surprise or consternation which here and there arose from persons who found their houses invaded by the storm.

Now and then, too, there would come a sudden gust of wind that in its strength, as it blew laterally, would, for a moment, hold millions of the hailstones suspended in mid air, but it was only to dash them with redoubled force in some new direction, where more mischief was to be done.

Oh, how the storm raged! Hail—rain—wind. It was, in very truth, an awful night.

There was an antique chamber in an ancient house. Curious and quaint carvings adorn the walls, and the large chimneypiece is a curiosity of itself. The ceiling is low, and a large bay window, from roof to floor, looks to the west. The window is latticed, and filled with curiously painted glass and rich stained pieces, which send in a strange, yet beautiful light, when sun or moon shines into the apartment. There is but one portrait in that room, although the walls seem paneled for the express purpose of containing a series of pictures. That portrait is of a young man, with a pale face, a stately brow, and a strange expression about the eyes, which no one cared to look on twice.

There is a stately bed in that chamber, of carved walnut-wood is it made, rich in design and elaborate in execution; one of those works which owe their existence to the Elizabethan era. It is hung with heavy silken and damask furnishing; nodding feathers are at its corners—covered with dust are they, and they lend a funereal aspect to the room. The floor is of polished oak.

God! How the hail dashes on the old bay window! Like an occasional discharge of mimic musketry, it comes clashing, beating, and cracking upon the small panes; but they resist it—their small size saves them; the wind, the hail, the rain, expend their fury in vain.

The bed in that old chamber is occupied. A creature formed in all fashions of loveliness lies in a half sleep upon that ancient couch—a girl young and beautiful as a spring morning. Her long hair has escaped from its confinement and streams over the blackened coverings of the bedstead; she has been restless in her sleep, for the clothing of the bed is in much confusion. One arm is over her head, the other hangs nearly off the side of the bed near to which she lies. A neck and bosom that would have formed a study for the rarest sculptor that ever Providence gave genius to, were half disclosed. She moaned slightly in her sleep, and once or twice the lips moved as if in prayer—at least one might judge so, for the name of Him who suffered for all came once faintly from them.

She had endured much fatigue, and the storm does not awaken her; but it can disturb the slumbers it does not possess the power to destroy entirely. The turmoil of the elements wakes the senses, although it cannot entirely break the repose they have lapsed into.

Oh, what a world of witchery was in that mouth, slightly parted, and exhibiting within the pearly teeth that glistened even in the faint light that came from that bay window. How sweetly the long silken eyelashes lay upon the cheek. Now she moves, and one shoulder is entirely visible—whiter, fairer than the spotless clothing of the bed on which she lies, is the smooth skin of that fair creature, just budding into womanhood, and in that transition state which presents to us all the charms of the girl—almost of the child, with the more matured beauty and gentleness of advancing years.

Was that lightning? Yes—an awful, vivid, terrifying flash—then a roaring peal of thunder, as if a thousand mountains were rolling one over the other in the blue vault of Heaven! Who sleeps now in that ancient city? Not one living soul. The dread trumpet of eternity could not more effectually have awakened any one.

The hail continues. The wind continues. The uproar of the elements seems at its height. Now she awakens—that beautiful girl on the antique bed; she opens those eyes of celestial blue, and a faint cry of alarm bursts from her lips. At least it is a cry which, amid the noise and turmoil without, sounds but faint and weak. She sits upon the bed and presses her hands upon her eyes. Heavens! What a wild torrent of wind, and rain, and hail! The thunder likewise seems intent upon awakening sufficient echoes to last until the next flash of forked lightning should again produce the wild concussion of the air. She murmurs a prayer—a prayer for those she loves best; the names of those dear to her gentle heart come from her lips; she weeps and prays; she thinks then of what devastation the storm must surely produce, and to the great God of Heaven she prays for all living things. Another flash—a wild, blue, bewildering flash of lightning streams across that bay window, for an instant bringing out every colour in it with terrible distinctness. A shriek bursts from the lips of the young girl, and then, with eyes fixed upon that window, which, in another moment, is all darkness, and with such an expression of terror upon her face as it had never before known, she trembled, and the perspiration of intense fear stood upon her brow.

"What—what was it?" she gasped, "real or delusion? Oh, God, what was it? A figure tall and gaunt, endeavouring from the outside to unclasp the window. I saw it. That flash of lightning revealed it to me. It stood the whole length of the window."

There was a lull of the wind. The hail was not falling so thickly—moreover, it now fell, what there was of it, straight, and yet a strange clattering sound came upon the glass of that long window. It could not be a delusion—she is awake, and she hears it. What can produce

it? Another flash of lightning—another shriek—there could be now
no delusion.

A tall figure is standing on the ledge immediately outside the long
window. It is its finger-nails upon the glass that produces the sound
so like the hail, now that the hail has ceased. Intense fear paralysed
the limbs of the beautiful girl. That one shriek is all she can utter—
with hand clasped, a face of marble, a heart beating so wildly in her
bosom, that each moment it seems as if it would break its confines,
eyes distended and fixed upon the window, she waits, froze with
horror. The pattering and clattering of the nails continue. No word
is spoken, and now she fancies she can trace the darker form of that
figure against the window, and she can see the long arms moving to
and fro, feeling for some mode of entrance. What strange light is that
which now gradually creeps up into the air? Red and terrible—
brighter and brighter it grows. The lightning has set fire to a mill,
and the reflection of the rapidly consuming building falls upon that
long window. There can be no mistake. The figure is there, still feeling for an entrance, and clattering against the glass with its long
nails, that appear as if the growth of many years had been untouched.
She tries to scream again but a choking sensation comes over her,
and she cannot. It is too dreadful—she tries to move—each limb
seems weighted down by tons of lead—she can but in a hoarse faint
whisper cry,—

"Help—help—help—help!"

And that one word she repeats like a person in a dream. The red
glare of the fire continues. It throws up the tall gaunt figure in hideous relief against the long window. It shows, too, upon the one
portrait that is in the chamber, and the portrait appears to fix its
eyes upon the attempting intruder, while the flickering light from
the fire makes it look fearfully lifelike. A small pane of glass is broken, and the form from without introduces a long gaunt hand,
which seems utterly destitute of flesh. The fastening is removed,
and one-half of the window, which opens like folding doors, is
swung wide open upon its hinges.

And yet now she could not scream—she could not move. "Help!—help!—help!" was all she could say. But, oh, that look of terror that sat upon her face, it was dreadful—a look to haunt the memory for a lifetime—a look to obtrude itself upon the happiest moments, and turn them to bitterness.

The figure turns half round, and the light falls upon its face. It is perfectly white—perfectly bloodless. The eyes look like polished tin; the lips are drawn back, and the principal feature next to those dreadful eyes is the teeth—the fearful-looking teeth—projecting like those of some wild animal, hideously, glaringly white, and fang-like. It approaches the bed with a strange, gliding movement. It clashes together the long nails that literally appear to hang from the finger ends. No sound comes from its lips. Is she going mad—that young and beautiful girl exposed to so much terror? She has drawn up all her limbs; she cannot even now say help. The power of articulation is gone, but the power of movement has returned to her; she can draw herself slowly along to the other side of the bed from that towards which the hideous appearance is coming.

But her eyes are fascinated. The glance of a serpent could not have produced a greater effect upon her than did the fixed gaze of those awful, metallic-looking eyes that were bent down on her face. Crouching down so that the gigantic height was lost, and the horrible, protruding white face was the most prominent object, came on the figure. What was it?—What did it want there?—What made it look so hideous—so unlike an inhabitant of the earth, and yet be on it?

Now she has got to the verge of the bed, and the figure pauses. It seemed as if when it paused she lost the power to proceed. The clothing of the bed was now clutched in her hands with unconscious power. She drew her breath short and thick. Her bosom heaves, and her limbs tremble, yet she cannot withdraw her eyes from that marble-looking face. He holds her with his glittering eye.

The storm has ceased—all is still. The winds are hushed; the church clock proclaims the hour of one: a hissing sound comes from the throat of the hideous being, and he raises his long, gaunt arms—the lips move. He advances. The girl places one small foot on to the floor. She is unconsciously dragging the clothing with her. The door of the room is in that direction—can she reach it? Has she power to walk?—can she withdraw her eyes from the face of the intruder, and so break the hideous charm? God of Heaven! Is it real, or some dream so like reality as to nearly overturn judgment forever?

The figure has paused again, and half on the bed and half out of it that young girl lies trembling. Her long hair streams across the entire width of the bed. As she has slowly moved along she has left it streaming across the pillows. The pause lasted about a minute—oh, what an age of agony. That minute was, indeed, enough for madness to do its full work in.

With a sudden rush that could not be foreseen—with a strange howling cry that was enough to awaken terror in every breast, the figure seized the long tresses of her hair, and twining them round his bony hands he held her to the bed. Then she screamed— Heaven granted her then power to scream. Shriek followed shriek in rapid succession. The bed-clothes fell in a heap by the side of the bed—she was dragged by her long silken hair completely on to it again. Her beautifully rounded limbs quivered with the agony of her soul. The glassy, horrible eyes of the figure ran over that angelic form with a hideous satisfaction—horrible profanation. He drags her head to the bed's edge. He forces it back by the long hair still entwined in his grasp. With a plunge he seizes her neck in his fang-like teeth—a gush of blood, and a hideous sucking noise follows. *The girl has swooned, and the vampyre is at his hideous repast!*

Fitz-James O'Brien

(1826?–1862)

"FITZ-JAMES O'BRIEN," WROTE JESSICA Amanda Salmonson in her two-volume collection of his writings, "is the most important figure after Poe and before Lovecraft in modern horror literature." Without him, she argues, "the flourishing of supernatural literature in the last half of the nineteenth century would never have occurred." Although these assertions seem rather grand, there is no doubt that O'Brien was hugely influential. His first-place position shows up among all sorts of critics. Science-fiction historian Sam Moskowitz, for example, called O'Brien's story "Horrors Unknown" "the single most striking example of surrealistic fiction to pre-date *Alice in Wonderland.*" His stories include "The Diamond Lens," about a man who kills to steal a diamond and employs it in the lens of a super-microscope that enables him to watch miniature worlds within the atom—where he sees, of course, a beautiful microscopic woman with whom he falls in love. More convincing and moving are moody tales such as "The Lost Room" and "The Wondersmith."

Born an only child to County Cork gentry, he came of age mid-century and took only two years to fritter away his inheritance. O'Brien wrote "What Was it?" at the home of his friend Thomas Bailey Aldrich. A novelist, poet, and editor, Aldrich befriended many young authors in midcentury New York, including Walt

Whitman. He took in O'Brien during one of the Irishman's bouts of humiliating poverty. O'Brien had a reputation among his friends as a man of great talent dissipated by laziness, unreliability, and vanity. One friend, the poet George Arnold, described O'Brien as "a disciple of the church of St. Biceps." In his time he was known as a bohemian dandy who invariably claimed to be younger than he was; the birth year of 1826 is debatable.

"What Was It?" was published in the March 1859 issue of *Harper's New Monthly Magazine*, the first incarnation of what is now *Harper's*, which at the time was only in its ninth year of publication. The magazine published at least sixty items by O'Brien, including both stories and poems. Also in 1859, O'Brien published a poem called "The Ghosts" in a New York monthly called the *Knickerbocker*, in which he nicely expresses the convincing empathy that distinguishes his writings on the supernatural:

> Pale shapes advancing from the midnight air . . .
> I seem to share
> your dim vitality—mine's well-nigh fled.
> I feel the human outlines melt away . . .

"What Was It?" became an immediate hit. One of the earliest stories to employ the concept of invisibility, it was clearly a direct influence on Maupassant's "The Horla." For his 1881 collection *Life, Poems and Stories of Fitz-James O'Brien*, William Winter cut and streamlined the story, and it was this unauthorized condensation that was anthologized many times over the next several decades. Salmonson was the first editor to reprint the original in its entirety, and this restored version follows. O'Brien's title reminds us that his brilliant and terrifying story is almost a riddle. By the time you finish it, you will know the answer, although the narrator never does.

What Was It?

A Mystery

I T IS, I CONFESS, with considerable diffidence that I approach the strange narrative which I am about to relate. The events which I propose detailing are of so extraordinary and unheard-of a character that I am quite prepared to meet with an unusual amount of incredulity and scorn. I accept all such beforehand. I have, I trust, the literary courage to face unbelief. I have, after mature consideration, resolved to narrate, in as simple and straightforward a manner as I can compass, some facts that passed under my observation in the month of July last, and which, in the annals of the mysteries of physical science, are wholly unparalleled.

I live at No. — Twenty-sixth Street, in this city. The house is in some respects a curious one. It has enjoyed for the last two years the reputation of being haunted. It is a large and stately residence, surrounded by what was once a garden, but which is now only a green inclosure used for bleaching clothes. The dry basin of what has been a fountain, and a few fruit-trees, ragged and unpruned, indicate that this spot, in past days, was a pleasant, shady retreat, filled with fruits and flowers and the sweet murmur of waters.

The house is very spacious. A hall of noble size leads to a vast spiral staircase winding through its centre; while the various apartments are of imposing dimensions. It was built some fifteen or twenty years since by Mr. A——, the well-known New York merchant, who five years ago threw the commercial world into convulsions by a stupendous bank fraud. Mr. A——, as every one knows, escaped to Europe, and died not long after of a broken heart. Almost immediately after the news of his decease reached this country, and was verified, the report spread in Twenty-sixth Street that No. —— was haunted. Legal measures had dispossessed the widow of its former owner, and it was inhabited merely by a care-taker and his wife, placed there by the house-agent into whose hands it had passed for purposes of renting or sale. These people declared that they were troubled with unnatural noises. Doors were opened without any visible agency. The remnants of furniture scattered through the various rooms were, during the night, piled one upon the other by unknown hands. Invisible feet passed up and down the stairs in broad daylight, accompanied by the rustle of unseen silk dresses and the gliding of viewless hands along the massive balusters. The caretaker and his wife declared they would live there no longer. The house-agent laughed, dismissed them, and put others in their place. The noises and supernatural manifestations continued. The neighborhood caught up the story, and the house remained untenanted for three years. Several parties negotiated for it; but somehow, always before the bargain was closed, they heard the unpleasant rumors, and declined to treat any further.

It was in this state of things that my landlady—who at that time kept a boardinghouse in Bleecker Street, and who wished to move farther uptown—conceived the bold idea of renting No. —— Twenty-sixth Street. Happening to have in her house rather a plucky and philosophical set of boarders, she laid her scheme before us, stating candidly every thing she had heard respecting the ghostly qualities of the establishment to which she wished to remove us. With the exception of one or two timid persons—a sea-captain and a returned Californian, who immediately gave notice that they would leave—every one of Mrs. Moffat's guests declared that they would accompany her in her chivalric incursion into the abode of spirits.

Our removal was effected in the month of May, and we were all charmed with our new residence. The portion of Twenty-sixth

Street where our house is situated—between Seventh and Eighth Avenues—is one of the pleasantest localities in New York. The gardens back of the houses, running down nearly to the Hudson, form, in the summertime, a perfect avenue of verdure. The air is pure and invigorating, sweeping, as it does, straight across the river from the Weehawken heights, and even the ragged garden which surrounded the house on two sides, although displaying on washing-days rather too much clothes-line, still gave us a piece of green sward to look at, and a cool retreat in the summer evenings, where we smoked our cigars in the dusk, and watched the fire-flies flashing their dark-lanterns in the long grass.

Of course we had no sooner established ourselves at No. — than we began to expect the ghosts. We absolutely awaited their advent with eagerness. Our dinner conversation was supernatural. One of the boarders, who had purchased Mrs. Crowe's *Night Side of Nature* for his own private delectation, was regarded as a public enemy by the entire household for not having bought twenty copies. The man led a life of supreme wretchedness while he was perusing the volume. A system of espionage was established, of which he was the victim. If he incautiously laid the book down for an instant and left the room, it was immediately seized and read aloud in secret places to a select few. I found myself a person of immense importance, it having leaked out that I was tolerably well versed in the history of supernaturalism, and had once written a story, entitled "The Pot of Tulips," for *Harper's Monthly*, the foundation of which was a ghost. If a table or a wainscot panel happened to warp when we were assembled in the large drawing-room, there was an instant silence, and every one was prepared for an immediate clanking of chains and a spectral form.

After a month of psychological excitement, it was with the utmost dissatisfaction that we were forced to acknowledge that nothing in the remotest degree approaching the supernatural had manifested itself. Once the black butler asseverated that his candle had been blown out by some invisible agency while in the act of undressing himself for the night; but as I had more than once discovered this colored gentleman in a condition when one candle must have appeared to him like two, I thought it possible that, by going a step farther in his potations, he might have reversed this phenomenon, and seen no candle at all where he ought to have beheld one.

Things were in this state when an incident took place so awful and inexplicable in its character that my reason fairly reels at the bare memory of the occurrence. It was the tenth of July. After dinner was over I repaired, with my friend Dr. Hammond, to the garden to smoke my evening pipe. Independent of certain mental sympathies which existed between the Doctor and myself, we were linked together by a secret vice. We both smoked opium. We knew each other's secret, and respected it. We enjoyed together that wonderful expansion of thought; that marvelous intensifying of the perceptive faculties; that boundless feeling of existence when we seem to have points of contact with the whole universe; in short, that unimaginable spiritual bliss, which I would not surrender for a throne, and which I hope you, reader, will never— never taste.

Those hours of opium happiness which the Doctor and I spent together in secret were regulated with a scientific accuracy. We did not blindly smoke the drug of Paradise, and leave our dreams to chance. While smoking we carefully steered our conversation through the brightest and calmest channels of thought. We talked of the East, and endeavored to recall the magical panorama of its glowing scenery. We criticised the most sensuous poets, those who painted life ruddy with health, brimming with passion, happy in the possession of youth, and strength, and beauty. If we talked of Shakespeare's *Midsummer Night's Dream,* we lingered over Ariel and avoided Caliban. Like the Gebers, we turned our faces to the East, and saw only the sunny side of the world.

This skillful coloring of our train of thought produced in our subsequent visions a corresponding tone. The splendors of Arabian fairy-land dyed our dreams. We paced that narrow strip of grass with the tread and port of kings. The song of the *Rana arborea* while he clung to the bark of the ragged plum-tree sounded like the strains of divine orchestras. Houses, walls, and streets melted like rain-clouds, and vistas of unimaginable glory stretched away before us. It was a rapturous companionship. We each of us enjoyed the vast delight more perfectly because, even in our most ecstatic moments, we were ever conscious of each other's presence. Our pleasures, while individual, were still twin, vibrating and moving in musical accord.

On the evening in question, the tenth of July, the Doctor and myself found ourselves in an unusually metaphysical mood. We lit our large meerschaums, filled with fine Turkish tobacco; in the core of which burned a little black nut of opium, that, like the nut in the fairy tale, held within its narrow limits wonders beyond the reach of kings; we paced to and fro, conversing. A strange perversity dominated the currents of our thought. They would *not* flow through the sun-lit channels into which we strove to divert them. For some unaccountable reason they constantly diverged into dark and lonesome beds, where a continual gloom brooded. It was in vain that, after our old fashion, we flung ourselves on the shores of the East, and talked of its gay bazaars, of the splendors of the time of Haroun, of harems and golden palaces. Black afreets continually arose from the depths of our talk, and expanded, like the one the fisherman released from the copper vessel, until they blotted every thing bright from our vision. Insensibly we yielded to the occult force that swayed us, and indulged in gloomy speculation. We had talked some time upon the proneness of the human mind to mysticism and the almost universal love of the Terrible, when Hammond suddenly said to me:

"What do you consider to be the greatest element of Terror?"

The question, I own, puzzled me. That many things were terrible, I knew. Stumbling over a corpse in the dark; beholding, as I once did, a woman floating down a deep and rapid river, with wildly-lifted arms and awful, upturned face, uttering, as she sank, shrieks that rent one's heart, while we, the spectators, stood frozen at a window which overhung the river at a height of sixty feet, unable to make the slightest effort to save her, but dumbly watching her last supreme agony and her disappearance. A shattered wreck, with no life visible, encountered floating listlessly on the ocean, is a terrible object, for it suggests a huge terror, the proportions of which are veiled. But it now struck me for the first time that there must be one great and ruling embodiment of fear, a King of Terrors to which all others must succumb. What might it be? To what train of circumstances would it owe its existence?

"I confess, Hammond," I replied to my friend, "I never considered the subject before. That there must be one Something more terrible than any other thing, I feel. I can not attempt, however, even the most vague definition."

"I am somewhat like you, Harry," he answered. "I feel my capacity to experience a terror greater than any thing yet conceived by the human mind. Something combining in fearful and unnatural amalgamation hitherto supposed incompatible elements. The calling of the voices in Brockden Brown's novel of *Wieland* is awful; so is the picture of the Dweller of the Threshold in Bulwer's *Zanoni*; but," he added, shaking his head gloomily, "there is something more horrible still than these."

"Look here, Hammond," I rejoined; "let us drop this kind of talk for Heaven's sake. We shall suffer for it, depend on it."

"I don't know what's the matter with me tonight," he replied, "but my brain is running upon all sorts of weird and awful thoughts. I feel as if I could write a story like Hoffmann tonight, if I were only master of a literary style."

"Well, if we are going to be Hoffmannesque in our talk I'm off to bed. Opium and nightmares should never be brought together. How sultry it is! Good-night, Hammond."

"Good-night, Harry. Pleasant dreams to you."

"To you, gloomy wretch, afreets, ghouls, and enchanters."

We parted, and each sought his respective chamber. I undressed quickly and got into bed, taking with me, according to my usual custom, a book, over which I generally read myself to sleep. I opened the volume as soon as I had laid my head upon the pillow, and instantly flung it to the other side of the room. It was Goudon's *History of Monsters*—a curious French work, which I had lately imported from Paris, but which, in the state of mind I was then in, was any thing but an agreeable companion. I resolved to go to sleep at once; so turning down my gas until nothing but a little blue point of light glimmered on the top of the tube, I composed myself to rest once more.

The room was in total darkness. The atom of gas that still remained lighted did not illuminate a distance of three inches round the burner. I desperately drew my arm across my eyes, as if to shut out even the darkness, and tried to think of nothing. It was in vain. The confounded themes touched on by Hammond in the garden kept obtruding themselves on my brain. I battled against them. I erected ramparts of would-be blankness of intellect to keep them out. They still crowded upon me. While I was lying still as a corpse, hoping that by a perfect physical inaction I would hasten mental repose, an awful incident occurred. A Something dropped, as it seemed, from the ceiling, plumb upon my chest, and the next instant I felt two bony hands encircling my throat, endeavoring to choke me.

I am no coward, and am possessed of considerable physical strength. The suddenness of the attack instead of stunning me strung every nerve to its highest tension. My body acted from instinct, before my brain had time to realize the terrors of my position. In an instant I wound two muscular arms around the creature, and squeezed it, with all the strength of despair, against my chest. In a few seconds the bony hands that had fastened on my throat loosened their hold, and I was free to breathe once more. Then commenced a struggle of awful intensity. Immersed in the most profound darkness, totally ignorant of the nature of the Thing by which I was so suddenly attacked, finding my grasp slipping every moment by reason, it seemed to me, of the entire nakedness of my assailant, bitten with sharp teeth in the shoulder, neck, and chest, having every moment to protect my throat against a pair of sinewy, agile hands, which my utmost efforts could not confine— these were a combination of circumstances to combat which required all the strength and skill and courage that I possessed.

At last, after a silent, deadly, exhausting struggle, I got my assailant under by a series of incredible efforts of strength. Once pinned, with my knee on what I made out to be its chest, I knew that I was victor. I rested for a moment to breathe. I heard the creature beneath me panting in the darkness, and felt the violent throbbing of a heart. It was apparently as exhausted as I was, that was one comfort. At this moment I remembered that I usually placed under my pillow, before going to bed, a large, yellow silk pocket-handkerchief, for use during the night. I felt for it instantly; it was there. In a few seconds more I had, after a fashion, pinioned the creature's arms.

I now felt tolerably secure. There was nothing more to be done but to turn on the gas, and having first seen what my midnight assailant was like, arouse the household. I will confess to being actuated by a certain pride in not giving the alarm before; I wished to make the capture alone and unaided.

Never loosing my hold for an instant, I slipped from the bed to the floor, dragging my captive with me. I had but a few steps to make to reach the gas-burner; these I made with the greatest caution, holding the creature in a grip like a vice. At last I got within arm's-length of the tiny speck of blue light, which told me where the gas burner lay. Quick as lightning I released my grasp with one hand and let on the full flood of light. Then I turned to look at my captive.

I can not even attempt to give any definition of my sensations the instant after I turned on the gas. I suppose I must have shrieked with terror, for in less than a minute afterward my room was crowded with the inmates of the house. I shudder now as I think of that awful moment. *I saw nothing!* Yes; I had one arm firmly clasped round a breathing, panting, corporeal shape, my other hand gripped with all its strength a throat as warm, and apparently fleshly, as my own; and yet, with this living substance in my grasp, with its body pressed against my own, and all in the bright glare of a large jet of gas, I absolutely beheld nothing! Not even an outline—a vapor!

I do not, even at this hour, realize the situation in which I found myself. I can not recall the astounding incident thoroughly. Imagination in vain tries to compass the awful paradox.

It breathed. I felt its warm breath upon my cheek. It struggled fiercely. It had hands. They clutched me. Its skin was smooth, just like my own. There it lay, pressed close up against me, solid as stone—and yet utterly invisible!

I wonder that I did not faint or go mad on the instant. Some wonderful instinct must have sustained me; for, absolutely, in place of loosening my hold on the terrible Enigma, I seemed to gain an additional strength in my moment of horror, and tightened my grasp with such wonderful force that I felt the creature shivering with agony.

Just then Hammond entered my room at the head of the household. As soon as he beheld my face—which, I suppose, must have been an awful sight to look at—he hastened forward, crying,

"Great Heaven, Harry! what has happened?"

"Hammond! Hammond!" I cried, "come here. Oh! this is awful! I have been attacked in bed by something or other, which I have hold of; but I can't see it—I can't see it!"

Hammond, doubtless struck by the unfeigned horror expressed in my countenance, made one or two steps forward with an anxious yet puzzled expression. A very audible titter burst from the remainder of my visitors. This suppressed laughter made me furious. To laugh at a human being in my position! It was the worst species of cruelty. *Now*, I can understand why the appearance of a man struggling violently, as it would seem, with an airy nothing, and calling for assistance against a vision, should have appeared ludicrous. *Then*, so great was my rage against the mocking crowd that had I the power I would have stricken them dead where they stood.

"Hammond! Hammond!" I cried again, despairingly, "for God's sake come to me. I can hold the—the Thing but a short while longer. It is overpowering me. Help me. Help me!"

"Harry," whispered Hammond, approaching me, "you have been smoking too much opium."

"I swear to you Hammond that this is no vision," I answered, in the same low tone. "Don't you see how it shakes my whole frame with its struggles? If you don't believe me convince yourself. Feel it—touch it."

Hammond advanced and laid his hand in the spot I indicated. A wild cry of horror burst from him. He had felt it!

In a moment he had discovered somewhere in my room a long piece of cord, and was the next instant winding it, and knotting it about the body of the unseen being that I clasped in my arms.

"Harry," he said, in a hoarse, agitated voice, for, though he preserved his presence of mind, he was deeply moved. "Harry, it's all safe now. You may let go, old fellow, if you're tired. The Thing can't move."

I was utterly exhausted, and I gladly loosed my hold.

Hammond stood holding the ends of the cord that bound the Invisible, twisted round his hand, while before him, self-supporting, as it were, he beheld a rope laced and interlaced, and stretching tightly around a vacant space. I never saw a man look so thoroughly stricken with awe. Nevertheless his face expressed all the courage and determination which I knew him to possess. His lips, although white, were set firmly, and one could perceive at a glance that, although stricken with fear, he was not daunted.

The confusion that ensued among the guests of the house, who were witnesses of this extraordinary scene between Hammond and myself—who beheld the pantomime of binding this struggling Something—who beheld me almost sinking from physical exhaustion when my task of jailer was over—the confusion and terror that took possession of the bystanders, when they saw all this, was beyond description. Many of the weaker ones fled from the apartment. The few who remained behind clustered near the door, and could not be induced to approach Hammond and his Charge. Still incredulity broke out through their terror. They had not the courage to satisfy themselves, and yet they doubted. It was in vain that I begged of some of the men to come near and convince themselves by touch of the existence of a living being in that room which was invisible. They were incredulous, but did not dare to undeceive themselves. How could a solid, living, breathing body be invisible? they asked. My reply was this. I gave a sign to Hammond, and both of us—conquering our fearful repugnance to touching the invisible creature—lifted it from the ground, manacled as it was, and took it to my bed. Its weight was about that of a boy of fourteen.

"Now my friends," I said, as Hammond and myself held the creature suspended over the bed, "I can give you self-evident proof that here is a solid, ponderable body which, nevertheless, you can not see. Be good enough to watch the surface of the bed attentively."

I was astonished at my own courage in treating this strange event so calmly; but I had recovered from my first terror, and felt a sort of scientific pride in the affair which dominated every other feeling.

The eyes of the by-standers were immediately fixed on my bed. At a given signal Hammond and I let the creature fall. There was the dull sound of a heavy body alighting on a soft mass. The timbers of the bed creaked. A deep impression marked itself distinctly on the pillow, and on the bed itself. The crowd who witnessed this gave a sort of low, universal cry, and rushed from the room. Hammond and I were left alone with our Mystery.

We remained silent for some time, listening to the low, irregular breathing of the creature on the bed, and watching the rustle of the bedclothes as it impotently struggled to free itself from confinement. Then Hammond spoke.

"Harry, this is awful."

"Ay, awful."

"But not unaccountable."

"Not unaccountable! What do you mean? Such a thing has never occurred since the birth of the world. I know not what to think, Hammond. God grant that I am not mad, and that this is not an insane fantasy!"

"Let us reason a little, Harry. Here is a solid body which we touch, but which we can not see. The fact is so unusual that it strikes us with terror. Is there no parallel, though, for such a phenomenon? Take a piece of pure glass. It is tangible and transparent. A certain chemical coarseness is all that prevents its being so entirely transparent as to be totally invisible. It is not *theoretically impossible*, mind you, to fabricate a glass which shall not reflect a single ray of light—a glass so pure and homogeneous in its atoms that the rays from the sun shall pass through it as they do through the air, refracted but not reflected. We do not see the air, and yet we feel it."

"That's all very well, Hammond, but these are inanimate substances. Glass does not breathe, air does not breathe. *This* thing has a heart that palpitates. A will that moves it. Lungs that play and inspire and respire."

"You forget the strange phenomena of which we have so often heard of late," answered the Doctor, gravely. "At the meetings called 'spirit circles,' invisible hands have been thrust into the hands of those persons round the table—warm, fleshly hands that seemed to pulsate with mortal life."

"What? Do you think, then, that this thing is—"

"I don't know what it is" was the solemn reply; "but please the gods I will, with your assistance, thoroughly investigate it."

We watched together, smoking many pipes, all night long by the bedside of the unearthly being that tossed and panted until it was apparently wearied out. Then we learned by the low, regular breathing that it slept.

The next morning the house was all astir. The boarders congregated on the landing outside my room, and Hammond and myself were lions. We had to answer a thousand questions as to the state of our extraordinary prisoner, for as yet not one person in the house except ourselves could be induced to set foot in the apartment.

The creature was awake. This was evidenced by the convulsive manner in which the bedclothes were moved in its efforts to escape. There was something truly terrible in beholding, as it were, those second-hand indications of the terrible writhings and agonized struggles for liberty, which themselves were invisible.

Hammond and myself had racked our brains during the long night to discover some means by which we might realize the shape and general appearance of the Enigma. As well as we could make out by passing our hands over the creature's form, its outlines and lineaments were human. There was a mouth; a round, smooth head without hair; a nose, which, however, was little elevated above the cheeks; and its hands and feel felt like those of a boy. At first we thought of placing the being on a smooth surface and tracing its outline with chalk, as shoemakers trace the outline of the foot. This plan was given up as being of no value. Such an outline would give not the slightest idea of its conformation.

A happy thought struck me. We would take a cast of it in plaster of Paris. This would give us the solid figure, and satisfy all our wishes. But how to do it? The movements of the creature would disturb the setting of the plastic covering, and distort the mould. Another thought. Why not give it chloroform? It had respiratory organs—that was evident by its breathing. Once reduced to a state of insensibility, we could do with it what we would. Doctor X—— was sent for; and after the worthy physician had recovered from the first shock of amazement, he proceeded to administer the chloroform. In three minutes afterward we were enabled to remove the fetters from the creature's body, and a well-known modeler of this city was busily engaged in covering the invisible form with the moist clay. In five minutes more we had a mould, and before evening a rough fac-simile of the Mystery. It was shaped like a man. Distorted, uncouth, and horrible, but still a man. It was small, not over four feet and some inches in height, and its limbs betrayed a muscular development that was unparalleled. Its face surpassed in hideousness any thing I had ever seen. Gustave Dore, or Callot, or Tony Johannot never conceived anything so horrible. There is a face in one of the latter's illustrations to *"Un voyage où il vous plaira,"* which somewhat approaches the countenance of this creature, but does not equal it. It was the physiognomy of what I should have fancied a ghoul to be. It looked as if it was capable of feeding on human flesh.

Having satisfied our curiosity, and bound every one in the house over to secrecy, it became a question what was to be done with our Enigma? It was impossible that we should keep such a horror in our house; it was equally impossible that such an awful being should be let loose upon the world. I confess that I would have gladly voted for the creature's destruction. But who would shoulder the responsibility? Who would undertake the execution of this horrible semblance of a human being? Day after day this question was deliberated gravely. The boarders all left the house. Mrs. Moffat was in despair, and threatened Hammond and myself with all sorts of legal penalties if we did not remove the Horror. Our answer was, "We will go if you like, but we decline taking this creature with us. Remove it yourself if you please. It appeared in your house. On you the responsibility rests." To this there was, of course, no answer. Mrs. Moffat could not obtain for love or money a person who would even approach the Mystery.

The most singular part of the transaction was, that we were entirely ignorant of what the creature habitually fed on. Every thing in the way of nutriment that we could think of was placed before it, but was never touched. It was awful to stand by, day after day, and see the clothes toss and hear the hard breathing, and know that it was starving.

Ten, twelve days, a fortnight passed, and it still lived. The pulsations of the heart, however, were daily growing fainter, and had now nearly ceased altogether. It was evident that the creature was dying for want of sustenance. While this terrible life-struggle was going on I felt miserable. I could not sleep of nights. Horrible as the creature was, it was pitiful to think of the pangs it was suffering.

At last it died. Hammond and I found it cold and stiff one morning in the bed. The heart had ceased to beat, the lungs to inspire. We hastened to bury it in the garden. It was a strange funeral, the dropping of that viewless corpse into the damp hole. The cast of its form I gave to Doctor X——, who keeps it in his museum in Tenth Street.

As I am on the eve of a long journey from which I may not return, I have drawn up this narrative of an event the most singular that has ever come to my knowledge.

Harry Escott

Note: It is rumored that the proprietors of a well-known museum in this city have made arrangements with Dr. X—— to exhibit to the public the singular cast which Mr. Escott deposited with him. So extraordinary a history can not fail to attract universal attention.

※

Anonymous

(dates unknown)

"The Mysterious Stranger" appeared in the English magazine *Odds and Ends* in 1860. Both the author and the translator
were anonymous then and remain so now, which is a shame, because it's a vivid and memorable story. One interesting point is its
use of the folkloric idea that vampires are unable to enter a home
unless first invited, no matter how innocently, by the victim. Leonard Woolf points out that this idea may relate to the conviction that
the devil proceeds by making deals with willing victims, but Leslie
S. Klinger remarks, "This consensual element is part of the
nineteenth-century image of the 'seductive' vampire but sounds a
lot like the archaic view that female rape victims always consent to
or invite the rape."

"You wish it?" asks the titular stranger in this story. "You press
the invitation?" But this isn't strictly a male-and-female dance. You
can see the same kind of situation in Bram Stoker's *Dracula*, when
the count invites Jonathan Harker to enter the castle:

> "Welcome to my house! Enter freely and of your own will." He
> made no motion of stepping to meet me, but stood like a statue,
> as though his gesture of welcome had fixed him into stone. The
> instant, however, that I had stepped over the threshold, he
> moved impulsively forward, and holding out his hand grasped

mine with a strength that made me wince, an effect which was not lessened by the fact that it seemed as cold as ice—more like the hand of a dead than a living man.

Critics have pointed out various indications that Stoker seems to have read this excellent anonymous story. Perhaps he even read it in his youth; he was thirteen when it was published and still a teenager when, as you will see in the biographical note about Stoker, he wrote a school paper on sensationalism in fiction.

The Mysterious Stranger

To die, to sleep,
To sleep, perchance to dream, ay, there's the rub . . .

Hamlet

BOREAS, THAT FEARFUL NORTH-WEST wind, which in the spring and autumn stirs up the lowest depths of the wild Adriatic, and is then so dangerous to vessels, was howling through the woods, and tossing the branches of the old knotty oaks in the Carpathian Mountains, when a party of five riders, who surrounded a litter drawn by a pair of mules, turned into a forest-path, which offered some protection from the April weather, and allowed the travellers in some degree to recover their breath. It was already evening, and bitterly cold; the snow fell every now and then in large flakes. A tall old gentleman, of aristocratic appearance, rode at the head of the troop. This was the Knight of Fahnenberg, in Austria. He had inherited from a childless brother a considerable property, situated in the Carpathian Mountains; and he had set out to take possession of it, accompanied by his daughter Franziska, and a niece about twenty years of age, who had been brought up with her. Next to the knight rode a fine young man of some twenty and odd years—the Baron Franz von Kronstein; he wore, like the former, the broad-brimmed

hat with hanging feathers, the leather collar, the wide riding-boots—
in short, the travelling-dress which was in fashion at the commencement of the seventeenth century. The features of the young
man had much about them that was open and friendly, as well as
some mind; but the expression was more that of dreamy and sensitive softness than of youthful daring, although no one could deny
that he possessed much of youthful beauty. As the cavalcade turned
into the oak wood the young man rode up to the litter, and chatted
with the ladies who were seated therein. One of these—and to her
his conversation was principally addressed—was of dazzling beauty.
Her hair flowed in natural curls round the fine oval of her face, out
of which beamed a pair of star-like eyes, full of genius, lively fancy,
and a certain degree of archness. Franziska von Fahnenberg seemed
to attend but carelessly to the speeches of her admirer, who made
many kind inquiries as to how she felt herself during the journey,
which had been attended with many difficulties: she always answered him very shortly, almost contemptuously; and at length remarked, that if it had not been for her father's objections, she would
long ago have requested the baron to take her place in their horrid
cage of a litter, for, to judge by his remarks, he seemed incom-
moded by the weather; and she would so much rather be mounted
on the spirited horse, and face wind and storm, than be mewed up
there, dragged up the hills by those long-eared animals, and mope
herself to death with ennui. The young lady's words, and, still
more, the half-contemptuous tone in which they were uttered, appeared to make the most painful impression on the young man: he
made her no reply at the moment, but the absent air with which he
attended to the kindly-intended remarks of the other young lady,
showed how much he was disconcerted.

"It appears, dear Franziska," said he at length in a kindly tone,
"that the hardships of the road have affected you more than you
will acknowledge. Generally so kind to others, you have been very
often out of humour during the journey, and particularly with regard to your humble servant and cousin, who would gladly bear a

double or triple share of the discomforts, if he could thereby save you from the smallest of them."

Franziska showed by her look that she was about to reply with some bitter jibe, when the voice of the knight was heard calling for his nephew, who galloped off at the sound.

"I should like to scold you well, Franziska," said her companion somewhat sharply, "for always plagueing your poor Cousin Franz in this shameful way; he who loves you so truly, and who, whatever you may say, will one day be your husband."

"My husband!" replied the other angrily. "I must either completely alter my ideas, or he his whole self, before that takes place. No, Bertha! I know that this is my father's darling wish, and I do not deny the good qualities Cousin Franz may have, or really has, since I see you are making a face; but to marry an effeminate man—never!"

"Effeminate! You do him great injustice," replied her friend quickly. "Just because instead of going off to the Turkish war, where little honour was to be gained, he attended to your father's advice, and stayed at home, to bring his neglected estate into order, which he accomplished with care and prudence; and because he does not represent this howling wind as a mild zephyr—for reasons such as these you are pleased to call him effeminate."

"Say what you will, it is so," cried Franziska obstinately. "Bold, aspiring, even despotic, must be the man who is to gain my heart; these soft, patient, and thoughtful natures are utterly distasteful to me. Is Franz capable of deep sympathy, either in joy or sorrow? He is always the same—always quiet, soft, and tiresome."

"He has a warm heart, and is not without genius," said Bertha.

"A warm heart! that may be," replied the other; "but I would rather be tyrannized over, and kept under a little by my future husband, than be loved in such a wearisome manner. You say he has genius, too. I will not exactly contradict you, since that would be impolite, but it is not easily discovered. But even allowing you are right in both statements, still the man who does not bring these qualities into action is a despicable creature. A man may do many foolish things, he may even be a little wicked now and then, provided it is in nothing dishonourable; and one can forgive him, if he is only acting on some fixed theory for some special object. There is, for instance, your own faithful admirer the Castellan of Glogau, Knight of Woislaw; he loves you most truly, and is now quite in a position to enable you to marry comfortably. The brave man has lost his right hand—reason enough for remaining seated behind the stove, or near the spinning-wheel of his Bertha; but what does he do?—He goes off to the war in Turkey; he fights for a noble thought—"

"And runs the chance of getting his other hand chopped off, and another great scar across his face," put in her friend.

"Leaves his lady-love to weep and pine a little," pursued Franziska, "but returns with fame, marries, and is all the more honoured and admired! This is done by a man of forty, a rough warrior, not bred at court, a soldier who has nothing but his cloak and sword. And Franz—rich, noble—but I will not go on. Not a word more on this detested point, if you love me, Bertha."

Franziska leaned back in the corner of the litter with a dissatisfied air, and shut her eyes as though, overcome by fatigue, she wished to sleep.

"This awful wind is so powerful, you say, that we must make a detour to avoid its full force," said the knight to an old man, dressed in a fur-cap and a cloak of rough skin, who seemed to be the guide of the party.

"Those who have never personally felt the Boreas storming over the country between Sessano and Trieste, can have no conception of the reality," replied the other. "As soon as it commences, the snow is blown in thick long columns along the ground. That is nothing to what follows. These columns become higher and higher, as the wind rises, and continue to do so until you see nothing but snow above, below, and on every side—unless, indeed, sometimes, when sand and gravel are mixed with the snow, and at length it is impossible to open your eyes at all. Your only plan for safety is to wrap your cloak around you, and lie down flat on the ground. If your home were but a few hundred yards off, you might lose your life in the attempt to reach it."

"Well, then, we owe you thanks, old Kumpan," said the knight, though it was with difficulty he made his words heard above the roaring of the storm; "we owe you thanks for taking us this round as we shall thus be enabled to reach our destination without danger."

"You may feel sure of that, noble sir," said the old man. "By midnight we shall have arrived, and that without any danger by the way, if—" Suddenly the old man stopped, he drew his horse sharply up, and remained in an attitude of attentive listening.

"It appears to me we must be in the neighborhood of some village," said Franz von Kronstein; "for between the gusts of the storm I hear a dog howling."

"It is no dog, it is no dog!" said the old man uneasily, and urged his horse to a rapid pace. "For miles around there is no human dwelling; and except in the castle of Klatka, which indeed lies in the neighborhood, but has been deserted for more than a century, probably no one has lived here since the creation.—But there again," he continued; "well, if I wasn't sure of it from the first."

"That howling seems to bother you, old Kumpan," said the knight, listening to a long-drawn fierce sound, which appeared nearer than before, and seemed to be answered from a distance.

"That howling comes from no dogs," replied the old guide uneasily. "Those are reed-wolves; they may be on our track; and it would be as well if the gentlemen looked to their firearms."

"Reed-wolves? What do you mean?" inquired Franz in surprise.

"At the edge of this wood," said Kumpan, "there lies a lake about a mile long, whose banks are covered with reeds. In these a number of wolves have taken up their quarters, and feed on wild birds, fish, and such like. They are shy in the summer-time, and a boy of twelve might scare them; but when the birds migrate, and the fish are frozen up, they prowl about at night, and then they are dangerous.

They are worst, however, when the Boreas rages, for then it is just as if the fiend himself possessed them: they are so mad and fierce that man and beast become alike their victims; and a party of them have been known even to attack the ferocious bears of these mountains, and, what is more, to come off victorious." The howl was now again repeated more distinctly, and from two opposite directions. The riders in alarm felt for their pistols and the old man grasped the spear which hung at his saddle.

"We must keep close to the litter; the wolves are very near us," whispered the guide. The riders turned their horses, surrounded the litter, and the knight informed the ladies, in a few quieting words, of the cause of this movement.

"Then we *shall* have an adventure—some little variety!" cried Franziska with sparkling eyes.

"How can you talk so foolishly?" said Bertha in alarm.

"Are we not under manly protection? Is not Cousin Franz on our side?" said the other mockingly.

"See, there is a light gleaming among the twigs; and there is another," cried Bertha. "There must be people close to us."

"No, no," cried the guide quickly. "Shut up the door, ladies. Keep close together, gentlemen. It is the eyes of wolves you see sparkling there." The gentlemen looked towards the thick underwood, in which every now and then little bright spots appeared, such as in summer would have been taken for glowworms; it was just the same greenish yellow light, but less unsteady, and there were always two flames together. The horses began to be restive, they kicked and dragged at the rein; but the mules behaved tolerably well.

"I will fire on the beasts, and teach them to keep their distance," said Franz, pointing to the spot where the lights were thickest.

"Hold, hold, Sir Baron!" cried Kumpan quickly, and seized the young man's arm. "You would bring such a host together by the report, that, encouraged by numbers, they would be sure to make the first assault. However, keep your arms in readiness, and if an old she-wolf springs out—for these always lead the attack—take

good aim and kill her, for then there must be no further hesitation." By this time the horses were almost unmanageable, and terror had also infected the mules. Just as Franz was turning towards
the litter to say a word to his cousin, an animal, about the size of a
large hound, sprang from the thicket and seized the foremost mule.

"Fire, baron! A wolf!" shouted the guide.

The young man fired, and the wolf fell to the ground. A fearful
howl rang through the wood.

"Now, forward! Forward without a moment's delay!" cried
Kumpan. "We have not above five minutes' time. The beasts will
tear their wounded comrade to pieces, and, if they are very hungry, partially devour her. We shall, in the meantime, gain a little
start, and it is not more than an hour's ride to the end of the forest.
There—do you see—there are the towers of Klatka between the
trees—out there where the moon is rising, and from that point the
wood becomes less dense."

The travellers endeavoured to increase their pace to the utmost,
but the litter retarded their progress. Bertha was weeping with fear,
and even Franziska's courage had diminished, for she sat very still.
Franz endeavoured to reassure them. They had not proceeded many
moments when the howling recommenced, and approached nearer
and nearer.

"There they are again and fiercer and more numerous than before," cried the guide in alarm.

The lights were soon visible again, and certainly in greater
numbers. The wood had already become less thick, and the snow-
storm having ceased, the moonbeams discovered many a dusky
form amongst the trees, keeping together like a pack of hounds and
advancing nearer and nearer till they were within twenty paces,
and on the very path of the travellers. From time to time a fierce
howl arose from their centre which was answered by the whole
pack, and was at length taken up by single voices in the distance.

The party now found themselves some few hundred yards from
the ruined castle of which Kumpan had spoken. It was, or seemed

by moonlight to be, of some magnitude. Near the tolerably preserved principal building lay the ruins of a church which must have
once been beautiful, placed on a little hillock dotted with single
oak-trees and bramble-bushes. Both castle and church were still
partially roofed in, and a path led from the castle gate to an old oak-
tree, where it joined at right angles the one along which the travellers were advancing.

The old guide seemed in much perplexity.

"We are in great danger, noble sir," said he. "The wolves will
very soon make a general attack. There will then be only one way
of escape: leaving the mules to their fate, and taking the young
ladies on your horses."

"That would be all very well, if I had not thought of a better
plan," replied the knight. "Here is the ruined castle; we can surely
reach that, and then, blocking up the gates, we must just await the
morning."

"Here? In the ruins of Klatka?—Not for all the wolves in the
world!" cried the old man. "Even by daylight no one likes to approach the place, and, now, by night!—The castle, Sir Knight, has a
bad name."

"On account of robbers?" asked Franz.

"No; it is haunted," replied the other.

"Stuff and nonsense!" said the baron. "Forward to the ruins;
there is not a moment to be lost."

And this was indeed the case. The ferocious beasts were but a few
steps behind the travellers. Every now and then they retired, and set
up a ferocious howl. The party had just arrived at the old oak before
mentioned and were about to turn into the path to the ruins, when
the animals, as though perceiving the risk they ran of losing their
prey, came so near that a lance could easily have struck them. The
knight and Franz faced sharply about, spurring their horses amidst
the advancing crowds, when suddenly, from the shadow of the oak
stepped forth a man who in a few strides placed himself between the
travellers and their pursuers. As far as one could see in the dusky

light the stranger was a man of a tall and well-built frame; he wore a
sword by his side and a broad-brimmed hat was on his head. If the
party were astonished at his sudden appearance, they were still more
so at what followed. As soon as the stranger appeared the wolves
gave over their pursuit, tumbled over each other, and set up a fearful
howl. The stranger now raised his hand, appeared to wave it, and the
wild animals crawled back into the thickets like a pack of beaten
hounds.

Without casting a glance at the travellers, who were too much
overcome by astonishment to speak, the stranger went up the path
which led to the castle and soon disappeared beneath the gateway.

"Heaven have mercy on us!" murmured old Kumpan in his
beard, as he made the sign of the cross.

"Who was that strange man?" asked the knight with surprise,
when he had watched the stranger as long as he was visible, and the
party had resumed their way.

The old guide pretended not to understand, and riding up to
the mules, busied himself with arranging the harness, which had
become disordered in their haste: more than a quarter of an hour
elapsed before he rejoined them.

"Did you know the man who met us near the ruins and who
freed us from our fourfooted pursuers in such a miraculous way?"
asked Franz of the guide.

"Do I know him? No, noble sir; I never saw him before," replied the guide hesitatingly.

"He looked like a soldier, and was armed," said the baron. "Is
the castle, then, inhabited?"

"Not for the last hundred years," replied the other. "It was dis-
mantled because the possessor in those days had iniquitous dealings
with some Turkish-Selavonian hordes, who had advanced as far as
this; or rather"—he corrected himself hastily—"he is *said* to have
had such, for he might have been as upright and good a man as ever
ate cheese fried in butter."

"And who is now the possessor of the ruins and of these woods?" inquired the knight.

"Who but yourself, noble sir?" replied Kumpan. "For more than two hours we have been on your estate, and we shall soon reach the end of the wood."

"We hear and see nothing more of the wolves," said the baron after a pause. "Even their howling has ceased. The adventure with the stranger still remains to me inexplicable, even if one were to suppose him a huntsman—"

"Yes, yes; that is most likely what he is," interrupted the guide hastily, whilst he looked uneasily round him. "The brave good man, who came so opportunely to our assistance, must have been a huntsman. Oh, there are many powerful woodsmen in this neighborhood! Heaven be praised!" he continued, taking a deep breath, "there is the end of the wood, and in a short hour we shall be safely housed."

And so it happened. Before an hour had elapsed the party passed through a well-built village, the principal spot on the estate, towards the venerable castle, the windows of which were brightly illuminated, and at the door stood the steward and other dependents, who, having received their new lord with every expression of respect, conducted the party to the splendidly furnished apartments.

Nearly four weeks passed before the travelling adventures again came on the *tapis*. The knight and Franz found such constant employment in looking over all the particulars of the large estate, and endeavouring to introduce various German improvements, that they were very little at home. At first Franziska was charmed with everything in a neighborhood so entirely new and unknown. It appeared to her so romantic, so very different from her German Father-land, that she took the greatest interest in everything, and often drew comparisons between the countries, which generally ended unfavourably for Germany. Bertha was of exactly the contrary opinion: she laughed at her cousin, and said that her liking for novelty and

strange sights must indeed have come to a pass when she preferred
hovels in which the smoke went out of the doors and windows instead of the chimney, walls covered with soot, and inhabitants not
much cleaner, and of unmannerly habits, to the comfortable dwellings and polite people of Germany. However, Franziska persisted in
her notions, and replied that everything in Austria was flat, *ennuyant*,
and common; and that a wild peasant here, with his rough coat of
skin, had ten times more interest for her than a quiet Austrian in his
holiday suit, the mere sight of whom was enough to make one yawn.

As soon as the knight had gotten the first arrangements into
some degree of order the party found themselves more together
again. Franz continued to show great attention to his cousin, which,
however, she received with little gratitude, for she made him the
butt of all her fanciful humours, that soon returned when after a
longer sojourn she had become more accustomed to her new life.
Many excursions into the neighborhood were undertaken but there
was little variety in the scenery, and these soon ceased to amuse.

The party were one day assembled in the old-fashioned hall,
dinner had just been removed, and they were arranging in which
direction they should ride. "I have it," cried Franziska suddenly, "I
wonder we never thought before of going to view by day the spot
where we fell in with our night-adventure with wolves and the
Mysterious Stranger."

"You mean a visit to the ruins—what were they called?" said
the knight.

"Castle Klatka," cried Franziska gaily. "Oh, we really must ride
there! It will be so charming to go over again by daylight, and in
safety, the ground where we had such a dreadful fright."

"Bring round the horses," said the knight to a servant; "and tell
the steward to come to me immediately." The latter, an old man,
soon after entered the room.

"We intend taking a ride to Klatka," said the knight: "we had
an adventure there on our road—"

"So old Kumpan told me," interrupted the steward.

"And what do you say about it?" asked the knight.

"I really don't know what to say," replied the old man, shaking his head. "I was a youth of twenty when I first came to this castle, and now my hair is grey; half a century has elapsed during that time. Hundreds of times my duty has called me into the neighbourhood of those ruins, but never have I seen the Fiend of Klatka."

"What do you say? Whom do you call by that name?" inquired Franziska, whose love of adventure and romance was strongly awakened.

"Why, people call by that name the ghost or spirit who is supposed to haunt the ruins," replied the steward. "They say he only shows himself on moon-light nights—"

"That is quite natural," interrupted Franz smiling. "Ghosts can never bear the light of day; and if the moon did not shine, how could the ghost be seen, for it is not supposed that any one for a mere freak would visit the ruins by torch-light."

"There are some credulous people who pretend to have seen this ghost," continued the steward. "Huntsmen and woodcutters say they have met him by the large oak on the crosspath. That, noble sir, is supposed to be the spot he inclines most to haunt, for the tree was planted in remembrance of the man who fell there."

"And who was he?" asked Franziska with increasing curiosity.

"The last owner of the castle, which at that time was a sort of robbers' den, and the headquarters of all depredators in the neighbourhood," answered the old man. "They say this man was of superhuman strength, and was feared not only on account of his passionate temper, but of his treaties with the Turkish hordes. Any young woman, too, in the neighbourhood to whom he took a fancy, was carried off to his tower and never heard of more. When the measure of his iniquity was full, the whole neighbourhood rose in a mass, besieged his stronghold, and at length he was slain on the spot where the huge oak-tree now stands."

"I wonder they did not burn the whole castle, so as to erase the very memory of it," said the knight.

"It was a dependency of the church, and that saved it," replied the other. "Your great-grandfather afterwards took possession of it, for it had fine lands attached. As the Knight of Klatka was of good family, a monument was erected to him in the church, which now lies as much in ruin as the castle itself."

"Oh, let us set off at once! Nothing shall prevent my visiting so interesting a spot," said Franziska eagerly. "The imprisoned damsels who never reappeared, the storming of the tower, the death of the knight, the nightly wanderings of his spirit round the old oak, and lastly, our own adventure, all draw me thither with an indescribable curiosity."

When a servant announced that the horses were at the door, the young girls tripped laughingly down the steps which led to the coach-yard. Franz, the knight, and a servant well acquainted with the country followed; and in a few minutes the party was on the road to the forest.

The sun was still high in the heavens when they saw the towers of Klatka rising above the trees. Everything in the wood was still except the cheerful twitterings of the birds as they hopped about amongst the bursting buds and leaves and announced that spring had arrived.

The party soon found themselves near the old oak at the bottom of the hill on which stood the towers, still imposing in their ruin. Ivy and bramble bushes had wound themselves over the walls, and forced their deep roots so firmly between the stones that they in a great measure held these together. On the top of the highest spot a small bush in its young fresh verdure swayed lightly in the breeze.

The gentlemen assisted their companions to alight, and leaving the horses to the care of the servant, ascended the hill to the castle. After having explored this in every nook and cranny, and spent much time in a vain search for some trace of the extraordinary stranger whom Franziska declared she was determined to discover, they proceeded to an inspection of the adjoining church. This they found to have better withstood the ravages of time and weather; the nave, indeed, was in complete dilapidation, but the chancel and altar were still under roof, as well as a sort of chapel which appeared to have been a place of honour for the families of the old knights of the castle. Few traces remained, however, of the magnificent painted glass which must once have adorned the windows, and the wind entered at pleasure through the open spaces.

The party were occupied for some time in deciphering the inscriptions on a number of tombstones, and on the walls, principally within the chancel. They were generally memorials of the ancient lords, with figures of men in armour, and women and children of all ages. A flying raven and various other devices were placed at the corners. One gravestone, which stood close to the entrance of the chancel, differed widely from the others: there was no figure sculptured on it, and the inscription, which on all besides was a mere mass of flattering eulogies, was here simple and unadorned; it contained only these words: "Ezzelin von Klatka fell like a knight at the storming of the castle"—on such a day and year.

"That must be the monument of the knight whose ghost is said to haunt these ruins," cried Franziska eagerly. "What a pity he is not represented in the same way as the others—I should so like to have known what he was like!"

"Oh, there is the family vault, with steps leading down to it, and the sun is lighting it up through a crevice," said Franz, stepping from the adjoining vestry.

The whole party followed him down the eight or nine steps which led to a tolerably airy chamber, where were placed a number of coffins of all sizes, some of them crumbling into dust. Here, again, one close to the door was distinguished from the others by the simplicity of its design, the freshness of its appearance, and the brief inscription: "Ezzelinus de Klatka, Eques."

As not the slightest effluvium was perceptible, they lingered some time in the vault; and when they reascended to the church, they had

a long talk over the old possessors, of whom the knight now remembered he had heard his parents speak. The sun had disappeared, and the moon was just rising as the explorers turned to leave
the ruins. Bertha had made a step into the nave, when she uttered a
slight exclamation of fear and surprise. Her eyes fell on a man who
wore a hat with drooping feathers, a sword at his side, and a short
cloak of somewhat old-fashioned cut over his shoulders. The
stranger leaned carelessly on a broken column at the entrance; he
did not appear to take any notice of the party; and the moon shone
full on his pale face.

The party advanced towards the stranger.

"If I am not mistaken," commenced the knight, "we have met
before."

Not a word from the unknown.

"You released us in an almost miraculous manner," said Franziska,
"from the power of those dreadful wolves. Am I wrong in suppos-
ing it is to you we are indebted for that great service?"

"The beasts are afraid of me," replied the stranger in a deep
fierce tone, while he fastened his sunken eyes on the girl, without
taking any notice of the others.

"Then you are probably a huntsman," said Franz, "and wage
war against the fierce brutes."

"Who is not either the pursuer or the pursued? All persecute or
are persecuted, and Fate persecutes all," replied the stranger without looking at him.

"Do you live in these ruins?" asked the knight hesitatingly.

"Yes; but not to the destruction of your game, as you may fear,
Knight of Fahnenberg," said the unknown contemptuously. "Be
quite assured of this; your property shall remain untouched—"

"Oh! my father did not mean that," interrupted Franziska, who
appeared to take the liveliest interest in the stranger. "Unfortunate
events and sad experiences have, no doubt, induced you to take up
your abode in these ruins, of which my father would by no means
dispossess you."

"Your father is very good, if that is what he meant," said the stranger in his former tone; and it seemed as though his dark features were drawn into a slight smile; "but people of my sort are rather difficult to turn out."

"You must live very uncomfortably here," said Franziska, half vexed, for she thought her polite speech had deserved a better reply.

"My dwelling is not exactly uncomfortable, only somewhat small—still quite suitable for quiet people," said the unknown with a kind of sneer. "I am not, however, always quiet; I sometimes pine to quit the narrow space, and then I dash away through forest and field, over hill and dale; and the time when I must return to my little dwelling always comes too soon for me."

"As you now and then leave your dwelling," said the knight, "I would invite you to visit us, if I knew—"

"That I was in a station to admit of your doing so," interrupted the other; and the knight started slightly, for the stranger had exactly expressed the half-formed thought. "I lament," he continued coldly, "that I am not able to give you particulars on this point—some difficulties stand in the way: be assured, however, that I am a knight, and of at least as ancient a family as yourself."

"Then you must not refuse our request," cried Franziska, highly interested in the strange manners of the unknown. "You must come and visit us."

"I am no boon-companion, and on that account few have invited me of late," replied the other with his peculiar smile; "besides, I generally remain at home during the day; that is my time for rest. I belong, you must know, to that class of persons who turn day into night, and night into day, and who love everything uncommon and peculiar."

"Really? So do I! And for that reason, you must visit us," cried Franziska. "Now," she continued smiling, "I suppose you have just risen, and you are taking your morning airing. Well, since the moon is your sun, pray pay a frequent visit to our castle by the light of its rays. I think we shall agree very well, and that it will be very nice for us to be acquainted."

"You wish it?—You press the invitation?" asked the stranger earnestly and decidedly.

"To be sure, for otherwise you will not come," replied the young lady shortly.

"Well, then, come I will!" said the other, again fixing his gaze on her. "If my company does not please you at any time, you will have yourself to blame for an acquaintance with one who seldom forces himself, but is difficult to shake off."

When the unknown had concluded these words he made a slight motion with his hand, as though to take leave of them, and passing under the doorway, disappeared among the ruins. The party soon after mounted their horses and took the road home.

It was evening of the following day, and all were again seated in the hall of the castle. Bertha had that day received good news. The knight Woislaw had written from Hungary that the war with the Turks would soon be brought to a conclusion during the year, and that although he had intended returning to Silesia, hearing of the Knight of Fahnenberg having gone to take possession of his new estates, he should follow the family there, not doubting that Bertha had accompanied her friend. He hinted that he stood so high in the opinion of his duke on account of his valuable services, that in future his duties would be even more important and extensive; but before settling down to them, he should come and claim Bertha's promise to become his wife. He had been much enriched by his master, as well as by booty taken from the Turks. Having formerly lost his right hand in the duke's service, he had essayed to fight with his left; but this did not succeed very admirably, and so he had an iron one made by a very clever artist. This hand performed many of the functions of a natural one, but there had been still much wanting; now, however, his master had presented him with one of gold, an extraordinary work of art, produced by a celebrated Italian mechanic. The knight described it as something marvellous, especially as to the superhuman strength with which it enabled him to use the sword and lance. Franziska naturally rejoiced in the happiness of her friend, who had had no news of her betrothed for a long time before. She launched out every now and then, partly to plague Franz, and partly to express her own feelings, in the highest praise and admiration of the bravery and enterprise of the knight, whose adventurous qualities she lauded to the skies. Even the scar on his face and his want of a right hand were reckoned as virtues; and Franziska at last saucily declared that a rather ugly man was infinitely more attractive to her than a handsome one, for as a general rule handsome men were conceited and effeminate. Thus, she added, no one could term their acquaintance of the night before handsome, but attractive and interesting he certainly was. Franz and Bertha simultaneously denied this. His gloomy appearance, the deadly hue of his complexion, the tone of his voice, were each in turn depreciated by Bertha, while Franz found fault with the contempt and arrogance obvious in his speech. The knight stood between the two parties. He thought there was something in his bearing that spoke of good family, though much could not be said for his politeness; however, the man might have had trials enough in his life to make him misanthropical. Whilst they were conversing in this way, the door suddenly opened and the subject of their remarks himself walked in.

"Pardon me, Sir Knight," he said coldly, "that I come, if not uninvited, at least unannounced; there was no one in the ante-chamber to do me that service."

The brilliantly lighted chamber gave a full view of the stranger. He was a man of about forty, tall, and extremely thin. His features could not be termed uninteresting—there lay in them something bold and daring—but the expression was on the whole anything but benevolent. There were contempt and sarcasm in the cold grey eyes, whose glance, however, was at times so piercing that no one could endure it long. His complexion was even more peculiar than the features: it could neither be called pale nor yellow; it was a sort of grey, or, so to speak, dirty white, like that of an Indian who has

been suffering long from fever; and was rendered still more remarkable by the intense blackness of his beard and short-cropped
hair. The dress of the unknown was knightly, but old-fashioned and
neglected; there were great spots of rust on the collar and breastplate
of his armour; and his dagger and the hilt of his finely worked
sword were marked in some places with mildew. As the party were
just going to supper, it was only natural to invite the stranger to
partake of it; he complied, however, only in so far that he seated
himself at the table, for he ate no morsel. The knight, with some
surprise, inquired the reason.

"For a long time past I have accustomed myself never to eat at
night," he replied with a strange smile. "My digestion is quite un-
used to solids, and indeed would scarcely confront them. I live
entirely on liquids."

"Oh, then we can empty a bumper of Rhine-wine together,"
cried the host.

"Thanks; but I neither drink wine nor any cold beverage," replied the other; and his tone was full of mockery. It appeared as if
there was some amusing association connected with the idea.

"Then I will order you a cup of hippocras"—a warm drink composed of herbs—"it shall be ready immediately," said Franziska.

"Many thanks, fair lady; not at present," replied the other. "But
if I refuse the beverage you offer me now, you may be assured that
as soon as I require it—perhaps very soon—I will request that, or
some other of you."

Bertha and Franz thought the man had something inexpressibly
repulsive in his whole manner, and they had no inclination to engage him in conversation; but the baron, thinking that perhaps
politeness required him to say something, turned towards the
guest, and commenced in a friendly tone: "It is now many weeks
since we first became acquainted with you; we then had to thank
you for a singular service—"

"And I have not yet told you my name, although you would

gladly know it," interrupted the other dryly. "I am called Azzo; and as"—this he said again with his ironical smile—"with the permission of the Knight of Fahnenberg, I live at the castle of Klatka, you can in future call me Azzo von Klatka."

"I only wonder you do not feel lonely and uncomfortable amongst those old walls," began Bertha. "I cannot understand—"

"Why my business is there? Oh, about that I will willingly give you some information, since you and the young gentleman there take such a kindly interest in my person," replied the unknown in his tone of sarcasm.

Franz and Bertha both started, for he had revealed their thoughts as though he could read their souls. "You see, my lady," he continued, "there are a variety of strange whims in the world. As I have already said, I love what is peculiar and uncommon, at least what would appear so to you. It is wrong in the main to be astonished at anything, for, viewed in one light, all things are alike; even life and death, this side of the grave and the other, have more resemblance than you would imagine. You perhaps consider me rather touched a little in my mind, for taking up my abode with the bat and the owl; but if so, why not consider every hermit and recluse insane? You will tell me that those are holy men. I certainly have no pretension that way; but as they find pleasure in praying and singing psalms, so I amuse myself with hunting. Oh, away in the pale moonlight, on a horse that never tires, over hill and dale, through forest and woodland! I rush among the wolves, which fly at my approach, as you yourself perceived, as though they were puppies fearful of the lash."

"But still it must be lonely, very lonely for you," remarked Bertha.

"So it would by day; but I am then asleep," replied the stranger dryly; "at night I am merry enough."

"You hunt in an extraordinary way," remarked Franz hesitatingly.

"Yes; but, nevertheless, I have no communication with robbers, as you seem to imagine," replied Azzo coldly.

Franz again started—that very thought had just crossed his mind. "Oh, I beg your pardon; I do not know—" he stammered.

"What to make of me," interrupted the other. "You would therefore do well to believe just what I tell you, or at least to avoid making conjectures of your own, which will lead to nothing."

"I understand you: I know how to value your ideas, if no one else does," cried Franziska eagerly. "The humdrum, everyday life of the generality of men is repulsive to you; you have tasted the joys and pleasures of life, at least what are so called, and you have found them tame and hollow. How soon one tires of the things one sees all around! Life consists in change. Only in what is new, uncommon, and peculiar, do the flowers of the spirit bloom and give forth scent. Even pain may become a pleasure if it saves one from the shallow monotony of everyday life—a thing I shall hate till the hour of my death."

"Right, fair lady—quite right! Remain in this mind: this was always my opinion, and the one from which I have derived the highest reward," cried Azzo; and his fierce eyes sparkled more intensely than ever. "I am doubly pleased to have found in you a person who shares my ideas. Oh, if you were a man, you would make me a splendid companion; but even a woman may have fine experiences when once these opinions take root in her, and bring forth action!"

As Azzo spoke these words in a cold tone of politeness, he turned from the subject, and for the rest of his visit only gave the knight monosyllabic replies to his inquiries, taking leave before the table was cleared. To an invitation from the knight, backed by a still more pressing one from Franziska to repeat his visit, he replied that he would take advantage of their kindness, and come sometimes.

When the stranger had departed, many were the remarks made on his appearance and general deportment. Franz declared his most decided dislike of him. Whether it was as usual to vex her cousin, or whether Azzo had really made an impression on her, Franziska took his part vehemently. As Franz contradicted her more eagerly than usual, the young lady launched out into still stronger expressions; and there is no knowing what hard words her cousin might have received had not a servant entered the room.

The following morning Franziska lay longer than usual in bed. When her friend went to her room, fearful lest she should be ill, she found her pale and exhausted. Franziska complained she had passed a very bad night; she thought the dispute with Franz about the stranger must have excited her greatly, for she felt quite feverish and exhausted, and a strange dream, too, had worried her, which was evidently a consequence of the evening's conversation. Bertha, as usual, took the young man's part, and added that a common dispute about a man whom no one knew, and about whom anyone might form his own opinion, could not possibly have thrown her into her present state. "At least," she continued, "you can let me hear this wonderful dream."

To her surprise, Franziska for a length of time refused to do so.

"Come, tell me," inquired Bertha, "what can possibly prevent you from relating a dream—a mere dream? I might almost think it credible, if the idea were not too horrid, that poor Franz is not very far wrong when he says that the thin, corpse-like, dried-up, old-fashioned stranger has made a greater impression on you than you will allow."

"Did Franz say so?" asked Franziska. "Then you can tell him he is not mistaken. Yes, the thin, corpse-like, dried-up, whimsical stranger is far more interesting to me than the rosy-cheeked, well-dressed, polite, and prosy cousin."

"Strange," cried Bertha. "I cannot at all comprehend the almost magic influence which this man, so repulsive, exercises over you."

"Perhaps the very reason I take his part, may be that you are all so prejudiced against him," remarked Franziska pettishly. "Yes, it must be so; for that his appearance should please my eyes is what no one in his senses could imagine. But," she continued, smiling and holding out her hand to Bertha, "is it not laughable that I should get out of temper even with you about this stranger?—I can more easily understand it with Franz—and that this unknown should spoil my morning, as he has already spoiled my evening and my night's rest?"

"By that dream, you mean?" said Bertha, easily appeased, as she put her arm round her cousin's neck and kissed her. "Now, do tell it to me. You know how I delight in hearing anything of the kind."

"Well, I will, as a sort of compensation for my peevishness towards you," said the other, clasping her friend's hands. "Now, listen! I had walked up and down my room for a long time; I was excited—out of spirits—I do not know exactly what. It was almost midnight ere I lay down, but I could not sleep. I tossed about, and at length it was only from sheer exhaustion that I dropped off. But what a sleep it was! An inward fear ran through me perpetually. I saw a number of pictures before me, as I used to do in childish sicknesses. I do not know whether I was asleep or half awake. Then I dreamed, but as clearly as if I had been wide awake, that a sort of mist filled the room, and out of it stepped the knight Azzo. He gazed at me for a time, and then letting himself slowly down on one knee, imprinted a kiss on my throat. Long did his lips rest there; and I felt a slight pain, which always increased, until I could bear it no more. With all my strength I tried to force the vision from me, but succeeded only after a long struggle. No doubt I uttered a scream, for that awoke me from my trance. When I came a little to my senses I felt a sort of superstitious fear creeping over me—how great you may imagine when I tell you that, with my eyes open and awake, it appeared to me as if Azzo's figure were still by my bed, and then disappearing gradually into the mist, vanished at the door!"

"You must have dreamed very heavily, my poor friend," began Bertha, but suddenly paused. She gazed with surprise at Franziska's throat. "Why, what is that?" she cried. "Just look: how extraordinary—a red streak on your throat!"

Franziska raised herself, and went to a little glass that stood in the window. She really saw a small red line about an inch long on her neck, which began to smart when she touched it with her finger.

"I must have hurt myself by some means in my sleep," she said after a pause; "and that in some measure will account for my dream."

The friends continued chatting for some time about this singular coincidence—the dream and the stranger; and at length it was all turned into a joke by Bertha.

Several weeks passed. The knight had found the estate and affairs in greater disorder than he at first imagined; and instead of remaining three or four weeks, as was originally intended, their departure was deferred to an indefinite period. This postponement was likewise in some measure occasioned by Franziska's continued indisposition. She who had formerly bloomed like a rose in its young fresh beauty was becoming daily thinner, more sickly and exhausted, and at the same time so pale, that in the space of a month not a tinge of red was perceptible on the once glowing cheek. The knight's anxiety about her was extreme, and the best advice was procured which the age and country afforded; but all to no purpose. Franziska complained from time to time that the horrible dream with which her illness commenced was repeated, and that always on the day following she felt an increased and indescribable weakness. Bertha naturally set this down to the effects of fever, but the ravages of that fever on the usually clear reason of her friend filled her with alarm.

The knight Azzo repeated his visits every now and then. He always came in the evening, and when the moon shone brightly. His manner was always the same. He spoke in monosyllables, and was coldly polite to the knight; to Franz and Bertha, particularly to the former, contemptuous and haughty; but to Franziska, friendliness itself. Often when, after a short visit, he again left the house, his peculiarities became the subject of conversation. Besides his odd way of speaking, in which Bertha said there lay a deep hatred, a cold detestation of all mankind with the exception of Franziska, two other singularities were observable. During none of his visits, which often took place at supper-time, had he been prevailed upon to eat or drink anything, and that without giving any good reason for his abstinence. A remarkable altera-tion, too, had taken place in his appearance: he seemed an entirely different creature. The skin, before so shrivelled and stretched, seemed smooth and soft, while a slight tinge of red appeared in his cheeks, which began to look round and plump. Bertha, who could not at all conceal her ill-will towards him, said often, that much as she hated his face before, when it was more like a death's-head than a human being's, it was now more than ever re-pulsive; she always felt a shudder run through her veins whenever his sharp piercing eyes rested on her. Perhaps it was owing to Franziska's partiality, or to the knight Azzo's own contemptuous way of replying to Franz, or to his haughty way of treating him in general, that made the young man dislike him more and more. It was quite observable that whenever Franz made a remark to his cousin in the presence of Azzo, the latter would immediately throw some ill-natured light on it or distort it to a totally differ-ent meaning. This increased from day to day, and at last Franz declared to Bertha that he would stand such conduct no longer, and that it was only out of consideration for Franziska that he had not already called him to account.

At this time the party at the castle was increased by the arrival of Bertha's long-expected guest. He came just as they were sitting down to supper one evening, and all jumped up to greet their old friend. The knight Woislaw was a true model of the soldier, hard-ened and strengthened by war with men and elements. His face would not have been termed ugly, if a Turkish sabre had not left a mark running from the right eye to the left cheek, and standing out bright red from the sunburned skin. The frame of the Castellan of Glogau might almost be termed colossal. Few would have been able to carry his armour, and still fewer move with his lightness and ease under its weight. He did not think little of this same armour, for it had been a present from the palatine of Hungary on his leaving the camp. The blue wrought-steel was ornamented all over with patterns in gold; and he had put it on to do honour to his bride-elect, together with the wonderful gold hand, the gift of the duke.

Woislaw was questioned by the knight and Franz on all the concerns of the campaign; and he entered into the most minute particulars relating to the battles, which, with regard to plunder, had been more successful than ever. He spoke much of the strength of the Turks in a hand-to-hand fight, and remarked that he owed the duke many thanks for his splendid gift, for in consequence of its strength many of the enemy regarded him as something superhuman. The sickliness and deathlike paleness of Franziska was too perceptible not to be immediately noticed by Woislaw; accustomed to see her so fresh and cheerful, he hastened to inquire into the cause of the change. Bertha related all that had happened, and Woislaw listened with the greatest interest. This increased to the utmost at the account of the often-repeated dream, and Franziska had to give him the most minute particulars of it; it appeared as though he had met with a similar case before, or at least had heard of one. When the young lady added that it was very remarkable that the wound on her throat which she had at first felt had never healed, and still pained her, the knight Woislaw looked at Bertha as much as to say that this last fact had greatly strengthened his idea as to the cause of Franziska's illness.

It was only natural that the discourse should next turn to the knight Azzo, about whom everyone began to talk eagerly. Woislaw inquired as minutely as he had done with regard to Franziska's illness about what concerned this stranger, from the first evening of their acquaintance down to his last visit, without, however, giving any opinion on the subject. The party were still in earnest conversation, when the door opened, and Azzo entered. Woislaw's eyes remained fixed on him, as he, without taking any particular notice of the new arrival, walked up to the table, and seating him-self, directed most of the conversation to Franziska and her father, and now and then made some sarcastic remark when Franz began to speak. The Turkish war again came on the *tapis,* and though Azzo only put in an occasional remark, Woislaw had much to say on the subject. Thus they had advanced late into the night, and Franz said smiling to Woislaw: "I should not wonder if day had surprised us, whilst listening to your entertaining adventures."

"I admire the young gentleman's taste," said Azzo, with an ironi-cal curl of the lip. "Stories of storm and shipwreck are, indeed, best heard on *terra firma,* and those of battle and death at a hospitable table or in the chimney corner. One has then the comfortable feel-ing of keeping a whole skin, and being in no danger, not even of taking cold." With the last words, he gave a hoarse laugh, and turning his back on Franz, rose, bowed to the rest of the company, and left the room. The knight, who always accompanied Azzo to the door, now expressed himself fatigued, and bade his friends good night.

"That Azzo's impertinence is unbearable," cried Bertha when he was gone. "He becomes daily more rough, unpolite, and presum-ing. If only on account of Franziska's dream, though of course he cannot help that, I detest him. Now, tonight, not one civil word has he spoken to anyone but Franziska, except, perhaps, some casual remark to my uncle."

"I cannot deny that you are right, Bertha," said her cousin. "One may forgive much to a man whom fate had probably made some-what misanthropical; but he should not overstep the bounds of common politeness. But where on earth is Franz?" added Franziska, as she looked uneasily round. The young man had quietly left the room whilst Bertha was speaking.

"He cannot have followed the knight Azzo to challenge him?" cried Bertha in alarm.

"It were better he entered a lion's den to pull his mane!" said

Woislaw vehemently. "I must follow him instantly," he added, as he rushed from the room.

He hastened over the threshold, out of the castle, and through the court before he came up to them. Here a narrow bridge with a slight balustrade passed over the moat by which the castle was surrounded. It appeared that Franz had only just addressed Azzo in a few hot words, for as Woislaw, unperceived by either, advanced under the shadow of the wall, Azzo said gloomily: "Leave me, foolish boy—leave me; for by that sun"—and he pointed to the full moon above them—"you will see those rays no more if you linger another moment on my path."

"And I tell you, wretch, that you either give me satisfaction for your repeated insolence, or you die," cried Franz, drawing his sword.

Azzo stretched forth his hand, and grasping the sword in the middle, it snapped like a broken reed. "I warn you for the last time," he said in a voice of thunder as he threw the pieces into the moat. "Now, away—away, boy, from my path, or, by those below us, you are lost!"

"You or I! you or I!" cried Franz madly as he made a rush at the sword of his antagonist and strove to draw it from his side. Azzo replied not; only a bitter laugh half escaped from his lips; then seizing Franz by the chest, he lifted him up like an infant, and was in the act of throwing him over the bridge when Woislaw stepped to his side. With a grasp of his wonderful hand, into the springs of which he threw all his strength, he seized Azzo's arm, pulled it down, and obliged him to drop his victim. Azzo seemed in the highest degree astonished. Without concerning himself further about Franz, he gazed in amazement on Woislaw.

"Who art thou who darest to rob me of my prey?" he asked hesitatingly. "Is it possible? Can you be—"

"Ask not, thou bloody one! Go, seek thy nourishment! Soon comes thy hour!" replied Woislaw in a calm but firm tone.

"Ha, now I know!" cried Azzo eagerly. "Welcome, blood-brother! I give up to you this worm, and for your sake will not crush him. Farewell; our paths will soon meet again."

"Soon, very soon; farewell!" cried Woislaw, drawing Franz towards him. Azzo rushed away and disappeared.

Franz had remained for some moments in a state of stupefaction, but suddenly started as from a dream. "I am dishonoured, dishonoured forever!" he cried, as he pressed his clenched hands to his forehead.

"Calm yourself; you could not have conquered," said Woislaw.

"But I will conquer, or perish!" cried Franz incensed. "I will seek this adventurer in his den, and he or I must fall."

"You could not hurt him," said Woislaw. "You would infallibly be the victim."

"Then show me a way to bring the wretch to judgment," cried Franz, seizing Woislaw's hands, while tears of anger sprang to his eyes. "Disgraced as I am, I cannot live."

"You shall be revenged, and that within twenty-four hours, I hope; but only on two conditions—"

"I agree to them! I will do anything—" began the young man eagerly.

"The first is, that you do nothing, but leave everything in my hands," interrupted Woislaw. "The second, that you will assist me in persuading Franziska to do what I shall represent to her as absolutely necessary. That young lady's life is in more danger from Azzo than your own."

"How? What?" cried Franz fiercely. "Franziska's life in danger! And from that man? Tell me, Woislaw, who is this fiend?"

"Not a word will I tell either the young lady or you, until the danger is passed," said Woislaw firmly. "The smallest indiscretion would ruin everything. No one can act here but Franziska herself, and if she refuses to do so she is irretrievably lost."

"Speak, and I will help you. I will do all you wish, but I must know—"

"Nothing, absolutely nothing," replied Woislaw. "I must have both you and Franziska yield to me unconditionally. Come now, come to her. You are to be mute on what has passed, and use every effort to induce her to accede to my proposal."

Woislaw spoke firmly, and it was impossible for Franz to make any further objection; in a few moments they both entered the hall, where they found the young girls still anxiously awaiting them.

"Oh, I have been so frightened," said Franziska, even paler than usual, as she held out her hand to Franz. "I trust all has ended peaceably."

"Everything is arranged; a couple of words were sufficient to settle the whole affair," said Woislaw cheerfully. "But Master Franz was less concerned in it than yourself, fair lady."

"I! How do you mean?" said Franziska in surprise.

"I allude to your illness," replied the other.

"And you spoke of that to Azzo? Does he, then, know a remedy which he could not tell me himself?" she inquired, smiling painfully.

"The knight Azzo must take part in your cure; but speak to you about it he cannot, unless the remedy is to lose all its efficacy," replied Woislaw quietly.

"So it is some secret elixir, as the learned doctors who have so long attended me say, and through whose means I only grow worse," said Franziska mournfully.

"It is certainly a secret, but is as certainly a cure," replied Woislaw.

"So said all, but none has succeeded," said the young lady peevishly.

"You might at least try it," began Bertha.

"Because your friend proposes it," said the other smiling. "I have no doubt that you, with nothing ailing you, would take all manner of drugs to please your knight; but with me the inducement is wanting, and therefore also the faith."

"I did not speak of any medicine," said Woislaw.

"Oh! a magical remedy! I am to be cured—what was it the quack who was here the other day called it?—'by sympathy.' Yes, that was it."

"I do not object to your calling it so, if you like," said Woislaw smiling; "but you must know, dear lady, that the measures I shall propose must be attended to literally, and according to the strictest directions."

"And you trust this to me?" asked Franziska.

"Certainly," said Woislaw hesitating; "but—"

"Well, why do you not proceed? Can you think that I shall fail in courage?" she asked.

"Courage is certainly necessary for the success of my plan," said Woislaw gravely; "and it is because I give you credit for a large share of that virtue, I venture to propose it at all, although for the real harmlessness of the remedy I will answer with my life, provided you follow my directions exactly."

"Well, tell me the plan, and then I can decide," said the young lady.

"I can only tell you that when we commence our operations," replied Woislaw.

"Do you think I am a child to be sent here, there, and everywhere, without a reason?" asked Franziska, with something of her old pettishness.

"You did me great injustice, dear lady, if you thought for a moment I would propose anything disagreeable to you, unless demanded by the sternest necessity," said Woislaw; "and yet I can only repeat my former words."

"Then I will not do it," cried Franziska. "I have already tried so much—and all ineffectually."

"I give you my honour as a knight, that your cure is certain, but you must pledge yourself solemnly and unconditionally to do implicitly what I shall direct," said Woislaw earnestly.

"Oh, I implore you to consent, Franziska. Our friend would not propose anything unnecessary," said Bertha, taking both her cousin's hands.

"And let me join my entreaties to Bertha's," said Franz.

"How strange you all are!" exclaimed Franziska, shaking her head. "You make such a secret of that which I must know if I am to accomplish it, and then you declare so positively that I shall recover, when my own feelings tell me it is quite hopeless."

"I repeat, that I will answer for the result," said Woislaw, "on the condition I mentioned before, and that you have courage to carry out what you commence."

"Ha! now I understand; this, after all, is the only thing which appears doubtful to you," cried Franziska. "Well, to show you that our sex are neither wanting in the will nor in the power to accomplish deeds of daring, I give my consent."

With the last words, she offered Woislaw her hand.

"Our compact is thus sealed," she pursued smiling. "Now say, Sir Knight, how am I to commence this mysterious cure?"

"It commenced when you gave your consent," said Woislaw gravely. "Now, I have only to request that you will ask no more questions, but hold yourself in readiness to take a ride with me tomorrow an hour before sunset. I also request that you will not mention to your father a word of what has passed."

"Strange!" said Franziska.

"You have made the compact; you are not wanting in resolution; and I will answer for everything else," said Woislaw encouragingly.

"Well, so let it be. I will follow your directions," said the lady, although she still looked incredulous.

"On our return you shall know everything; before that, it is quite impossible," said Woislaw in conclusion. "Now go, dear lady, and take some rest; you will need strength for tomorrow."

It was on the morning of the following day; the sun had not risen above an hour, and the dew still lay like a veil of pearls on the grass or dripped from the petals of the flowers swaying in the early breeze, when the knight Woislaw hastened over the fields towards the forest, and turned into a gloomy path, which by the direction one could perceive led towards the towers of Klatka. When he arrived at the old oak-tree we have before had occasion to mention, he sought carefully along the road for traces of human footsteps, but only a deer had passed that way. Seemingly satisfied with his search, he proceeded on his way, though not before he had half drawn his dagger from its sheath, as though to assure himself that it was ready for service in time of need.

Slowly he ascended the path; it was evident he carried something beneath his cloak. Arrived in the court, he left the ruins of the castle to the left, and entered the old chapel. In the chancel he looked eagerly and earnestly around. A deathlike stillness reigned in the deserted sanctuary, only broken by the whispering of the wind in an old thorn-tree which grew outside. Woislaw had looked round him ere he perceived the door leading down to the vault; he hurried towards it and descended. The sun's position enabled its rays to penetrate the crevices, and made the subterranean chamber so light that one could read easily the inscriptions at the head and feet of the coffins. The knight first laid on the ground the packet he had hitherto carried under his cloak, and then going from coffin to coffin, at last remained stationary before the oldest of them. He read the inscription carefully, drew his dagger thoughtfully from its case, and endeavoured to raise the lid with its point. This was no difficult matter, for the rusty iron nails kept but a slight hold of the rotten wood. On looking in, only a heap of ashes, some remnants of dress, and a skull were the contents. He quickly closed it again, and went on to the next, passing over those of a woman and two children. Here things had much the same appearance, except that the corpse held together till the lid was raised, and then fell into dust, a few linen rags and bones being alone perceptible. In the third, fourth, and nearly the next half-dozen, the bodies were in better preservation: in some, they looked a sort of yellow-brown mummy; whilst in others a skinless skull covered with hair grinned from the coverings of velvet, silk, or mildewed embroideries; all, however, were touched with the loathsome marks of decay. Only one more coffin now remained to be inspected; Woislaw approached it, and read the inscription. It was the same that had before attracted the Knight of Fahnenberg: Ezzelin von Klatka, the last possessor of the tower, was described as lying therein. Woislaw found it more difficult to raise the lid here; and it was only by the exertion of much strength that he at length succeeded in extracting the nails. He did all, however, as quietly as if afraid of rousing some sleeper within; he then raised the cover, and cast a glance on the corpse. An involuntary "Ha!" burst from his lips as he stepped back a pace. If he had less expected the sight that met his eyes, he would have been far more overcome. In the coffin lay Azzo as he lived and breathed, and as Woislaw had seen him at the supper-table only the evening before. His appearance, dress, and all were the same; besides, he had more the semblance of sleep than of death—no trace of decay was visible—there was even a rosy tint on his cheeks. Only the circumstance that the breast did not heave distinguished him from one who slept. For a few moments Woislaw did not move; he could only stare into the coffin. With a hastiness in his movements not usual with him, he suddenly seized the lid, which had fallen from his hands, and laying it on the coffin, knocked the nails into their places. As soon as he had completed this work, he fetched the packet he had left at the entrance, and laying it on the top of the coffin, hastily ascended the steps, and quitted the church and the ruins.

The day passed. Before evening, Franziska requested her father to allow her to take a ride with Woislaw, under pretense of showing him the country. He, only too happy to think this a sign of amendment in his daughter, readily gave his consent; so followed by a single servant, they mounted and left the castle. Woislaw was unusually silent and serious. When Franziska began to rally him about his gravity and the approaching sympathetic cure, he replied that what was before her was no laughing matter; and that although the result would be certainly a cure, still it would leave an impression on her whole future life. In such discourse they reached the wood, and at length the oak, where they left their horses. Woislaw gave Franziska his arm, and they ascended the hill slowly and silently. They had just reached one of the half-dilapidated outworks where they could catch a glimpse of the open country, when Woislaw, speaking more to himself than to his companion, said: "In a quarter of an hour, the sun will set, and in another hour the moon will have risen; then all must be accomplished. It will soon be time to commence the work."

"Then, I should think it was time to entrust me with some idea of what it is," said Franziska, looking at him.

"Well, my lady," he replied, turning towards her, and his voice was very solemn, "I entreat you, Franziska von Fahnenberg, for your own good, and as you love the father who clings to you with his whole soul, that you will weigh well my words, and that you will not interrupt me with questions which I cannot answer until the work is completed. Your life is in the greatest danger from the illness under which you are laboring; indeed, you are irrecoverably lost if you do not fully carry out what I shall now impart to you. Now, promise me to do implicitly as I shall tell you; I pledge you my knightly word it is nothing against Heaven, or the honour of your house; and, besides, it is the sole means for saving you." With these words, he held out his right hand to his companion, while he raised the other to heaven in confirmation of his oath.

"I promise you," said Franziska, visibly moved by Woislaw's solemn tone, as she laid her little white and wasted hand in his.

"Then, come; it is time," was his reply, as he led her towards the church. The last rays of the sun were just pouring through the broken windows. They entered the chancel, the best preserved part of the whole building; here there were still some old kneeling-stools, placed before the high altar, although nothing remained of that but the stonework and a few steps; the pictures and decorations had all vanished.

"Say an *Ave*; you will have need of it," said Woislaw, as he himself fell on his knees.

Franziska knelt beside him, and repeated a short prayer. After a few moments, both rose.

"The moment has arrived! The sun sinks, and before the moon rises, all must be over," said Woislaw quickly.

"What am I to do?" asked Franziska cheerfully.

"You see there that open vault!" replied the knight Woislaw, pointing to the door and flight of steps. "You must descend. You must go alone; I may not accompany you. When you have reached the vault you will find, close to the entrance, a coffin, on which is placed a small packet. Open this packet, and you will find three long iron nails and a hammer. Then pause for a moment; but when I begin to repeat the *Credo* in a loud voice, knock with all your might, first one nail, then a second, and then a third, into the lid of the coffin, right up to their heads."

Franziska stood thunderstruck; her whole body trembled, and she could not utter a word. Woislaw perceived it.

"Take courage, dear lady!" said he. "Think that you are in the hands of Heaven, and that, without the will of your Creator, not a hair can fall from your head. Besides, I repeat, there is no danger."

"Well, then, I will do it," cried Franziska, in some measure regaining courage.

"Whatever you may hear, whatever takes place inside the coffin," continued Woislaw, "must have no effect upon you. Drive the nails well in, without flinching: your work must be finished before my prayer comes to an end."

Franziska shuddered, but again recovered herself. "I will do it; Heaven will send me strength," she murmured softly.

"There is one thing more," said Woislaw hesitatingly; "perhaps it is the hardest of all I have proposed, but without it your cure will not be complete. When you have done as I have told you, a sort of"—he hesitated—"a sort of liquid will flow from the coffin; in this dip your finger, and besmear the scratch on your throat."

"Horrible!" cried Franziska. "This liquid is blood. A human being lies in the coffin."

"An *unearthly one* lies therein! That blood is your own, but it flows in other veins," said Woislaw gloomily. "Ask no more; the sand is running out."

Franziska summoned up all her powers of mind and body, went towards the steps which led to the vault, and Woislaw sank on his knees before the altar in quiet prayer. When the lady had descended, she found herself before the coffin on which lay the packet before mentioned. A sort of twilight reigned in the vault, and everything around was so still and peaceful, that she felt more calm, and going up to the coffin, opened the packet. She had hardly seen that a hammer and three long nails were its contents when suddenly Woislaw's voice rang through the church, and broke the stillness of the aisles. Franziska started, but recognized the appointed prayer. She seized one of the nails, and with one stroke of the hammer drove it at least an inch into the cover. All was still; nothing was heard but the echo of the stroke. Taking heart, the maiden grasped the hammer with both hands, and struck the nail twice with all her might, right up to the head into the wood. At this moment commenced a rustling noise; it seemed as though something in the interior began to move and to struggle. Franziska drew back in alarm. She was already on the point of throwing away the hammer and flying up the steps, when Woislaw raised his voice so powerfully, and so entreatingly, that in a sort of excitement, such as would induce one to rush into a lion's den, she returned to the coffin, determined to bring things to a conclusion. Hardly knowing what she did, she placed a second nail in the centre of the lid, and after some strokes this was likewise buried to its head. The struggle now increased fearfully, as if some living creature were striving to burst the coffin. This was so shaken by it, that it cracked and split on all sides. Half distracted, Franziska seized the third nail; she thought no more of her ailments, she only knew herself to be in terrible danger, of what kind she could not guess: in an agony that threatened to rob her of her senses and in the midst of the turning and cracking of the coffin, in which low groans were now heard, she struck the third nail in equally tight. At this moment, she began to lose consciousness. She wished to hasten away, but staggered; and mechanically grasping at something to save herself by, seized the corner of the coffin, and sank fainting beside it on the ground.

A quarter of an hour might have elapsed when she again opened her eyes. She looked around her. Above was the starry sky, and the moon, which shed her cold light on the ruins and on the tops of the old oak-trees. Franziska was lying outside the church walls, Woislaw on his knees beside her, holding her hand in his.

"Heaven be praised that you live!" he cried, with a sigh of relief. "I was beginning to doubt whether the remedy had not been too severe, and yet it was the only thing to save you."

Franziska recovered her full consciousness very gradually. The past seemed to her like a dreadful dream. Only a few moments before, that fearful scene; and now this quiet all around her. She hardly dared at first to raise her eyes, and shuddered when she found herself only a few paces removed from the spot where she had undergone such terrible agony. She listened half unconsciously, now to the pacifying words Woislaw addressed to her, now to the whistling of the servant, who stood by the horses, and who, to while away his time, was imitating the evening-song of a belated cowherd.

"Let us go," whispered Franziska, as she strove to raise herself. "But what is this? My shoulder is wet, my throat, my hand—"

"It is probably the evening dew on the grass," said Woislaw gently.

"No; it is blood!" she cried, springing up with horror in her tone. "See, my hand is full of blood!"

"Oh, you are mistaken—surely mistaken," said Woislaw, stammering. "Or perhaps the wound on your neck may have opened!

Pray, feel whether this is the case." He seized her hand and directed it to the spot.

"I do not perceive anything; I feel no pain," she said at length, somewhat angrily.

"Then, perhaps, when you fainted you may have struck a corner of the coffin, or have torn yourself with the point of one of the nails," suggested Woislaw.

"Oh, of what do you remind me!" cried Franziska shuddering. "Let us away—away! I entreat you, come! I will not remain a moment longer near this dreadful, dreadful place."

They descended the path much quicker than they came. Woislaw placed his companion on her horse, and they were soon on their way home.

When they approached the castle, Franziska began to inundate her protector with questions about the preceding adventure; but he declared that her present state of excitement must make him defer all explanations till the morning, when her curiosity should be satisfied. On their arrival, he conducted her at once to her room, and told the knight his daughter was too much fatigued with her ride to appear at the supper table. On the following morning, Franziska rose earlier than she had done for a long time. She assured her friend it was the first time since her illness commenced that she had been really refreshed by her sleep, and, what was still more remarkable, she had not been troubled by her old terrible dream. Her improved looks were not only remarked by Bertha, but by Franz and the knight; and with Woislaw's permission, she related the adventures of the previous evening. No sooner had she concluded, than Woislaw was completely stormed with questions about such a strange occurrence.

"Have you," said the latter, turning towards his host, "ever heard of Vampires?"

"Often," replied he; "but I have never believed in them."

"Nor did I," said Woislaw; "but I have been assured of their existence by experience."

"Oh, tell us what occurred," cried Bertha eagerly, as a light seemed to dawn on her.

"It was during my first campaign in Hungary," began Woislaw, "when I was rendered helpless for some time by this sword-cut of a janizary across my face, and another on my shoulder. I had been taken into the house of a respectable family in a small town. It consisted of the father and mother, and a daughter about twenty years of age. They obtained their living by selling the very good wine of the country, and the taproom was always full of visitors. Although the family were well-to-do in the world, there seemed to brood over them a continual melancholy, caused by the constant illness of the only daughter, a very pretty and excellent girl. She had always bloomed like a rose, but for some months she had been getting so thin and wasted, and that without any satisfactory reason: they tried every means to restore her, but in vain. As the army had encamped quite in the neighbourhood, of course a number of people of all countries assembled in the tavern. Amongst these there was one man who came every evening, when the moon shone, who struck everybody by the peculiarity of his manners and appearance; he looked dried up and deathlike, and hardly spoke at all; but what he did say was bitter and sarcastic. Most attention was excited towards him by the circumstance, that although he always ordered a cup of the best wine, and now and then raised it to his lips, the cup was always as full after his departure as at first."

"This all agrees wonderfully with the appearance of Azzo," said Bertha, deeply interested.

"The daughter of the house," continued Woislaw, "became daily worse, despite the aid not only of Christian doctors, but of many amongst the heathen prisoners, who were consulted in the hope that they might have some magical remedy to propose. It was singular that the girl always complained of a dream, in which the unknown guest worried and plagued her."

"Just the same as your dream, Franziska," cried Bertha.

"One evening," resumed Woislaw, "an old Selavonian—who

had made many voyages to Turkey and Greece, and had even seen the New World—and I were sitting over our wine, when the stranger entered, and sat down at the table. The bottle passed quickly between my friend and me, whilst we talked of all manner of things, of our adventures, and of passages in our lives, both horrible and amusing. We went on chatting thus for about an hour, and drank a tolerable quantity of wine. The unknown had remained perfectly silent the whole time, only smiling contemptuously every now and then. He now paid his money, and was going away. All this had quietly worried me—perhaps the wine had gotten a little into my head—so I said to the stranger: 'Hold, you stony stranger; you have hitherto done nothing but listen, and have not even emptied your cup. Now you shall take your turn in telling us something amusing, and if you do not drink up your wine, it shall produce a quarrel between us.' 'Yes,' said the Selavonian, 'you must remain; you shall chat and drink, too'; and he grasped— for although no longer young, he was big and very strong—the stranger by the shoulder, to pull him down to his seat again: the latter, however, although as thin as a skeleton, with one movement of his hand flung the Selavonian to the middle of the room, and half stunned him for a moment. I now approached to hold the stranger back. I caught him by the arm; and although the springs of my iron hand were less powerful than those I have at present, I must have gripped him rather hard in my anger, for after looking grimly at me for a moment, he bent towards me and whispered in my ear: 'Let me go: from the grip of your fist, I see you are my brother, therefore do not hinder me from seeking my bloody nourishment. I am hungry!' Surprised by such words, I let him loose, and almost before I was aware of it, he had left the room. As soon as I had in some degree recovered from my astonishment, I told the Selavonian what I had heard. He started, evidently alarmed. I asked him to tell me the cause of his fears, and pressed him for an explanation of those extraordinary words. On our way to his lodging, he complied with my request. 'The stranger,' said he, 'is a Vampire!' "

"How?" cried the knight, Franziska, and Bertha simultaneously, in a voice of horror. "So this Azzo was—"

"Nothing less. He also was a Vampire!" replied Woislaw. "But at all events *his* hellish thirst is quenched for ever; he will never return. But I have not finished. As in my country Vampires had never been heard of, I questioned the Selavonian minutely. He said that in Hungary, Croatia, Dalmatia, and Bosnia, these hellish guests were not uncommon. They were deceased persons, who had either once served as nourishment to Vampires, or who had died in deadly sin, or under excommunication; and that whenever the moon shone, they rose from their graves, and sucked the blood of the living."

"Horrible!" cried Franziska. "If you had told me all this before-hand, I should never have accomplished the work."

"So I thought; and yet it must be executed by the sufferers them-selves, while someone else performs the devotions," replied Wois-law. "The Selavonian," he continued after a short pause, "added many other facts with regard to these unearthly visitants. He said that whilst their victim wasted, they themselves improved in ap-pearance, and that a Vampire possessed enormous strength—"

"Now I can understand the change your false hand produced on Azzo," interrupted Franz.

"Yes, that was it," replied Woislaw. "Azzo, as well as the other Vampire, mistook its great power for that of a natural one, and con-cluded I was one of his own species. You may now imagine, dear lady," he continued, turning to Franziska, "how alarmed I was at your appearance when I arrived: all you and Bertha told me in-creased my anxiety; and when I saw Azzo, I could doubt no longer that he was a Vampire. As I learned from your account that a grave with the name Ezzelin von Klatka lay in the neighbourhood, I had no doubt that you might be saved if I could only induce you to as-sist me. It did not appear to me advisable to impart the whole facts of the case, for your bodily powers were so impaired, that an idea of the horrors before you might have quite unfitted you for the exertion; for this reason, I arranged everything in the manner in which it has taken place."

"You did wisely," replied Franziska shuddering. "I can never be grateful enough to you. Had I known what was required of me, I never could have undertaken the deed."

"That was what I feared," said Woislaw; "but fortune has favored us all through."

"And what became of the unfortunate girl in Hungary?" inquired Bertha.

"I know not," replied Woislaw. "That very evening there was an alarm of Turks, and we were ordered off. I never heard anything more of her."

The conversation upon these strange occurrences continued for some time longer. The knight determined to have the vault at Klatka walled up for ever. This took place on the following day; the knight alleging as a reason that he did not wish the dead to be disturbed by irreverent hands.

Franziska recovered gradually. Her health had been so severely shaken, that it was long ere her strength was so much restored as to allow of her being considered out of danger. The young lady's character underwent a great change in the interval. Its former strength was, perhaps, in some degree diminished, but in place of that, she had acquired a benevolent softness, which brought out all her best qualities. Franz continued his attentions to his cousin; but, perhaps owing to a hint from Bertha, he was less assiduous in his exhibition of them. His inclinations did not lead him to the battle, the camp, or the attainment of honours; his great aim was to increase the good condition and happiness of his tenants, and to this he contributed the whole energy of his mind. Franziska could not withstand the unobtrusive signs of the young man's continued attachment; and it was not long ere the credit she was obliged to yield to his noble efforts for the welfare of his fellow-creatures, changed into a liking, which went on increasing, until at length it assumed the character of love. As Woislaw insisted on making Bertha his wife before he returned to Silesia, it was arranged that the marriage should take place at their present abode. How joyful was the surprise of the Knight of Fahnenberg, when his daughter and Franz likewise entreated his blessing, and expressed their desire of being united on the same day! That day soon came round, and it saw the bright looks of two happy couples.

✳︎

Anne Crawford

(1846–?)

ANNE CRAWFORD CAME FROM an American family distinguished in the arts. Her father was the sculptor Thomas Crawford, whose public works include the robed and plumed bronze figure atop the dome of the U.S. Capitol in Washington, D.C. Her aunt was the poet Julia Ward Howe, author of the rousing abolitionist anthem "The Battle Hymn of the Republic." The artistic Crawford family produced a trio of writers—F. Marion, who wrote memorable horror stories such as "For the Blood Is the Life"; Mary, who, under her married name, Mrs. Hugh Fraser, wrote novels and memoirs and travel books; and Anne, who became Baroness Von Rabe and wrote under the pseudonym Von Degen. Both Marion and Mary were more prolific and successful writers than Anne, but neither wrote a better ghost story than "A Mystery of the Campagna." Although there is also a small Italian town called Campagna, Crawford's title refers to a populous region in southern Italy now usually spelled Campania. On the peninsula south of Rome, it is an area rich in history that dates well before the Roman Empire.

This elegant tale first appeared in late 1886, in *The Witching Time: Tales for the Year's End*, a compilation edited by Sir Henry Norman and published around Christmas as *Unwin's Annual for 1887*. The volume also included her brother Marion's story "By the Waters of Paradise," as well as "The Hidden Door," by a great writer of supernatural stories, Vernon Lee (the pseudonym of another important woman in the field, Violet Paget). *Unwin's Annual* was a noble venue. The year before, it had included Marion's now famous horror story "The Upper Berth," as well as "Markheim," by Robert Louis Stevenson.

Unwin's was published by the firm of T. Fisher Unwin, who in 1891 reprinted the following story and one other by Crawford in a double volume entitled *A Mystery of the Campagna and A Shadow on the Wave*. It was the nephew of this Unwin who founded the famous twentieth-century British publisher Allen and Unwin, who published such books as Tolkien's *Lord of the Rings*.

A Mystery of the Campagna

I

Martin Detaille's Account
of What Happened at the Vigna Marziali

MARCELLO'S VOICE IS PLEADING with me now, perhaps because after years of separation I have met an old acquaintance who had a part in his strange story. I have a longing to tell it, and have asked Monsieur Sutton to help me. He noted down the circumstances at the time, and he is willing to join his share to mine, that Marcello may be remembered.

One day, it was in spring, he appeared in my little studio amongst the laurels and green alleys of the Villa Medici. "Come, *mon enfant*," he said, "put up your paints"; and he unceremoniously took my palette out of my hand. "I have a cab waiting outside, and we are going in search of a hermitage." He was already washing my brushes as he spoke, and this softened my heart, for I hate to do it myself. Then he pulled off my velvet jacket and took down my respectable coat from a nail on the wall. I let him dress me like a child. We always did his will, and he knew it, and in a moment we were sitting in the cab, driving through the Via Sistina on our way to the Porta San Giovanni, whither he had directed the coachman to go.

I MUST TELL MY story as I can, for though I have been told by my comrades, who cannot know very well, that I can speak good English, writing it is another thing. Monsieur Sutton has asked me to use his tongue, because he has so far forgotten mine that he will not trust himself in it, though he has promised to correct my mistakes, that what I have to tell you may not seem ridiculous, and make people laugh when they read of Marcello. I tell him I wish to write this for my countrymen, not his; but he reminds me that Marcello had many English friends who still live, and that the English do not forget as we do. It is of no use to reason with him, for neither do they yield as we do, and so I have consented to his wish. I think he has a reason which he does not tell me, but let it go. I will translate it all into my own language for my own people. Your English phrases seem to me to be always walking sideways, or trying to look around the corner or stand upon their heads, and they have as many little tails as a kite. I will try not to have recourse to my own language, but he must pardon me if I forget myself. He may be sure I do not do it to offend him. Now that I have explained so much, let me go on.

When we had passed out of the Porta San Giovanni, the coachman drove as slowly as possible; but Marcello was never practical. How could he be, I ask you, with an Opera in his head? So we crawled along, and he gazed dreamily before him. At last, when we had reached the part where the little villas and vineyards begin, he began to look about him.

You all know how it is out there; iron gates with rusty names or initials over them, and beyond them straight walks bordered with roses and lavender leading up to a forlorn little casino, with trees and a wilderness behind it sloping down to the Campagna, lonely enough to be murdered in and no one to hear you cry. We stopped at several of these gates and Marcello stood looking in, but none of the places were to his taste. He seemed not to doubt that he might have whatever pleased him, but nothing did so. He would jump out and run to the gate, and return saying, "The shape of those windows would disturb my inspiration," or, "That yellow paint would make me fail my duet in the second Act"; and once he liked the air of the house well enough, but there were marigolds growing in the walk, and he hated them. So we drove on and on, until I thought we should find nothing more to reject. At last we came to one which suited him, though it was terribly lonely, and I should have fancied it very *agaçant* to live so far away from the world with nothing but those melancholy olives and green oaks—ilexes, you call them—for company.

"I shall live here and become famous!" he said, decidedly, as he pulled the iron rod which rang a great bell inside. We waited, and then he rang again very impatiently and stamped his foot.

"No one lives here, *mon vieux*! Come, it is getting late, and it is so damp out here, and you know that the damp for a tenor voice—" He stamped his foot again and interrupted me angrily.

"Why, then, have you got a tenor? You are stupid! A bass would be more sensible; nothing hurts it. But you have not got one, and you call yourself my friend! Go home without me." How could I, so far on foot? "Go and sing your lovesick songs to your lean English misses! They will thank you with a cup of abominable tea, and you will be in Paradise! This is *my* Paradise, and I shall stay until the angel comes to open it!"

He was very cross and unreasonable, and those were just the times when one loved him most, so I waited and enveloped my throat in my pocket handkerchief and sang a passage or two just to prevent my voice from becoming stiff in that damp air.

"Be still! silence yourself!" he cried. "I cannot hear if anyone is coming."

Someone came at last, a rough-looking sort of keeper, or *guardiano* as they are called there, who looked at us as though he thought we were mad. One of us certainly was, but it was not I. Marcello spoke pretty good Italian, with a French accent, it is true, but the man understood him, especially as he held his purse in his hand. I heard him say a great many impetuously persuasive things all in one breath, then he slipped a gold piece into the *guardiano*'s horny hand, and the two turned towards the house, the man shrugging his shoulders in a resigned sort of way, and Marcello called out to me over his shoulder—

"Go home in the cab, or you will be late for your horrible English party! I am going to stay here tonight." *Ma foi!* I took his permission and left him; for a tenor voice is as tyrannical as a jealous woman. Besides, I was furious, and yet I laughed. His was the artist temperament, and appeared to us by turns absurd, sublime, and intensely irritating; but this last never for long, and we all felt that were we more like him our pictures would be worth more. I had not got as far as the city gate when my temper had cooled, and I began to reproach myself for leaving him in that lonely place with his purse full of money, for he was not poor at all, and tempting the dark *guardiano* to murder him. Nothing could be easier than to kill him in his sleep and bury him away somewhere under the olive trees or in some old vault of a ruined catacomb, so common on the borders of the Campagna. There were sure to be a hundred convenient places. I stopped the coachman and told him to turn back, but he shook his head and said something about having to be in the Piazza of St. Peter at eight o'clock. His horse began to go lame, as though he had understood his master and was his accomplice. What could I do? I said to myself that it was fate, and let him take me back to the Villa Medici, where I had to pay him a pretty sum for our crazy expedition, and then he rattled off, the horse not lame at all, leaving me bewildered at this strange afternoon.

I did not sleep well that night, though my tenor song had been applauded, and the English misses had caressed me much. I tried not to think of Marcello, and he did not trouble me much until I went to bed; but then I could not sleep, as I have told you.

I fancied him already murdered, and being buried in the darkness by the *guardiano*. I saw the man dragging his body, with the
beautiful head thumping against the stones, down dark passages,
and at last leaving it all bloody and covered with earth under a black
arch in a recess, and coming back to count the gold pieces. But then
again I fell asleep, and dreamed that Marcello was standing at the
gate and stamping his foot; and then I slept no more, but got up as
soon as the dawn came, and dressed myself and went to my studio
at the end of the laurel walk. I took down my painting jacket, and
remembered how he had pulled it off my shoulders. I took up the
brushes he had washed for me; they were only half cleaned after all,
and stiff with paint and soap. I felt glad to be angry with him, and
sacré'd a little, for it made me sure that he was yet alive if I could scold
at him. Then I pulled out my study of his head for my picture of
Mucius Scaevola holding his hand in the flame, and then I forgave
him; for who could look upon that face and not love it?

I worked with the fire of friendship in my brush, and did my best
to endow the features with the expression of scorn and obstinacy I
had seen at the gate. It could not have been more suitable to my
subject! Had I seen it for the last time? You will ask me why I did
not leave my work and go to see if anything had happened to him,
but against this there were several reasons. Our yearly exhibition
was not far off and my picture was barely painted in, and my comrades had sworn that it would not be ready. I was expecting a model
for the King of the Etruscans; a man who cooked chestnuts in the
Piazza Montanara, and who had consented to stoop to sit to me as a
great favour; and then, to tell the truth, the morning was beginning
to dispel my fancies. I had a good northern light to work by, with
nothing sentimental about it, and I was not fanciful by nature; so
when I sat down to my easel I told myself that I had been a fool, and
that Marcello was perfectly safe: the smell of the paints helping
me to feel practical again. Indeed, I thought every moment that he
would come in, tired of his caprice already, and even was preparing

and practising a little lecture for him. Some one knocked at my door, and I cried *"Entrez!"* thinking it was he at last, but no, it was Pierre Magnin.

"There is a curious man, a man of the country, who wants you," he said. "He has your address on a dirty piece of paper in Marcello's handwriting, and a letter for you, but he won't give it up. He says he must see 'il Signor Martino.' He'd make a superb model for a murderer! Come and speak to him, and keep him while I get a sketch of his head."

I followed Magnin through the garden, and outside, for the porter had not allowed him to enter, I found the *guardiano* of yesterday. He showed his white teeth, and said, 'Good day, signore,' like a Christian; and here in Rome he did not look half so murderous, only a stupid, brown, country fellow. He had a rough peasant-cart waiting, and he had tied up his shaggy horse to a ring in the wall. I held out my hand for the letter and pretended to find it difficult to read, for I saw Magnin standing with his sketch-book in the shadow of the entrance hall. The note said this: I have it still and I will copy it. It was written in pencil on a leaf torn from his pocketbook:

Mon vieux! I have passed a good night here, and the man will keep me as long as I like. Nothing will happen to me, except that I shall be divinely quiet, and I already have a famous motif in my head. Go to my lodgings and pack up some clothes and all my manuscripts, with plenty of music paper and a few bottles of Bordeaux, and give them to my messenger. Be quick about it!

Fame is preparing to descend upon me! If you care to see me, do not come before eight days. The gate will not be opened if you come sooner. The guardiano is my slave, and he has instructions to kill any intruder who in the guise of a friend tries to get in uninvited. He will do it, for he has confessed to me that he has murdered three men already.

(Of course this was a joke. I knew Marcello's way.)

When you come, go to the poste restante and fetch my letters. Here is my card to legitimate you. Don't forget pens and a bottle of ink! Your Marcello.

There was nothing for it but to jump into the cart, tell Magnin, who had finished his sketch, to lock up my studio, and go bumping off to obey these commands. We drove to his lodgings in the Via del Governo Vecchio, and there I made a bundle of all that I could think of; the landlady hindering me by a thousand questions about when the Signore would return. He had paid for the rooms in advance, so she had no need to be anxious about her rent. When I told her where he was, she shook her head, and talked a great deal about the bad air out there, and said 'Poor Signorino!' in a melancholy way, as though he were already buried, and looked mournfully after us from the window when we drove away. She irritated me, and made me feel superstitious. At the corner of the Via del Tritone I jumped down and gave the man a franc out of pure sentimentality, and cried after him, 'Greet the Signore!' but he did not hear me, and jogged away stupidly whilst I was longing to be with him. Marcello was a cross to us sometimes, but we loved him always.

THE EIGHT DAYS WENT by sooner than I had thought they would, and Thursday came, bright and sunny, for my expedition. At one o'clock I descended into the Piazza di Spagna, and made a bargain with a man who had a well-fed horse, remembering how dearly Marcello's want of good sense had cost me a week ago, and we drove off at a good pace to the Vigna Marziali, as I was almost forgetting to say that it was called. My heart was beating, though I did not know why I should feel so much emotion. When we reached the iron gate the *guardiano* answered my ring directly, and I had no sooner set foot in the long flower-walk than I saw Marcello hastening to meet me.

"I knew you would come," he said, drawing my arm within his, and so we walked towards the little grey house, which had a sort of portico and several balconies, and a sun-dial on its front. There were grated windows down to the ground floor, and the place, to my relief, looked safe and habitable. He told me that the man did not sleep there, but in a little hut down towards the Campagna, and that he, Marcello, locked himself in safely every night, which I was also relieved to know.

"What do you get to eat?" said I.

"Oh, I have goat's flesh, and dried beans and polenta, with pecorino cheese, and there is plenty of black bread and sour wine," he answered smilingly. "You see I am not starved."

"Do not overwork yourself, *mon vieux*," I said; "you are worth more than your opera will ever be."

"Do I look overworked?" he said, turning his face to me in the broad, outdoor light. He seemed a little offended at my saying that about his opera, and I was foolish to do it.

I examined his face critically, and he looked at me half defiantly. "No, not yet," I answered rather unwillingly, for I could not say that he did; but there was a restless, inward look in his eyes, and an almost imperceptible shadow lay around them. It seemed to me as though the full temples had grown slightly hollow, and a sort of faint mist lay over his beauty, making it seem strange and far off. We were standing before the door, and he pushed it open, the *guardiano* following us with slow, loud-resounding steps.

"Here is my Paradise," said Marcello, and we entered the house, which was like all the others of its kind. A hall, with stucco bas-reliefs, and a stairway adorned with antique fragments, gave access to the upper rooms. Marcello ran up the steps lightly, and I heard him lock a door somewhere above and draw out the key, then he came and met me on the landing.

"This," he said, "is my workroom," and he threw open a low door. The key was in the lock, so this room could not be the one I heard him close. "Tell me I shall not write like an angel here!" he cried. I was so dazzled by the flood of bright sunshine after the dusk of the passage, that I blinked like an owl at first, and then I saw a large room, quite bare except for a rough table and chair, the chair covered with manuscript music.

"You are looking for the furniture," he said, laughing; "it is outside. Look here!" and he drew me to a rickety door of worm-eaten wood and coarse greenish glass, and flung it open on to a rusty iron balcony. He was right; the furniture was outside: that is to say, a divine view met my eyes. The Sabine Mountains, the Alban Hills, and broad Campagna, with its mediaeval towers and ruined aqueducts, and the open plain to the sea. All this glowing and yet calm in the sunlight. No wonder he could write there! The balcony ran round the corner of the house, and to the right I looked down upon an alley of ilexes, ending in a grove of tall laurel trees—very old, apparently. There were bits of sculpture and some ancient sarcophagi standing gleaming against them, and even from so high I could hear a little stream of water pouring from an antique mask into a long, rough trough. I saw the brown *guardiano* digging at his cabbages and onions, and I laughed to think that I could fancy him a murderer! He had a little bag of relics, which dangled to and fro over his sunburned breast, and he looked very innocent when he sat down upon an old column to eat a piece of black bread with an onion which he had just pulled out of the ground, slicing it with a knife not at all like a dagger. But I kept my thoughts to myself, for Marcello would have laughed at them. We were standing together, looking down at the man as he drank from his hands at the running fountain, and Marcello now leaned down over the balcony, and called out a long *"Ohé!"* The lazy *guardiano* looked up, nodded, and then got up slowly from the stone where he had been half-kneeling to reach the jet of water.

"We are going to dine," Marcello explained. "I have been waiting for you." Presently he heard the man's heavy tread upon the stairs, and he entered bearing a strange meal in a basket.

There came to light pecorino cheese made from ewe's milk, black bread of the consistency of a stone, a great bowl of salad apparently composed of weeds, and a sausage which filled the room with a

strong smell of garlic. Then he disappeared and came back with a
dish full of ragged-looking goat's flesh cooked together with a
mass of smoking polenta, and I am not sure that there was not oil
in it.

"I told you I lived well, and now you see!" said Marcello. It was
a terrible meal, but I had to eat it, and was glad to have some rough,
sour wine to help me, which tasted of earth and roots. When we
had finished I said, "And your opera! How are you getting on?"

"Not a word about that!" he cried. "You see how I have written!" and he turned over a heap of manuscript; "but do not talk to
me about it. I will not lose my ideas in words." This was not like
Marcello, who loved to discuss his work, and I looked at him astonished.

"Come," he said, "we will go down into the garden, and you
shall tell me about the comrades. What are they doing? Has Magnin
found a model for his Clytemnestra?"

I humoured him, as I always did, and we sat upon a stone bench
behind the house, looking towards the laurel grove, talking of the
pictures and the students. I wanted to walk down the ilex alley, but
he stopped me.

"If you are afraid of the damp, don't go down there," he said,
"the place is like a vault. Let us stay here and be thankful for this
heavenly view."

"Well, let us stay here," I answered, resigned as ever. He lit a
cigar and offered me one in silence. If he did not care to talk, I
could be still too. From time to time he made some indifferent
observation, and I answered it in the same tone. It almost seemed
to me as though we, the old heart-comrades, had become strangers
who had not known each other a week, or as though we had been
so long apart that we had grown away from each other. There was
something about him which escaped me. Yes, the days of solitude
had indeed put years and a sort of shyness, or rather ceremony, between us! It did not seem natural to me now to clap him on the
back, and make the old, harmless jokes at him. He must have felt

the constraint too, for we were like children who had looked forward to a game, and did not know now what to play at.

At six o'clock I left him. It was not like parting with Marcello. I felt rather as though I should find my old friend in Rome that evening, and here only left a shadowy likeness of him. He accompanied me to the gate, and pressed my hand, and for a moment the true Marcello looked out of his eyes; but we called out no last word to each other as I drove away. I had only said, "Let me know when you want me," and he said, *"Merci!"* and all the way back to Rome I felt a chill upon me, his hand had been so cold, and I thought and thought what could be the matter with him.

That evening I spoke out my anxiety to Pierre Magnin, who shook his head and declared that malaria fever must be taking hold of him, and that people often begin to show it by being a little odd.

"He must not stay there! We must get him away as soon as possible," I cried.

"We both know Marcello, and that nothing can make him stir against his will," said Pierre. "Let him alone, and he will get tired of his whim. It will not kill him to have a touch of malaria, and some evening he will turn up amongst us as merry as ever."

But he did not. I worked hard at my picture and finished it, but for a few touches, and he had not yet appeared. Perhaps it was the extreme application, perhaps the sitting out in that damp place, for I insist upon tracing it to something more material than emotion. Well, whatever it was, I fell ill; more ill than I had even been in my life. It was almost twilight when it overtook me, and I remember it distinctly, though I forget what happened afterwards, or, rather, I never knew, for I was found by Magnin quite unconscious, and he has told me that I remained so for some time, and then became delirious, and talked of nothing but Marcello. I have told you that it was very nearly twilight; but just at the moment when the sun is gone the colours show in their true value. Artists know this, and I was putting last touches here and there to my picture and especially to my head of Mucius Scaevola, or rather, Marcello.

The rest of the picture came out well enough; but that head, which should have been the principal one, seemed faded and sunk in. The face appeared to grow paler and paler, and to recede from me; a strange veil spread over it, and the eyes seemed to close. I am not easily frightened, and I know what tricks some peculiar methods of colour will play by certain lights, for the moment I spoke of had gone, and the twilight greyness had set in; so I stepped back to look at it. Just then the lips, which had become almost white, opened a little, and sighed! An illusion, of course. I must have been very ill and quite delirious already, for to my imagination it was a real sigh, or, rather, a sort of exhausted gasp. Then it was that I fainted, I suppose, and when I came to myself I was in my bed, with Magnin and Monsieur Sutton standing by me, and a Soeur de Charité moving softly about among medicine bottles, and speaking in whispers. I stretched out my hands, and they were thin and yellow, with long, pale nails; and I heard Magnin's voice, which sounded very far away, say, *"Dieu merci!"* And now Monsieur Sutton will tell you what I did not know until long afterwards.

II

Robert Sutton's Account of What Happened
at the Vigna Marziali

I am attached to Detaille, and was very glad to be of use to him, but I never fully shared his admiration for Marcello Souvestre, though I appreciated his good points. He was certainly very promising—I must say that. But he was an odd, flighty sort of fellow, not of the kind which we English care to take the trouble to understand. It is my business to write stories, but not having need of such characters I have never particularly studied them. As I say, I was glad to be of use to Detaille, who is a thorough good fellow, and I willingly gave up my work to go and sit by his bedside. Magnin knew that I was a friend of his, and very properly came to me when he found that Detaille's illness was a serious one and likely to last for a long time. I found him perfectly delirious, and raving about Marcello.

"Tell me what the *motif* is! I know it is a *Marche Funèbre*!" And here he would sing a peculiar melody, which, as I have a knack at music, I noted down, it being like nothing I had heard before. The Sister of Charity looked at me with severe eyes; but how could she know that all is grist for our mill, and that observation becomes with us a mechanical habit? Poor Detaille kept repeating this curious melody over and over, and then would stop and seem to be looking at his picture, crying that it was fading away.

"Marcello! Marcello! You are fading too! Let me come to you!" He was as weak as a baby, and could not have moved from his bed unless in the strength of delirium.

"I cannot come!" he went on; "they have tied me down." And here he made as though he were trying to gnaw through a rope at his wrists, and then burst into tears. "Will no one go for me and bring me a word from you? Ah! if I could know that you are alive!"

Magnin looked at me. I knew what he was thinking. He would not leave his comrade, but I must go. I don't mind acknowledging that I did not undertake this unwillingly. To sit by Detaille's bedside and listen to his ravings enervated me, and what Magnin wanted struck me as troublesome but not uninteresting to one of my craft, so I agreed to go. I had heard all about Marcello's strange seclusion from Magnin and Detaille himself, who lamented over it openly in his simple way at supper at the Academy, where I was a frequent guest.

I knew that it would be useless to ring at the gate of the Vigna Marziali. Not only should I not be admitted, but I should arouse Marcello's anger and suspicion, for I did not for a moment believe that he was not alive, though I thought it very possible that he was becoming a little crazy, as his countrymen are so easily put off their balance. Now, odd people are oddest late in the day and at evening time. Their nerves lose the power of resistance then, and the real man gets the better of them. So I determined to try to discover something at night, reflecting also that I should be safer from detection then. I knew his liking for wandering about when he ought to be in his bed, and I did not doubt that I should get a glimpse of him, and that was really all I needed.

My first step was to take a long walk out of the Porta San Giovanni, and this I did in the early morning, tramping along steadily until I came to an iron gate on the right of the road, with VIGNA MARZIALI over it; and then I walked straight on, never stopping until I had reached a little bushy lane running down towards the Campagna to the right. It was pebbly, and quite shut in by luxuriant ivy and elder bushes, and it bore deep traces of the last heavy rains. These had evidently been effaced by no footprints, so I concluded that it was little used. Down this path I made my way cautiously, looking behind and before me, from a habit contracted in my lonely wanderings in the Abruzzi. I had a capital revolver with me—an old friend—and I feared no man; but I began to feel a dramatic interest in my undertaking, and determined that it should not be crossed by any disagreeable surprises. The lane led me further down the plain than I had reckoned upon, for the bushy edge shut out the view; and when I had got to the bottom and faced round, the Vigna Marziali was lying quite far to my left. I saw at a glance that behind the grey casino an alley of ilexes ended in a laurel grove; then there were plantations of kitchen stuff, with a sort of thatched cabin in their midst, probably that of a gardener. I looked about for a kennel, but saw none, so there was no watchdog. At the end of this primitive kitchen garden was a broad patch of grass, bounded by a fence, which I could take at a spring. Now, I knew my way, but I could not resist tracing it out a little further. It was well that I did so, for I found just within the fence a sunken stream, rather full at the time, in consequence of the rains, too deep to wade and too broad to jump. It struck me that it would be easy enough to take a board from the fence and lay it over for a bridge. I measured the breadth with my eye, and decided the board would span it; then I went back as I had come, and returned to find Detaille still raving.

As he could understand nothing it seemed to me rather a fool's errand to go off in search of comfort for him; but a conscious moment might come, and moreover, I began to be interested in my undertaking; and so I agreed with Magnin that I should go and take some food and rest and return to the Vigna that night. I told my landlady that I was going into the country and should return the next day, and I went to Nazarri's and laid in a stock of sandwiches and filled my flask with something they called sherry, for, though I was no great wine-drinker, I feared the night chill.

It was about seven o'clock when I started, and I retraced my morning's steps exactly. As I reached the lane, it occurred to me that it was still too light for me to pass unobserved over the stream, and I made a place for myself under the hedge and lay down, quite screened by the thick curtain of tangled overhanging ivy.

I must have been out of training, and tired by the morning's walk, for I fell asleep. When I awoke it was night; the stars were shining, a dank mist made its way down my throat, and I felt stiff and cold. I took a pull at my flask, finding it nasty stuff, but it warmed me. Then I rang my repeater, which struck a quarter to eleven, got up and shook myself free of the leaves and brambles, and went on down the lane. When I got to the fence I sat down and thought the thing over. What did I expect to discover? What *was* there to discover? Nothing! Nothing but that Marcello was alive; and that was no discovery at all for I felt sure of it. I was a fool, and had let myself be allured by the mere stage nonsense and mystery of the business, and a mouse would creep out of this mountain of precautions! Well, at least, I could turn it to account by describing my own absurd behaviour in some story yet to be written, and, as it was not enough for a chapter, I would add to it by further experience. "Come along!" I said to myself. "You're an ass, but it may prove instructive." I raised the top board from the fence noiselessly. There was a little stile there, and the boards were easily moved. I laid down my bridge with some difficulty, and stepped carefully across, and made my way to the laurel grove as quickly and noiselessly as possible.

There all was thick darkness, and my eyes only grew slowly accustomed to it. After all there was not much to see; some stone seats in a semi-circle, and some fragments of columns set upright with antique busts upon them. Then a little to the right a sort of arch, with apparently some steps descending into the ground, probably the entrance to some discovered branch of a catacomb. In the midst of the enclosure, not a very large one, stood a stone table, deeply fixed in the earth. No one was there; of that I felt certain, and I sat down, having now got used to the gloom, and fell to eat my sandwiches, for I was desperately hungry.

Now that I had come so far, was nothing to take place to repay me for my trouble? It suddenly struck me that it was absurd to expect Marcello to come out to meet me and perform any mad antics he might be meditating there before my eyes for my especial satisfaction. Why had I supposed that something would take place in the grove I do not know, except that this seemed a fit place for it. I would go and watch the house, and if I saw a light anywhere I might be sure he was within. Any fool might have thought of that, but a novelist lays the scene of his drama and expects his characters to slide about in the grooves like puppets. It is only when mine surprise me that I feel they are alive. When I reached the end of the ilex alley I saw the house before me. There were more cabbages and onions after I had left the trees, and I saw that in this open space I could easily be perceived by any one standing on the balcony above. As I drew back again under the ilexes, a window above, not the one on the balcony, was suddenly lighted up; but the light did not remain long, and presently a gleam shone through the glass oval over the door below.

I had just time to spring behind the thickest trunk near me when the door opened. I took advantage of its creaking to creep up the slanting tree like a cat, and lie out upon a projecting branch.

As I expected, Marcello came out. He was very pale, and moved mechanically like a sleepwalker. I was shocked to see how hollow his face had become as he held the candle still lighted in his hand, and it cast deep shadows on his sunken cheeks and fixed eyes, which burned wildly and seemed to see nothing. His lips were quite white, and so drawn that I could see his gleaming teeth. Then the candle fell from his hand, and he came slowly and with a curiously regular step on into the darkness of the ilexes, I watching him from above. But I scarcely think he would have noticed me had I been standing in his path. When he had passed I let myself down and followed him. I had taken off my shoes, and my tread was absolutely noiseless; moreover, I felt sure he would not turn around.

On he went with the same mechanical step until he reached the grove. There I knelt behind an old sarcophagus at the entrance, and waited. What would he do? He stood perfectly still, not looking about him, but as though the clockwork within him had suddenly stopped. I felt that he was becoming psychologically interesting, after all. Suddenly he threw up his arms as men do when they are mortally wounded on the battlefield, and I expected to see him fall at full length. Instead of this he made a step forward.

I looked in the same direction, and saw a woman, who must have concealed herself there while I was waiting before the house, come from out of the gloom, and as she slowly approached and laid her head upon his shoulder, the outstretched arms clasped themselves closely around her, so that her face was hidden upon his neck.

So this was the whole matter, and I had been sent off on a wild-goose chase to spy out a common love affair! His opera and his seclusion for the sake of work, his tyrannical refusal to see Detaille unless he sent for him—all this was but a mask to a vulgar intrigue which, for reasons best known to himself, could not be indulged in, in the city. I was thoroughly angry! If Marcello passed his time mooning about in that damp hole all night, no wonder that he looked so wretchedly ill, and seemed half mad! I knew very well that Marcello was no saint. Why should he be? But I had not taken him for a fool! He had had plenty of romantic episodes, and as he was discreet without being uselessly mysterious, no one had ever unduly pryed into them, nor should we have done so now. I said to myself that that mixture of French and Italian blood was at the bottom of it; French flimsiness and light-headedness and Italian love of cunning! I looked back upon all the details of my mysterious expedition. I suppose at the root of my anger lay a certain dramatic disappointment at not finding him lying murdered, and I despised myself for all the trouble I had taken to this ridiculous end: just to see him holding a woman in his arms. I could not see her face, and her figure was enveloped from head to foot in something long and dark; but I could make out that she was tall and slender, and that a pair of white hands gleamed from her drapery. As I was looking intently, for all my indignation, the couple moved on, and still clinging to one another descended the steps. So even the solitude of the lonely laurel grove could not satisfy Marcello's insane love of secrecy! I kept still awhile; then I stole to where they had disappeared, and listened; but all was silent, and I cautiously struck a match and peered down. I could see the steps for a short distance below me, and then the darkness seemed to rise and swallow them. It must be a catacomb as I had imagined, or an old Roman bath, perhaps, which Marcello had made comfortable enough, no doubt, and as likely as not they were having a nice little cold supper there. My empty stomach told me that I could have forgiven him even then could I have shared it; I was in truth frightfully hungry as well as angry, and sat down on one of the stone benches to finish my sandwiches.

The thought of waiting to see this love-sick pair return to upper earth never for a moment occurred to me. I had found out the whole thing, and a great humbug it was! Now I wanted to get back to Rome before my temper had cooled, and to tell Magnin on what a fool's errand he had sent me. If he liked to quarrel with me, all the better!

All the way home I composed cutting French speeches, but they suddenly cooled and petrified like a gust of lava from a volcano when I discovered that the gate was closed. I had never thought of getting a pass, and Magnin ought to have warned me. Another grievance against the fellow! I enjoyed my resentment, and it kept me warm as I patrolled up and down. There are houses, and even small eating-shops outside the gate, but no light was visible, and I did not care to attract attention by pounding at the doors in the middle of the night; so I crept behind a bit of wall. I was getting used to hiding by this time, and made myself as comfortable as I could with my ulster, took another pull at my flask, and waited. At last the gate was opened and I slipped through, trying not to look as though I had been out all night like a bandit. The guard looked at me narrowly, evidently wondering at my lack of luggage. Had I had a knapsack I might have been taken for some innocently mad English tourist indulging in the mistaken pleasure of trudging in from Frascati or Albano; but a man in an ulster, with his hands in his pockets, sauntering in at the gate of the city at break of day as though returning from a stroll, naturally puzzled the officials, who looked at me and shrugged their shoulders.

Luckily I found an early cab in the Piazza of the Lateran, for I was dead-beat, and was soon at my lodgings in the Via della Croce, where my landlady let me in very speedily. Then at last I had the comfort of throwing off my clothes, all damp with the night dew, and turning in. My wrath had cooled to a certain point, and I did not fear to lower its temperature too greatly by yielding to an over-whelming desire for sleep. An hour or two could make no great difference to Magnin—let him fancy me still hanging about the Vigna Marziali! Sleep I must have, no matter what he thought.

I slept long, and was awakened at last by my landlady, Sora Nanna, standing over me, and saying, "There is a Signore who wants you."

"It is I, Magnin!" said a voice behind her. "I could not wait for you to come!" He looked haggard with anxiety and watching.

"Detaille is raving still," he went on, "only worse than before. Speak, for Heaven's sake! Why don't you tell me something?" And he shook me by the arm as though he thought I was still asleep.

"Have you nothing to say? You must have seen something! Did you see Marcello?"

"Oh! yes, I saw him."

"Well?"

"Well, he was very comfortable—quite alive. He had a woman's arms around him."

I heard my door violently slammed to, a ferocious *"Sacré gamin!"* and then steps springing down the stairs. I felt perfectly happy at having made such an impression, and turned and resumed my broken sleep with almost a kindly feeling towards Magnin, who was at that moment probably tearing up the Spanish Scalinata two steps at a time, and making himself horribly hot. It could not help Detaille, poor fellow! He could not understand my news. When I had slept long enough I got up, refreshed myself with a bath and something to eat, and went off to see Detaille. It was not his fault that I had been made a fool of, so I felt sorry for him.

I found him raving just as I had left him the day before, only worse, as Magnin said. He persisted in continually crying, "Marcello, take care! no one can save you!" in hoarse, weak tones, but with the regularity of a knell, keeping up a peculiar movement with his feet, as though he were weary with a long road, but must press forward to his goal. Then he would stop and break into childish sobs.

"My feet are so sore," he murmured piteously, "and I am so tired! But I will come! They are following me, but I am strong!" Then a violent struggle with his invisible pursuers, in which he would break off into that singing of his, alternating with the warning cry. The singing voice was quite another from the speaking one. He went on and on repeating the singular air which he had himself called A Funeral March, and which had become intensely disagreeable to me. If it was one indeed, it surely was intended for no Christian burial. As he sang, the tears kept trickling down his cheeks, and Magnin sat wiping them away as tenderly as a woman. Between his song he would clasp his hands, feebly enough, for he was very weak when the delirium did not make him violent, and cry in heart-rending tones, "Marcello, I shall never see you again! Why did you leave us?" At last, when he stopped for a moment, Magnin left his side, beckoning the Sister to take it, and drew me into the other room, closing the door behind him.

"Now tell me exactly how you saw Marcello," said he; so I related my whole absurd experience—forgetting, however, my personal irritation, for he looked too wretched and worn for anybody to be angry with him. He made me repeat several times my description of Marcello's face and manner as he had come out of the house. That seemed to make more impression upon him than the love-business.

"Sick people have strange intuitions," he said gravely; "and I persist in thinking that Marcello is very ill and in danger. *Tenez!*" And here he broke off, went to the door, and called, *"Ma Sœur!"* under his breath. She understood, and after having drawn the bedclothes straight, and once more dried the trickling tears, she came noiselessly to where we stood, the wet handkerchief still in her hand. She was a singularly tall and strong-looking woman, with piercing black eyes and a self-controlled manner. Strange to say, she bore the adopted name of Claudius, instead of a more feminine one.

"Ma Sœur," said Magnin, "at what o'clock was it that he sprang out of bed and we had to hold him for so long?"

"Half-past eleven and a few minutes," she answered promptly. Then he turned to me.

"At what time did Marcello come out into the garden?"

"Well, it might have been half-past eleven," I answered unwillingly. "I should say that three-quarters of an hour might possibly have passed since I rang my repeater. Mind you, I won't swear it!" I hate to have people try to prove mysterious coincidences, and this was just what they were attempting.

"Are you sure of the hour, *ma Sœur?*" I asked, a little tartly.

She looked at me calmly with her great, black eyes, and said:

"I heard the Trinità de' Monti strike the half-hour just before it happened."

"Be so good as to tell Monsieur Sutton exactly what took place," said Magnin.

"One moment, Monsieur," and she went swiftly and softly to Detaille, raised him on her strong arm, and held a glass to his lips, from which he drank mechanically. Then she came and stood where she could watch him through the open door.

"He hears nothing," she said, as she hung the handkerchief to dry over a chair; and then she went on. "It was half-past eleven, and my patient had been very uneasy—that is to say, more so even than before. It might have been four or five minutes after the dock had finished striking that he became suddenly quite still, and then began to tremble all over, so that the bed shook with him." She spoke admirable English, as many of the Sisters do, so I need not translate, but will give her own words.

"He went on trembling until I thought he was going to have a fit, and told Monsieur Magnin to be ready to go for the doctor, when just then the trembling stopped, he became perfectly stiff, his hair stood up upon his head, and his eyes seemed coming out of their sockets, though he could see nothing, for I passed the candle before them. All at once he sprang out of his bed and rushed to the door. I did not know he was so strong. Before he got there I had him in my arms, for he has become very light, and I carried him back to bed again, though he was struggling, like a child. Monsieur Magnin came in from the next room just as he was trying to get up again, and we held him down until it was past, but he screamed Monsieur Souvestre's name for a long time after that. Afterwards he was very cold and exhausted, of course, and I gave him some beef-tea, though it was not the hour for it."

"I think you had better tell the Sister all about it," said Magnin turning to me. "It is the best that the nurse should know every-thing."

"Very well," said I; "though I do not think it's much in her line."
She answered me herself: "Everything which concerns our patients
is our business. Nothing shocks me." Thereupon she sat down and
thrust her hands into her long sleeves, prepared to listen. I repeated
the whole affair as I had done to Magnin. She never took her brilliant eyes from off my face, and listened as coolly as though she had
been a doctor hearing an account of a difficult case, though to me it
seemed almost sacrilege to be describing the behaviour of a love-
stricken youth to a Sister of Charity.

"What do you say to that, *ma Sœur?*" asked Magnin, when I had
done.

"I say nothing, monsieur. It is sufficient that I know it"; and she
withdrew her hands from her sleeves, took up the handkerchief,
which was dry by this time, and returned quietly to her place at the
bedside.

"I wonder if I have shocked her, after all?" I said to Magnin.

"Oh, no," he answered. "They see many things, and a *Sœur* is as
abstract as a confessor; they do not allow themselves any personal
feelings. I have seen Sœur Claudius listen perfectly unmoved to the
most abominable ravings, only crossing herself beneath her cape at
the most hideous blasphemies. It was late summer when poor Justin
Revol died. You were not here." Magnin put his hand to his forehead.

"You are looking ill yourself," I said. "Go and try to sleep, and
I will stay."

"Very well," he answered; "but I cannot rest unless you promise to remember everything he says, that I may hear it when I
wake"; and he threw himself down on the hard sofa like a sack, and
was asleep in a moment; and I, who had felt so angry with him but
a few hours ago, put a cushion under his head and made him comfortable.

I sat down in the next room and listened to Detaille's monotonous ravings, while Sœur Claudius read in her book of prayers. It
was getting dusk, and several of the academicians stole in and stood

over the sick man and shook their heads. They looked around for Magnin, but I pointed to the other room with my finger on my lips, and they nodded and went away on tiptoe.

It required no effort of memory to repeat Detaille's words to Magnin when he woke, for they were always the same. We had another Sister that night, and as Sœur Claudius was not to return till the next day at midday, I offered to share the watch with Magnin, who was getting very nervous and exhausted, and who seemed to think that some such attack might be expected as had occurred the night before. The new sister was a gentle, delicate-looking little woman, with tears in her soft brown eyes as she bent over the sick man, and crossed herself from time to time, grasping the crucifix which hung from the beads at her waist. Nevertheless she was calm and useful, and as punctual as Sœur Claudius herself in giving the medicines.

The doctor had come in the evening, and prescribed a change in these. He would not say what he thought of his patient, but only declared that it was necessary to wait for a crisis. Magnin sent for some supper, and we sat over it together in the silence, neither of us hungry. He kept looking at his watch.

"If the same thing happens tonight, he will die!" said he, and laid his head on his arms.

"He will die in a most foolish cause, then," I said angrily, for I thought he was going to cry, as those Frenchmen have a way of doing, and I wanted to irritate him by way of a tonic; so I went on—

"It would be dying for a *vaurien* who is making an ass of himself in a ridiculous business which will be over in a week! Souvestre may get as much fever as he likes! Only don't ask me to come and nurse him."

"It is not the fever," said he slowly, "it is a horrible nameless dread that I have; I suppose it is listening to Detaille that makes me nervous. Hark!" he added, "it strikes eleven. We must watch!"

"If you really expect another attack you had better warn the Sister," I said; so he told her in a few words what might happen.

"Very well, monsieur," she answered, and sat down quietly near the bed, Magnin at the pillow and I near him. No sound was to be heard but Detaille's ceaseless lament.

And now, before I tell you more, I must stop to entreat you to believe me. It will be almost impossible for you to do so, I know, for I have laughed myself at such tales, and no assurances would have made me credit them. But I, Robert Sutton, swear that this thing happened. More I cannot do. It is the truth.

We had been watching Detaille intently. He was lying with closed eyes, and had been very restless. Suddenly he became quite still, and then began to tremble, exactly as Sœur Claudius had described. It was a curious, uniform trembling, apparently in every fibre, and his iron bedstead shook as though strong hands were at its head and foot. Then came the absolute rigidity she had also described, and I do not exaggerate when I say that not only did his short-cropped hair seem to stand erect, but that it literally did so. A lamp cast the shadow of his profile against the wall to the left of his bed, and as I looked at the immovable outline which seemed painted on the wall, I saw the hair slowly rise until the line where it joined the forehead was quite a different one—abrupt instead of a smooth sweep. His eyes opened wide and were frightfully fixed, then as frightfully strained, but they certainly did not see us.

We waited breathlessly for what might follow. The little Sister was standing close to him, her lips pressed together and a little pale, but very calm. "Do not be frightened, *ma Sœur*," whispered Magnin; and she answered in a business-like tone, "No, monsieur," and drew still nearer to her patient, and took his hands, which were stiff as those of a corpse, between her own to warm them. I laid mine upon his heart; it was beating so imperceptibly that I almost thought it had stopped, and as I leaned my face to his lips I could feel no breath issue from them. It seemed as though the rigour would last for ever.

Suddenly, without any transition, he hurled himself with enormous force, and literally at one bound, almost into the middle of the room, scattering us aside like leaves in the wind. I was upon

him in a moment, grappling with him with all my strength, to prevent him from reaching the door. Magnin had been thrown backwards against the table, and I heard the medicine bottles crash with
his fall. He had flung back his hand to save himself, and rushed to
help me with blood dripping from a cut in his wrist. The little Sister
sprang to us. Detaille had thrown her violently back upon her knees,
and now, with a nurse's instinct, she tried to throw a shawl over his
bare breast. We four must have made a strange group!

Four? *We were five!* Marcello Souvestre stood before us, just within
the door! We all saw him, for he was there. His bloodless face was
turned towards us unmoved; his hands hung by his side as white as
his face; only his eyes had life in them; they were fixed on Detaille.

"Thank God you have come at last!" I cried. "Don't stand there
like a fool! Help us, can't you?" But he never moved. I was furiously angry, and, leaving my hold, sprang upon him to drag him
forwards. My outstretched hands struck hard against the door, and
I felt a thing like a spider's web envelop me. It seemed to draw itself
over my mouth and eyes, and to blind and choke me, and then to
flutter and tear and float from me.

Marcello was gone!

Detaille had slipped from Magnin's hold, and lay in a heap upon
the floor, as though his limbs were broken. The Sister was trembling violently as she knelt over him and tried to raise his head. We
gazed at one another, stooped and lifted him in our arms, and carried him back to his bed, while Sœur Marie quietly collected the
broken phials.

"You saw it, *ma Sœur*?" I heard Magnin whisper hoarsely.

"Yes, monsieur!" she only answered, in a trembling voice, holding on to her crucifix. Then she said in a professional tone—

"Will monsieur let me bind up his wrist?" And though her
fingers trembled and his hand was shaking, the bandage was an
irreproachable one.

Magnin went into the next room, and I heard him throw himself
heavily into a chair. Detaille seemed to be sleeping. His breath came

regularly; his eyes were closed with a look of peace about the lids, his hands lying in a natural way upon the quilt. He had not moved since we laid him there. I went softly to where Magnin was sitting in the dark. He did not move, but only said: "Marcello is dead!"

"He is either dead or dying," I answered, "and we must go to him."

"Yes," Magnin whispered, "we must go to him, but we shall not reach him."

"We will go as soon as it is light," I said, and then we were still again.

When the morning came at last he went and found a comrade to take his place, and only said to Sœur Marie, "It is not necessary to speak of this night"; and at her quiet, "You are right, monsieur," we felt we could trust her. Detaille was still sleeping. Was this the crisis the doctor had expected? Perhaps; but surely not in such fearful form. I insisted upon my companion having some breakfast before we started, and I breakfasted myself, but I cannot say I tasted what passed between my lips.

We engaged a closed carriage, for we did not know what we might bring home with us, though neither of us spoke out his thoughts. It was early morning still when we reached the Vigna Marziali, and we had not exchanged a word all the way. I rang at the bell, while the coachman looked on curiously. It was answered promptly by the *guardiano*, of whom Detaille has already told you.

"Where is the Signore?" I asked through the gate.

"Chi lo sa?" he answered, "He is here, of course; he has not left the Vigna. Shall I call him?"

"Call him?" I knew that no mortal voice could reach Marcello now, but I tried to fancy he was still alive.

"No," I said. "Let us in. We want to surprise him; he will be pleased."

The man hesitated, but he finally opened the gate, and we entered, leaving the carriage to wait outside. We went straight to the house; the door at the back was wide-open. There had been a gale in the night, and it had torn some leaves and bits of twigs from the trees and blown them into the entrance hall. They lay scattered across the threshold, and were evidence that the door had remained open ever since they had fallen. The *guardiano* left us, probably to escape Marcello's anger at having let us in, and we went up the stairs unhindered, Magnin foremost, for he knew the house better than I, from Detaille's description. He had told him about the corner room with the balcony, and we pretended that Marcello might be there, absorbed betimes in his work, but we did not call him.

He was not there. His papers were strewn over the table as though he had been writing, but the inkstand was dry and full of dust; he could not have used it for days. We went silently into the other chambers. Perhaps he was still asleep? But, no! We found his bed untouched, so he could not have lain in it that night. The rooms were all unlocked but one, and this closed door made our hearts beat. Marcello could scarcely be there, however, for there was no key in the lock; I saw the daylight shining through the key-hole. We called his name, but there came no answer. We knocked loudly; still no sign from within; so I put my shoulder to the door, which was old and cracked in several places, and succeeded in bursting it open.

Nothing was there but a sculptor's modelling-stand, with something upon it covered with a white cloth, and the modelling-tools on the floor. At the sight of the cloth, still damp, we drew a deep breath. It could have hung there for many hours, certainly not for twenty-four. We did not raise it. "He would be vexed," said Magnin, and I nodded, for it is accounted almost a crime in the artists' world to unveil a sculptor's work behind his back. We expressed no surprise at the fact of his modelling: a ban seemed to lie upon our tongues. The cloth hung tightly to the object beneath it, and showed us the outline of a woman's head and rounded-bust, and so veiled we left her. There was a little winding stair leading out of the passage, and we climbed it, to find ourselves in a sort of belvedere, commanding a superb view. It was a small, open terrace, on the roof of the house, and we saw at a glance that no one was there.

We had now been all over the casino, which was small and simply built, being evidently intended only for short summer use. As we stood leaning over the balustrade we could look down into the garden. No one was there but the *guardiano*, lying amongst his cabbages with his arms behind his head, half asleep. The laurel grove had been in my mind from the beginning, only it had seemed more natural to go to the house first. Now we descended the stairs silently and directed our steps thither.

As we approached it, the *guardiano* came towards us lazily.

"Have you seen the Signore?" he asked, and his stupidly placid face showed me that he, at least, had no hand in his disappearance.

"No, not yet," I answered, "but we shall come across him somewhere, no doubt. Perhaps he has gone to take a walk, and we will wait for him. What is this?" I went on, trying to seem careless. We were standing now by the little arch of which you know.

"This?" said he; "I have never been down there, but they say it is something old. Do the Signori want to see it? I will fetch a lantern."

I nodded, and he went off to his cabin. I had a couple of candles in my pocket, for I had intended to explore the place, should we not find Marcello. It was there that he had disappeared that night, and my thoughts had been busy with it; but I kept my candles concealed, reflecting that they would give our search an air of premeditation which would excite curiosity.

"When did you see the Signore last?" I asked, when he had returned with the lantern.

"I brought him his supper yesterday evening."

"At what o'clock?"

"It was the Ave Maria, Signore," he replied. "He always sups then."

It would be useless to put any more questions. He was evidently utterly unobserving, and would lie to please us.

"Let me go first," said Magnin, taking the lantern. We set our feet upon the steps; a cold air seemed to fill our lungs and yet to choke us, and a thick darkness lay beneath. The steps, as I could see by the light of my candle, were modern, as well as the vaulting above them. A tablet was let into the wall, and in spite of my excitement I paused to read it, perhaps because I was glad to delay whatever awaited us below. It ran thus:

Questo antico sepolcro Romano scoprì il Conte Marziali nell' anno 1853, e piamente conservò. In plain English:

"Count Marziali discovered this ancient Roman sepulchre in the year 1853, and piously preserved it."

I read it more quickly than it has taken time to write here, and hurried after Magnin, whose footsteps sounded faintly below me. As I hastened, a draught of cold air extinguished my candle, and I was trying to make my way down by feeling along the wall, which was horribly dark and clammy, when my heart stood still at a cry from far beneath me—a cry of horror!

"Where are you?" I shouted; but Magnin was calling my name, and could not hear me. "I am here. I am in the dark!"

I was making haste as fast as I could, but there were several turnings.

"I have found him!" came up from below.

"Alive?" I shouted. No answer.

One last short flight brought me face to face with the gleam of the lantern. It came from a low doorway, and within stood Magnin, peering into the darkness. I knew by his face, as he held the light high above him, that our fears were realized.

Yes; Marcello was there. He was lying stretched upon the floor, staring at the ceiling, dead, and already stiff, as I could see at a glance. We stood over him, saying not a word, then I knelt down and felt him, for mere form's sake, and said, as though I had not known it before, "He has been dead for some hours."

"Since yesterday evening," said Magnin, in a horror-stricken voice, yet with a certain satisfaction in it, as though to say, "You see, I was right."

Marcello was lying with his head slightly thrown back, no

contortions in his handsome features; rather the look of a person who has quietly died of exhaustion—who has slipped unconsciously from life to death. His collar was thrown open and a part of his breast, of a ghastly white, was visible. Just over the heart was a small spot.

"Give me the lantern," I whispered, as I stooped over it. It was a very little spot, of a faint purplish brown, and must have changed colour within the night.

I examined it intently, and should say that the blood had been sucked to the surface, and then a small prick or incision made. The slight subcutaneous effusion led me to this conclusion. One tiny drop of coagulated blood closed the almost imperceptible wound. I probed it with the end of one of Magnin's matches. It was scarcely more than skin-deep, so it could not be the stab of a stiletto, however slender, or the track of a bullet. Still, it was strange, and with one impulse we turned to see if no one were concealed there, or if there were no second exit. It would be madness to suppose that the murderer, if there was one, would remain by his victim. Had Marcello been making love to a pretty *contadina*, and was this some jealous lover's vengeance? But it was not a stab. Had one drop of poison in the little wound done this deadly work?

We peered about the place, and I saw that Magnin's eyes were blinded by tears and his face as pale as that upturned one on the floor, whose lids I had vainly tried to close. The chamber was low, and beautifully ornamented with stucco bas-reliefs, in the manner of the well-known one not far from there upon the same road. Winged genii, griffins, and arabesques, modelled with marvellous lightness, covered the walls and ceiling. There was no other door than the one we had entered by. In the centre stood a marble sarcophagus, with the usual subjects sculptured upon it, on the one side Hercules conducting a veiled figure, on the other a dance of nymphs and fauns. A space in the middle contained the following inscription, deeply cut in the stone, and still partially filled with red pigment:

D. M.
VESPERTILIAE·THC·AIMA–
TOΠΩTIΛOC·Q·FLAVIVS·
VIX·IPSE·SOSPES·MON·
POSVIT

"What is this?" whispered Magnin. It was only a pickaxe and a long crowbar, such as the country people use in hewing out their blocks of tufa, and his foot had struck against them. Who could have brought them here? They must belong to the *guardiano* above, but he said that he had never come here, and I believed him, knowing the Italian horror of darkness and lonely places; but what had Marcello wanted with them? It did not occur to us that archaeological curiosity could have led him to attempt to open the sarcophagus, the lid of which had evidently never been raised, thus justifying the expression *piously preserved*.

As I rose from examining the tools my eyes fell upon the line of mortar where the cover joined to the stone below, and I noticed that some of it had been removed, perhaps with the pickaxe which lay at my feet. I tried it with my nails and found that it was very crumbly. Without a word I took the tool in my hand, Magnin instinctively following my movements with the lantern. What impelled us I do not know. I had myself no thought, only an irresistible desire to see what was within. I saw that much of the mortar had been broken away, and lay in small fragments upon the ground, which I had not noticed before. It did not take long to complete the work. I snatched the lantern from Magnin's hand and set it upon the ground, where it shone full upon Marcello's dead face, and by its light I found a little break between the two masses of stone and managed to insert the end of my crowbar, driving it in with a blow of the pickaxe. The stone chipped and then cracked a little. Magnin was shivering.

"What are you going to do?" he said, looking around at where Marcello lay.

"Help me!" I cried, and we two bore with all our might upon the crowbar. I am a strong man, and I felt a sort of blind fury as the stone refused to yield. What if the bar should snap? With another blow I drove it in still further, then using it as a lever, we weighed upon it with our outstretched arms until every muscle was at its highest tension. The stone moved a little, and almost fainting we stopped to rest.

From the ceiling hung the rusty remnant of an iron chain which must once have held a lamp. To this, by scrambling upon the sarcophagus, I contrived to make fast the lantern.

"Now!" said I, and we heaved again at the lid. It rose, and we alternately heaved and pushed until it lost its balance and fell with a thundering crash upon the other side; such a crash that the walls seemed to shake, and I was for a moment utterly deafened, while little pieces of stucco rained upon us from the ceiling. When we had paused to recover from the shock we leaned over the sarcophagus and looked in.

The light shone full upon it, and we saw—how is it possible to tell? We saw lying there, amidst folds of mouldering rags, the body of a woman, perfect as in life, with faintly rosy face, soft crimson lips, and a breast of living pearl, which seemed to heave as though stirred by some delicious dream. The rotten stuff swathed about her was in ghastly contrast to this lovely form, fresh as the morning! Her hands lay stretched at her side, the pink palms were turned a little outwards, her eyes were closed as peacefully as those of a sleeping child, and her long hair, which shone red-gold in the dim light from above, was wound around her head in numberless finely plaited tresses, beneath which little locks escaped in rings upon her brow. I could have sworn that the blue veins on that divinely perfect bosom held living blood!

We were absolutely paralyzed, and Magnin leaned gasping over the edge as pale as death, paler by far than this living, almost smiling face to which his eyes were glued. I do not doubt that I was as pale as he at this inexplicable vision. As I looked the red lips seemed to grow redder. They *were* redder! The little pearly teeth showed between them. I had not seen them before, and now a clear ruby drop trickled down to her rounded chin and from there slipped sideways and fell upon her neck. Horror-struck I gazed upon the living corpse, till my eyes could not bear the sight any longer. As I looked away my glance fell once more upon the inscription, but now I could see—*and read*—it all. "To Vespertilia"—that was in Latin, and even the Latin name of the woman suggested a thing of evil flitting in the dusk. But the full horror of the nature of that thing had been veiled to Roman eyes under the Greek τησαίματοπωτίδος, "The blood-drinker, the vampire woman." And Flavius—her lover—*vix ipse sospes,* "himself hardly saved" from that deadly embrace, had buried her here, and set a seal upon her sepulchre, trusting to the weight of stone and the strength of clinging mortar to imprison for ever the beautiful monster he had loved.

"Infamous murderess!" I cried, "you have killed Marcello!" and a sudden, vengeful calm came over me.

"Give me the pickaxe," I said to Magnin; I can hear myself saying it still. He picked it up and handed it to me as in a dream; he seemed little better than an idiot, and the beads of sweat were shining on his forehead. I took my knife, and from the long wooden handle of the pickaxe I cut a fine, sharp stake. Then I clambered, scarcely feeling any repugnance, over the side of the sarcophagus, my feet amongst the folds of Vespertilia's decaying winding-sheet, which crushed like ashes beneath my boot.

I looked for one moment at that white breast, but only to choose the loveliest spot, where the network of azure veins shimmered like veiled turquoises, and then with one blow I drove the pointed stake deep down through the breathing snow and stamped it in with my heel.

An awful shriek, so ringing and horrible that I thought my ears must have burst; but even then I felt neither fear nor horror. There are times when these cannot touch us. I stopped and gazed once again at the face, now undergoing a fearful change—fearful and final!

"Foul vampire!" I said quietly in my concentrated rage. "You will do no more harm now!" And then, without looking back upon her cursed face, I clambered out of the horrible tomb.

We raised Marcello, and slowly carried him up the steep stairs—a difficult task, for the way was narrow and he was so stiff. I noticed that the steps were ancient up to the end of the second flight; above, the modern passage was somewhat broader. When we reached the top, the *guardiano* was lying upon one of the stone benches; he did not mean us to cheat him out of his fee. I gave him a couple of francs.

"You see that we have found the signore," I tried to say in a natural voice. "He is very weak, and we will carry him to the carriages." I had thrown my handkerchief over Marcello's face, but the man knew as well as I did that he was dead. Those stiff feet told their own story, but Italians are timid of being involved in such affairs. They have a childish dread of the police, and he only answered, "Poor Signorino! He is very ill; it is better to take him to Rome," and kept cautiously clear of us as we went up to the ilex alley with our icy burden, and he did not go to the gate with us, not liking to be observed by the coachman who was dozing on his box. With difficulty we got Marcello's corpse into the carriage, the driver turning to look at us suspiciously. I explained we had found our friend very ill, and at the same time slipped a gold piece into his hand, telling him to drive to the Via del Governo Vecchio. He pocketed the money, and whipped his horses into a trot, while we sat supporting the stiff body, which swayed like a broken doll at every pebble in the road. When we reached the Via del Governo Vecchio at last, no one saw us carry him into the house. There was no step before the door, and we drew up so close to it that it was possible to screen our burden from sight. When we had brought him into his room and laid him upon his bed, we noticed that his eyes were closed; from the movement of the carriage, perhaps, though that was scarcely possible. The landlady behaved very much as I had expected her to do, for, as I told you, I know the Italians. She pretended, too, that the signore was very ill, and made a pretence of offering to fetch a doctor, and when I thought it best to tell her that he was dead, declared that it must have happened that very moment, for she had seen him look at us and close his eyes again. She had always told him that he ate too little and that he would be ill. Yes, it was weakness and that bad air out there which had killed him; and then he worked too hard. When she had successfully established this fiction, which we were glad enough to agree to, for neither did we wish for the publicity of an inquest, she ran out and fetched a gossip to come and keep her company.

So died Marcello Souvestre, and so died Vespertilia the blood-drinker at last.

THERE IS NOT MUCH more to tell. Marcello lay calm and beautiful upon his bed, and the students came and stood silently looking at him, then knelt down for a moment to say a prayer, crossed themselves, and left him for ever.

We hastened to the Villa Medici, where Detaille was sleeping, and Sister Claudius watching him with a satisfied look on her strong face. She rose noiselessly at our entrance, and came to us at the threshold.

"He will recover," said she, softly. She was right. When he awoke and opened his eyes he knew us directly, and Magnin breathed a devout "Thank God!"

"Have I been ill, Magnin?" he asked, very feebly.

"You have had a little fever," answered Magnin, promptly; "but it is over now. Here is Monsieur Sutton come to see you."

"Has Marcello been here?" was the next question. Magnin looked at him very steadily.

"No," he only said, letting his face tell the rest.

"Is he dead, then?" Magnin only bowed his head. "Poor friend!"

Detaille murmured to himself, then closed his heavy eyes and slept again.

A few days after Marcello's funeral we went to the fatal Vigna Marziali to bring back the objects which had belonged to him. As I laid the manuscript score of the opera carefully together, my eye fell upon a passage which struck me as the identical one which Detaille had so constantly sung in his delirium, and which I noted down. Strange to say, when I reminded him of it later, it was perfectly new to him, and he declared that Marcello had not let him examine his manuscript. As for the veiled bust in the other room, we left it undisturbed, and to crumble away unseen.

❉

Emily Gerard

(1849–1905)

EMILY GERARD APPEARS IN this anthology, and is often mentioned by scholars of vampire lore, because her anthropological travel memoir *The Land Beyond the Forest* helped inspire Bram Stoker's novel *Dracula* and provided background description for it. Emily's sister Dorothea also wrote novels, and Emily's first three were collaborations with her, under the joined initials E. D. Gerard. In fact, Dorothea was more prolific and more commercially successful. But she didn't help inspire *Dracula*, so she is forgotten.

But Emily Gerard was an interesting character in her own right, aside from her role as inspiration. Born in Scotland and educated in the Tyrol (now divided between Italy and Austria), she wound up in vampire territory because she married an officer in the Austro-Hungarian cavalry, Chevalier Miecislas de Laszowski. After a stint in Poland, he was transferred to Transylvania, where his wife learned all she could about local history and culture—and clearly took extensive notes. *The Land Beyond the Forest: Facts, Figures, and Fancies* was published in 1888. Three years earlier, part of the book had appeared, under the title "Transylvanian Superstitions," in the British monthly *The Nineteenth Century* (which, as of the beginning of the twentieth century in 1901, blithely added to its title the phrase *and After*).

Gerard's book disproves the rule that nothing is more out-of-date than an old travel book—or perhaps, to be new again, it has to become old enough to preserve snapshots of a lost era. Biased at times, condescending at times, and not always as well-informed as she thought she was, Gerard was nonetheless an engaging writer. Like many Western European commentators visiting the more isolated Romania, she bemoaned the loss of "the old world charm" in the wake of "that nineteenth-century monster, the steam engine." And she coins some memorable phrases, such as her description of posthumous activities as "restlessness upon the part of the defunct."

These excerpts include the first known use of the word *nosferatu*, which Gerard presents as the Romanian word for vampire. Bram Stoker found the word in Gerard's writings and snapped it up for use in *Dracula*. The popularity of F. W. Murnau's brilliant 1922 silent film, *Nosferatu*, which was largely an unauthorized adaptation of *Dracula*, helped promote the word. One version of the film's English subtitles begins, "Nosferatu—Does not this word sound like the call of the death bird at midnight?" But unfortunately, as the omnipresent horror scholar David J. Skal and others have pointed out, there is no such word; Emily Gerard mistranslated or misconstrued. "The Romanian word for vampire," Skal points out bluntly, "is *vampir*." Nominees for the original word—such as *necuratal*, the Romanian word for "devil," and *nosophoros*, the Greek word for "plague-bearer"—remain far-fetched. Nonetheless, *nosferatu* is firmly established now as a synonym for *vampire*.

The following excerpts derive from Chapter XXV of *The Land Beyond the Forest*, "The Roumanians: Death and Burial—Vampires and Were-Wolves."

Death and Burial—Vampires and
Were-Wolves

NOWHERE DOES THE INHERENT superstition of the Romanian peasant find stronger expression than in his mourning and funeral rites, which are based upon a totally original conception of death.

Among the various omens of approaching death are the groundless barking of a dog, the shriek of an owl, the falling down of a picture from the wall, and the crowing of a black hen. The influence of this latter may, however, be annulled, and the catastrophe averted, if the bird be put in a sack and carried sunwise thrice round the dwelling house.

It is likewise prognostic of death to break off the smaller portion of a fowl's merry-thought, to dream of troubled water or of teeth falling out,* or to be merry without apparent reason.

A falling star always denotes that a soul is leaving the earth—for, according to Lithuanian mythology, to each star is attached the thread of some man's life, which, breaking at his death, causes the star to fall. In some places it is considered unsafe to point at a falling star.

A dying man may be restored to life if he be laid on Holy Saturday

---

*Both Greeks and Romans attached an ominous meaning to a dream of falling-out teeth.

outside the church-door, where the priest passing with the procession may step over him; or else let him eat of a root which has
been dug up from the church-yard on Good Friday; but if these
and other remedies prove inefficient, then must the doomed man
be given a burning candle into his hand, for it is considered to be
the greatest of all misfortunes if a man die without a light—a favor
the Roumanian durst not refuse to his deadliest enemy.

The corpse must be washed immediately after death, and the
dirt, if necessary, scraped off with knives, because the dead man
will be more likely to find favor above if he appear in a clean state
before the Creator. Then he is attired in his best clothes, in doing
which great care must be taken not to tie anything in a knot, for
that would disturb his rest by keeping him bound down to the
earth. Nor must he be suffered to carry away any particle of iron
about his person, such as buttons, boot-nails, etc., for that would
assuredly prevent him from reaching Paradise, the road to which is
long, and, moreover, divided off by several tolls or ferries. To enable the soul to pass through these a piece of money must be laid
in the hand, under the pillow, or beneath the tongue of the corpse.
In the neighborhood of Forgaras, where the ferries or toll-bars are
supposed to amount to twenty-five, the hair of the defunct is divided into as many plaits, and a piece of money secured in each.
Likewise a small provision of needles, thread, pins, etc., is put into
the coffin, to enable the pilgrim to repair any damages his clothes
may receive on the way.

The family must also be careful not to leave a knife lying with
the sharpened edge uppermost as long as the corpse remains in the
house, or else the soul will be forced to ride on the blade.

The mourning songs, called *Bocete*, usually performed by paid
mourners, are directly addressed to the corpse, and sung into his
ear on either side. This is the last attempt made by the survivors to
wake the dead man to life by reminding him of all he is leaving,
and urging him to make a final effort to arouse his dormant
faculties—the thought which underlies these proceedings being that

the dead man hears and sees all that goes on around him, and that it only requires the determined effort of a strong will in order to restore elasticity to the stiffened limbs, and cause the torpid blood to flow anew in the veins.

Here is a fragment of one of these mourning songs, which are often very pathetic and fanciful:

> Mother dear, arise, arise,
> Dry the tearful household's eyes!
> Waken, waken from thy trance,
> Speak a word or cast a glance!
> Pity thou thy children's lot!
> Rise, O mother, leave us not!
> Death triumphant, woe is me,
> From thy children snatcheth thee!
> To the wall hast turned thee now,
> Son nor daughter heedest thou.
> Laid the church-yard sod beneath,
> Thou shalt feel no breeze's breath
> On the surface of thy grave;
> From thy brow shall grasses wave,
> From those eyes so mild and true
> Nodding harebells take their blue.

Women alone are allowed to take part in these lamentations, and all women related to the deceased by ties of blood or friendship are bound to assist as mourners; likewise, those whose families have been on unfriendly terms with the dead man now appear to ask his forgiveness.

The corpse must remain exposed a full day and night in the chamber of death, and during that time must never be left alone, nor should the lamentations be suffered to cease for a single moment. For this reason it is customary to have hired women to act the part of mourners, by relieving each other at intervals in singing

the mourning songs. Often the deceased himself, in his last testa-
mentary disposition, has ordered the details of his funeral, and fixed
the payment—sometimes very considerable—which the mourning
women are to receive.

The men related to the deceased are also bound to spend the
night in the house, keeping watch over the corpse. This is called
keeping the *privegghia*, which, however, has not necessarily a mournful character, as they mostly pass the time with various games, or else
seated at table with food and wine.

Before the funeral the priest is called in, who, reciting the words
of the fiftieth psalm, pours wine over the corpse. After this the coffin is closed, and must not be reopened unless the deceased be
suspected to have died of a violent death, in which case the man
accused of the crime is confronted with the corpse of his supposed
victim, whose wounds will, at his sight, begin to bleed afresh.

In many places two openings corresponding to the ears of the
deceased are cut in the wood of the coffin, to enable him to hear
the songs of mourning which are sung on either side of him as he
is carried to the grave. This singing into the ears has passed into a
proverb, and when the Roumanian says, *"I-a-cantat la urechia"* (they
have sung into his ear), it is tantamount to saying that prayer, advice, and remonstrance have all been used in vain.

Whoever dies unmarried must not be carried by married bearers to the grave: a married man or woman is carried by married
men, and a youth by other youths, while a maiden is carried by
other maidens with hanging, dishevelled hair. In every case the
rank of the bearer should correspond to that of the deceased, and a
fruntas can as little be carried by *mylocasi* as the bearers of a *codas*
may be higher than himself in rank.

In many villages no funeral takes place in the forenoon, as the
people believe that the soul will reach its destination more easily
by following the march of the sinking sun.

The mass for the departed soul should, if possible, be said in the
open air; and when the coffin is lowered into the grave, the earthen

jar containing the water in which the corpse has been washed must be shattered to atoms on the spot.

A thunder-storm during the funeral denotes that another death will shortly follow.

It is often customary to place bread and wine on the fresh grave-mound; and in the case of young people, small fir-trees or gay-colored flags are placed beside the cross, to which in the case of a shepherd a tuft of wool is always attached.

Seven copper coins, and seven loaves of bread with a lighted candle sticking in each, are often distributed to seven poor people at the grave. This also is intended to signify the tolls to be cleared on the way to heaven.

In some places it is usual for the procession returning from a funeral to take its way through a river or stream of running water, sometimes going a mile or two out of their way to avoid all bridges, thus making sure that the vagrant soul of the beloved deceased will not follow them back to the house.

Earth taken from a fresh grave-mound and laid behind the neck at night will bring pleasant dreams; it may also serve as a cure for fever if made use of in the following manner: The person afflicted with fever repairs to the grave of some beloved relative, where, calling upon the defunct in the most tender terms, he begs of him or her the loan of a winding-sheet for a strange and unwelcome guest. Taking, then, from the grave a handful of earth, which he is careful to tie up tightly and place inside his shirt, the sick man goes away, and for three days and nights he carries this talisman about with him wherever he goes. On the fourth day he returns to the grave by a different route, and replacing the earth on the mound, thanks the dead man for the service rendered.

A still more efficacious remedy for fever is to lay a string or thread the exact length of your own body into the coffin of some one newly deceased, saying these words, "May I shiver only when this dead man shivers." Sore eyes may be cured by anointing them with the dew gathered off the grass of the grave of a just man on a fine evening in early spring; and a bone taken from the deceased's right arm will cure boils and sores by its touch. Whoever would keep sparrows off his field must between eleven o'clock and midnight collect earth from off seven different graves and scatter it over his field; while the same earth, if thrown over a dog addicted to hunting, will cure him of this defect.

The *pomeana*, or funeral feast, is invariably held after the funeral, for much of the peace of the defunct depends upon the strict observance of this ancient custom. All the favorite dishes of the dead man are served at this banquet, and each guest receives a cake, a jug of wine, and a wax candle in his memory. Similar pomeanas are repeated after a fortnight, six weeks, and on each anniversary of the death for the next seven years. On the first anniversary it is usual to bring bread and wine to the church-yard. The bread is distributed to the poor, and the wine poured down through the earth into the grave.

During six weeks after the funeral the women of the family let their hair hang uncombed and unplaited in sign of mourning. It is, moreover, no uncommon thing for Roumanians to bind themselves down to a mourning of ten or twenty years, or even for life, in memory of some beloved deceased one. Thus in one of the villages there still lived, two years ago, an old man who for the last forty years had worn no head covering, summer or winter, in memory of his only son, who had died in early youth.

In the case of a man who has died a violent death, or in general of all such as have expired without a light, none of these ceremonies take place. Such a man has neither right to bocete, privegghia, mass, or pomeana, nor is his body laid in consecrated ground. He is buried wherever the body may be found, on the bleak hill-side or in the heart of the forest where he met his death, his last resting-place only marked by a heap of dry branches, to which each passer-by is expected to add by throwing a handful of twigs—usually a thorny branch—on the spot. This handful of thorns—*o mână de spini*, as the Roumanian calls it—being the only mark of attention to which the deceased can lay claim, therefore to the mind of this people no thought is so dreadful as that of dying deprived of light.

The attentions due to such as have received orthodox burial often extend even beyond the first seven years after death; for whenever the defunct appears in a dream to any of the family, this likewise calls for another pomeana, and when this condition is not complied with, the soul thus neglected is apt to wander complaining about the earth, unable to find rest.

This restlessness on the part of the defunct may either be caused by his having concealed treasures during his lifetime, in which case he is doomed to haunt the place where he has hidden his riches until they are discovered; or else he may have died with some secret sin on his conscience—such, for instance, as having removed the boundary stone from a neighbor's field in order to enlarge his own. He will then probably be compelled to pilger about with a sack of the stolen earth on his back until he has succeeded in selling the whole of it to the people he meets in his nightly wanderings.

These restless spirits, called *strigoi*, are not malicious, but their appearance bodes no good, and may be regarded as omens of sickness or misfortune.

More decidedly evil is the *nosferatu,* or vampire, in which every Roumanian peasant believes as firmly as he does in heaven or hell. There are two sorts of vampires, living and dead. The living vampire is generally the illegitimate offspring of two illegitimate persons; but even a flawless pedigree will not insure any one against the intrusion of a vampire into their family vault, since every person killed by a nosferatu becomes likewise a vampire after death, and will continue to suck the blood of other innocent persons till the spirit has been exorcised by opening the grave of the suspected person, and either driving a stake through the corpse, or else firing a pistol-shot into the coffin. To walk smoking round the grave on each anniversary of the death is also supposed to be effective in confining the vampire. In very obstinate cases of vampirism it is recommended to cut off the head, and replace it in the coffin with the mouth filled with garlic, or to extract the heart and burn it, strewing its ashes over the grave.

That such remedies are often resorted to even now is a well-attested fact, and there are probably few Roumanian villages where such have not taken place within memory of the inhabitants. There is likewise no Roumanian village which does not count among its inhabitants some old woman (usually a midwife) versed in the precautions to be taken in order to counteract vampires, and who makes of this science a flourishing trade. She is frequently called in by the family who has lost a member, and requested to "settle" the corpse securely in its coffin, so as to insure it against wandering. The means by which she endeavors to counteract any vampirelike instincts which may be lurking are various. Sometimes she drives a nail through the forehead of the deceased, or else rubs the body with the fat of a pig which has been killed on the Feast of St. Ignatius, five days before Christmas. It is also very usual to lay the thorny branch of a wild-rose bush across the body to prevent it leaving the coffin.

First-cousin to the vampire, the long-exploded were-wolf of the Germans, is here to be found lingering under the name of *prikolitsch*. Sometimes it is a dog instead of a wolf whose form a man has taken, or been compelled to take, as penance for his sins. In one village a story is still told—and believed—of such a man, who, driving home one Sunday with his wife, suddenly felt that the time for his transformation had come. He therefore gave over the reins to her and stepped aside into the bushes, where, murmuring the mystic formula, he turned three somersaults over a ditch. Soon after, the woman, waiting vainly for her husband, was attacked by a furious dog, which rushed barking out of the bushes and succeeded in biting her severely as well as tearing her dress. When, an hour or two later, the woman reached home after giving up her husband as lost, she was surprised to see him come smiling to meet her; but when between his teeth she caught sight of the shreds of her dress bitten out by the dog, the horror of this discovery caused her to faint away.

Another man used gravely to assert that for several years he had gone about in the form of a wolf, leading on a troop of these animals, till a hunter, in striking off his head, restored him to his natural shape.

This superstition once proved nearly fatal to a harmless botanist, who, while collecting plants on a hill-side many years ago, was observed by some peasants, and, in consequence of his crouching attitude, mistaken for a wolf. Before they had time to reach him, however, he had risen to his feet and disclosed himself in the form of a man; but this in the minds of the Roumanians, who now regarded him as an aggravated case of wolf, was but additional motive for attacking him. They were quite sure that he must be a prikolitsch, for only such could change his shape in this unaccountable manner; and in another minute they were all in full cry after the wretched victim of science, who might have fared badly indeed had he not succeeded in gaining a carriage on the high-road before his pursuers came up.

I once inquired of an old Saxon woman, whom I had visited with a view to extracting various pieces of superstitious information, whether she had ever come across a prikolitsch herself.

"Bless you!" she said, "when I was young there was no village without two or three of them at least, but now there seem to be fewer."

"So there is no prikolitsch in this village?" I asked, feeling particularly anxious to make the acquaintance of a real live were-wolf.

"No," she answered, doubtfully, "not that I know of for certain, though of course there is no saying with those Roumanians. But close by here in the next street, round the corner, there lives the widow of a prikolitsch whom I knew. She is still a young woman, and lost her husband five or six years ago. In ordinary life he was a quiet enough fellow, rather weak and sickly-looking; but sometimes he used to disappear for a week or ten days at a time, and though his wife tried to deceive people by telling them that her husband was lying drunk in the loft, of course we knew better, for those were the times when he used to be away *wolving* in the mountains."

Thinking that the relict of a were-wolf was the next best thing to the were-wolf himself, I determined on paying my respects to the interesting widow; but on reaching her house the door was closed, and I had the cruel disappointment of learning that Madame Prikolitsch was not at home.

We do not require to go far for the explanation of the extraordinary tenacity of the were-wolf legend in a country like Transylvania, where real wolves still abound. Every winter here brings fresh proof of the boldness and cunning of these terrible animals, whose attacks on flocks and farms are often conducted with a skill which would do honor to a human intellect. Sometimes a whole village is kept in trepidation for weeks together by some particularly audacious leader of a flock of wolves, to whom the peasants not unnaturally attribute a more than animal nature; and it is safe to prophesy that as long as the flesh-and-blood wolf continues to haunt the Transylvanian forests, so long will his spectre brother survive in the minds of the people.

❋

Mary Cholmondeley

(1859–1925)

MARY CHOLMONDELEY (PRONOUNCED "CHUMLEY") was a popu-
lar British novelist now remembered mostly for *Red Pottage*, her 1899
satirical novel sympathetic to the aspirations of the New Woman. It
opens memorably:

> "I can't get out," said Sterne's starling, through the bars of his
> cage.
> "I will get out," said Hugh Scarlett to himself, seeing no
> bars, but half conscious of a cage.

Cholmondeley understood the urge to escape. The daughter of
a vicar, she was born in Shropshire, in the tiny village of Hodnet.
As the eldest daughter among eight siblings, she was handed the
thankless role of caretaker for an invalid mother. Literature ran in
the family, however—one ancestor was a poet and her uncle was a
friend of Mark Twain's—and eventually it rescued her as well. She
began writing in her teens and wound up publishing many novels
and stories.

Emerging from the borderlands of vampire tales, "Let Loose" is
a stylish and witty story, with unexpected twists and quotable lines
such as this comment on a crypt full of skeletons: "I attribute my
present determination to be cremated to the painful impression

produced on me by this spectacle." P. G. Wodehouse himself would have been proud to have invented the village of Wet Waste-on-the-Wolds. And "Let Loose" reminds us again that the vicious, having not caused enough trouble while alive, are the most likely to return undead.

The story first appeared in 1890 in *Temple Bar* ("A London Magazine for Town and Country Readers"), a monthly that had gained fame in the 1860s by publishing sensation novelist Mary Elizabeth Braddon, whose 1896 story "Good Lady Ducayne" appears in this anthology. *Temple Bar* continued to specialize in serialized fiction by such luminaries as Robert Louis Stevenson and Wilkie Collins. Years after "Let Loose" appeared, some readers suggested that Cholmondeley had patterned it on F. G. Loring's story "The Tomb of Sarah." Actually Cholmondeley's story appeared first, and as you will soon discover in these pages, the two stories bear little resemblance beyond their major themes. Because the epigraph that opens "Let Loose" appears without attribution, it is worth noting that many of Cholmondeley's readers would have recognized the lines as coming from "The Dead," a sonnet by the popular Victorian poet Mathilde Blind.

Let Loose

THE DEAD ABIDE WITH US!
THOUGH STARK AND COLD
EARTH SEEMS TO GRIP THEM,
THEY ARE WITH US STILL . . .

SOME YEARS AGO I took up architecture, and made a tour through Holland, studying the buildings of that interesting country. I was not then aware that it is not enough to take up art. Art must take you up, too. I never doubted but that my passing enthusiasm for her would be returned. When I discovered that she was a stern mistress, who did not immediately respond to my attentions, I naturally transferred them to another shrine. There are other things in the world besides art. I am now a landscape gardener.

But at the time of which I write I was engaged in a violent flirtation with architecture. I had one companion on this expedition, who has since become one of the leading architects of the day. He was a thin, determined-looking man with a screwed-up face and heavy jaw, slow of speech, and absorbed in his work to a degree which I quickly found tiresome. He was possessed of a certain quiet power of overcoming obstacles which I have rarely seen equalled. He has since become my brother-in-law, so I ought to know; for my parents did not like him much and opposed the marriage, and my sister did not like him at all, and refused him over and over again; but, nevertheless, he eventually married her.

I have thought since that one of his reasons for choosing me as his travelling companion on this occasion was because he was getting up steam for what he subsequently termed "an alliance with my family," but the idea never entered my head at the time. A more careless man as to dress I have rarely met, and yet, in all the heat of July in Holland, I noticed that he never appeared without a high, starched collar, which had not even fashion to commend it at that time.

I often chaffed him about his splendid collars, and asked him why he wore them, but without eliciting any response. One evening, as we were walking back to our lodgings in Middeburg, I attacked him for about the thirtieth time on the subject.

"Why on earth do you wear them?" I said.

"You have, I believe, asked me that question many times," he replied, in his slow, precise utterance; "but always on occasions when I was occupied. I am now at leisure, and I will tell you."

And he did.

I have put down what he said, as nearly in his own words as I can remember them.

TEN YEARS AGO, I was asked to read a paper on English Frescoes at the Institute of British Architects. I was determined to make the paper as good as I could, down to the slightest details, and I consulted many books on the subject, and studied every fresco I could find. My father, who had been an architect, had left me, at his death, all his papers and note-books on the subject of architecture. I searched them diligently, and found in one of them a slight unfinished sketch of nearly fifty years ago that specially interested me. Underneath was noted, in his clear, small hand—*Frescoed east wall of crypt. Parish Church. Wet Waste-on-the-Wolds, Yorkshire (viâ Pickering).*

The sketch had such a fascination for me that I decided to go there and see the fresco for myself. I had only a very vague idea as to where Wet Waste-on-the-Wolds was, but I was ambitious for the success of my paper; it was hot in London, and I set off on my long journey not without a certain degree of pleasure, with my dog Brian, a large nondescript brindled creature, as my only companion.

I reached Pickering, in Yorkshire, in the course of the afternoon, and then began a series of experiments on local lines which ended, after several hours, in my finding myself deposited at a little out-of-the-world station within nine or ten miles of Wet Waste. As no conveyance of any kind was to be had, I shouldered my portmanteau, and set out on a long white road that stretched away into the distance over the bare, treeless wold. I must have walked for several hours, over a waste of moorland patched with heather, when a doctor passed me, and gave me a lift to within a mile of my destination. The mile was a long one, and it was quite dark by the time I saw the feeble glimmer of lights in front of me, and found that I had reached Wet Waste. I had considerable difficulty in getting any one to take me in; but at last I persuaded the owner of the public-house to give me a bed, and, quite tired out, I got into it as soon as possible, for fear he should change his mind, and fell asleep to the sound of a little stream below my window.

I was up early next morning, and inquired directly after breakfast the way to the clergyman's house, which I found was close at hand. At Wet Waste everything was close at hand. The whole village seemed composed of a straggling row of one-storeyed grey stone houses, the same colour as the stone walls that separated the few fields enclosed from the surrounding waste, and as the little bridges over the beck that ran down one side of the grey wide street. Everything was grey. The church, the low tower of which I could see at a little distance, seemed to have been built of the same stone; so was the parsonage when I came up to it, accompanied on my way by a mob of rough, uncouth children, who eyed me and Brian with half-defiant curiosity.

The clergyman was at home, and after a short delay I was admitted. Leaving Brian in charge of my drawing materials, I followed the servant into a low panelled room, in which, at a latticed window, a very old man was sitting. The morning light fell on his white head bent low over a litter of papers and books.

"Mr. er —?" he said, looking up slowly, with one finger keeping his place in a book.

"Blake."

"Blake," he repeated after me, and was silent.

I told him that I was an architect; that I had come to study a fresco in the crypt of his church, and asked for the keys.

"The crypt," he said, pushing up his spectacles and peering hard at me. "The crypt has been closed for thirty years. Ever since—" and he stopped short.

"I should be much obliged for the keys," I said again.

He shook his head. "No," he said. "No one goes in there now."

"It is a pity," I remarked, "for I have come a long way with that one object"; and I told him about the paper I had been asked to read, and the trouble I was taking with it.

He became interested. "Ah!" he said, laying down his pen, and removing his finger from the page before him, "I can understand that. I also was young once, and fired with ambition. The lines have fallen to me in somewhat lonely places, and for forty years I have held the cure of souls in this place, where, truly, I have seen but little of the world, though I myself may be not unknown in the paths of literature. Possibly you may have read a pamphlet, written by myself, on the Syrian version of the *Three Authentic Epistles* of Ignatius?"

"Sir," I said, "I am ashamed to confess that I have not time to read even the most celebrated books. My one object in life is my art. *Ars longa, vita brevis*, you know."

"You are right, my son," said the old man, evidently disappointed, but looking at me kindly. "There are diversities of gifts, and if the Lord has entrusted you with a talent, look to it. Lay it not up in a napkin."

I said I would not do so if he would lend me the keys of the crypt. He seemed startled by my recurrence to the subject and looked undecided.

"Why not?" he murmured to himself. "The youth appears a good youth. And superstition! What is it but distrust in God!"

He got up slowly, and taking a large bunch of keys out of his pocket, opened with one of them an oak cupboard in the corner of the room.

"They should be here," he muttered, peering in; "but the dust of many years deceives the eye. See, my son, if among these parchments there be two keys; one of iron and very large, and the other steel, and of a long thin appearance."

I went eagerly to help him, and presently found in a back drawer two keys tied together, which he recognised at once.

"Those are they," he said. "The long one opens the first door at the bottom of the steps which go down against the outside wall of the church yard by the sword graven in the wall. The second opens (but it is hard of opening and of shutting) the iron door within the passage leading to the crypt itself. My son, is it necessary to your treatise that you should enter this crypt?"

I replied that it was absolutely necessary.

"Then take them," he said, "and in the evening you will bring them to me again."

I said I might want to go several days running, and asked if he would not allow me to keep them till I had finished my work; but on that point he was firm.

"Likewise," he added, "be careful that you lock the first door at the foot of the steps before you unlock the second, and lock the second also while you are within. Furthermore, when you come out lock the iron inner door as well as the wooden one."

I promised I would do so, and, after thanking him, hurried away, delighted at my success in obtaining the keys. Finding Brian and my sketching materials waiting for me in the porch, I eluded the vigilance of my escort of children by taking the narrow private

path between the parsonage and the church which was close at
hand, standing in a quadrangle of ancient yews.

The church itself was interesting, and I noticed that it must have
arisen out of the ruins of a previous building, judging from the
number of fragments of stone caps and arches, bearing traces of very
early carving, now built into the walls. There were incised crosses,
too, in some places, and one especially caught my attention, being
flanked by a large sword. It was in trying to get a nearer look at this
that I stumbled, and, looking down, saw at my feet a flight of narrow stone steps green with moss and mildew. Evidently this was the
entrance to the crypt. I at once descended the steps, taking care of
my footing, for they were damp and slippery in the extreme. Brian
accompanied me, as nothing would induce him to remain behind.
By the time I had reached the bottom of the stairs, I found myself
almost in darkness, and I had to strike a light before I could find the
keyhole and the proper key to fit into it. The door, which was of
wood, opened inwards fairly easily, although an accumulation of
mould and rubbish on the ground outside showed it had not been
used for many years. Having got through it, which was not altogether an easy matter, as nothing would induce it to open more than
about eighteen inches, I carefully locked it behind me, although I
should have preferred to leave it open, as there is to some minds an
unpleasant feeling in being locked in anywhere, in case of a sudden
exit seeming advisable.

I kept my candle alight with some difficulty, and after groping
my way down a low and of course exceedingly dank passage, came
to another door. A toad was squatting against it, who looked as if
he had been sitting there about a hundred years. As I lowered the
candle to the floor, he gazed at the light with unblinking eyes,
and then retreated slowly into a crevice in the wall, leaving against
the door a small cavity in the dry mud which had gradually silted
up round his person. I noticed that this door was of iron, and had
a long bolt, which, however, was broken. Without delay, I fitted
the second key into the lock, and pushing the door open after

considerable difficulty, I felt the cold breath of the crypt upon my face. I must own I experienced a momentary regret at locking the second door again as soon as I was well inside, but I felt it my duty to do so. Then, leaving the key in the lock, I seized my candle and looked round. I was standing in a low vaulted chamber with groined roof, cut out of the solid rock. It was difficult to see where the crypt ended, as further light thrown on any point only showed other rough archways or openings, cut in the rock, which had probably served at one time for family vaults. A peculiarity of the Wet Waste crypt, which I had not noticed in other places of that description, was the tasteful arrangement of skulls and bones which were packed about four feet high on either side. The skulls were symmetrically built up to within a few inches of the top of the low archway on my left, and the shin bones were arranged in the same manner on my right. But the fresco! I looked round for it in vain. Perceiving at the further end of the crypt a very low and very massive archway, the entrance to which was not filled up with bones, I passed under it, and found myself in a second smaller chamber. Holding my candle above my head, the first object its light fell upon was—the fresco, and at a glance I saw that it was unique. Setting down some of my things with a trembling hand on a rough stone shelf hard by, which had evidently been a credence table, I examined the work more closely. It was a reredos over what had probably been the altar at the time the priests were proscribed. The fresco belonged to the earliest part of the fifteenth century, and was so perfectly preserved that I could almost trace the limits of each day's work in the plaster, as the artist had dashed it on and smoothed it out with his trowel. The subject was the Ascension, gloriously treated. I can hardly describe my elation as I stood and looked at it, and reflected that this magnificent specimen of English fresco painting would be made known to the world by myself. Recollecting myself at last, I opened my sketching bag, and, lighting all the candles I had brought with me, set to work.

Brian walked about near me, and though I was not otherwise

than glad of his company in my rather lonely position, I wished several times I had left him behind. He seemed restless, and even the sight of so many bones appeared to exercise no soothing effect upon him. At last, however, after repeated commands, he lay down, watchful but motionless, on the stone floor.

I must have worked for several hours, and I was pausing to rest my eyes and hands, when I noticed for the first time the intense stillness that surrounded me. No sound from me reached the outer world. The church clock which had clanged out so loud and ponderously as I went down the steps, had not since sent the faintest whisper of its iron tongue down to me below. All was silent as the grave. This was the grave. Those who had come here had indeed gone down into silence. I repeated the words to myself, or rather they repeated themselves to me.

Gone down into silence.

I was awakened from my reverie by a faint sound. I sat still and listened. Bats occasionally frequent vaults and underground places.

The sound continued, a faint, stealthy, rather unpleasant sound. I do not know what kinds of sounds bats make, whether pleasant or otherwise. Suddenly there was a noise as of something falling, a momentary pause and then—an almost imperceptible but distant jangle as of a key.

I had left the key in the lock after I had turned it, and I now regretted having done so. I got up, took one of the candles, and went back into the larger crypt—for though I trust I am not so effeminate as to be rendered nervous by hearing a noise for which I cannot instantly account; still, on occasions of this kind, I must honestly say I should prefer that they did not occur. As I came towards the iron door, there was another distinct (I had almost said hurried) sound. The impression on my mind was one of great haste. When I reached the door, and held the candle near the lock to take out the key, I perceived that the other one, which hung by a short string to its fellow, was vibrating slightly. I should have preferred not to find it vibrating, as there seemed no occasion for such a course; but I put them both into my pocket, and turned to go back to my work. As I turned, I saw on the ground what had occasioned the louder noise I had heard, namely, a skull which had evidently just slipped from its place on the top of one of the walls of bones, and had rolled almost to my feet. There, disclosing a few more inches of the top of an archway behind, was the place from which it had been dislodged. I stooped to pick it up, but fearing to displace any more skulls by meddling with the pile, and not liking to gather up its scattered teeth, I let it lie, and went back to my work, in which I was soon so completely absorbed that I was only roused at last by my candles beginning to burn low and go out one after another.

Then, with a sigh of regret, for I had not nearly finished, I turned to go. Poor Brian, who had never quite reconciled himself to the place, was beside himself with delight. As I opened the iron door he pushed past me, and a moment later I heard him whining and scratching, and I had almost added, beating, against the wooden one. I locked the iron door, and hurried down the passage as quickly as I could, and almost before I had got the other one ajar there seemed to be a rush past me into the open air, and Brian was bounding up the steps and out of sight. As I stopped to take out the key, I felt quite deserted and left behind. When I came out once more into the sunlight, there was a vague sensation all about me in the air of exultant freedom.

It was already late in the afternoon, and after I had sauntered back to the parsonage to give up the keys, I persuaded the people of the public-house to let me join in the family meal, which was spread out in the kitchen. The inhabitants of Wet Waste were primitive people, with the frank, unabashed manner that flourishes still in lonely places, especially in the wilds of Yorkshire; but I had no idea that in these days of penny posts and cheap newspapers such entire ignorance of the outer world could have existed in any corner, however remote, of Great Britain.

When I took one of the neighbour's children on my knee—a pretty little girl with the palest aureole of flaxen hair I had ever seen—and began to draw pictures for her of the birds and beasts of other countries, I was instantly surrounded by a crowd of children, and even grown-up people, while others came to their doorways and looked on from a distance, calling to each other in the strident unknown tongue which I have since discovered goes by the name of "Broad Yorkshire."

The following morning, as I came out of my room, I perceived that something was amiss in the village. A buzz of voices reached me as I passed the bar, and in the next house I could hear through the open window a high-pitched wail of lamentation.

The woman who brought me my breakfast was in tears, and in answer to my questions, told me that the neighbour's child, the little girl whom I had taken on my knee the evening before, had died in the night.

I felt sorry for the general grief that the little creature's death seemed to arouse, and the uncontrolled wailing of the poor mother took my appetite away.

I hurried off early to my work, calling on my way for the keys, and with Brian for my companion descended once more into the crypt, and drew and measured with an absorption that gave me no time that day to listen for sounds real or fancied. Brian, too, on this occasion seemed quite content, and slept peacefully beside me on the stone floor. When I had worked as long as I could, I put away my books with regret that even then I had not quite finished, as I had hoped to do. It would be necessary come again for a short time on the morrow. When I returned the keys late that afternoon, the old clergyman met me at the door, and asked me to come in and have tea with him.

"And has the work prospered?" he asked, as we sat down in the long, low room, into which I had just been ushered, and where he seemed to live entirely.

I told him it had, and showed it to him.

"You have seen the original, of course?" I said.

"Once," he replied, gazing fixedly at it. He evidently did not care to be communicative, so I turned the conversation to the age of the church.

"All here is old," he said. "When I was young, forty years ago, and came here because I had no means of mine own, and was much moved to marry at that time, I felt oppressed that all was so old; and that this place was so far removed from the world, for which I had at times longing grievous to be borne; but I had chosen my lot, and with it I was forced to be content. My son, marry not in youth, for love, which truly in that season is a mighty power, turns away the heart from study, and young children break the back of ambition. Neither marry in middle life, when woman is seen to be but a woman and her talk a weariness, so you will not be burdened with a wife in your old age."

I had my own views on the subject of marriage, for I am of opinion that a well-chosen companion of domestic tastes and docile and devoted temperament may be of material assistance to a professional man. But my opinions once formulated, it is not of moment to me to discuss them with others, so I changed the subject, and asked if the neighbouring villages were as antiquated as Wet Waste.

"Yes, all about here is old," he repeated. "The paved road leading to Dyke Fens is an ancient pack road, made even in the time of the Romans. Dyke Fens, which is very near here, a matter of but four or five miles, is likewise old, and forgotten by the world. The Reformation never reached it. It stopped here. And at Dyke Fens they still have a priest and a bell, and bow down before the saints. It is a damnable heresy, and weekly I expound it as such to my people, showing them true doctrines; and I have heard that this same priest has so far yielded himself to the Evil One that he has preached against me as withholding gospel truths from my flock; but I take no heed of it, neither of his pamphlet touching the Clementine Homilies, in which he vainly contradicts that which I have plainly set forth and proven beyond doubt, concerning the word *Asaph*."

The old man was fairly off on his favourite subject, and it was some time before I could get away. As it was, he followed me to the door, and I only escaped because the old clerk hobbled up at that moment, and claimed his attention.

The following morning I went for the keys for the third and last time. I had decided to leave early the next day. I was tired of Wet Waste, and a certain gloom seemed to my fancy to be gathering over the place. There was a sensation of trouble in the air, as if, although the day was bright and clear, a storm were coming.

This morning, to my astonishment, the keys were refused to me when I asked for them. I did not, however, take the refusal as final—I make it a rule never to take a refusal as final—and after a short delay I was shown into the room where, as usual, the clergyman was sitting, or rather, on this occasion, was walking up and down.

"My son," he said with vehemence, "I know wherefore you have come, but it is of no avail. I cannot lend the keys again."

I replied that, on the contrary, I hoped he would give them to me at once.

"It is impossible," he repeated. "I did wrong, exceeding wrong. I will never part with them again."

"Why not?"

He hesitated, and then said slowly:

"The old clerk, Abraham Kelly, died last night." He paused, and then went on: "The doctor has just been here to tell me of that which is a mystery to him. I do not wish the people of the place to know it, and only to me he has mentioned it, but he has discovered plainly on the throat of the old man, and also, but more faintly on the child's, marks as of strangulation. None but he has observed it, and he is at a loss how to account for it. I, alas! can account for it but in one way, but in one way!"

I did not see what all this had to do with the crypt, but to humour the old man, I asked what that way was.

"It is a long story, and, haply, to a stranger it may appear but foolishness, but I will even tell it; for I perceive that unless I furnish a reason for withholding the keys, you will not cease to entreat me for them.

"I told you at first when you inquired of me concerning the crypt, that it had been closed these thirty years, and so it was. Thirty years ago a certain Sir Roger Despard departed this life, even the Lord of the manor of Wet Waste and Dyke Fens, the last of his family, which is now, thank the Lord, extinct. He was a man of a vile life, neither fearing God nor regarding man, nor having compassion or innocence, and the Lord appeared to have given him over to the tormentors even in this world, for he suffered many things of his vices, more especially from drunkenness, in which seasons, and they were many, he was as one possessed by seven devils, being an abomination to his household and a root of bitterness to all, both high and low.

"And, at last, the cup of his iniquity being full to the brim, he came to die, and I went to exhort him on his death-bed; for I heard that terror had come upon him, and that evil imaginations encompassed him so thick on every side, that few of them that were with him could abide in his presence. But when I saw him I perceived that there was no place of repentance left for him, and he scoffed at me and my superstition, even as he lay dying, and swore there was no God and no angel, and all were damned even as he was. And the next day, towards evening, the pains of death came upon him, and he raved the more exceedingly, inasmuch as he said he was being strangled by the Evil One. Now on his table was his hunting knife, and with his last strength he crept and laid hold upon it, no man withstanding him, and swore a great oath that if he went down to burn in hell, he would leave one of his hands behind on earth, and that it would never rest until it had drawn blood from the throat of another and strangled him, even as he himself was being strangled. And he cut off his own right hand at the wrist, and no man dared go near him to stop him, and the blood went through the floor, even down to the ceiling of the room below, and thereupon he died.

"And they called me in the night, and told me of his oath, and I counselled that no man should speak of it, and I took the dead hand, which none had ventured to touch, and I laid it beside him in his coffin; for I thought it better he should take it with him, so that he might have it, if haply some day after much tribulation he should perchance be moved to stretch forth his hands towards God. But the story got spread about, and the people were affrighted, so, when he came to be buried in the place of his fathers, he being the last of his family, and the crypt likewise full, I had it closed, and kept the keys myself, and suffered no man to enter therein any more; for truly he was a man of an evil life, and the devil is not yet wholly overcome, nor cast chained into the lake of fire. So in time the story died out, for in thirty years much is forgotten. And when you came and asked me for the keys, I was at the first minded to withhold them; but I thought it was a vain superstition, and I perceived that you do but ask a second time for what is first refused; so I let you have them, seeing it was not an idle curiosity, but a desire to improve the talent committed to you, that led you to require them."

The old man stopped, and I remained silent, wondering what would be the best way to get them just once more.

"Surely, sir," I said at last, "one so cultivated and deeply read as yourself cannot be biased by an idle superstition."

"I trust not," he replied, "and yet—it is a strange thing that since the crypt was opened two people have died, and the mark is plain upon the throat of the old man and visible on the young child. No blood was drawn, but the second time the grip was stronger than the first. The third time, perchance—"

"Superstition such as that," I said with authority, "is an entire want of faith in God. You once said so yourself."

I took a high moral tone which is often efficacious with conscientious, humble-minded people.

He agreed, and accused himself of not having faith as a grain of mustard seed; but even when I had got him so far as that, I had a severe struggle for the keys. It was only when I finally explained to him that if any malign influence had been let loose the first day, at any rate, it was out now for good or evil, and no further going or coming of mine could make any difference, that I finally gained my point. I was young, and he was old; and, being much shaken by what had occurred, he gave way at last, and I wrested the keys from him.

I will not deny that I went down the steps that day with a vague, indefinable repugnance, which was only accentuated by the closing of the two doors behind me. I remembered then, for the first time, the faint jangling of the key and other sounds which I had noticed the first day, and how one of the skulls had fallen. I went to the place where it still lay. I have already said these walls of skulls were built up so high as to be within a few inches of the top of the low arch- ways that led into more distant portions of the vault. The displace- ment of the skull in question had left a small hole just large enough for me to put my hand through. I noticed for the first time, over the archway above it, a carved coat-of-arms, and the name, now almost obliterated, of Despard. This, no doubt, was the Despard vault. I could not resist moving a few more skulls and looking in, holding my candle as near the aperture as I could. The vault was full. Piled high, one upon another, were old coffins, and remnants of coffins, and strewn bones. I attribute my present determination to be cre- mated to the painful impression produced on me by this spectacle. The coffin nearest the archway alone was intact, save for a large crack across the lid. I could not get a ray from my candle to fall on the brass plates, but I felt no doubt this was the coffin of the wicked Sir Roger. I put back the skulls, including the one which had rolled down, and carefully finished my work. I was not there much more than an hour, but I was glad to get away.

If I could have left Wet Waste at once I should have done so, for I had a totally unreasonable longing to leave the place; but I found that only one train stopped during the day at the station from which I had come, and that it would not be possible to be in time for it that day.

Accordingly I submitted to the inevitable, and wandered about with Brian for the remainder of the afternoon and until late in the evening, sketching and smoking. The day was oppressively hot, and even after the sun had set across the burnt stretches of the wolds, it seemed to grow very little cooler. Not a breath stirred. In the evening, when I was tired of loitering in the lanes, I went up to my own room, and after contemplating afresh my finished study of the fresco, I suddenly set to work to write the part of my paper bearing upon it. As a rule, I write with difficulty, but that evening words came to me with winged speed, and with them a hovering impression that I must make haste, that I was much pressed for time. I wrote and wrote, until my candles guttered out and left me trying to finish by the moonlight, which, until I endeavoured to write by it, seemed as clear as day.

I had to put away my MS., and, feeling it was too early to go to bed, for the church clock was just counting out ten, I sat down by the open window and leaned out to try and catch a breath of air. It was a night of exceptional beauty; and as I looked out my nervous haste and hurry of mind were allayed. The moon, a perfect circle, was—if so poetic an expression be permissible—as it were, sailing across a calm sky. Every detail of the little village was as clearly illuminated by its beams as if it were broad day; so, also, was the adjacent church with its primeval yews, while even the wolds beyond were dimly indicated, as if through tracing paper.

I sat a long time leaning against the window-sill. The heat was still intense. I am not, as a rule, easily elated or readily cast down; but as I sat that night in the lonely village on the moors, with Brian's head against my knee, how, or why, I know not, a great depression gradually came upon me.

My mind went back to the crypt and the countless dead who had been laid there. The sight of the goal to which all human life, and strength, and beauty, travel in the end, had not affected me at the time, but now the very air about me seemed heavy with death.

What was the good, I asked myself, of working and toiling, and grinding down my heart and youth in the mill of long and strenuous effort, seeing that in the grave folly and talent, idleness and labour lie together, and are alike forgotten? Labour seemed to stretch before me till my heart ached to think of it, to stretch before me even to the end of life, and then came, as the recompense of my labour—the grave. Even if I succeeded, if, after wearing my life threadbare with toil, I succeeded, what remained to me in the end? The grave. A little sooner, while the hands and eyes were still strong to labour, or a little later, when all power and vision had been taken from them; sooner or later only—the grave.

I do not apologise for the excessively morbid tenor of these reflections, as I hold that they were caused by the lunar effects which I have endeavoured to transcribe. The moon in its various quarterings has always exerted a marked influence on what I may call the sub-dominant, namely, the poetic side of my nature.

I roused myself at last, when the moon came to look in upon me where I sat, and, leaving the window open, I pulled myself together and went to bed.

I fell asleep almost immediately, but I do not fancy I could have been asleep very long when I was wakened by Brian. He was growling in a low, muffled tone, as he sometimes did in his sleep, when his nose was buried in his rug. I called out to him to shut up; and as he did not do so, turned in bed to find my match box or something to throw at him. The moonlight was still in the room, and as I looked at him I saw him raise his head and evidently wake up. I admonished him, and was just on the point of falling asleep when he began to growl again in a low, savage manner that waked me most effectually. Presently he shook himself and got up, and began prowling about the room. I sat up in bed and called to him, but he paid no attention. Suddenly I saw him stop short in the moonlight; he showed his teeth, and crouched down, his eyes following something in the air. I looked at him in horror. Was he going mad? His eyes were glaring, and his head moved slightly as if he were following the rapid movements of an enemy. Then, with a furious snarl, he suddenly sprang from the ground, and rushed in great leaps across the room towards me, dashing himself against the furniture, his eyes rolling, snatching and tearing wildly in the air with his teeth. I saw he had gone mad. I leaped out of bed, and rushing at him, caught him by the throat. The moon had gone behind a cloud; but in the darkness I felt him turn upon me, felt him rise up, and his teeth close in my throat. I was being strangled. With all the strength of despair, I kept my grip of his neck, and, dragging him across the room, tried to crush in his head against the iron rail of my bedstead. It was my only chance. I felt the blood running down my neck. I was suffocating. After one moment of frightful struggle, I beat his head against the bar and heard his skull give way. I felt him give one strong shudder, a groan, and then I fainted away.

When I came to myself I was lying on the floor, surrounded by the people of the house, my reddened hands still clutching Brian's throat. Someone was holding a candle towards me, and the draught from the window made it flare and waver. I looked at Brian. He was stone dead. The blood from his battered head was trickling slowly over my hands. His great jaw was fixed in something that—in the uncertain light—I could not see.

They turned the light a little.

"Oh, God!" I shrieked. "There! Look! Look!"

"He's off his head," said some one, and I fainted again.

I was ill for about a fortnight without regaining consciousness, a waste of time of which even now I cannot think without poignant regret. When I did recover consciousness, I found I was being carefully nursed by the old clergyman and the people of the house. I have often heard the unkindness of the world in general inveighed against, but for my part I can honestly say that I have received many more kindnesses than I have time to repay. Country people especially are remarkably attentive to strangers in illness.

I could not rest until I had seen the doctor who attended me, and had received his assurance that I should be equal to reading my paper on the appointed day. This pressing anxiety removed, I told him of what I had seen before I fainted the second time. He listened attentively, and then assured me, in a manner that was intended to be soothing, that I was suffering from an hallucination, due, no doubt, to the shock of my dog's sudden madness.

"Did you see the dog after it was dead?" I asked. He said he did. The whole jaw was covered with blood and foam; the teeth certainly seemed convulsively fixed, but the case being evidently one of extraordinarily virulent hydrophobia, owing to the intense heat, he had had the body burned immediately.

MY COMPANION STOPPED SPEAKING as we reached our lodgings, and went upstairs. Then, lighting a candle, he slowly turned down his collar.

"You see I have the marks still," he said, "but I have no fear of dying of hydrophobia. I am told such peculiar scars could not have been made by the teeth of a dog. If you look closely you see the pressure of the five fingers. That is the reason why I wear high collars."

Eric, Count Stenbock

(1860–1895)

LATER IN THIS ANTHOLOGY, you will find M. R. James's story "Count Magnus." A real (and considerably less frightening) Count Magnus appears in the true story of Eric Stenbock—his grandfather, who administered the paternal trust fund left behind by Eric's father, who died when the boy was only a year old. Like Aleksei Tolstoy, Stenbock was born into a world of social advantages and material comfort, including other trust funds and his inheritance of both the title Count Eric and a vast family estate in Estonia. His father was an aristocratic Swede whose titles included Baron de Torpa and Count de Bogesun. Another grandfather was a Bremen-born textile businessman who emigrated to sooty Manchester and built Thirlestaine Hall in Cheltenham, where Erik Magnus Andreas Harry Stenbock was born. To this already formidable parade of names, he added Stanislaus when he converted to Catholicism.

Upon inheriting the Estonian estate at the age of twenty-five, Stenbock moved there and settled into a lifestyle reminiscent of that of Oscar Wilde, or perhaps of his creation Dorian Gray. Visitors to his home first passed a fox and a bear and a small herd of reindeer that lived in the garden, only to find their host lounging in a silk smoking gown with a snake around his neck. Stenbock smoked the air with incense, seduced his muse with opium, mixed famously toxic cocktails, cavorted in outlandish costumes, and populated the house with decadent statues of Eros and Buddha. His home was also a shrine to the Pre-Raphaelite works of Simeon Solomon, a painter of unconvincingly winged young men who sport shaggy rock-star locks and the requisite pouty Pre-Raphaelite lips. Stenbock knew Solomon, with whom he is thought to have been romantically (or at least sexually) involved. Stenbock's sexual orientation was well-known within his circle, but he never suffered Solomon's Wildean fate—hard labor for soliciting sexual favors from men.

After a couple of years in Estonia, Stenbock moved back to England and became a popular member of bohemian literary circles. He knew illustrator Aubrey Beardsley and poet William Butler Yeats. The latter memorably described Stenbock: "Scholar, connoisseur, drunkard, poet, pervert, most charming of men." Stenbock published a single volume of dark but lively stories and three books of moody verse. In 1893, a newspaper review of his third volume of poems, *The Shadow of Death*, denounced it for "the maudlin sentiment, the affected preciousness, the sham mysticism," and finally decided "it must be a parody." Two years later, Stenbock died on the first day of Oscar Wilde's trial.

"A True Story of a Vampire" first appeared in 1894 in his story collection *Studies of Death*, which is subtitled *Romantic Tales*. Interestingly, the female narrator is named Carmela; Le Fanu's "Carmilla" had appeared only twenty-two years before. Stenbock also reverses the gender of the vampire and the victim, returning to the tense male-male attraction that showed up in vampire fiction as early as Byron and Polidori.

A True Story of a Vampire

V AMPIRE STORIES ARE GENERALLY located in Styria; mine is also. Styria is by no means the romantic kind of place described by those who have certainly never been there. It is a flat, uninteresting country, only celebrated by its turkeys, its capons, and the stupidity of its inhabitants. Vampires generally arrive by night, in carriages drawn by two black horses.

Our Vampire arrived by the commonplace means of the railway train, and in the afternoon. You must think that I am joking, or perhaps that by the word "Vampire" I mean a financial vampire. No, I am quite serious. The Vampire of whom I am speaking, who laid waste our hearth and home, was a real vampire.

Vampires are generally described as dark, sinister-looking, and singularly handsome. Our Vampire was, on the contrary, rather fair, and certainly not at first sight sinister-looking, and though decidedly attractive in appearance, not what one would call singularly handsome.

Yes, he desolated our home, killed my brother—the one object of my adoration—also my dear father. Yet, at the same time, I must say that I myself came under the spell of his fascination, and, in spite of all, have no ill-will towards him now.

Doubtless you have read in the papers *passim* of "the Baroness

and her beasts." It is to tell how I came to spend most of my useless
wealth on an asylum for stray animals that I am writing this.

I am old now; what happened then was when I was a little girl
of about thirteen. I will begin by describing our household. We
were Poles; our name was Wronski: we lived in Styria, where we
had a castle. Our household was very limited. It consisted, with
the exclusion of domestics, of only my father, my governess—a
worthy Belgian named mademoiselle Vonnaert—my brother, and
myself. Let me begin with my father: He was old, and both my
brother and I were children of his old age. Of my mother I remember nothing: she died in giving birth to my brother, who is only
one year, or not as much, younger than myself. Our father was stu-
dious, continually occupied in reading books, chiefly on recondite
subjects and in all kinds of unknown languages. He had a long
white beard, and wore habitually a black velvet skull-cap.

How kind he was to us! It was more than I could tell. Still it was
not I who was the favourite. His whole heart went out to Gabriel—
Gabryel as we spelt it in Polish. He was always called by the Russian abbreviation Gavril—I mean, of course, my brother, who had
a resemblance to the only portrait of my mother, a slight chalk
sketch which hung in my father's study. But I was by no means
jealous: my brother was and has been the only love of my life. It is
for his sake that I am now keeping in Westbourne Park a home for
stray cats and dogs.

I was at that time, as I said before, a little girl; my name was
Carmela. My long tangled hair was always all over the place, and
never would be combed straight. I was not pretty—at least, looking at a photograph of me at that time, I do not think I could describe myself as such. Yet at the same time, when I look at my
photograph, I think my expression may have been pleasing to some
people: irregular features, large mouth, and large wild eyes.

I was by way of being naughty—not so naughty as Gabriel in
the opinion of Mlle. Vonnaert. Mlle. Vonnaert, I may intercalate,

was a wholly excellent person, middle-aged, who really did speak good French, although she was a Belgian, and could make herself understood in German, which, as you may or may not know, is the current language of Styria.

I find it difficult to describe my brother, Gabriel; there was something about him strange and superhuman, or perhaps I should rather say praeter-human, something between the animal and the divine. Perhaps the Greek idea of the Faun might illustrate what I mean; but that will not do either. He had large, wild, gazelle-like eyes: his hair, like mine, was in a perpetual tangle—that point he had in common with me, and indeed, as I afterwards heard, our mother having been of gypsy race, it will account for much of the innate wildness there was in our natures. I was wild enough, but Gabriel was much wilder. Nothing would induce him to put on shoes and socks, except on Sundays—when he also allowed his hair to be combed, but only by me. How shall I describe the grace of that lovely mouth, shaped verily en arc d'amour. I always think of the text in the Psalm, "Grace is shed forth on thy lips, therefore has God blessed thee eternally"—lips that seemed to exhale the very breath of life. Then that beautiful, lithe, living, elastic form!

He could run faster than any deer: spring like a squirrel to the topmost branch of a tree: he might have stood for the sign and symbol of vitality itself. But seldom could he be induced by Mlle. Vonnaert to learn lessons, but when he did so, he learned with extraordinary quickness. He would play upon every conceivable instrument, holding a violin here, there, and everywhere except the right place: manufacturing instruments for himself out of reeds—even sticks. Mlle. Vonnaert made futile efforts to induce him to learn to play the piano. I suppose he was what was called spoilt, though merely in the superficial sense of the word. Our father allowed him to indulge in every caprice.

One of his peculiarities, when quite a little child, was horror at the sight of meat. Nothing on earth would induce him to taste it. Another thing which was particularly remarkable about him was his extraordinary power over animals. Everything seemed to come tame to his hand. Birds would sit on his shoulder. Then sometimes Mlle. Vonnaert and I would lose him in the woods—he would suddenly dart away. Then we would find him singing softly or whistling to himself, with all manner of woodland creatures around him,—hedgehogs, little foxes, wild rabbits, marmots, squirrels, and such like. He would frequently bring these things home with him and insist on keeping them. This strange menagerie was the terror of poor Mlle. Vonnaert's heart. He chose to live in a little room at the top of a turret; but which, instead of going upstairs, he chose to reach by means of a very tall chestnut tree, through the window. But in contradiction to all this, it was his custom to serve every Sunday Mass in the parish church, with hair nicely combed and with white surplice and red cassock. He looked as demure and tamed as possible. Then came the element of the divine. What an expression of ecstasy there was in those glorious eyes!

Thus far I have not been speaking about the Vampire. However, let me begin with my narrative at last. One day my father had to go to the neighboring town—as he frequently had. This time he returned accompanied by a guest. The gentleman, he said, had missed his train, through the late arrival of another at our station, which was a junction, and he would therefore, as trains were not frequent in our parts, have had to wait there all night. He had joined in conversation with my father in the too-late-arriving train from the town: and had consequently accepted my father's invitation to stay the night at our house. But of course, you know, in those out-of-the-way parts we are almost patriarchal in our hospitality.

He was announced under the name of Count Vardalek—the name being Hungarian. But he spoke German well enough: not with the monotonous accentuation of Hungarians, but rather, if anything, with a slight Slavonic intonation. His voice was particularly soft and insinuating. We soon afterwards found out he could talk Polish, and Mlle. Vonnaert vouched for his good French. Indeed he seemed to know all languages. But let me give my first impressions. He was rather tall, with fair wavy hair, rather long, which accentuated a certain effeminacy about his smooth face. His figure had something—I cannot say what—serpentine about it. The features were refined; and he had long, slender, magnetic-looking hands, a somewhat long sinuous nose, a graceful mouth, and an attractive smile, which belied the intense sadness of the expression of the eyes. When he arrived his eyes were half closed—indeed they were habitually so—so that I could not decide their colour. He looked worn and wearied. I could not possibly guess his age.

Suddenly Gabriel burst into the room: a yellow butterfly was clinging to his hair. He was carrying in his arms a little squirrel. Of course he was bare-legged as usual. The stranger looked up at his approach; then I noticed his eyes. They were green: they seemed to dilate and grow larger. Gabriel stood stock-still, with a startled look, like that of a bird fascinated with a serpent. But nevertheless he held out his hand to the newcomer Vardalek, taking his hand—I don't know why I noticed this trivial thing,—pressed the pulse with his forefinger. Suddenly Gabriel darted from the room and upstairs, going to his turret-room this time by the staircase instead of the tree. I was in terror of what the Count might think of him. Great was my relief when he came down in his velvet Sunday suit, and shoes and stockings. I combed his hair, and set him generally right.

When the stranger came to dinner his appearance had somewhat altered; he looked much younger. There was an elasticity of the skin, combined with a delicate complexion, rarely to be found in a man. Before, he had struck me as very pale.

Well, at dinner we were all charmed with him, especially my father. He seemed to be thoroughly acquainted with all my father's peculiar hobbies. Once, when my father was relating some of his military experiences, he said something about a drummer-boy who was wounded in battle. His eyes opened completely again and dilated: this time with a particularly disagreeable expression, dull and dead, yet at the same time animated by some horrible excitement. But this was only momentary.

The chief subject of his conversation with my father was about certain curious mystical books which my father had just lately picked up, and which he could not make out, but Vardalek seemed completely to understand. At dessert-time my father asked him if he were in a great hurry to reach his destination: if not, would he not stay on with us a little while: though our place was out of the way, he would find much that would interest him in his library.

He answered, "I am in no hurry. I have no particular reason for going to that place at all, and if I can be of service to you in deciphering these books, I shall be only too glad." He added with a smile that was bitter, very very bitter: "You see, I am a cosmopolitan, a wanderer on the face of the earth."

After dinner my father asked him if he played the piano. He said, "Yes, I can do a little," and he sat down at the piano. Then he played a Hungarian *czardas*—wild, rhapsodic, wonderful.

That is the music which makes men mad. He went on in the same strain.

Gabriel stood stock still by the piano, his eyes dilated and fixed, his form quivering. At last he said very slowly, at one particular motive—for want of a better word you may call it the *relâche* of a *czardas* by which I mean that point where the original quasi-slow movement begins again—"Yes, I think I could play that."

Then he quickly fetched his fiddle and self-made xylophone, and did actually, alternating the instruments, render the same very well indeed.

Vardalek looked at him, and said in a very sad voice, "Poor child! You have the soul of music within you."

I could not understand why he should seem to commiserate instead of congratulate Gabriel on what certainly showed an extraordinary talent.

Gabriel was shy even as the wild animals who were tame to him. Never before had he taken to a stranger. Indeed, as a rule, if any stranger came to the house by any chance, he would hide himself, and I had to bring him up his food to the turret chamber. You may imagine what was my surprise when I saw him walking about hand in hand with Vardalek the next morning, in the garden, talking livelily with him, and showing his collection of pet animals, which he had gathered from the woods, and for which we had had to fit up a regular zoological gardens. He seemed utterly under the domination of Vardalek. What surprised us was (for otherwise we liked the stranger, especially for being kind to him) that he seemed, though not noticeably at first—except to me, who noticed everything with regard to him—to be gradually losing his health and vitality. He did not become pale as yet; but there was a certain languor about his movements which certainly there was by no means before.

My father got more and more devoted to Count Vardalek. He helped him in his studies: and my father would hardly allow him to go away, which he did sometimes—to Trieste, he said—he always came back, bringing us presents of strange Oriental jewellery or textures.

I knew all kinds of people came to Trieste, Orientals included. Still, there was a strangeness and magnificence about these things which I was sure even then could not have possibly come from such a place as Trieste, memorable to me chiefly for its necktie shops.

When Vardalek was away, Gabriel was continually asking for him and talking about him. Then at the same time he seemed to regain his old vitality and spirits. Vardalek always returned looking much older, wan, and weary. Gabriel would rush to meet him, and kiss him on the mouth. Then he gave a slight shiver, and after a little while began to look quite young again.

Things continued like this for some time. My father would not hear of Vardalek's going away permanently. He came to be an inmate of our house. I indeed, and Mlle. Vonnaert also, could not help noticing what a difference there was altogether about Gabriel. But my father seemed totally blind to it.

One night I had gone downstairs to fetch something which I had left in the drawing room. As I was going up again I passed

Vardalek's room. He was playing on a piano, which had been specially put there for him, one of Chopin's nocturnes, very beautifully; I stopped, leaning on the banisters to listen.

Something white appeared on the dark staircase. We believed in ghosts in our part. I was transfixed with terror, and clung to the banisters. What was my astonishment to see Gabriel walking slowly down the staircase, his eyes fixed as though in a trance! This terrified me even more than a ghost would. Could I believe my senses? Could that be Gabriel?

I simply could not move. Gabriel, clad in his long white nightshirt, came downstairs and opened the door. He left it open. Vardalek still continued playing, but talked as he played.

He said—this time speaking in Polish—*Nie umiem wyrazic jak ciehie kocham,*—"My darling, I fain would spare thee; but thy life is my life, and I must live, I who would rather die. Will God not have *any* mercy on me? Oh! oh! life; oh, the torture of life!" Here he struck one agonised and strange chord, then continued playing softly, "Oh, Gabriel, my beloved! My life, yes *life*—oh, why life? I am sure this is but a little of what I demand of thee. Surely thy superabundance of life can spare a little to one who is already dead. No, stay," he said now almost harshly, "what must be, must be!"

Gabriel stood there quite still, with the same fixed vacant expression, in the room. He was evidently walking in his sleep. Vardalek played on: then said, "Ah!" with a sigh of terrible agony. Then, very gently, "Go now, Gabriel; it is enough." And Gabriel went out of the room and ascended the staircase at the same slow pace, with the same unconscious stare. Vardalek struck the piano, and although he did not play loudly, it seemed as though the strings would break. You never heard music so strange and so heart-rending!

I only know I was found by Mlle. Vonnaert in the morning, in an unconscious state, at the foot of the stairs. Was it a dream after all? I am sure now that it was not. I thought then it might be, and said nothing to any-one about it. Indeed, what could I say?

Well, to let me cut a long story short, Gabriel, who had never known a moment's sickness in his life, grew ill; and we had to send to Gratz for a doctor, who could give no explanation of Gabriel's strange illness. Gradual wasting away, he said: absolutely no organic complaint. What could this mean?

My father at last became conscious of the fact that Gabriel was ill. His anxiety was fearful. The last trace of grey faded from his hair, and it became quite white. We sent to Vienna for doctors. But all with the same result.

Gabriel was generally unconscious, and when conscious, only seemed to recognize Vardalek, who sat continually by his bedside, nursing him with the utmost tenderness.

One day I was alone in the room: and Vardalek cried suddenly, almost fiercely, "Send for a priest at once, at once," he repeated. "It is now almost too late!"

Gabriel stretched out his arms spasmodically, and put them around Vardalek's neck. This was the only movement he had made for some time. Vardalek bent down and kissed him on the lips. I rushed downstairs: and the priest was sent for. When I came back Vardalek was not there. The priest administered extreme unction. I think Gabriel was already dead, although we did not think so at the time.

Vardalek had utterly disappeared; and when we looked for him he was nowhere to be found; nor have I seen or heard of him since.

My father died very soon afterwards: suddenly aged, and bent down with grief. And so the whole of the Wronski property came into my sole possession. And here I am, an old woman, generally laughed at for keeping, in memory of Gabriel, an asylum for stray animals—and—people do not, as a rule, believe in Vampires!

Mary Elizabeth Braddon

(1835–1915)

MARY ELIZABETH BRADDON WAS one of those indefatigable Victorian novelists who make other writers look like layabouts. Scholars estimate that she wrote more than eighty novels; they're uncertain because some were published under pseudonyms. Famous especially for *Lady Audley's Secret* and *Aurora Floyd*, in her prime Braddon was considered the queen of sensation novelists.

The term arose in response to such novels as *The Woman in White*, by Wilkie Collins, and *East Lynne*, by Ellen Wood, both of which were built around outrageous plots involving family secrets and violence. Sensation novelists inherited Gothic writers' penchant for melodrama, but brought it down-to-earth, situating their midnight intrigues not in Transylvanian castles but in Regent's Park. Instead of doomed barons, their villains might be City businessmen. The public couldn't get enough; writers such as Braddon reaped a new financial harvest with every book. She admitted that she cranked out some volumes as bill-paying hack work. Once she complained to Bulwer Lytton that "the amount of crime, treachery, murder, slow poisoning & general infamy required by the halfpenny reader is something terrible," but she was willing to meet the demand, under several pseudonyms when necessary.

Her most famous novel, still read in the twenty-first century, was *Lady Audley's Secret*, inspired in part by a visit to Ingatestone

Hall, the sixteenth-century manor house that you can still see in Essex. (A popular actor in the still thriving category of Victorian melodrama, Ingatestone played Bleak House in a recent television adaptation of Dickens's novel.) *Audley's* and several of her other books are much better crafted and more stylish than the manufactured potboilers, but they are never tame or well behaved. Even Queen Victoria was a fan, despite the critics who decried Braddon's topics and popularity.

"Good Lady Ducayne" demonstrates Braddon's lively and literate style and her gift for dialogue. It was published late in her career, in 1896, in the February issue of the *Strand*. Braddon weaves together several concerns about blood that were prevalent in late-nineteenth-century England, many of which Bram Stoker would address the following year in *Dracula*. Never have such innocent-sounding questions been so fraught with doom as these, asked of Braddon's heroine, naïve young Bella Rolleston: "Have you good health? Are you strong and active, able to eat well, sleep well, walk well, able to enjoy all that there is good in life?"

Good Lady Ducayne

BELLA ROLLESTON HAD MADE up her mind that her only chance of earning her bread and helping her mother to an occasional crust was by going out into the great unknown world as companion to a lady. She was willing to go to any lady rich enough to pay her a salary and so eccentric as to wish for a hired companion. Five shillings told off reluctantly from one of those sovereigns which were so rare with the mother and daughter, and which melted away so quickly, five solid shillings, had been handed to a smartly-dressed lady in an office in Harbeck Street, London, W., in the hope that this very Superior Person would find a situation and a salary for Miss Rolleston. The Superior Person glanced at the two half-crowns as they lay on the table where Bella's hand had placed them, to make sure they were neither of them florins, before she wrote a description of Bella's qualifications and requirements in a formidable-looking ledger.

"Age?" she asked, curtly.

"Eighteen, last July."

"Any accomplishments?"

"No; I am not at all accomplished. If I were I should want to be a governess—a companion seems the lowest stage."

"We have some highly accomplished ladies on our books as companions, or chaperon companions."

"Oh, I know!" babbled Bella, loquacious in her youthful candor. "But that is quite a different thing. Mother hasn't been able to afford a piano since I was twelve years old, so I'm afraid I've forgotten how to play. And I have had to help mother with her needlework, so there hasn't been much time to study."

"Please don't waste time upon explaining what you can't do, but kindly tell me anything you can do," said the Superior Person, crushingly, with her pen poised between delicate fingers waiting to write. "Can you read aloud for two or three hours at a stretch? Are you active and handy, an early riser, a good walker, sweet tempered, and obliging?"

"I can say yes to all those questions except about the sweetness. I think I have a pretty good temper, and I should be anxious to oblige anybody who paid for my services. I should want them to feel that I was really earning my salary."

"The kind of ladies who come to me would not care for a talkative companion," said the Person, severely, having finished writing in her book. "My connection lies chiefly among the aristocracy, and in that class considerable deference is expected."

"Oh, of course," said Bella; "but it's quite different when I'm talking to you. I want to tell you all about myself once and forever."

"I am glad it is to be only once!" said the Person, with the edges of her lips.

The Person was of uncertain age, tightly laced in a black silk gown. She had a powdery complexion and a handsome clump of somebody else's hair on the top of her head. It may be that Bella's girlish freshness and vivacity had an irritating effect upon nerves weakened by an eight-hour day in that overheated second floor in Harbeck Street. To Bella the official apartment, with its Brussels carpet, velvet curtains and velvet chairs, and French clock, ticking loud on the marble chimney-piece, suggested the luxury of a palace, as compared with another second floor in Walworth where

Mrs. Rolleston and her daughter had managed to exist for the last six years.

"Do you think you have anything on your books that would suit me?" faltered Bella, after a pause.

"Oh, dear, no; I have nothing in view at present," answered the Person, who had swept Bella's half-crowns into a drawer, absent-mindedly, with the tips of her fingers. "You see, you are so very unformed—so much too young to be companion to a lady of position. It is a pity you have not enough education for a nursery governess; that would be more in your line."

"And do you think it will be very long before you can get me a situation?" asked Bella, doubtfully.

"I really cannot say. Have you any particular reason for being so impatient—not a love affair, I hope?"

"A love affair!" cried Bella, with flaming cheeks. "What utter nonsense. I want a situation because mother is poor, and I hate being a burden to her. I want a salary that I can share with her."

"There won't be much margin for sharing in the salary you are likely to get at your age—and with your—very—unformed manners," said the Person, who found Bella's peony cheeks, bright eyes, and unbridled vivacity more and more oppressive.

"Perhaps if you'd be kind enough to give me back the fee I could take it to an agency where the connection isn't quite so aristocratic," said Bella, who—as she told her mother in her recital of the interview—was determined not to be sat upon.

"You will find no agency that can do more for you than mine," replied the Person, whose harpy fingers never relinquished coin. "You will have to wait for your opportunity. Yours is an exceptional case: but I will bear you in mind, and if anything suitable offers I will write to you. I cannot say more than that."

The half-contemptuous bend of the stately head, weighted with borrowed hair, indicated the end of the interview. Bella went back to Walworth—tramped sturdily every inch of the way in the September afternoon—and "took off" the Superior Person for the amusement of her mother and the landlady, who lingered in the shabby little sitting-room after bringing in the tea-tray, to applaud Miss Rolleston's "taking off."

"Dear, dear, what a mimic she is!" said the landlady. "You ought to have let her go on the stage, mum. She might have made her fortune as an actress."

II

BELLA WAITED AND HOPED, and listened for the postman's knocks which brought such store of letters for the parlors and the first floor, and so few for that humble second floor, where mother and daughter sat sewing with hand and with wheel and treadle, for the greater part of the day. Mrs. Rolleston was a lady by birth and education; but it had been her bad fortune to marry a scoundrel; for the last half-dozen years she had been that worst of widows, a wife whose husband had deserted her. Happily, she was courageous, industrious, and a clever needlewoman; and she had been able just to earn a living for herself and her only child, by making mantles and cloaks for a West-end house. It was not a luxurious living. Cheap lodgings in a shabby street off the Walworth Road, scanty dinners, homely food, well-worn raiment, had been the portion of mother and daughter; but they loved each other so dearly, and Nature had made them both so light-hearted, that they had contrived somehow to be happy.

But now this idea of going out into the world as companion to some fine lady had rooted itself into Bella's mind, and although she idolized her mother, and although the parting of mother and daughter must needs tear two loving hearts into shreds, the girl longed for enterprise and change and excitement, as the pages of old longed to be knights, and to start for the Holy Land to break a lance with the infidel.

She grew tired of racing downstairs every time the postman

knocked, only to be told "nothing for you, miss," by the smudgy-faced drudge who picked up the letters from the passage floor. "Nothing for you, miss," grinned the lodging-house drudge, till at last Bella took heart of grace and walked up to Harbeck Street, and asked the Superior Person how it was that no situation had been found for her.

"You are too young," said the Person, "and you want a salary."

"Of course I do," answered Bella; "don't other people want salaries?"

"Young ladies of your age generally want a comfortable home."

"I don't," snapped Bella: "I want to help mother."

"You can call again this day week," said the Person; "or, if I hear of anything in the meantime, I will write to you."

No letter came from the Person, and in exactly a week Bella put on her neatest hat, the one that had been seldomest caught in the rain, and trudged off to Harbeck Street.

It was a dull October afternoon, and there was a greyness in the air which might turn to fog before night. The Walworth Road shops gleamed brightly through that grey atmosphere, and though to a young lady reared in Mayfair or Belgravia such shop-windows would have been unworthy of a glance, they were a snare and temptation for Bella. There were so many things that she longed for, and would never be able to buy.

Harbeck Street is apt to be empty at this dead season of the year, a long, long street, an endless perspective of eminently respectable houses. The Person's office was at the further end, and Bella looked down that long, grey vista almost despairingly, more tired than usual with the trudge from Walworth. As she looked, a carriage passed her, an old-fashioned, yellow chariot, on cee springs, drawn by a pair of high grey horses, with the stateliest of coachmen driving them, and a tall footman sitting by his side.

"It looks like the fairy godmother's coach," thought Bella. "I shouldn't wonder if it began by being a pumpkin."

It was a surprise when she reached the Person's door to find the yellow chariot standing before it, and the tall footman waiting near the doorstep. She was almost afraid to go in and meet the owner of that splendid carriage. She had caught only a glimpse of its occupant as the chariot rolled by, a plumed bonnet, a patch of ermine.

The Person's smart page ushered her upstairs and knocked at the official door. "Miss Rolleston," he announced, apologetically, while Bella waited outside.

"Show her in," said the Person, quickly; and then Bella heard her murmuring something in a low voice to her client.

Bella went in fresh, blooming, a living image of youth and hope, and before she looked at the Person her gaze was riveted by the owner of the chariot.

Never had she seen anyone as old as the old lady sitting by the Person's fire: a little old figure, wrapped from chin to feet in an ermine mantle; a withered, old face under a plumed bonnet—a face so wasted by age that it seemed only a pair of eyes and a peaked chin. The nose was peaked, too, but between the sharply pointed chin and the great, shining eyes, the small, aquiline nose was hardly visible.

"This is Miss Rolleston, Lady Ducayne."

Claw-like fingers, flashing with jewels, lifted a double eyeglass to Lady Ducayne's shining black eyes, and through the glasses Bella saw those unnaturally bright eyes magnified to a gigantic size, and glaring at her awfully.

"Miss Torpinter has told me all about you," said the old voice that belonged to the eyes. "Have you good health? Are you strong and active, able to eat well, sleep well, walk well, able to enjoy all that there is good in life?"

"I have never known what it is to be ill, or idle," answered Bella.

"Then I think you will do for me."

"Of course, in the event of references being perfectly satisfactory," put in the Person.

"I don't want references. The young woman looks frank and innocent. I'll take her on trust."

"So like you, dear Lady Ducayne," murmured Miss Torpinter.

"I want a strong young woman whose health will give me no trouble."

"You have been so unfortunate in that respect," cooed the Person, whose voice and manner were subdued to a melting sweetness by the old woman's presence.

"Yes, I've been rather unlucky," grunted Lady Ducayne.

"But I am sure Miss Rolleston will not disappoint you, though certainly after your unpleasant experience with Miss Tomson, who looked the picture of health—and Miss Blandy, who said she had never seen a doctor since she was vaccinated—"

"Lies, no doubt," muttered Lady Ducayne, and then turning to Bella, she asked, curtly, "You don't mind spending the winter in Italy, I suppose?"

In Italy! The very word was magical. Bella's fair young face flushed crimson.

"It has been the dream of my life to see Italy," she gasped.

From Walworth to Italy! How far, how impossible such a journey had seemed to that romantic dreamer.

"Well, your dream will be realized. Get yourself ready to leave Charing Cross by the train deluxe this day week at eleven. Be sure you are at the station a quarter before the hour. My people will look after you and your luggage."

Lady Ducayne rose from her chair, assisted by her crutch-stick, and Miss Torpinter escorted her to the door.

"And with regard to salary?" questioned the Person on the way.

"Salary, oh, the same as usual—and if the young woman wants a quarter's pay in advance you can write to me for a check," Lady Ducayne answered, carelessly.

Miss Torpinter went all the way downstairs with her client, and waited to see her seated in the yellow chariot. When she came upstairs again she was slightly out of breath, and she had resumed that superior manner which Bella had found so crushing.

"You may think yourself uncommonly lucky, Miss Rolleston,"

she said. "I have dozens of young ladies on my books whom I might have recommended for this situation—but I remembered having told you to call this afternoon—and I thought I would give you a chance. Old Lady Ducayne is one of the best people on my books. She gives her companion a hundred a year, and pays all traveling expenses. You will live in the lap of luxury."

"A hundred a year! How too lovely! Shall I have to dress very grandly? Does Lady Ducayne keep much company?"

"At her age! No, she lives in seclusion—in her own apartments—her French maid, her footman, her medical attendant, her courier."

"Why did those other companions leave her?" asked Bella.

"Their health broke down!"

"Poor things, and so they had to leave?"

"Yes, they had to leave. I suppose you would like a quarter's salary in advance?"

"Oh, yes, please. I shall have things to buy."

"Very well, I will write for Lady Ducayne's check, and I will send you the balance—after deducting my commission for the year."

"To be sure, I had forgotten the commission."

"You don't suppose I keep this office for pleasure."

"Of course not," murmured Bella, remembering the five shillings entrance fee; but nobody could expect a hundred a year and a winter in Italy for five shillings.

III

FROM MISS ROLLESTON, AT Cap Ferrino, to Mrs. Rolleston, in Beresford Street, Walworth, London.

How I wish you could see this place, dearest; the blue sky, the olive woods, the orange and lemon orchards between the cliffs and the sea—sheltering in the hollow of the great hills—and with summer waves dancing up to the narrow ridge of pebbles and weeds which is the Italian idea of a beach! Oh, how I wish you could see it all, mother dear, and bask in this sunshine, that makes it so difficult to believe the date at the head of this paper. November! The air is like an English June—the sun is so hot that I can't walk a few yards without an umbrella. And to think of you at Walworth while I am here! I could cry at the thought that perhaps you will never see this lovely coast, this wonderful sea, these summer flowers that bloom in winter. There is a hedge of pink geraniums under my window, mother—a thick, rank hedge, as if the flowers grew wild—and there are Dijon roses climbing over arches and palisades all along the terrace—a rose garden full of bloom in November! Just picture it all! You could never imagine the luxury of this hotel. It is nearly new, and has been built and decorated regardless of expense. Our rooms are upholstered in pale blue satin, which shows up Lady Ducayne's parchment complexion; but as she sits all day in a corner of the balcony basking in the sun, except when she is in her carriage, and all the evening in her armchair close to the fire, and never sees anyone but her own people, her complexion matters very little.

She has the handsomest suite of rooms in the hotel. My bedroom is inside hers, the sweetest room—all blue satin and white lace—white enameled furniture, looking-glasses on every wall, till I know my pert little profile as I never knew it before. The room was really meant for Lady Ducayne's dressing-room, but she ordered one of the blue satin couches to be arranged as a bed for me—the prettiest little bed, which I can wheel near the window on sunny mornings, as it is on casters and easily moved about. I feel as if Lady Ducayne were a funny old grandmother, who had suddenly appeared in my life, very, very rich, and very, very kind.

She is not at all exacting. I read aloud to her a good deal, and she dozes and nods while I read. Sometimes I hear her moaning in her sleep—as if she had troublesome dreams. When she is tired of my reading she orders Francine, her maid, to read a French novel to her, and I hear her chuckle and groan now and then, as if she were more interested in those books than in Dickens or Scott. My French is not good enough to follow Francine, who reads very quickly. I have a great deal of liberty, for Lady Ducayne often tells me to run away and amuse myself; I roam about the hills for hours. Everything is so lovely. I lose myself in olive woods, always climbing up and up towards the pine woods above—and above the pines there are the snow mountains that just show their white peaks above the dark hills. Oh, you poor dear, how can I ever make you understand what this place is like—you, whose poor, tired eyes have only the opposite side of Beresford Street? Sometimes I go no farther than the terrace in front of the hotel, which is a favorite lounging-place with everybody. The gardens lie below, and the tennis courts where I some- times play with a very nice girl, the only person in the hotel with whom I have made friends. She is a year older than I, and has come to Cap Ferrino with her brother, a doctor—or a medical student, who is going to be a doctor. He passed his M.B. exam. at Edinburgh just before they left home, Lotta told me. He came to Italy entirely on his sister's account. She had a troublesome chest attack last summer and was ordered to win- ter abroad. They are orphans, quite alone in the world, and so fond of each other. It is very nice for me to have such a friend as Lotta. She is so thoroughly respectable. I can't help using that word, for some of the girls in this hotel go on in a way that I know you would shudder at. Lotta was brought up by an aunt, deep down in the country, and knows hardly anything about life. Her brother won't allow her to read a novel, French or English, that he has not read and approved.

"He treats me like a child," she told me, "but I don't mind, for it's nice to know somebody loves me, and cares about what I do, and even about my thoughts."

Perhaps this is what makes some girls so eager to marry—the want of someone strong and brave and honest and true to care for them and order them about. I want no one, mother darling, for I have you, and you are all the world to me. No husband could ever come between us two. If I ever were to marry he would have only the second place in my heart. But I don't suppose I ever shall marry, or even know what it is like to have an offer of marriage. No young man can afford to marry a penniless girl nowadays. Life is too expensive.

Mr. Stafford, Lotta's brother, is very clever, and very kind. He thinks it is rather hard for me to have to live with such an old woman as Lady Ducayne, but then he does not know how poor we are—you and I—and what a wonderful life this seems to me in this lovely place. I feel a selfish wretch for enjoying all my luxuries, while you, who want them so much more than I, have none of them—hardly know what they are like—do you, dearest?—for my scamp of a father began to go to the dogs soon after you were married, and since then life has been all trouble and care and struggle for you.

This letter was written when Bella had been less than a month at Cap Ferrino, before the novelty had worn off the landscape, and before the pleasure of luxurious surroundings had begun to cloy. She wrote to her mother every week, such long letters as girls who have lived in closest companionship with a mother alone can write; letters that are like a diary of heart and mind. She wrote gaily always; but when the new year began Mrs. Rolleston thought she detected a note of melancholy under all those lively details about the place and the people.

"My poor girl is getting homesick," she thought. "Her heart is in Beresford Street."

It might be that she missed her new friend and companion, Lotta Stafford, who had gone with her brother for a little tour to Genoa and Spezia, and as far as Pisa. They were to return before February; but in the meantime Bella might naturally feel very solitary among all those strangers, whose manners and doings she described so well.

The mother's instinct had been true. Bella was not so happy as she had been in that first flush of wonder and delight which followed the change from Walworth to the Riviera. Somehow, she knew not how, lassitude had crept upon her. She no longer loved to climb the hills, no longer flourished her orange stick in sheer gladness of heart as her light feet skipped over the rough ground and the coarse grass on the mountainside. The odor of rosemary and thyme, the fresh breath of the sea, no longer filled her with rapture. She thought of Beresford Street and her mother's face with a sick longing. They were so far—so far away! And then she thought of Lady Ducayne, sitting by the heaped-up olive logs in the overheated salon—thought of that wizened-nutcracker profile, and those gleaming eyes, with an invincible horror.

Visitors at the hotel had told her that the air of Cap Ferrino was relaxing—better suited to age than to youth, to sickness than to health. No doubt it was so. She was not so well as she had been at Walworth; but she told herself that she was suffering only from the pain of separation from the dear companion of her girlhood, the mother who had been nurse, sister, friend, flatterer, all things in this world to her. She had shed many tears over that parting, had spent many a melancholy hour on the marble terrace with yearning eyes looking westward, and with her heart's desire a thousand miles away.

She was sitting in her favorite spot, an angle at the eastern end of the terrace, a quiet little nook sheltered by orange trees, when she heard a couple of Riviera habitués talking in the garden below. They were sitting on a bench against the terrace wall.

She had no idea of listening to their talk, till the sound of Lady Ducayne's name attracted her, and then she listened without any thought of wrong-doing. They were talking no secrets—just casually discussing a hotel acquaintance.

They were two elderly people whom Bella only knew by sight. An English clergyman who had wintered abroad for half his lifetime; a stout, comfortable, well-to-do spinster, whose chronic bronchitis obliged her to migrate annually.

"I have met her about Italy for the last ten years," said the lady; "but have never found out her real age."

"I put her down at a hundred—not a year less," replied the parson. "Her reminiscences all go back to the Regency. She was evidently then in her zenith; and I have heard her say things that showed she was in Parisian society when the First Empire was at its best—before Josephine was divorced."

"She doesn't talk much now."

"No; there's not much life left in her. She is wise in keeping herself secluded. I only wonder that wicked old quack, her Italian doctor, didn't finish her off years ago."

"I should think it must be the other way, and that he keeps her alive."

"My dear Miss Manders, do you think foreign quackery ever kept anybody alive?"

"Well, there she is—and she never goes anywhere without him. He certainly has an unpleasant countenance."

"Unpleasant," echoed the parson, "I don't believe the foul fiend himself can beat him in ugliness. I pity that poor young woman who has to live between old Lady Ducayne and Dr. Parravicini."

"But the old lady is very good to her companions."

"No doubt. She is very free with her cash; the servants call her good Lady Ducayne. She is a withered old female Croesus, and knows she'll never be able to get through her money, and doesn't relish the idea of other people enjoying it when she's in her coffin. People who live to be as old as she is become slavishly attached to life. I daresay she's generous to those poor girls—but she can't make them happy. They die in her service."

"Don't say they, Mr. Carton; I know that one poor girl died at Mentone last spring."

"Yes, and another poor girl died in Rome three years ago. I was there at the time. Good Lady Ducayne left her there in an English family. The girl had every comfort. The old woman was very liberal to her—but she died. I tell you, Miss Manders, it is not good for any young woman to live with two such horrors as Lady Ducayne and Parravicini."

They talked of other things—but Bella hardly heard them. She sat motionless, and a cold wind seemed to come down upon her from the mountains and to creep up to her from the sea, till she shivered as she sat there in the sunshine, in the shelter of the orange trees in the midst of all that beauty and brightness.

Yes, they were uncanny, certainly, the pair of them—she so like an aristocratic witch in her withered old age; he of no particular age, with a face that was more like a waxen mask than any human countenance Bella had ever seen. What did it matter? Old age is venerable, and worthy of all reverence; and Lady Ducayne had been very kind to her. Dr. Parravicini was a harmless, inoffensive student, who seldom looked up from the book he was reading. He had his private sitting-room, where he made experiments in chemistry and natural science—perhaps in alchemy. What could it matter to Bella? He had always been polite to her, in his far-off way. She could not be more happily placed than she was—in this palatial hotel, with this rich old lady.

No doubt she missed the young English girl who had been so friendly, and it might be that she missed the girl's brother, for Mr. Stafford had talked to her a good deal—had interested himself in the books she was reading, and her manner of amusing herself when she was not on duty.

"You must come to our little salon when you are 'off,' as the hospital nurses call it, and we can have some music. No doubt you play and sing?" Upon which Bella had to own with a blush of shame that she had forgotten how to play the piano ages ago.

"Mother and I used to sing duets sometimes between the lights, without accompaniment," she said, and the tears came into her eyes as she thought of the humble room, the half-hour's respite from work, the sewing machine standing where a piano ought to have been, and her mother's plaintive voice, so sweet, so true, so dear.

Sometimes she found herself wondering whether she would ever see that beloved mother again. Strange forebodings came into her mind. She was angry with herself for giving way to melancholy thoughts.

One day she questioned Lady Ducayne's French maid about those two companions who had died within three years.

"They were poor, feeble creatures," Francine told her. "They looked fresh and bright enough when they came to Milady; but they ate too much, and they were lazy. They died of luxury and idleness. Milady was too kind to them. They had nothing to do; and so they took to fancying things; fancying the air didn't suit them, that they couldn't sleep."

"I sleep well enough, but I have had a strange dream several times since I have been in Italy."

"Ah, you had better not begin to think about dreams, or you will be like those other girls. They were dreamers—and they dreamt themselves into the cemetery."

The dream troubled her a little, not because it was a ghastly or frightening dream, but on account of sensations which she had never felt before in sleep—a whirring of wheels that went round in her brain, a great noise like a whirlwind, but rhythmical like the ticking of a gigantic clock: and then in the midst of this uproar as of winds and waves she seemed to sink into a gulf of unconsciousness, out of sleep into far deeper sleep—total extinction. And then, after that black interval, there had come the sound of voices, and then again the whirr of wheels, louder and louder—and again the black—and then she awoke, feeling languid and oppressed.

She told Dr. Parravicini of her dream one day, on the only occasion when she wanted his professional advice. She had suffered rather severely from the mosquitoes before Christmas—and had been almost frightened at finding a wound upon her arm which she could only attribute to the venomous sting of one of these torturers. Parravicini put on his glasses, and scrutinized the angry mark on the round, white arm, as Bella stood before him and Lady Ducayne with her sleeve rolled up above her elbow.

"Yes, that's rather more than a joke," he said; "he has caught you on the top of a vein. What a vampire! But there's no harm done, signorina, nothing that a little dressing of mine won't heal. You must always show me any bite of this nature. It might be dangerous if neglected. These creatures feed on poison and disseminate it."

"And to think that such tiny creatures can bite like this," said Bella; "my arm looks as if it had been cut by a knife."

"If I were to show you a mosquito's sting under my microscope you wouldn't be surprised at that," replied Parravicini.

Bella had to put up with the mosquito bites, even when they came on the top of a vein, and produced that ugly wound. The wound recurred now and then at longish intervals, and Bella found Dr. Parravicini's dressing a speedy cure. If he were the quack his enemies called him, he had at least a light hand and a delicate touch in performing this small operation.

"Bella Rolleston to Mrs. Rolleston—April 14th.

EVER DEAREST,

Behold the check for my second quarter's salary—five and twenty pounds. There is no one to pinch off a whole tenner for a year's commission as there was last time, so it is all for you, mother, dear. I have plenty of pocket-money in hand from the cash I brought away with me, when you insisted on my keeping more than I wanted. It isn't possible to spend money here—except on occasional tips to servants, or sous to beggars and children—unless one had lots to spend, for everything one would like to buy—tortoise-shell, coral, lace—is so ridiculously dear that only a millionaire ought to look at it. Italy is a dream of beauty: but for shopping, give me Newington Causeway.

You ask me so earnestly if I am quite well that I fear my letters must have been very dull lately. Yes, dear, I am well—but I am not quite so strong as I was when I used to trudge to the West-end to buy half a pound of tea—just for a constitutional walk—or to Dulwich to look at the pictures. Italy is relaxing; and I feel what the people here call "slack." But I fancy I can see your dear face looking worried as you read this. Indeed, and indeed, I am not ill. I am only a little tired of this lovely scene—as I *suppose one might get tired of looking at one of Turner's pictures if it hung on a wall that was always opposite one. I think of you every hour in every day—think of you and our homely little room—our dear little shabby parlor, with the armchairs from the wreck of your old home, and Dick singing in his cage over the sewing machine. Dear, shrill, maddening Dick, who, we flattered ourselves, was so passionately fond of us. Do tell me in your next letter that he is well.*

My friend Lotta and her brother never came back after all. They went from Pisa to Rome. Happy mortals! And they are to be on the Italian lakes in May; which lake was not decided when Lotta last wrote to me. She has been a charming correspondent, and has confided all her little flirtations to me. We are all to go to Bellaggio next week—by Genoa and Milan. Isn't that lovely? Lady Ducayne travels by the easiest stages—except when she is bottled up in the train deluxe. We shall stop two days at Genoa and one at Milan. What a bore I shall be to you with my talk about Italy when I come home.

Love and love—and ever more love from your adoring, BELLA.

IV

HERBERT STAFFORD AND HIS sister had often talked of the pretty English girl with her fresh complexion, which made such a pleasant touch of rosy color among all those sallow faces at the Grand Hotel. The young doctor thought of her with a compassionate tenderness— her utter loneliness in that great hotel where there were so many people, her bondage to that old, old woman, where everybody else was free to think of nothing but enjoying life. It was a hard fate; and the poor child was evidently devoted to her mother, and felt the pain of separation—"only two of them, and very poor, and all the world to each other," he thought.

Lotta told him one morning that they were to meet again at Bellaggio. "The old thing and her court are to be there before we are," she said. "I shall be charmed to have Bella again. She is so bright and gay—in spite of an occasional touch of homesickness. I never took to a girl on a short acquaintance as I did to her."

"I like her best when she is homesick," said Herbert; "for then I am sure she has a heart."

"What have you to do with hearts, except for dissection? Don't forget that Bella is an absolute pauper. She told me in confidence that her mother makes mantles for a West-end shop. You can hardly have a lower depth than that."

"I shouldn't think any less of her if her mother made matchboxes."

"Not in the abstract—of course not. Matchboxes are honest labor. But you couldn't marry a girl whose mother makes mantles."

"We haven't come to the consideration of that question yet," answered Herbert, who liked to provoke his sister.

In two years' hospital practice he had seen too much of the grim realities of life to retain any prejudices about rank. Cancer, phthisis, gangrene, leave a man with little respect for the humanity. The kernel is always the same—fearfully and wonderfully made—a subject for pity and terror.

Mr. Stafford and his sister arrived at Bellaggio in a fair May evening. The sun was going down as the steamer approached the pier; and all that glory of purple bloom which curtains every wall at this season of the year flushed and deepened in the glowing light. A group of ladies were standing on the pier watching the arrivals, and among them Herbert saw a pale face that startled him out of his wonted composure.

"There she is," murmured Lotta, at his elbow, "but how dreadfully changed. She looks a wreck."

They were shaking hands with her a few minutes later, and a flush had lighted up her poor pinched face in the pleasure of meeting.

"I thought you might come this evening," she said. "We have been here a week."

She did not add that she had been there every evening to watch the boat in, and a good many times during the day. The Grand Bretagne was close by, and it had been easy for her to creep to the pier when the boat bell rang. She felt a joy in meeting these people again; a sense of being with friends; a confidence which Lady Ducayne's goodness had never inspired in her.

"Oh, you poor darling, how awfully ill you must have been," exclaimed Lotta, as the two girls embraced.

Bella tried to answer, but her voice was choked with tears.

"What has been the matter, dear? That horrid influenza, I suppose?"

"No, no, I have not been ill—I have only felt a little weaker than I used to be. I don't think the air of Cap Ferrino quite agreed with me."

"It must have disagreed with you abominably. I never saw such a change in anyone. Do let Herbert doctor you. He is fully qualified, you know. He prescribed for ever so many influenza patients at the Londres. They were glad to get advice from an English doctor in a friendly way."

"I am sure he must be very clever!" faltered Bella, "but there is really nothing the matter. I am not ill, and if I were ill, Lady Ducayne's physician—"

"That dreadful man with the yellow face? I would as soon one of the Borgias prescribed for me. I hope you haven't been taking any of his medicines."

"No, dear, I have taken nothing. I have never complained of being ill."

This was said while they were all three walking to the hotel. The Staffords' rooms had been secured in advance, pretty ground-floor rooms, opening into the garden. Lady Ducayne's statelier apartments were on the floor above.

"I believe these rooms are just under ours," said Bella.

"Then it will be all the easier for you to run down to us," replied Lotta, which was not really the case, as the grand staircase was in the center of the hotel.

"Oh, I shall find it easy enough," said Bella. "I'm afraid you'll have too much of my society. Lady Ducayne sleeps away half the day in this warm weather, so I have a good deal of idle time; and I get awfully moped thinking of mother and home."

Her voice broke upon the last word. She could not have thought of that poor lodging which went by the name of home more tenderly had it been the most beautiful that art and wealth ever created. She moped and pined in this lovely garden, with the sunlit lake and the romantic hills spreading out their beauty before her. She was homesick and she had dreams; or, rather, an occasional recurrence of that one bad dream with all its strange sensations—it was more like a hallucination than dreaming—the whirring of wheels, the sinking into an abyss, the struggling back to consciousness. She had the dream shortly before she left Cap Ferrino, but not since she had come to Bellaggio, and she began to hope the air in this lake district suited her better, and that those strange sensations would never return.

Mr. Stafford wrote a prescription and had it made up at the chemist's near the hotel. It was a powerful tonic, and after two bottles, and a row or two on the lake, and some rambling over the hills and in the meadows where the spring flowers made earth seem paradise, Bella's spirits and looks improved as if by magic.

"It is a wonderful tonic," she said, but perhaps in her heart of hearts she knew that the doctor's kind voice, and the friendly hand that helped her in and out of the boat, and the lake, had something to do with her cure.

"I hope you don't forget that her mother makes mantles," Lotta said warningly.

"Or matchboxes; it is just the same thing, so far as I am concerned."

"You mean that in no circumstances could you think of marrying her?"

"I mean that if ever I love a woman well enough to think of

marrying her, riches or rank will count for nothing with me. But I fear—I fear your poor friend may not live to be any man's wife."

"Do you think her so very ill?"

He sighed, and left the question unanswered.

One day, while they were gathering wild hyacinths in an upland meadow, Bella told Mr. Stafford about her bad dream.

"It is curious only because it is hardly like a dream," she said. "I daresay you could find some commonsense reason for it. The position of my head on my pillow, or the atmosphere, or something."

And then she described her sensations; how in the midst of sleep there came a sudden sense of suffocation; and then those whirring wheels, so loud, so terrible; and then a blank, and then a coming back to waking consciousness.

"Have you ever had chloroform given you—by a dentist, for instance?"

"Never—Dr. Parravicini asked me that question one day."

"Lately?"

"No, long ago, when we were in the train deluxe."

"Has Dr. Parravicini prescribed for you since you began to feel weak and ill?"

"Oh, he has given me a tonic from time to time, but I hate medicine, and took very little of the stuff. And then I am not ill, only weaker than I used to be. I was ridiculously strong and well when I lived at Walworth, and used to take long walks every day. Mother made me take those tramps to Dulwich or Norwood, for fear I should suffer from too much sewing machine; sometimes— but very seldom—she went with me. She was generally toiling at home while I was enjoying fresh air and exercise. And she was very careful about our food—that, however plain it was, it should be always nourishing and ample. I owe it to her care that I grew up such a great, strong creature."

"You don't look great or strong now, you poor dear," said Lotta.

"I'm afraid Italy doesn't agree with me."

"Perhaps it is not Italy, but being cooped up with Lady Ducayne that has made you ill."

"But I am never cooped up. Lady Ducayne is absurdly kind, and lets me roam about or sit in the balcony all day if I like. I have read more novels since I have been with her than in all the rest of my life."

"Then she is very different from the average old lady, who is usually a slave driver," said Stafford. "I wonder why she carries a companion about with her if she has so little need of society."

"Oh, I am only part of her state. She is inordinately rich—and the salary she gives me doesn't count. Apropos of Dr. Parravicini, I know he is a clever doctor, for he cures my horrid mosquito bites."

"A little ammonia would do that, in the early stage of the mischief. But there are no mosquitoes to trouble you now."

"Oh, yes, there are; I had a bite just before we left Cap Ferrino." She pushed up her loose lawn sleeve, and exhibited a scar, which he scrutinized intently, with a surprised and puzzled look.

"This is no mosquito bite," he said.

"Oh, yes, it is—unless there are snakes or adders at Cap Ferrino."

"It is not a bite at all. You are trifling with me. Miss Rolleston—you have allowed that wretched Italian quack to bleed you. They killed the greatest man in modern Europe that way, remember. How very foolish of you."

"I was never bled in my life, Mr. Stafford."

"Nonsense! Let me look at your other arm. Are there any more mosquito bites?"

"Yes; Dr. Parravicini says I have a bad skin for healing, and that the poison acts more virulently with me than with most people."

Stafford examined both her arms in the broad sunlight, scars new and old.

"You have been very badly bitten, Miss Rolleston," he said, "and if ever I find the mosquito I shall make him smart. But, now tell me, my dear girl, on your word of honor, tell me as you would tell a friend who is sincerely anxious for your health and happiness—as you would tell your mother if she were here to question you—have you no knowledge of any cause for these scars except mosquito bites—no suspicion even?"

"No, indeed! No, upon my honor! I have never seen a mosquito biting my arm. One never does see the horrid little fiends. But I have heard them trumpeting under the curtains and I know that I have often had one of the pestilent wretches buzzing about me."

Later in the day Bella and her friends were sitting at tea in the garden, while Lady Ducayne took her afternoon drive with her doctor.

"How long do you mean to stop with Lady Ducayne, Miss Rolleston?" Herbert Stafford asked, after a thoughtful silence, breaking suddenly upon the trivial talk of the two girls.

"As long as she will go on paying me twenty-five pounds a quarter."

"Even if you feel your health breaking down in her service?"

"It is not the service that has injured my health. You can see that I have really nothing to do—to read aloud for an hour or so once or twice a week; to write a letter once in a while to a London tradesman. I shall never have such an easy time with anybody. And nobody else would give me a hundred a year."

"Then you mean to go on till you break down; to die at your post?"

"Like the other two companions? No! If ever I feel seriously ill—really ill—I shall put myself in a train and go back to Walworth without stopping."

"What about the other two companions?"

"They both died. It was very unlucky for Lady Ducayne. That's why she engaged me; she chose me because I was ruddy and robust. She must feel rather disgusted at my having grown white and weak. By-the-bye, when I told her about the good your tonic had done me, she said she would like to see you and have a little talk with you about her own case."

"And I should like to see Lady Ducayne. When did she say this?"

"The day before yesterday."

"Will you ask her if she will see me this evening?"

"With pleasure! I wonder what you will think of her? She looks rather terrible to a stranger; but Dr. Parravicini says she was once a famous beauty."

It was nearly ten o'clock when Mr. Stafford was summoned by message from Lady Ducayne, whose courier came to conduct him to her ladyship's salon. Bella was reading aloud when the visitor was admitted; and he noticed the languor in the low, sweet tones, the evident effort.

"Shut up the book," said the querulous old voice. "You are beginning to drawl like Miss Blandy."

Stafford saw a small, bent figure crouching over the piled-up olive logs; a shrunken old figure in a gorgeous garment of black and crimson brocade, a skinny throat emerging from a mass of old Venetian lace, clasped with diamonds that flashed like fireflies as the trembling old head turned towards him.

The eyes that looked at him out of the face were almost as bright as the diamonds—the only living feature in that narrow parchment mask. He had seen terrible faces in the hospital—faces on which disease had set dreadful marks—but he had never seen a face that impressed him so painfully as this withered countenance, with its indescribable horror of death outlived, a face that should have been hidden under a coffin-lid years and years ago.

The Italian physician was standing on the other side of the fire-place, smoking a cigarette, and looking down at the little old woman brooding over the hearth as if he were proud of her.

"Good evening, Mr. Stafford; you can go to your room, Bella, and write your everlasting letter to your mother at Walworth," said Lady Ducayne. "I believe she writes a page about every wild flower she discovers in the woods and meadows. I don't know what else she can find to write about," she added, as Bella quietly withdrew to the pretty little bedroom opening out of Lady Ducayne's spacious apartment. Here, as at Cap Ferrino, she slept in a room adjoining the old lady's.

"You are a medical man, I understand, Mr. Stafford."

"I am a qualified practitioner, but I have not begun to practice."

"You have begun upon my companion, she tells me."

"I have prescribed for her, certainly, and I am happy to find my prescription has done her good; but I look upon that improvement as temporary. Her case will require more drastic treatment."

"Never mind her case. There is nothing the matter with the girl—absolutely nothing—except girlish nonsense; too much liberty and not enough work."

"I understand that two of your ladyship's previous companions died of the same disease," said Stafford, looking first at Lady Ducayne, who gave her tremulous old head an impatient jerk, and then at Parravicini, whose yellow complexion had paled a little under Stafford's scrutiny.

"Don't bother me about my companions, sir," said Lady Ducayne. "I sent for you to consult you about myself—not about a parcel of anemic girls. You are young, and medicine is a progressive science, the newspapers tell me. Where have you studied?"

"In Edinburgh—and in Paris."

"Two good schools. And know all the new-fangled theories, the modern discoveries—that remind one of the medieval witchcraft, of Albertus Magnus, and George Ripley; you have studied hypnotism—electricity?"

"And the transfusion of blood," said Stafford, very slowly, looking at Parravicini.

"Have you made any discovery that teaches you to prolong human life—any elixir—any mode of treatment? I want my life prolonged, young man. That man there has been my physician for thirty years. He does all he can to keep me alive—after his lights. He studies all the new theories of all the scientists—but he is old;

he gets older every day—his brainpower is going—he is bigoted—prejudiced—can't receive new ideas—can't grapple with new systems. He will let me die if I am not on my guard against him."

"You are of an unbelievable ingratitude, Ecclenza," said Parravicini.

"Oh, you needn't complain. I have paid you thousands to keep me alive. Every year of my life has swollen your hoards; you know there is nothing to come to you when I am gone. My whole fortune is left to endow a home for indigent women of quality who have reached their ninetieth year. Come, Mr. Stafford, I am a rich woman. Give me a few years more in the sunshine, a few years more aboveground, and I will give you the price of a fashionable London practice—I will set you up at the West-End."

"How old are you, Lady Ducayne?"

"I was born the day Louis XVI was guillotined."

"Then I think you have had your share of the sunshine and the pleasures of the earth, and that you should spend your few remaining days in repenting your sins and trying to make atonement for the young lives that have been sacrificed to your love of life."

"What do you mean by that, sir?"

"Oh, Lady Ducayne, need I put your wickedness and your physician's still greater wickedness in plain words? The poor girl who is now in your employment has been reduced from robust health to a condition of absolute danger by Dr. Parravicini's experimental surgery; and I have no doubt those other two young women who broke down in your service were treated by him in the same manner. I could take upon myself to demonstrate—by most convincing evidence, to a jury of medical men—that Dr. Parravicini has been bleeding Miss Rolleston after putting her under chloroform, at intervals, ever since she has been in your service. The deterioration in the girl's health speaks for itself; the lancet marks upon the girl's arms are unmistakable; and her description of a series of sensations, which she calls a dream, points unmistakably to the administration of chloroform while she was sleeping. A practice so nefarious, so murderous, must, if exposed, result in a sentence only less severe than the punishment of murder."

"I laugh," said Parravicini, with an airy motion of his skinny fingers; "I laugh at once at your theories and at your threats. I, Parravicini Leopold, have no fear that the law can question anything I have done."

"Take the girl away, and let me hear no more of her," cried Lady Ducayne, in the thin, old voice, which so poorly matched the energy and fire of the wicked old brain that guided its utterances. "Let her go back to her mother—I want no more girls to die in my service. There are girls enough and to spare in the world, God knows."

"If you ever engage another companion—or take another English girl into your service, Lady Ducayne, I will make all England ring with the story of your wickedness."

"I want no more girls. I don't believe in his experiments. They have been full of danger for me as well as for the girl—an air bubble, and I should be gone. I'll have no more of his dangerous quackery. I'll find some new man—a better man than you, sir, a discoverer like Pasteur, or Virchow, a genius—to keep me alive. Take your girl away, young man. Marry her if you like. I'll write a check for a thousand pounds, and let her go and live on beef and beer, and get strong and plump again. I'll have no more such experiments. Do you hear, Parravicini?" she screamed, vindictively, the yellow, wrinkled face distorted with fury, the eyes glaring at him.

THE STAFFORDS CARRIED BELLA Rolleston off to Varese next day, she very loath to leave Lady Ducayne, whose liberal salary afforded such help for the dear mother. Herbert Stafford insisted, however, treating Bella as coolly as if he had been the family physician, and she had been given over wholly to his care.

"Do you suppose your mother would let you stop here to die?" he asked. "If Mrs. Rolleston knew how ill you are, she would come post haste to fetch you."

"I shall never be well again till I get back to Walworth," answered Bella, who was low-spirited and inclined to tears this morning, a reaction after her good spirits of yesterday.

"We'll try a week or two at Varese first," said Stafford. "When you can walk halfway up Monte Generoso without palpitation of the heart, you shall go back to Walworth."

"Poor mother, how glad she will be to see me, and how sorry that I've lost such a good place."

This conversation took place on the boat when they were leaving Bellaggio. Lotta had gone to her friend's room at seven o'clock that morning, long before Lady Ducayne's withered eyelids had opened to the daylight, before even Francine, the French maid, was astir, and had helped to pack a Gladstone bag with essentials, and hustled Bella downstairs and out of doors before she could make any strenuous resistance.

"It's all right," Lotta assured her. "Herbert had a good talk with Lady Ducayne last night, and it was settled for you to leave this morning. She doesn't like invalids, you see."

"No," sighed Bella, "she doesn't like invalids. It was very unlucky that I should break down, just like Miss Tomson and Miss Blandy."

"At any rate, you are not dead, like them," answered Lotta, "and my brother says you are not going to die."

IT SEEMED RATHER A dreadful thing to be dismissed in that offhand way, without a word of farewell from her employer.

"I wonder what Miss Torpinter will say when I go to her for another situation," Bella speculated, ruefully, while she and her friends were breakfasting on board the steamer.

"Perhaps you may never want another situation," said Stafford.

"You mean that I may never be well enough to be useful to anybody?"

"No, I don't mean anything of the kind."

It was after dinner at Varese, when Bella had been induced to take a whole glass of Chianti, and quite sparkled after that unaccustomed stimulant, that Mr. Stafford produced a letter from his pocket.

"I forgot to give you Lady Ducayne's letter of adieu!" he said.

"What, did she write to me? I am so glad—I hated to leave her in such a cool way; for after all she was very kind to me, and if I didn't like her it was only because she was too dreadfully old."

She tore open the envelope. The letter was short and to the point:—

Goodbye, child. Go and marry your doctor. I enclose a farewell gift for your trousseau.

—ADELINE DUCAYNE

"A hundred pounds, a whole year's salary—no—why, it's for a—a check for a thousand!" cried Bella. "What a generous old soul! She really is the dearest old thing."

"She just missed being very dear to you, Bella," said Stafford.

He had dropped into the use of her Christian name while they were on board the boat. It seemed natural now that she was to be in his charge till they all three went back to England.

"I shall take upon myself the privileges of an elder brother till we land at Dover," he said; "after that—well, it must be as you please."

The question of their future relations must have been satisfactorily settled before they crossed the Channel, for Bella's next letter to her mother communicated three startling facts.

First, that the inclosed check for £1,000 was to be invested in debenture stock in Mrs. Rolleston's name, and was to be her very own, income and principal, for the rest of her life.

Next, that Bella was going home to Walworth immediately.

And last, that she was going to be married to Mr. Herbert Stafford in the following autumn.

"And I am sure you will adore him, mother, as much as I do," wrote Bella.

"It is all good Lady Ducayne's doing. I never could have married if I had not secured that little nest-egg for you. Herbert says we shall be able to add to it as the years go by, and that wherever we live there shall be always a room in our house for you. The word *mother-in-law* has no terrors for him."

✣

Augustus Hare

(1834–1903)

BORN IN ROME AND educated at Harrow and Oxford, Augustus John Cuthbert Hare grew up in the village of Hurstmonceaux in East Sussex. He was an impressionable child and his nutty family provided him with plenty of material to write about. For a while, every Sunday, he was locked in the vestry of the local Hurstmonceaux Church between services. He spent his time crawling across the tombs of the Lords Dacre, although terrified by their supine effigies, and trying to avoid returning the stare of the two cautionary skulls that grinned upon the tombs (until Hare's aunt buried them despite their alleged provenance as founders of the church). "In the winter holidays," Hare recalled, "the intense cold of the unwarmed church made me so ill, that it led to my miserable penance being remitted."

One would think that such experiences would have driven him straight into confessional fiction, but instead Hare wrote rather admiring volumes about his family members and a long line of travel books, including *Walks in London, Days near Rome, Wanderings in Spain*. They are full of admiring but not particularly exciting sentences such as this one: "It is in its secluded valleys, or its deep orange-groves, along the hanks of its torrents, or amid the heights of the wild mountain-chain which forms its background, that the principal charm of Mentone is to be found." He was also a lover of art. His will comprised mainly bequests of paintings and prints to various friends.

In his autobiography, cleverly titled *The Story of My Life*, Hare recounted a vampire story that he said had been told to him by one Captain Fisher. It appears in the fourth of the six volumes, which were published between 1896 and 1900.

And the Creature Came In

Fisher may sound a very plebeian name, but this family is of a very ancient lineage, and for many hundreds of years they have possessed a very curious old place in Cumberland, which bears the weird name of Croglin Grange. The great characteristic of the house is that never at any period of its very long existence has it been more than one story high, but it has a terrace from which large grounds sweep away towards the church in the hollow, and a fine distant view.

When, in lapse of years, the Fishers outgrew Croglin Grange in family and fortune, they were wise enough not to destroy the long-standing characteristic of the place by adding another story to the house, but they went away to the south, to reside at Thorncombe near Guildford, and they let Croglin Grange.

They were extremely fortunate in their tenants, two brothers and a sister. They heard their praises from all quarters. To their poorer neighbours they were all that is most kind and beneficent, and their neighbours of a higher class spoke of them as a most welcome addition to the little society of the neighbourhood. On their part, the tenants were greatly delighted with their new residence. The arrangement of the house, which would have been a trial to many, was not so to them. In every respect Croglin Grange was exactly suited to them.

The winter was spent most happily by the new inmates of Croglin Grange, who shared in all the little social pleasures of the district, and made themselves very popular. In the following summer there was one day which was dreadfully, annihilatingly hot. The brothers lay under the trees with their books, for it was too hot for any active occupation. The sister sat in the veranda and worked, or tried to work, for in the intense sultriness of that summer day, work was next to impossible. They dined early, and after dinner they still sat out on the veranda, enjoying the cool air which came with the evening, and they watched the sun set, and the moon rise over the belt of trees which separated the grounds from the churchyard, seeing it mount the heavens till the whole lawn was bathed in silver light, across which the long shadows from the shrubbery fell as if embossed, so vivid and distinct were they.

When they separated for the night, all retiring to their rooms on the ground floor (for, as I said, there was no upstairs in that house), the sister felt that the heat was still so great that she could not sleep, and having fastened her window, she did not close the shutters—in that very quiet place it was not necessary—and, propped against the pillows, she still watched the wonderful, the marvellous beauty of that summer night. Gradually she became aware of two lights, two lights which flickered in and out in the belt of trees which separated the lawn from the churchyard, and, as her gaze became fixed upon them, she saw them emerge, fixed in a dark substance, a definite ghastly something, which seemed every moment to become nearer, increasing in size and substance as it approached. Every now and then it was lost for a moment in the long shadows which stretched across the lawn from the trees, and then it emerged larger than ever, and still coming on. As she watched it, the most uncontrollable horror seized her. She longed to get away, but the door was close to the window, and the door was locked on the inside, and while she was unlocking it she must be for an instant nearer to it. She longed to scream, but her voice seemed paralysed, her tongue glued to the roof of her mouth.

Suddenly—she could never explain why afterwards—the terrible object seemed to turn to one side, seemed to be going round the house, not to be coming to her at all, and immediately she jumped out of bed and rushed to the door, but as she was unlocking it she heard scratch, scratch, scratch upon the window, and saw a hideous brown face with flaming eyes glaring in at her. She rushed back to the bed, but the creature continued to scratch, scratch, scratch upon the window.

She felt a sort of mental comfort in the knowledge that the window was securely fastened on the inside. Suddenly the scratching sound ceased, and a kind of pecking sound took its place. Then, in her agony, she became aware that the creature was unpicking the lead! The noise continued, and a diamond pane of glass fell into the room. Then a long bony finger of the creature came in and turned the handle of the window, and the window opened, and the creature came in; and it came across the room, and her terror was so great that she could not scream, and it came up to the bed, and it twisted its long, bony fingers into her hair, and it dragged her head over the side of the bed, and—it bit her violently in the throat.

As it bit her, her voice was released, and she screamed with all her might and main. Her brothers rushed out of their rooms, but the door was locked on the inside. A moment was lost while they got a poker and broke it open. Then the creature had already escaped through the window, and the sister, bleeding violently from a wound in the throat, was lying unconscious over the side of the bed. One brother pursued the creature, which fled before him through the moonlight with gigantic strides, and eventually seemed to disappear over the wall into the churchyard. Then he rejoined his brother by the sister's bedside. She was dreadfully hurt, and her wound was a very definite one, but she was of strong disposition, not even given to romance or superstition, and when she came to herself she said, "What has happened is most extraordinary and I am very much hurt. It seems inexplicable, but of course there is an explanation, and we must wait for it. It will turn out that a lunatic has escaped from some asylum and found his way here." The wound healed, and she appeared to get well, but the doctor who was sent for to her would not believe that she could bear so terrible a shock so easily, and insisted that she must have change, mental and physical; so her brothers took her to Switzerland.

Being a sensible girl, when she went abroad she threw herself at once into the interests of the country she was in. She dried plants, she made sketches, she went up mountains, and as autumn came on, she was the person who urged that they should return to Croglin Grange. "We have taken it," she said, "for seven years, and we have only been there one; and we shall always find it difficult to let a house which is only one story high, so we had better return there; lunatics do not escape every day." As she urged it, her brothers wished nothing better, and the family returned to Cumberland. From there being no upstairs in the house it was impossible to make any great change in their arrangements. The sister occupied the same room, but it is unnecessary to say she always closed the shutters, which, however, as in many old houses, always left one top pane of the window uncovered. The brothers moved, and occupied a room together, exactly opposite that of their sister, and they always kept loaded pistols in their room.

The winter passed most peacefully and happily. In the following March, the sister was suddenly awakened by a sound she remembered only too well—scratch, scratch, scratch upon the window, and, looking up, she saw, climbed up to the topmost pane of the window, the same hideous brown shrivelled face, with glaring eyes, looking in at her. This time she screamed as loud as she could. Her brothers rushed out of their room with pistols, and out of the front door.

The creature was already scudding away across the lawn. One of the brothers fired and hit it in the leg, but still with the other leg it continued to make way, scrambled over the wall into the churchyard, and seemed to disappear into a vault which belonged to a family long extinct.

The next day the brothers summoned all the tenants of Croglin Grange, and in their presence the vault was opened. A horrible scene revealed itself. The vault was full of coffins; they had been broken open, and their contents, horribly mangled and distorted, were scattered over the floor. One coffin alone remained intact. Of that the lid had been lifted, but still lay loose upon the coffin. They raised it, and there, brown, withered, shrivelled, mummified, but quite entire, was the same hideous figure which had looked in at the windows of Croglin Grange, with the marks of a recent pistol-shot in the leg: and they did the only thing that can lay a vampire— they burnt it.

✳

F. G. Loring

(1869–1951)

"THE TOMB OF SARAH" was published in December 1897 in *Pall Mall*, an eclectic British monthly. Lushly illustrated by serious artists, and featuring writers from Hardy to Swinburne (whose "Astrophel" opened the first issue in 1893), *Pall Mall* maintained its high standards until it merged with another magazine on the eve of World War I. It's easier to describe the magazine than the author, because little is known about Frederick George Loring, except that he became a commander in Britain's Royal Navy. In a 2004 article, literary critic Nina Auerbach, author of *Our Vampires, Ourselves* and other books in the field, referred to "the elusive F. G. Loring." Auerbach also said of "The Tomb of Sarah" that the "female vampire is so revolting a schlurper that I assume the author was male." That much we know. Montague Summers, the controversial scholar of witches, were-wolves, vampires, and other monsters, called the following "one of the best vampire stories I know."

The Tomb of Sarah

M Y FATHER WAS THE head of a celebrated firm of church restor-
ers and decorators about sixty years ago. He took a keen interest in his work, and made an especial study of any old legends or
family histories that came under his observation. He was necessarily very well read and thoroughly well posted in all questions of
folk-lore and mediaeval legend. As he kept a careful record of every case he investigated the manuscripts he left at his death have a
special interest. From amongst them I have selected the following,
as being a particularly weird and extraordinary experience. In presenting it to the public I feel it is superfluous to apologize for its
supernatural character.

My Father's Diary

1841.—*JUNE 17TH*. RECEIVED a commission from my old friend
Peter Grant to enlarge and restore the chancel of his church at
Hagarstone, in the wilds of the West Country.

July 5th. Went down to Hagarstone with my head man, Somers.
A very long and tiring journey.

July 7th. Got the work well started. The old church is one of special interest to the antiquarian, and I shall endeavour while restoring

it to alter the existing arrangements as little as possible. One large tomb, however, must be moved bodily ten feet at least to the southward. Curiously enough, there is a somewhat forbidding inscription upon it in Latin, and I am sorry that this particular tomb should have to be moved. It stands amongst the graves of the Kenyons, an old family which has been extinct in these parts for centuries. The inscription on it runs thus:

SARAH

1630.

FOR THE SAKE OF THE DEAD AND THE WELFARE
OF THE LIVING, LET THIS SEPULCHRE REMAIN
UNTOUCHED AND ITS OCCUPANT UNDISTURBED TILL
THE COMING OF CHRIST.
IN THE NAME OF THE FATHER, THE SON,
AND THE HOLY GHOST.

July 8th. Took counsel with Grant concerning the "Sarah Tomb." We are both very loath to disturb it, but the ground has sunk so beneath it that the safety of the church is in danger; thus we have no choice. However, the work shall be done as reverently as possible under our own direction.

Grant says there is a legend in the neighbourhood that it is the tomb of the last of the Kenyons, the evil Countess Sarah, who was murdered in 1630. She lived quite alone in the old castle, whose ruins still stand three miles from here on the road to Bristol. Her reputation was an evil one even for those days. She was a witch or were-woman, the only companion of her solitude being a familiar in the shape of a huge Asiatic wolf. This creature was reputed to seize upon children, or failing these, sheep and other small animals, and convey them to the castle, where the Countess used to suck their blood. It was popularly supposed that she could never be killed. This, however, proved a fallacy, since she was strangled one day by a mad peasant woman who had lost two children, she declaring that they had both been seized and carried off by the Countess's familiar. This is a very interesting story, since it points to a local superstition very similar to that of the Vampire, existing in Slavonic and Hungarian Europe.

The tomb is built of black marble, surmounted by an enormous slab of the same material. On the slab is a magnificent group of figures. A young and handsome woman reclines upon a couch; round her neck is a piece of rope, the end of which she holds in her hand. At her side is a gigantic dog with bared fangs and lolling tongue. The face of the reclining figure is a cruel one: the corners of the mouth are curiously lifted, showing the sharp points of long canine or dog teeth. The whole group, though magnificently executed, leaves a most unpleasant sensation.

If we move the tomb it will have to be done in two pieces, the covering slab first and then the tomb proper. We have decided to remove the covering slab tomorrow.

July 9th.—6 P.M. A very strange day.

By noon everything was ready for lifting off the covering stone, and after the men's dinner we started the jacks and pulleys. The slab lifted easily enough, though it fitted closely into its seat and was further secured by some sort of mortar or putty, which must have kept the interior perfectly air-tight.

None of us were prepared for the horrible rush of foul, mouldy air that escaped as the cover lifted clear of its seating. And the contents that gradually came into view were more startling still. There lay the fully dressed body of a woman, wizened and shrunk and ghastly pale as if from starvation. Round her neck was a loose cord, and, judging by the scars still visible, the story of death by strangulation was true enough.

The most horrible part, however, was the extraordinary freshness of the body. Except for the appearance of starvation, life might have been only just extinct. The flesh was soft and white, the eyes were wide-open and seemed to stare at us with a fearful understanding in them. The body itself lay on mould, without any pretence to coffin or shell.

For several moments we gazed with horrible curiosity, and then it became too much for my work-men, who implored us to replace the covering slab. That, of course, we would not do; but I set the carpenters to work at once to make a temporary cover while we moved the tomb to its new position. This is a long job, and will take two or three days at least.

July 9th.—9 P.M. Just at sunset we were startled by the howling of, seemingly, every dog in the village. It lasted for ten minutes or a quarter of an hour, and then ceased as suddenly as it began. This, and a curious mist that has risen round the church, makes me feel rather anxious about the Sarah Tomb. According to the best established traditions of the Vampire-haunted countries, the disturbance of dogs or wolves at sunset is supposed to indicate the presence of one of these fiends, and local fog is always considered to be a certain sign. The Vampire has the power of producing it for the purpose of concealing its movements near its hiding-place at any time.

I dare not mention or even hint my fears to the Rector, for he is, not unnaturally perhaps, a rank disbeliever in many things that I know, from experience, are not only possible but even probable. I must work this out alone at first, and get his aid without his knowing in what direction he is helping me. I shall now watch till midnight at least.

10.15 P.M. As I feared and half expected. Just before ten there was another outburst of the hideous howling. It was commenced most distinctly by a particularly horrible and blood-curdling wail from the vicinity of the churchyard. The chorus lasted only a few minutes, however, and at the end of it I saw a large dark shape, like a huge dog, emerge from the fog and lope away at a rapid canter towards the open country. Assuming this to be what I fear, I shall see it return soon after midnight.

12.30 P.M. I was right. Almost as midnight struck I saw the beast returning. It stopped at the spot where the fog seemed to commence, and lifting up its head, gave tongue to that particularly horrible long-drawn wail that I had noticed as preceding the outburst earlier in the evening.

To-morrow I shall tell the Rector what I have seen; and if, as I expect, we hear of some neighbouring sheep-fold having been raided, I shall get him to watch with me for this nocturnal marauder. I shall also examine the Sarah Tomb for something which he may notice without any previous hint from me.

July 10th. I found the workmen this morning much disturbed in mind about the howling of the dogs. "We doan't like it, zur," one of them said to me—"we doan't like it; there was summat abroad last night that was unholy." They were still more uncomfortable when the news came round that a large dog had made a raid upon a flock of sheep, scattering them far and wide, and leaving three of them dead with torn throats in the field.

When I told the Rector of what I had seen and what was being said in the village, he immediately decided that we must try and catch or at least identify the beast I had seen. "Of course," said he, "it is some dog lately imported into the neighbourhood, for I know of nothing about here nearly as large as the animal you describe, though its size may be due to the deceptive moonlight."

This afternoon I asked the Rector, as a favour, to assist me in lifting the temporary cover that was on the tomb, giving as an excuse the reason that I wished to obtain a portion of the curious mortar with which it had been sealed. After a slight demur he consented, and we raised the lid. If the sight that met our eyes gave me a shock, at least it appalled Grant.

"Great God!" he exclaimed; "the woman is alive!"

And so it seemed for a moment. The corpse had lost much of its starved appearance and looked hideously fresh and alive. It was still wrinkled and shrunken, but the lips were firm, and of the rich red hue of health. The eyes, if possible, were more appalling than ever, though fixed and staring. At one corner of the mouth I thought I noticed a slight dark-colored froth, but I said nothing about it then.

"Take your piece of mortar, Harry," gasped Grant, "and let us shut the tomb again. God help me! Parson though I am, such dead faces frighten me!"

Nor was I sorry to hide that terrible face again; but I got my bit of mortar, and I have advanced a step towards the solution of the mystery.

This afternoon the tomb was moved several feet towards its new position, but it will be two or three days yet before we shall be ready to replace the slab.

10.15 P.M. Again the same howling at sunset, the same fog enveloping the church, and at ten o'clock the same great beast slipping silently out into the open country. I must get the Rector's help and watch for its return. But precautions we must take, for if things are as I believe, we take our lives in our hands when we venture out into the night to waylay the—Vampire. Why not admit it at once? For that the beast I have seen is the Vampire of that evil thing in the tomb I can have no reasonable doubt.

Not yet come to its full strength, thank Heaven! after the starvation of nearly two centuries, for at present it can only maraud as wolf apparently. But, in a day or two, when full power returns, that dreadful woman in new strength and beauty will be able to leave her refuge. Then it would not be sheep merely that would satisfy her disgusting lust for blood, but victims that would yield their life-blood without a murmur to her caressing touch—victims that, dying of her foul embrace, themselves must become Vampires in their turn to prey on others.

Mercifully my knowledge gives me a safeguard; for that little piece of mortar that I rescued to-day from the tomb contains a portion of the Sacred Host, and who holds it, humbly and firmly believing in its virtue, may pass safely through such an ordeal as I intend to submit myself and the Rector to to-night.

12.30 P.M. Our adventure is over for the present, and we are back safe.

After writing the last entry recorded above, I went off to find Grant and tell him that the marauder was out on the prowl again. "But, Grant," I said, "before we start out tonight I must insist that you will let me prosecute this affair in my own way; you must promise to put yourself completely under my orders, without asking any questions as to the why and wherefore."

After a little demur, and some excusable chaff on his part at the serious view I was taking of what he called a "dog hunt," he gave me his promise. I then told him that we were to watch to-night and try and track the mysterious beast, but not to interfere with it in any way. I think, in spite of his jests, that I impressed him with the fact that there might be, after all, good reason for my precautions.

It was just after eleven when we stepped out into the still night.

Our first move was to try and penetrate the dense fog round the church, but there was something so chilly about it, and a faint smell so disgustingly rank and loathsome, that neither our nerves nor our stomachs were proof against it. Instead, we stationed ourselves in the dark shadow of a yew tree that commanded a good view of the wicket entrance to the churchyard.

At midnight the howling of the dogs began again, and in a few minutes we saw a large grey shape, with green eyes shining like lamps, shamble swiftly down the path towards us.

The Rector started forward, but I laid a firm hand upon his arm and whispered a warning: "Remember!" Then we both stood very still and watched as the great beast cantered swiftly by. It was real enough, for we could hear the clicking of its nails on the stone flags. It passed within a few yards of us, and seemed to be nothing more nor less than a great grey wolf, thin and gaunt, with bristling hair and dripping jaws. It stopped where the mist commenced, and turned round. It was truly a horrible sight, and made one's blood run cold. The eyes burnt like fires, the upper lip was snarling and raised, showing the great canine teeth, while round the mouth hung and dripped a dark-coloured froth.

It raised its head and gave tongue to its long wailing howl, which was answered from afar by the village dogs.

After standing for a few moments it turned and disappeared into the thickest part of the fog.

Very shortly afterwards the atmosphere began to clear, and within ten minutes the mist was all gone, the dogs in the village were silent, and the night seemed to reassume its normal aspect. We examined the spot where the beast had been standing and found, plainly enough upon the stone flags, dark spots of froth and saliva.

"Well, Rector," I said, "will you admit now, in view of the things you have seen today, in consideration of the legend, the woman in the tomb, the fog, the howling dogs, and, last but not least, the mysterious beast you have seen so close, that there is something not quite normal in it all? Will you put yourself unreservedly in my hands and help me, *whatever I may do*, to first make assurance doubly sure, and finally take the necessary steps for putting an end to this horror of the night?" I saw that the uncanny influence of the night was strong upon him, and wished to impress it as much as possible.

"Needs must," he replied, "when the Devil drives: and in the face of what I have seen I must believe that some unholy forces are at work. Yet, how can they work in the sacred precincts of a church? Shall we not call rather upon Heaven to assist us in our need?"

"Grant," I said solemnly, "that we must do, each in his own way. God helps those who help themselves, and by His help and the light of my knowledge we must fight this battle for Him and the poor lost soul within."

We then returned to the rectory and to our rooms, though I have sat up to write this account while the scene is fresh in my mind.

July 11th. Found the workmen again very much disturbed in their minds, and full of a strange dog that had been seen during the night by several people, who had hunted it. Farmer Stotman, who had been watching his sheep (the same flock that had been raided the night before), had surprised it over a fresh carcase and tried to drive it off, but its size and fierceness so alarmed him that he had beaten a hasty retreat for a gun. When he returned the animal was gone, though he found that three more sheep from his flock were dead and torn.

The Sarah Tomb was moved to-day to its new position; but it was a long, heavy business, and there was not time to replace the covering slab. For this I was glad, as in the prosaic light of day the Rector almost disbelieves the events of the night, and is prepared to think everything to have been magnified and distorted by our imagination.

As, however, I could not possibly proceed with my war of extermination against this foul thing without assistance, and as there is nobody else I can rely upon, I appealed to him for one more night—to convince him that it was no delusion, but a ghastly, horrible truth, which must be fought and conquered for our own sakes, as well as that of all those living in the neighbourhood.

"Put yourself in my hands, Rector," I said, "for to-night at least. Let us take those precautions which my study of the subject tells me are the right ones. To-night you and I must watch in the church; and I feel assured that to-morrow you will be as convinced as I am, and be equally prepared to take those awful steps which I know to be proper, and I must warn you that we shall find a more startling change in the body lying there than you noticed yesterday."

My words came true; for on raising the wooden cover once more the rank stench of a slaughter-house arose, making us feel positively sick. There lay the Vampire, but how changed from the starved and shrunken corpse we saw two days ago for the first time! The wrinkles had almost disappeared, the flesh was firm and full, the crimson lips grinned horribly over the long pointed teeth, and a distinct smear of blood had trickled down one corner of the mouth. We set our teeth, however, and hardened our hearts. Then we replaced the cover and put what we had collected into a safe place in the vestry. Yet even now Grant could not believe that there was any real or pressing danger concealed in that awful tomb, as he raised strenuous objections to any apparent desecration of the body without further proof. This he shall have to-night. God grant that I am not taking too much on myself! If there is any truth in old legends it would be easy enough to destroy the Vampire now; but Grant will not have it.

I hope for the best of this night's work, but the danger in waiting is very great.

6 P.M. I have prepared everything: the sharp knives, the pointed stake, fresh garlic, and the wild dog-roses. All these I have taken and concealed in the vestry, where we can get at them when our solemn vigil commences.

If either or both of us die with our fearful task undone, let those reading my record see that this is done. I lay it upon them as a solemn obligation. "That the Vampire be pierced through the heart with the stake, then let the Burial Service be read over the poor clay at last released from its doom. Thus shall the Vampire cease to be, and a lost soul rest."

July 12th. All is over. After the most terrible night of watching and horror one Vampire at least will trouble the world no more. But how thankful should we be to a merciful Providence that that awful tomb was not disturbed by anyone not having the knowledge necessary to deal with its dreadful occupant! I write this with no feelings of self-complacency, but simply with a great gratitude for the years of study I have been able to devote to this special subject.

And now to my tale.

Just before sunset last night the Rector and I locked ourselves into the church, and took up our position in the pulpit. It was one of those pulpits, to be found in some churches, which is entered from the vestry, the preacher appearing at a good height through an arched opening in the wall. This gave us a sense of security (which we felt we needed), a good view of the interior, and direct access to the implements which I had concealed in the vestry.

The sun set and the twilight gradually deepened and faded. There was, so far, no sign of the usual fog, nor any howling of the dogs. At nine o'clock the moon rose, and her pale light gradually flooded the aisles, and still no sign of any kind from the "Sarah Tomb." The Rector had asked me several times what he might expect, but I was determined that no words or thought of mine should influence him, and that he should be convinced by his own senses alone.

By half-past ten we were both getting very tired, and I began to think that perhaps after all we should see nothing that night. However, soon after eleven we observed a light mist rising from the Sarah Tomb. It seemed to scintillate and sparkle as it rose, and curled in a sort of pillar or spiral

I said nothing, but I heard the Rector give a sort of gasp as he clutched my arm feverishly. "Great Heaven!" he whispered, "it is taking shape."

And, true enough, in a very few moments we saw standing erect by the tomb the ghastly figure of the Countess Sarah!

She looked thin and haggard still, and her face was deadly white; but the crimson lips looked like a hideous gash in the pale cheeks, and her eyes glared like red coals in the gloom of the church.

It was a fearful thing to watch as she stepped unsteadily down the aisle, staggering a little as if from weakness and exhaustion. This was perhaps natural, as her body must have suffered much physically from her long incarceration, in spite of the unholy forces which kept it fresh and well.

We watched her to the door, and wondered what would happen; but it appeared to present no difficulty, for she melted through it and disappeared.

"Now, Grant," I said, "do you believe?"

"Yes," he replied, "I must. Everything is in your hands, and I will obey your commands to the letter, if you can only instruct me how to rid my poor people of this unnameable terror."

"By God's help I will," said I; "but you shall be yet more convinced first, for we have a terrible work to do, and much to answer for in the future, before we leave the church again this morning.

And now to work, for in its present weak state the Vampire will not wander far, but may return at any time, and must not find us unprepared."

We stepped down from the pulpit and, taking dog-roses and garlic from the vestry, proceeded to the tomb. I arrived first and, throwing off the wooden cover, cried, "Look! it is empty!" There was nothing there! Nothing except the impress of the body in the loose damp mould!

I took the flowers and laid them in a circle round the tomb, for legend teaches us that Vampires will not pass over these particular blossoms if they can avoid it.

Then, eight or ten feet away, I made a circle on the stone pavement, large enough for the Rector and myself to stand in, and within the circle I placed the implements that I had brought into the church with me.

"Now," I said, "from this circle, which nothing unholy can step across, you shall see the Vampire face-to-face, and see her afraid to cross that other circle of garlic and dog roses to regain her unholy refuge. But on no account step beyond the holy place you stand in, for the Vampire has a fearful strength not her own, and, like a snake, can draw her victim willingly to his own destruction."

Now so far my work was done, and, calling the Rector, we stepped into the Holy Circle to await the Vampire's return.

Nor was this long delayed. Presently a damp, cold odour seemed to pervade the church, which made our hair bristle and flesh to creep. And then, down the aisle with noiseless feet came that which we watched for.

I heard the Rector mutter a prayer, and I held him tightly by the arm, for he was shivering violently.

Long before we could distinguish the features we saw the glowing eyes and the crimson sensual mouth. She went straight to her tomb, but stopped short when she encountered my flowers. She walked right round the tomb seeking a place to enter, and as she walked she saw us. A spasm of diabolical hate and fury passed over her face; but it quickly vanished, and a smile of love, more devilish still, took its place. She stretched out her arms towards us. Then we saw that round her mouth gathered a bloody froth, and from under her lips long pointed teeth gleamed and champed.

She spoke: a soft soothing voice, a voice that carried a spell with it, and affected us both strangely, particularly the Rector. I wished to test as far as possible, without endangering our lives, the Vampire's power.

Her voice had a soporific effect, which I resisted easily enough, but which seemed to throw the Rector into a sort of trance. More than this: it seemed to compel him to her in spite of his efforts to resist.

"Come!" she said—"come! I give sleep and peace—sleep and peace—sleep and peace."

She advanced a little towards us; but not far, for I noted that the Sacred Circle seemed to keep her back like an iron hand.

My companion seemed to become demoralized and spellbound. He tried to step forward and, finding me detain him, whispered, "Harry, let go! I must go! She is calling me! I must! I must! Oh, help me! help me!" And he began to struggle.

It was time to finish.

"Grant!" I cried, in a loud, firm voice, "in the name of all that you hold sacred, have done and play the man!" He shuddered violently and gasped, "Where am I?" Then he remembered, and clung to me convulsively for a moment.

At this a look of damnable hate changed the smiling face before us, and with a sort of shriek she staggered back.

"Back!" I cried: "back to your unholy tomb! No longer shall you molest the suffering world! Your end is near."

It was fear that now showed itself in her beautiful face (for it was beautiful in spite of its horror) as she shrank back, back and over the circlet of flowers, shivering as she did so. At last, with a low mournful cry, she appeared to melt back again into her tomb.

As she did so the first gleams of the rising sun lit up the world, and I knew all danger was over for the day.

Taking Grant by the arm, I drew him with me out of the circle and led him to the tomb. There lay the Vampire once more, still in her living death as we had a moment before seen her in her devilish life. But in the eyes remained that awful expression of hate, and cringing, appalling fear.

Grant was pulling himself together.

"Now," I said, "will you dare the last terrible act and rid the world for ever of this horror?"

"By God!" he said solemnly, "I will. Tell me what to do."

"Help me to lift her out of her tomb. She can harm us no more," I replied.

With averted faces we set to our terrible task, and laid her out upon the flags.

"Now," I said, "read the Burial Service over the poor body, and then let us give it its release from this living hell that holds it."

Reverently the Rector read the beautiful words, and reverently I made the necessary responses. When it was over I took the stake and, without giving myself time to think, plunged it with all my strength through the heart.

As though really alive, the body for a moment writhed and kicked convulsively, and an awful heart-rending shriek woke the silent church; then all was still.

Then we lifted the poor body back; and, thank God! the consolation that legend tells is never denied to those who have to do such awful work as ours came at last. Over the face stole a great and solemn peace; the lips lost their crimson hue, the prominent sharp teeth sank back into the mouth, and for a moment we saw before us the calm, pale face of a most beautiful woman, who smiled as she slept. A few minutes more, and she faded away to dust before our eyes as we watched. We set to work and cleaned up every trace of our work, and then departed for the rectory. Most thankful were we to step out of the church, with its horrible associations, into the rosy warmth of the summer morning.

With the above end the notes in my father's diary, though a few days later this further entry occurs:

JULY 15TH. SINCE THE 12th everything has been quiet and as usual. We replaced and sealed up the Sarah Tomb this morning. The workmen were surprised to find the body had disappeared, but took it to be the natural result of exposing it to the air.

One odd thing came to my ears to-day. It appears that the child of one of the villagers strayed from home the night of the 11th inst., and was found asleep in a coppice near the church, very pale and quite exhausted. There were two small marks on her throat, which have since disappeared.

What does this mean? I have, however, kept it to myself, as, now that the Vampire is no more, no further danger either to that child or any other is to be apprehended. It is only those who die of the Vampire's embrace that become Vampires at death in their turn.

❋

Hume Nisbet

(1849–1923)

JAMES HUME NISBET WAS one of several authors in this volume
who achieved considerable notice in their own time but have since
faded into obscurity. Born in Stirling, he studied art, taught drawing and painting, and even exhibited with the Royal Scottish Academy. He achieved no particular success with his own artwork, other
than in illustrating his own books and those of other writers, but he
wrote five books about the visual arts. He also produced four collections of verse. In his mid-teens, he began a lifetime of travel
when he ventured from his native Scotland to Australia, to which
he returned several times during his life. Nisbet also enjoyed traveling through New Guinea and New Zealand. He often denounced
racial prejudice and other social ills; the first of his forty-odd novels,
The Land of the Hibiscus Blossom, is said to be an unusually sympathetic portrayal of native Papuans. Other novels bore such titles as *A
Desert Bride: A Story of Adventure in India and Persia*. His sole contribution to the literature of the undead, "The Vampire Maid," first
appeared in Hume's 1900 collection *Stories Weird and Wonderful*.

The Vampire Maid

I T WAS THE EXACT kind of abode that I had been looking after for weeks, for I was in that condition of mind when absolute renunciation of society was a necessity. I had become diffident of myself, and wearied of my kind. A strange unrest was in my blood; a barren dearth in my brains. Familiar objects and faces had grown distasteful to me. I wanted to be alone. This is the mood which comes upon every sensitive and artistic mind when the possessor has been overworked or living too long in one groove. It is Nature's hint for him to seek pastures new; the sign that a retreat has become needful.

If he does not yield, he breaks down and becomes whimsical and hypochondriacal, as well as hypercritical. It is always a bad sign when a man becomes over-critical and censorious about his own or other people's work, for it means that he is losing the vital portions of work, freshness and enthusiasm.

Before I arrived at the dismal stage of criticism I hastily packed up my knapsack, and taking the train to Westmorland, I began my tramp in search of solitude, bracing air, and romantic surroundings.

Many places I came upon during that early summer wandering that appeared to have almost the required conditions, yet some petty drawback prevented me from deciding. Sometimes it was the scenery that I did not take kindly to. At other places I took sudden antipathies to the landlady or landlord, and felt I would abhor them before a week was spent under their charge. Other places which might have suited me I could not have, as they did not want a lodger. Fate was driving me to this Cottage on the Moor, and no one can resist destiny.

One day I found myself on a wide and pathless moor near the sea. I had slept the night before at a small hamlet, but that was already eight miles in my rear, and since I had turned my back upon it I had not seen any signs of humanity; I was alone with a fair sky above me, a balmy ozone-filled wind blowing over the stony and heather-clad mounds, and nothing to disturb my meditations.

How far the moor stretched I had no knowledge; I only knew that by keeping in a straight line I would come to the ocean cliffs, then perhaps after a time arrive at some fishing village.

I had provisions in my knapsack, and being young did not fear a night under the stars. I was inhaling the delicious summer air and once more getting back the vigour and happiness I had lost; my city-dried brains were again becoming juicy.

Thus hour after hour slid past me, with the paces, until I had covered about fifteen miles since morning, when I saw before me in the distance a solitary stone-built cottage with roughly slated roof. "I'll camp there if possible," I said to myself as I quickened my steps towards it.

To one in search of a quiet, free life, nothing could have possibly been more suitable than this cottage. It stood on the edge of lofty cliffs, with its front door facing the moor and the back-yard wall overlooking the ocean. The sound of the dancing waves struck upon my ears like a lullaby as I drew near; how they would thunder when the autumn gales came on and the seabirds fled shrieking to the shelter of the sedges.

A small garden spread in front, surrounded by a dry-stone wall just high enough for one to lean lazily upon when inclined. This garden was a flame of colour, scarlet predominating, with those other soft shades that cultivated poppies take on in their blooming, for this was all that the garden grew.

As I approached, taking notice of this singular assortment of poppies, and the orderly cleanness of the windows, the front door opened and a woman appeared who impressed me at once favourably as she leisurely came along the pathway to the gate, and drew it back as if to welcome me.

She was of middle age, and when young must have been remarkably good-looking. She was tall and still shapely, with smooth clear skin, regular features and a calm expression that at once gave me a sensation of rest.

To my inquiries she said that she could give me both a sitting and bedroom, and invited me inside to see them. As I looked at her smooth black hair, and cool brown eyes, I felt that I would not be too particular about the accommodation. With such a landlady, I was sure to find what I was after here.

The rooms surpassed my expectation, dainty white curtains and bedding with the perfume of lavender about them, a sitting-room homely yet cosy without being crowded. With a sigh of infinite relief I flung down my knapsack and clinched the bargain.

She was a widow with one daughter, whom I did not see the first day, as she was unwell and confined to her own room, but on the next day she was somewhat better, and then we met.

The fare was simple, yet it suited me exactly for the time, delicious milk and butter with home-made scones, fresh eggs and bacon; after a hearty tea I went early to bed in a condition of perfect content with my quarters.

Yet happy and tired out as I was I had by no means a comfortable night. This I put down to the strange bed. I slept certainly, but my sleep was filled with dreams so that I woke late and unrefreshed; a good walk on the moor, however, restored me, and I returned with a fine appetite for breakfast.

Certain conditions of mind, with aggravating circumstances,

are required before even a young man can fall in love at first sight, as Shakespeare has shown in his *Romeo and Juliet*. In the city, where many fair faces passed me every hour, I had remained like a stoic, yet no sooner did I enter the cottage after that morning walk than I succumbed instantly before the weird charms of my landlady's daughter, Ariadne Brunnell.

She was somewhat better this morning and able to meet me at breakfast, for we had our meals together while I was their lodger. Ariadne was not beautiful in the strictly classical sense, her complexion being too lividly white and her expression too set to be quite pleasant at first sight; yet, as her mother had informed me, she had been ill for some time, which accounted for that defect. Her features were not regular, her hair and eyes seemed too black with that strangely white skin, and her lips too red for any except the decadent harmonies of an Aubrey Beardsley.

Yet my fantastic dreams of the preceding night, with my morning walk, had prepared me to be enthralled by this modern poster-like invalid.

The loneliness of the moor, with the singing of the ocean, had gripped my heart with a wistful longing. The incongruity of those flaunting and evanescent poppy flowers, dashing the giddy tints in the face of that sober heath, touched me with a shiver as I approached the cottage, and lastly that weird embodiment of startling contrasts completed my subjugation.

She rose from her chair as her mother introduced her, and smiled while she held out her hand. I clasped that soft snowflake, and as I did so a faint thrill tingled over me and rested on my heart, stopping for the moment its beating.

This contact seemed also to have affected her as it did me; a clear flush, like a white flame, lighted up her face, so that it glowed as if an alabaster lamp had been lit; her black eyes became softer and more humid as our glances crossed, and her scarlet lips grew moist. She was a living woman now, while before she had seemed half a corpse.

She permitted her white slender hand to remain in mine longer than most people do at an introduction, and then she slowly withdrew it, still regarding me with steadfast eyes for a second or two afterwards.

Fathomless velvety eyes these were, yet before they were shifted from mine they appeared to have absorbed all my willpower and made me her abject slave. They looked like deep dark pools of clear water, yet they filled me with fire and deprived me of strength. I sank into my chair almost as languidly as I had risen from my bed that morning.

Yet I made a good breakfast, and although she hardly tasted anything, this strange girl rose much refreshed and with a slight glow of colour on her cheeks, which improved her so greatly that she appeared younger and almost beautiful.

I had come here seeking solitude, but since I had seen Ariadne it seemed as if I had come for her only. She was not very lively; indeed, thinking back, I cannot recall any spontaneous remark of hers; she answered my questions by monosyllables and left me to lead in words; yet she was insinuating and appeared to lead my thoughts in her direction and speak to me with her eyes. I cannot describe her minutely, I only know that from the first glance and touch she gave me I was bewitched and could think of nothing else.

It was a rapid, distracting, and devouring infatuation that possessed me; all day long I followed her about like a dog, every night I dreamed of that white glowing face, those steadfast black eyes, those moist scarlet lips, and each morning I rose more languid than I had been the day before. Sometimes I dreamt that she was kissing me with those red lips, while I shivered at the contact of her silky black tresses as they covered my throat; sometimes that we were floating in the air, her arms about me and her long hair enveloping us both like an inky cloud, while I lay supine and helpless.

She went with me after breakfast on that first day to the moor, and before we came back I had spoken my love and received her assent. I held her in my arms and had taken her kisses in answer to mine, nor did I think it strange that all this had happened so quickly. She was mine, or rather I was hers, without a pause. I told her it was fate that had sent me to her, for I had no doubts about my love, and she replied that I had restored her to life.

Acting upon Ariadne's advice, and also from a natural shyness, I did not inform her mother how quickly matters had progressed between us, yet although we both acted as circumspectly as possible, I had no doubt Mrs. Brunnell could see how engrossed we were in each other. Lovers are not unlike ostriches in their modes of concealment. I was not afraid of asking Mrs. Brunnell for her daughter, for she already showed her partiality towards me, and had bestowed upon me some confidences regarding her own position in life, and I therefore knew that, so far as social position was concerned, there could be no real objection to our marriage. They lived in this lonely spot for the sake of their health, and kept no servant because they could not get any to take service so far away from other humanity. My coming had been opportune and welcome to both mother and daughter.

For the sake of decorum, however, I resolved to delay my confession for a week or two and trust to some favourable opportunity of doing it discreetly.

Meantime Ariadne and I passed our time in a thoroughly idle and lotus-eating style. Each night I retired to bed meditating starting work next day, each morning I rose languid from those disturbing dreams with no thought for anything outside my love. She grew stronger every day, while I appeared to be taking her place as the invalid, yet I was more frantically in love than ever, and only happy when with her. She was my lone-star, my only joy—my life.

We did not go great distances, for I liked best to lie on the dry heath and watch her glowing face and intense eyes while I listened to the surging of the distant waves. It was love made me lazy, I thought, for unless a man has all he longs for beside him, he is apt to copy the domestic cat and bask in the sunshine.

I had been enchanted quickly. My disenchantment came as rapidly, although it was long before the poison left my blood.

One night, about a couple of weeks after my coming to the cottage, I had returned after a delicious moonlight walk with Ariadne. The night was warm and the moon at the full, therefore I left my bedroom window open to let in what little air there was.

I was more than usually fagged out, so that I had only strength enough to remove my boots and coat before I flung myself wearily on the coverlet and fell almost instantly asleep without tasting the nightcap draught that was constantly placed on the table, and which I had always drained thirstily.

I had a ghastly dream this night. I thought I saw a monster bat, with the face and tresses of Ariadne, fly into the open window and fasten its white teeth and scarlet lips on my arm. I tried to beat the horror away, but could not, for I seemed chained down and thralled also with drowsy delight as the beast sucked my blood with a gruesome rapture.

I looked out dreamily and saw a line of dead bodies of young men lying on the floor, each with a red mark on their arms, on the same part where the vampire was then sucking me, and I remembered having seen and wondered at such a mark on my own arm for the past fortnight. In a flash I understood the reason for my strange weakness, and at the same moment a sudden prick of pain roused me from my dreamy pleasure.

The vampire in her eagerness had bitten a little too deeply that night, unaware that I had not tasted the drugged draught. As I woke I saw her fully revealed by the midnight moon, with her black tresses flowing loosely, and with her red lips glued to my arm. With a shriek of horror I dashed her backwards, getting one last glimpse of her savage eyes, glowing white face and blood-stained red lips; then I rushed out to the night, moved on by my fear and hatred, nor did I pause in my mad flight until I had left miles between me and that accursed Cottage on the Moor.

III

The Fruit

❄

Mary E. Wilkins Freeman

(1852–1930)

THE FIRST WORDS IN the story "Luella Miller" are "Close to the village street stood the one-story house . . ." It's the kind of image for which Mary E. Wilkins Freeman (sometimes referred to by her earlier name, Mary Eleanor Wilkins) is remembered, from her stories—whether realistic or supernatural—about unknown lives in undistinguished places. But Luella Miller stands out from the parade of ordinary folk who populate Freeman's stories. Luella is one of those people who somehow always gets what she wants.

Mary E. Wilkins lost her parents and sister at a young age, which seems to have understandably fostered both sadness and compassion in her writing. Born in Massachusetts, Freeman spent most of her life there, working for decades as private secretary to the medical reformer and author Oliver Wendell Holmes Sr. In her fiction, she portrays the narrow-minded religious orthodoxy that suffocated her own childhood, the ties that bind small communities, and a long line of abandoned and abused children. Her initial writing was for children, after she won a story prize during her own teen years and decided to pursue writing. She sold her first adult story to Mary Louise Booth, the legendary editor of *Harper's Bazaar*.

For several decades, Freeman was sidelined by male critics, who of course comprised most of the critics until the late twentieth century. But of late she has been reconsidered as an original voice and a sharp talent. Readers and editors in her own time both knew her value; she was the first writer to whom the American Academy of Arts and Letters awarded its William Dean Howells Medal for Distinction in Fiction. In 1892 she was profiled in *Ladies' Home Journal* in a series called "Literary Women in Their Homes." Less than a decade later, another magazine wrote, "It is natural to suppose that any reader of current English literature would know Miss Wilkins."

Stories such as "The Lost Ghost" and "The Wind in the Rose-Bush" demonstrate her ability to anchor the supernatural in the ordinary, as well as her trademark theme of the abandoned child. She also wrote "The Long Arm," an extraordinary detective story. "Luella Miller" reads like a fragment of a supernatural *Winesburg, Ohio* or *Main Street*. It was published in 1902—the year that she married Charles M. Freeman and adopted a new writing name—in the December issue of *Everybody's Magazine*. The story was illustrated with a spooky drawing by Peter Newell (who had not yet published his now classic *The Hole Book*). The next year Freeman reprinted it in her collection *The Wind in the Rose-Bush and Other Stories of the Supernatural*.

Luella Miller

CLOSE TO THE VILLAGE street stood the one-story house in which
Luella Miller, who had an evil name in the village, had dwelt.
She had been dead for years, yet there were those in the village
who, in spite of the clearer light which comes on a vantage-point
from a long-past danger, half believed in the tale which they had
heard from their childhood. In their hearts, although they scarcely
would have owned it, was a survival of the wild horror and frenzied
fear of their ancestors who had dwelt in the same age with Luella
Miller. Young people even would stare with a shudder at the old
house as they passed, and children never played around it as was their
wont around an untenanted building. Not a window in the old
Miller house was broken: the panes reflected the morning sunlight
in patches of emerald and blue, and the latch of the sagging front
door was never lifted, although no bolt secured it. Since Luella
Miller had been carried out of it, the house had had no tenant except
one friendless old soul who had no choice between that and the far-
off shelter of the open sky. This old woman, who had survived her
kindred and friends, lived in the house one week, then one morning
no smoke came out of the chimney, and a body of neighbours, a
score strong, entered and found her dead in her bed. There were
dark whispers as to the cause of her death, and there were those who
testified to an expression of fear so exalted that it showed forth the

state of the departing soul upon the dead face. The old woman had been hale and hearty when she entered the house, and in seven days she was dead; it seemed that she had fallen a victim to some uncanny power. The minister talked in the pulpit with covert severity against the sin of superstition; still the belief prevailed. Not a soul in the village but would have chosen the almshouse rather than that dwelling. No vagrant, if he heard the tale, would seek shelter beneath that old roof, unhallowed by nearly half a century of superstitious fear.

There was only one person in the village who had actually known Luella Miller. That person was a woman well over eighty, but a marvel of vitality and unextinct youth. Straight as an arrow, with the spring of one recently let loose from the bow of life, she moved about the streets, and she always went to church, rain or shine. She had never married, and had lived alone for years in a house across the road from Luella Miller's.

This woman had none of the garrulousness of age, but never in all her life had she ever held her tongue for any will save her own, and she never spared the truth when she essayed to present it. She it was who bore testimony to the life, evil, though possibly wittingly or designedly so, of Luella Miller, and to her personal appearance. When this old woman spoke—and she had the gift of description, although her thoughts were clothed in the rude vernacular of her native village—one could seem to see Luella Miller as she had really looked. According to this woman, Lydia Anderson by name, Luella Miller had been a beauty of a type rather unusual in New England. She had been a slight, pliant sort of creature, as ready with a strong yielding to fate and as unbreakable as a willow. She had glimmering lengths of straight, fair hair, which she wore softly looped round a long, lovely face. She had blue eyes full of soft pleading, little slender, clinging hands, and a wonderful grace of motion and attitude.

"Luella Miller used to sit in a way nobody else could if they sat up and studied a week of Sundays," said Lydia Anderson, "and it was a sight to see her walk. If one of them willows over there on the edge of the brook could start up and get its roots free of the ground, and move off, it would go just the way Luella Miller used to. She had a green shot silk she used to wear, too, and a hat with green ribbon streamers, and a lace veil blowing across her face and out sideways, and a green ribbon flyin' from her waist. That was what she came out bride in when she married Erastus Miller. Her name before she was married was Hill. There was always a sight of *l's* in her name, married or single. Erastus Miller was good-lookin', too, better lookin' than Luella. Sometimes I used to think that Luella wa'n't so handsome after all. Erastus just about worshiped her. I used to know him pretty well. He lived next door to me, and we went to school together. Folks used to say he was waitin' on me, but he wa'n't. I never thought he was except once or twice when he said things that some girls might have suspected meant somethin'. That was before Luella came here to teach the district school. It was funny how she came to get it, for folks said she hadn't any education, and that one of the big girls, Lottie Henderson, used to do all the teachin' for her, while she sat back and did embroidery work on a cambric pocket-handkerchief. Lottie Henderson was a real smart girl, a splendid scholar, and she just set her eyes by Luella, as all the girls did. Lottie would have made a real smart woman, but she died when Luella had been here about a year—just faded away and died: nobody knew what ailed her. She dragged herself to that schoolhouse and helped Luella teach till the very last minute. The committee all knew how Luella didn't do much of the work herself, but they winked at it. It wa'n't long after Lottie died that Erastus married her. I always thought he hurried it up because she wa'n't fit to teach. One of the big boys used to help her after Lottie died, but he hadn't much government, and the school didn't do very well, and Luella might have had to give it up, for the committee couldn't have shut their eyes to things much longer. The boy that helped her was a real honest, innocent sort of fellow, and he was a good scholar, too. Folks said he overstudied, and that was the reason he was took crazy the year after Luella married, but I don't know. And I don't know what made Erastus Miller go into consumption of the blood the year after he was married: consumption wa'n't in his family. He just grew weaker and weaker, and went almost bent double when he tried to wait on Luella, and he spoke feeble, like an old man. He worked terrible hard till the last trying to save up a little to leave Luella. I've seen him out in the worst storms on a wood-sled—he used to cut and sell wood—and he was hunched up on top lookin' more dead than alive. Once I couldn't stand it: I went over and helped him pitch some wood on the cart—I was always strong in my arms. I wouldn't stop for all he told me to, and I guess he was glad enough for the help. That was only a week before he died. He fell on the kitchen floor while he was gettin' breakfast. He always got the breakfast and let Luella lay abed. He did all the sweepin' and the washin' and the ironin' and most of the cookin'. He couldn't bear to have Luella lift her finger, and she let him do for her. She lived like a queen for all the work she did. She didn't even do her sewin'. She said it made her shoulder ache to sew, and poor Erastus's sister Lily used to do all her sewin'. She wa'n't able to, either; she was never strong in her back, but she did it beautifully. She had to, to suit Luella, she was so dreadful particular. I never saw anythin' like the fagottin' and hemstitchin' that Lily Miller did for Luella. She made all Luella's weddin' outfit, and that green silk dress, after Maria Babbit cut it. Maria she cut it for nothin', and she did a lot more cuttin' and fittin' for nothin' for Luella, too. Lily Miller went to live with Luella after Erastus died. She gave up her home, though she was real attached to it and wa'n't a mite afraid to stay alone. She rented it and she went to live with Luella right away after the funeral."

Then this old woman, Lydia Anderson, who remembered Lu-ella Miller, would go on to relate the story of Lily Miller. It seemed that on the removal of Lily Miller to the house of her dead brother, to live with his widow, the village people first began to talk. This Lily Miller had been hardly past her first youth, and a most robust and blooming woman, rosy-cheeked, with curls of strong, black hair overshadowing round, candid temples and bright dark eyes. It was not six months after she had taken up her residence with her sister-in-law that her rosy colour faded and her pretty curves become wan hollows. White shadows began to show in the black rings of her hair, and the light died out of her eyes, her features sharpened, and there were pathetic lines at her mouth, which yet wore always an expression of utter sweetness and even happiness. She was devoted to her sister; there was no doubt that she loved her with her whole heart, and was perfectly content in her service. It was her sole anxiety lest she should die and leave her alone.

"The way Lily Miller used to talk about Luella was enough to make you mad and enough to make you cry," said Lydia Anderson. "I've been in there sometimes toward the last when she was too feeble to cook and carried her some blanc-mange or custard—somethin' I thought she might relish, and she'd thank me, and when I asked her how she was, say she felt better than she did yesterday, and asked me if I didn't think she looked better, dreadful pitiful, and say poor Luella had an awful time takin' care of her and doin' the work—she wa'n't strong enough to do anythin'—when all the time Luella wa'n't liftin' her finger and poor Lily didn't get any care except what the neighbours gave her, and Luella eat up everythin' that was carried in for Lily. I had it real straight that she did. Luella used to just sit and cry and do nothin'. She did act real fond of Lily, and she pined away considerable, too. There was those that thought she'd go into a decline herself. But after Lily died, her aunt Abby Mixter came, and then Luella picked up and grew as fat and rosy as ever. But poor Aunt Abby begun to droop just the way Lily had, and I guess somebody wrote to her married daughter, Mrs. Sam Abbot, who lived in Barre, for she wrote her mother that she must leave right away and come and make her a visit, but Aunt Abby wouldn't go. I can see her now. She was a real good-lookin' woman, tall and large, with a big, square face and a high forehead that looked of itself kind of benevolent and good. She just tended out on Luella as if she had been a baby, and when her married daughter sent for her she wouldn't stir one inch. She'd always thought a lot of her daughter, too, but she said Luella needed her and her married daughter didn't. Her daughter kept writin' and writin', but it didn't do any good. Finally she came, and when she saw how bad her mother looked, she broke down and cried and all but went on her knees to have her come away. She spoke her mind out to Luella, too. She told her that she'd killed her husband and everybody that had anythin' to do with her, and she'd thank her to leave her mother alone. Luella went into hysterics, and Aunt Abby was so frightened that she called me after her daughter went. Mrs. Sam Abbot she went away fairly cryin' out loud in the buggy, the neighbours heard her, and well she might, for she never saw her mother again alive. I went in that night when Aunt Abby called for me, standin' in the door with her little green-checked shawl over her head. I can see her now. 'Do come over here, Miss Anderson,' she sung out, kind of gasping for breath. I didn't stop for anythin'. I put over as fast as I could, and when I got there, there was Luella laughin' and cryin' all together, and Aunt Abby trying to hush her, and all the time she herself was white as a sheet and shakin' so she could hardly stand. 'For the land sakes, Mrs. Mixter,' says I, 'you look worse than she does. You ain't fit to be up out of your bed.'

"'Oh, there ain't anythin' the matter with me,' says she. Then she went on talkin' to Luella. 'There, there, don't, don't, poor little lamb,' says she. 'Aunt Abby is here. She ain't goin' away and leave you. Don't, poor little lamb.'

"'Do leave her with me, Mrs. Mixter, and you get back to bed,' says I, for Aunt Abby had been layin' down considerable lately, though somehow she contrived to do the work.

"'I'm well enough,' says she. 'Don't you think she had better have the doctor, Miss Anderson?'

"'The doctor,' says I, 'I think *you* had better have the doctor. I think you need him much worse than some folks I could mention.' And I looked right straight at Luella Miller laughin' and cryin' and goin' on as if she was the centre of all creation. All the time she was actin' so—seemed as if she was too sick to sense anythin'—she was keepin' a sharp lookout as to how we took it out of the corner of one eye. I see her. You could never cheat me about Luella Miller. Finally I got real mad and I run home and I got a bottle of valerian I had, and I poured some boilin' hot water on a handful of catnip, and I mixed up that catnip tea with most half a wineglass of valerian, and I went with it over to Luella's. I marched right up to Luella, a-holdin' out of that cup, all smokin'. 'Now,' says I, 'Luella Miller, *you swaller this!*'

"'What is—what is it, oh, what is it?' she sort of screeches out. Then she goes off a-laughin' enough to kill.

"'Poor lamb, poor little lamb,' says Aunt Abby, standin' over her, all kind of tottery, and tryin' to bathe her head with camphor.

"'*You swaller this right down,*' says I. And I didn't waste any cere- mony. I just took hold of Luella Miller's chin and I tipped her head back, and I caught her mouth open with laughin', and I clapped that cup to her lips and I fairly hollered at her: 'Swaller, swaller, swaller!' and she gulped it right down. She had to, and I guess it did her good. Anyhow, she stopped cryin' and laughin' and let me put her to bed, and she went to sleep like a baby inside of half an hour. That was more than poor Aunt Abby did. She lay awake all that night and I stayed with her, though she tried not to have me; said she wa'n't sick enough for watchers. But I stayed, and I made some good cornmeal gruel and I fed her a teaspoon every little while all night long. It seemed to me as if she was jest dyin' from bein' all wore out. In the mornin' as soon as it was light I run over to the Bisbees and sent Johnny Bisbee for the doctor. I told him to tell the doctor to hurry, and he come pretty quick. Poor Aunt Abby didn't seem to know much of anythin' when he got there. You couldn't hardly tell she breathed, she was so used up. When the doctor had gone, Luella came into the room lookin' like a baby in her ruffled nightgown. I can see her now. Her eyes were as blue and her face all pink and white like a blossom, and she looked at Aunt Abby in the bed sort of innocent and surprised. 'Why,' says she, 'Aunt Abby ain't got up yet?'

"'No, she ain't,' says I, pretty short.

" 'I thought I didn't smell the coffee,' says Luella.

" 'Coffee,' says I. 'I guess if you have coffee this mornin' you'll make it yourself.'

" 'I never made the coffee in all my life,' says she, dreadful astonished. 'Erastus always made the coffee as long as he lived, and then Lily she made it, and then Aunt Abby made it. I don't believe I *can* make the coffee, Miss Anderson.'

" 'You can make it or go without, jest as you please,' says I.

" 'Ain't Aunt Abby goin' to get up?' says she.

" 'I guess she won't get up,' says I, 'sick as she is.' I was gettin' madder and madder. There was somethin' about that little pink-and-white thing standin' there and talkin' about coffee, when she had killed so many better folks than she was, and had jest killed another, that made me feel 'most as if I wished somebody would up and kill her before she had a chance to do any more harm.

" 'Is Aunt Abby sick?' says Luella, as if she was sort of aggrieved and injured.

" 'Yes,' says I, 'she's sick, and she's goin' to die, and then you'll be left alone, and you'll have to do for yourself and wait on yourself, or do without things.' I don't know but I was sort of hard, but it was the truth, and if I was any harder than Luella Miller had been I'll give up. I ain't never been sorry that I said it. Well, Luella, she up and had hysterics again at that, and I jest let her have 'em. All I did was to bundle her into the room on the other side of the entry where Aunt Abby couldn't hear her, if she wa'n't past it—I don't know but she was—and set her down hard in a chair and told her not to come back into the other room, and she minded. She had her hysterics in there till she got tired. When she found out that nobody was comin' to coddle her and do for her she stopped. At least I suppose she did. I had all I could do with poor Aunt Abby tryin' to keep the breath of life in her. The doctor had told me that she was dreadful low, and give me some very strong medicine to give to her in drops real often, and told me real particular about the nourishment. Well, I did as he told me real faithful till she wa'n't able to swaller any longer. Then I had her daughter sent for. I had begun to realize that she wouldn't last any time at all. I hadn't realized it before, though I spoke to Luella the way I did. The doctor he came, and Mrs. Sam Abbot, but when she got there it was too late; her mother was dead. Aunt Abby's daughter just give one look at her mother layin' there, then she turned sort of sharp and sudden and looked at me.

" 'Where is she?' says she, and I knew she meant Luella.

" 'She's out in the kitchen,' says I. 'She's too nervous to see folks die. She's afraid it will make her sick.'

"The Doctor he speaks up then. He was a young man. Old Doctor Park had died the year before, and this was a young fellow just out of college. 'Mrs. Miller is not strong,' says he, kind of severe, 'and she is quite right in not agitating herself.'

" 'You are another, young man; she's got her pretty claw on you,' thinks I, but I didn't say anythin' to him. I just said over to Mrs. Sam Abbot that Luella was in the kitchen, and Mrs. Sam Abbot she went out there, and I went, too, and I never heard anythin' like the way she talked to Luella Miller. I felt pretty hard to Luella myself, but this was more than I ever would have dared to say. Luella she was too scared to go into hysterics. She jest flopped. She seemed to jest shrink away to nothin' in that kitchen chair, with Mrs. Sam Abbot standin' over her and talkin' and tellin' her the truth. I guess the truth was most too much for her and no mistake, because Luella presently actually did faint away, and there wa'n't any sham about it, the way I always suspected there was about them hysterics. She fainted dead away and we had to lay her flat on the floor, and the Doctor he came runnin' out and he said somethin' about a weak heart dreadful fierce to Mrs. Sam Abbot, but she wa'n't a mite scared. She faced him jest as white as even Luella was layin' there lookin' like death and the Doctor feelin' of her pulse.

" 'Weak heart,' says she, 'weak heart; weak fiddlesticks! There ain't nothin' weak about that woman. She's got strength enough to hang onto other folks till she kills 'em. Weak? It was my poor mother that was weak: this woman killed her as sure as if she had taken a knife to her.'

"But the Doctor he didn't pay much attention. He was bendin' over Luella layin' there with her yellow hair all streamin' and her pretty pink-and-white face all pale, and her blue eyes like stars gone out, and he was holdin' onto her hand and smoothin' her forehead, and tellin' me to get the brandy in Aunt Abby's room, and I was sure as I wanted to be that Luella had got somebody else to hang onto, now Aunt Abby was gone, and I thought of poor Erastus Miller, and I sort of pitied the poor young Doctor, led away by a pretty face, and I made up my mind I'd see what I could do.

"I waited till Aunt Abby had been dead and buried about a month, and the Doctor was goin' to see Luella steady and folks were beginnin' to talk; then one evenin', when I knew the Doctor had been called out of town and wouldn't be round, I went over to Luella's. I found her all dressed up in a blue muslin with white polka dots on it, and her hair curled jest as pretty, and there wa'n't a young girl in the place could compare with her. There was somethin' about Luella Miller seemed to draw the heart right out of you, but she didn't draw it out of *me*. She was settin' rocking in the chair by her sittin'-room window, and Maria Brown had gone home. Maria Brown had been in to help her, or rather to do the work, for Luella wa'n't helped when she didn't do anythin'. Maria Brown was real capable and she didn't have any ties; she wa'n't married, and lived alone, so she'd offered. I couldn't see why she should do the work any more than Luella; she wa'n't any too strong; but she seemed to think she could and Luella seemed to think so, too, so she went over and did all the work—washed, and ironed, and baked, while Luella sat and rocked. Maria didn't live long afterward. She began to fade away just the same fashion the others had. Well, she was warned, but she acted real mad when folks said anythin': said Luella was a poor, abused woman, too delicate to help herself, and they'd ought to be ashamed, and if she died helpin' them that couldn't help themselves she would—and she did.

"'I s'pose Maria has gone home,' says I to Luella, when I had gone in and sat down opposite her.

"'Yes, Maria went half an hour ago, after she had got supper and washed the dishes,' says Luella, in her pretty way.

"'I suppose she has got a lot of work to do in her own house to-night,' says I, kind of bitter, but that was all thrown away on Luella Miller. It seemed to her right that other folks that wa'n't any better able than she was herself should wait on her, and she couldn't get it through her head that anybody should think it *wa'n't* right.

"'Yes,' says Luella, real sweet and pretty, 'yes, she said she had to do her washin' to-night. She has let it go for a fortnight along of comin' over here.'

"'Why don't she stay home and do her washin' instead of comin' over here and doin' *your* work, when you are just as well able, and enough sight more so, than she is to do it?' says I.

"Then Luella she looked at me like a baby who has a rattle shook at it. She sort of laughed as innocent as you please. 'Oh, I can't do the work myself, Miss Anderson,' says she. 'I never did. Maria *has* to do it.'

"Then I spoke out: 'Has to do it!' says I. 'Has to do it! She don't have to do it, either. Maria Brown has her own home and enough to live on. She ain't beholden to you to come over here and slave for you and kill herself.'

"Luella she jest set and stared at me for all the world like a doll-baby that was so abused that it was comin' to life.

"'Yes,' says I, 'she's killin' herself. She's goin' to die just the way Erastus did, and Lily, and your Aunt Abby. You're killin' her jest as you did them. I don't know what there is about you, but you seem to bring a curse,' says I. 'You kill everybody that is fool enough to care anythin' about you and do for you.'

"She stared at me and she was pretty pale.

" 'And Maria ain't the only one you're goin' to kill,' says I. 'You're goin' to kill Doctor Malcom before you're done with him.'

"Then a red colour came flamin' all over her face. 'I ain't goin' to kill him, either,' says she, and she begun to cry.

" 'Yes, you *be*!' says I. Then I spoke as I had never spoke before. You see, I felt it on account of Erastus. I told her that she hadn't any business to think of another man after she'd been married to one that had died for her: that she was a dreadful woman; and she was, that's true enough, but sometimes I have wondered lately if she knew it—if she wa'n't like a baby with scissors in its hand cuttin' everybody without knowin' what it was doin'.

"Luella she kept gettin' paler and paler, and she never took her eyes off my face. There was somethin' awful about the way she looked at me and never spoke one word. After awhile I quit talkin' and I went home. I watched that night, but her lamp went out before nine o'clock, and when Doctor Malcom came drivin' past and sort of slowed up he see there wa'n't any light and he drove along. I saw her sort of shy out of meetin' the next Sunday, too, so he shouldn't go home with her, and I begun to think mebbe she did have some conscience after all. It was only a week after that that Maria Brown died—sort of sudden at the last, though everybody had seen it was comin'. Well, then there was a good deal of feelin' and pretty dark whispers. Folks said the days of witchcraft had come again, and they were pretty shy of Luella. She acted sort of offish to the Doctor and he didn't go there, and there wa'n't anybody to do anythin' for her. I don't know how she *did* get along. I wouldn't go in there and offer to help her—not because I was afraid of dyin' like the rest but I thought she was just as well able to do her own work as I was to do it for her, and I thought it was about time that she did it and stopped killin' other folks. But it wa'n't very long before folks began to say that Luella herself was goin' into a decline jest the way her husband, and Lily, and Aunt Abby and the others had, and I saw myself that she looked pretty bad. I used to see her goin' past from the store with a bundle as if she could hardly crawl, but I remembered how Erastus used to wait and 'tend when he couldn't hardly put one foot before the other, and I didn't go out to help her.

"But at last one afternoon I saw the Doctor come drivin' up like mad with his medicine chest, and Mrs. Babbit came in after supper and said that Luella was real sick.

"'I'd offer to go in and nurse her,' says she, 'but I've got my children to consider, and mebbe it ain't true what they say, but it's queer how many folks that have done for her have died.'

"I didn't say anythin', but I considered how she had been Erastus's wife and how he had set his eyes by her, and I made up my mind to go in the next mornin', unless she was better, and see what I could do; but the next mornin' I see her at the window, and pretty soon she came steppin' out as spry as you please, and a little while afterward Mrs. Babbit came in and told me that the Doctor had got a girl from out of town, a Sarah Jones, to come there, and she said she was pretty sure that the Doctor was goin' to marry Luella.

"I saw him kiss her in the door that night myself, and I knew it was true. The woman came that afternoon, and the way she flew around was a caution. I don't believe Luella had swept since Maria died. She swept and dusted, and washed and ironed; wet clothes and dusters and carpets were flyin' over there all day, and every time Luella set her foot out when the Doctor wa'n't there there was that Sarah Jones helpin' of her up and down the steps, as if she hadn't learned to walk.

"Well, everybody knew that Luella and the Doctor were goin' to be married, but it wa'n't long before they began to talk about his lookin' so poorly, jest as they had about the others; and they talked about Sarah Jones, too.

"Well, the Doctor did die, and he wanted to be married first, so as to leave what little he had to Luella, but he died before the minister could get there, and Sarah Jones died a week afterward.

"Well, that wound up everything for Luella Miller. Not another soul in the whole town would lift a finger for her. There got to be a sort of panic. Then she began to droop in good earnest. She used to have to go to the store herself, for Mrs. Babbit was afraid to let Tommy go for her, and I've seen her goin' past and stoppin' every two or three steps to rest. Well, I stood it as long as I could, but one day I see her comin' with her arms full and stoppin' to lean against the Babbit fence, and I run out and took her bundles and carried them to her house. Then I went home and never spoke one word to her though she called after me dreadful kind of pitiful. Well, that night I was taken sick with a chill, and I was sick as I wanted to be for two weeks. Mrs. Babbit had seen me run out to help Luella and she came in and told me I was goin' to die on account of it. I didn't know whether I was or not, but I considered I had done right by Erastus's wife.

"That last two weeks Luella she had a dreadful hard time, I guess. She was pretty sick, and as near as I could make out nobody dared go near her. I don't know as she was really needin' anythin' very much, for there was enough to eat in her house and it was warm weather, and she made out to cook a little flour gruel every day, I know, but I guess she had a hard time, she that had been so petted and done for all her life.

"When I got so I could go out, I went over there one morning. Mrs. Babbit had just come in to say she hadn't seen any smoke and she didn't know but what it was somebody's duty to go in, but she couldn't help thinkin' of her children, and I got right up, though I hadn't been out of the house for two weeks, and I went in there, and Luella she was layin' on the bed, and she was dyin'.

"She lasted all that day and into the night. But I sat there after the new doctor had gone away. Nobody else dared to go there. It was about midnight that I left her for a minute to run home and get some medicine I had been takin', for I begun to feel rather bad.

"It was a full moon that night, and just as I started out of my door to cross the street back to Luella's, I stopped short, for I saw something."

Lydia Anderson at this juncture always said with a certain

defiance that she did not expect to be believed, and then proceeded in a hushed voice:

"I saw what I saw, and I know I saw it, and I will swear on my death bed that I saw it. I saw Luella Miller and Erastus Miller, and Lily, and Aunt Abby, and Maria, and the Doctor, and Sarah, all goin' out of her door, and all but Luella shone white in the moonlight, and they were all helpin' her along till she seemed to fairly fly in the midst of them. Then it all disappeared. I stood a minute with my heart poundin', then I went over there. I thought of goin' for Mrs. Babbit, but I thought she'd be afraid. So I went alone, though I knew what had happened. Luella was layin' real peaceful, dead on her bed."

This was the story that the old woman, Lydia Anderson, told, but the sequel was told by the people who survived her, and this is the tale which has become folklore in the village.

Lydia Anderson died when she was eighty-seven. She had continued wonderfully hale and hearty for one of her years until about two weeks before her death.

One bright moonlight evening she was sitting beside a window in her parlour when she made a sudden exclamation, and was out of the house and across the street before the neighbour who was taking care of her could stop her. She followed as fast as possible and found Lydia Anderson stretched on the ground before the door of Luella Miller's deserted house, and she was quite dead.

The next night there was a red gleam of fire athwart the moonlight and the old house of Luella Miller was burned to the ground. Nothing is now left of it except a few old cellar stones and a lilac bush, and in summer a helpless trail of morning glories among the weeds, which might be considered emblematic of Luella herself.

M. R. James

(1862–1936)

MONTAGUE RHODES JAMES WAS born in Kent, the fourth child of an evangelical vicar who never got over his disappointment when his youngest son chose academic church history over active soul-saving. After preparatory school, James attended Eton and Cambridge, where in time he would wind up director of the Fitzwilliam Museum and ultimately provost of King's College. He was only seventeen when he published his first article, launching a lifetime of scholarship in dusty corners of ecclesiastical history and medieval manuscripts. In college James discovered the twelfth-century writer Walter Map, whose arcane *De Nugis Curialium* he described, in a letter home to his parents, as containing "extraordinary stories about Ghosts, Vampires, Woodnymphs, etc." As both a scholar and an elegant stylist, James stands out from the crowd in his genre. Not surprisingly, he was a devout fan of another deity in the pantheon of eerie writers, Sheridan Le Fanu, and James seems to have been the prime mover in a revival of interest in the author of "Carmilla."

In the early 1890s, James fell into the habit of reading his own ghostly tales aloud to fellow members of Cambridge's Chitchat Society, especially at Christmas. Ghost stories are always about the past, but James's tales are often explicitly set amid an antiquarian's explorations into the physical remnants of lost ages—musty cathedral ruins, crumbling leather-bound tomes. One of his most popular stories bears the misleadingly dry title "An Episode of Cathedral History," and he titled his 1904 debut collection *Ghost Stories of an Antiquary.* His introduction to this volume modestly expresses a goal for his tales: "If any of them succeed in causing their readers to feel pleasantly uncomfortable when walking along a solitary road at nightfall, or sitting over a dying fire in the small hours, my purpose in writing them will have been attained."

Both critics and fans agree, however, that James transcended his modest portrait of himself as a mere purveyor of goose bumps. "The central story of M. R. James, reiterated with inexhaustible inventiveness," remarks novelist Michael Chabon, "is ultimately the breathtaking fragility of life, of 'reality,' of all of the structures that we have erected to defend ourselves from our constant nagging suspicion that underlying everything is chaos, brutal and unreasoning. It is hard to conceive of a more serious theme, or a more contemporary plot, than this."

"Count Magnus," into which James wove details from his two visits to Sweden around the turn of the century, first appeared in *Ghost Stories of an Antiquary.* Although he advocated narrative restraint, James also confessed that he had little use for amiable specters, that he preferred ghost stories in which the spirit is "malevolent or odious." No ghouls could be more blindly spiteful than his—nor, when finally glimpsed, more viscerally repugnant. James's donnish but chatty narrative sneaks up on a reader and, in a way, on the spirit at its center, but he calmly divulges grisly details when he feels that the story needs them to make the reader pleasantly uncomfortable.

Count Magnus

By what means the papers out of which I have made a connected story came into my hands is the last point which the reader
will learn from these pages. But it is necessary to prefix to my ex-
tracts from them a statement of the form in which I possess them.

They consist, then, partly of a series of collections for a book of
travels, such a volume as was a common product of the forties and
fifties. Horace Marryat's *Journal of a Residence in Jutland and the Danish
Isles* is a fair specimen of the class to which I allude. These books
usually treated of some unfamiliar district on the Continent. They
were illustrated with woodcuts or steel plates. They gave details of
hotel accommodation, and of means of communication, such as we
now expect to find in any well-regulated guide-book, and they
dealt largely in reported conversations with intelligent foreigners,
racy innkeepers and garrulous peasants. In a word, they were
chatty.

Begun with the idea of furnishing material for such a book, my
papers as they progressed assumed the character of a record of one
single personal experience, and this record was continued up to the
very eve, almost, of its termination.

The writer was a Mr. Wraxall. For my knowledge of him I have
to depend entirely on the evidence his writings afford, and from

these I deduce that he was a man past middle age, possessed of some private means, and very much alone in the world. He had, it seems, no settled abode in England, but was a denizen of hotels and boarding-houses. It is probable that he entertained the idea of settling down at some future time which never came; and I think it also likely that the Pantechnicon fire in the early seventies must have destroyed a great deal that would have thrown light on his antecedents, for he refers once or twice to property of his that was warehoused at that establishment.

It is further apparent that Mr. Wraxall had published a book, and that it treated of a holiday he had once taken in Brittany. More than this I cannot say about his work, because a diligent search in bibliographical works has convinced me that it must have appeared either anonymously or under a pseudonym.

As to his character, it is not difficult to form some superficial opinion. He must have been an intelligent and cultivated man. It seems that he was near being a Fellow of his college at Oxford— Brasenose, as I judge from the Calendar. His besetting fault was pretty clearly that of over-inquisitiveness, possibly a good fault in a traveller, certainly a fault for which this traveller paid dearly enough in the end.

On what proved to be his last expedition, he was plotting another book. Scandinavia, a region not widely known to Englishmen forty years ago, had struck him as an interesting field. He must have lighted on some old books of Swedish history or memoirs, and the idea had struck him that there was room for a book descriptive of travel in Sweden, interspersed with episodes from the history of some of the great Swedish families. He procured letters of introduction, therefore, to some persons of quality in Sweden, and set out thither in the early summer of 1863.

Of his travels in the North there is no need to speak, nor of his residence of some weeks in Stockholm. I need only mention that some *savant* resident there put him on the track of an important collection of family papers belonging to the proprietors of an ancient manor-house in Vestergothland, and obtained for him permission to examine them.

The manor-house, or *herrgård*, in question is to be called Råbäck (pronounced something like Roebeck), though that is not its name. It is one of the best buildings of its kind in all the country, and the picture of it in Dahlenberg's *Suecia antiqua et moderna,* engraved in 1694, shows it very much as the tourist may see it to-day. It was built soon after 1600, and is, roughly speaking, very much like an English house of that period in respect of material—red-brick with stone facings—and style. The man who built it was a scion of the great house of de la Gardie, and his descendants possess it still. De la Gardie is the name by which I will designate them when mention of them becomes necessary.

They received Mr. Wraxall with great kindness and courtesy, and pressed him to stay in the house as long as his researches lasted. But, preferring to be independent, and mistrusting his powers of conversing in Swedish, he settled himself at the village inn, which turned out quite sufficiently comfortable, at any rate during the summer months. This arrangement would entail a short walk daily to and from the manor-house of something under a mile. The house itself stood in a park, and was protected—we should say grown up—with large old timber. Near it you found the walled garden, and then entered a close wood fringing one of the small lakes with which the whole country is pitted. Then came the wall of the demesne, and you climbed a steep knoll—a knob of rock lightly covered with soil—and on the top of this stood the church, fenced in with tall dark trees. It was a curious building to English eyes. The nave and aisles were low, and filled with pews and galleries. In the western gallery stood the handsome old organ, gaily painted, and with silver pipes. The ceiling was flat, and had been adorned by a seventeenth-century artist with a strange and hideous "Last Judgment," full of lurid flames, falling cities, burning ships, crying souls, and brown and smiling demons. Handsome brass coronæ hung from the roof;

the pulpit was like a doll's house, covered with little painted wooden cherubs and saints; a stand with three hour-glasses was hinged to the preacher's desk. Such sights as these may be seen in many a church in Sweden now, but what distinguished this one was an addition to the original building. At the eastern end of the north aisle the builder of the manor-house had erected a mausoleum for himself and his family. It was a largish eight-sided building, lighted by a series of oval windows, and it had a domed roof, topped by a kind of pumpkin-shaped object rising into a spire, a form in which Swedish architects greatly delighted. The roof was of copper externally, and was painted black, while the walls, in common with those of the church, were staringly white. To this mausoleum there was no access from the church. It had a portal and steps of its own on the northern side.

Past the churchyard the path to the village goes, and not more than three or four minutes bring you to the inn door.

On the first day of his stay at Råbäck Mr. Wraxall found the church door open, and made those notes of the interior which I have epitomized. Into the mausoleum, however, he could not make his way. He could by looking through the keyhole just descry that there were fine marble effigies and sarcophagi of copper, and a wealth of armorial ornament, which made him very anxious to spend some time in investigation.

The papers he had come to examine at the manor-house proved to be of just the kind he wanted for his book. There were family correspondence, journals, and account-books of the earliest owners of the estate, very carefully kept and clearly written, full of amusing and picturesque detail. The first de la Gardie appeared in them as a strong and capable man. Shortly after the building of the mansion there had been a period of distress in the district, and the peasants had risen and attacked several châteaux and done some damage. The owner of Råbäck took a leading part in suppressing the trouble, and there was reference to executions of ringleaders and severe punishments inflicted with no sparing hand.

The portrait of this Magnus de la Gardie was one of the best in the house, and Mr. Wraxall studied it with no little interest after his day's work. He gives no detailed description of it, but I gather that the face impressed him rather by its power than by its beauty or goodness; in fact, he writes that Count Magnus was an almost phenomenally ugly man.

On this day Mr. Wraxall took his supper with the family, and walked back in the late but still bright evening.

"I must remember," he writes, "to ask the sexton if he can let me into the mausoleum at the church. He evidently has access to it himself, for I saw him to-night standing on the steps, and, as I thought, locking or unlocking the door."

I find that early on the following day Mr. Wraxall had some conversation with his landlord. His setting it down at such length as he does surprised me at first; but I soon realized that the papers I was reading were, at least in their beginning, the materials for the book he was meditating, and that it was to have been one of those quasi-journalistic productions which admit of the introduction of an admixture of conversational matter.

His object, he says, was to find out whether any traditions of Count Magnus de la Gardie lingered on in the scenes of that gentleman's activity, and whether the popular estimate of him were favourable or not. He found that the Count was decidedly not a favourite. If his tenants came late to their work on the days which they owed to him as Lord of the Manor, they were set on the wooden horse, or flogged and branded in the manor-house yard. One or two cases there were of men who had occupied lands which encroached on the lord's domain, and whose houses had been mysteriously burnt on a winter's night, with the whole family inside. But what seemed to dwell on the innkeeper's mind most— for he returned to the subject more than once—was that the Count had been on the Black Pilgrimage, and had brought something or someone back with him.

You will naturally inquire, as Mr. Wraxall did, what the Black

Pilgrimage may have been. But your curiosity on the point must remain unsatisfied for the time being, just as his did. The landlord was evidently unwilling to give a full answer, or indeed any answer, on the point, and, being called out for a moment, trotted off with obvious alacrity, only putting his head in at the door a few minutes afterwards to say that he was called away to Skara, and should not be back till evening.

So Mr. Wraxall had to go unsatisfied to his day's work at the manor-house. The papers on which he was just then engaged soon put his thoughts into another channel, for he had to occupy himself with glancing over the correspondence between Sophia Albertina in Stockholm and her married cousin Ulrica Leonora at Råbäck in the years 1705–1710. The letters were of exceptional interest from the light they threw upon the culture of that period in Sweden, as anyone can testify who has read the full edition of them in the publications of the Swedish Historical Manuscripts Commission.

In the afternoon he had done with these, and after returning the boxes in which they were kept to their places on the shelf, he proceeded, very naturally, to take down some of the volumes nearest to them, in order to determine which of them had best be his principal subject of investigation next day. The shelf he had hit upon was occupied mostly by a collection of account-books in the writing of the first Count Magnus. But one among them was not an account-book, but a book of alchemical and other tracts in another sixteenth-century hand. Not being very familiar with alchemical literature, Mr. Wraxall spends much space which he might have spared in setting out the names and beginnings of the various treatises: The book of the Phœnix, book of the Thirty Words, book of the Toad, book of Miriam, Turba philosophorum, and so forth; and then he announces with a good deal of circumstance his delight at finding, on a leaf originally left blank near the middle of the book, some writing of Count Magnus himself headed "Liber nigræ peregrinationis." It is true that only a few lines were written, but there was quite enough to show that the landlord had that morning been referring to a belief at least as old as the time of Count Magnus, and probably shared by him. This is the English of what was written:

"If any man desires to obtain a long life, if he would obtain a faithful messenger and see the blood of his enemies, it is necessary that he should first go into the city of Chorazin, and there salute the prince . . ." Here there was an erasure of one word, not very thoroughly done, so that Mr. Wraxall felt pretty sure that he was right in reading it as *aëris* ("of the air"). But there was no more of the text copied, only a line in Latin: "Quære reliqua hujus materiei inter secretiora" (See the rest of this matter among the more private things).

It could not be denied that this threw a rather lurid light upon the tastes and beliefs of the Count; but to Mr. Wraxall, separated from him by nearly three centuries, the thought that he might have added to his general forcefulness alchemy, and to alchemy something like magic, only made him a more picturesque figure; and when, after a rather prolonged contemplation of his picture in the hall, Mr. Wraxall set out on his homeward way, his mind was full of the thought of Count Magnus. He had no eyes for his surroundings, no perception of the evening scents of the woods or the evening light on the lake; and when all of a sudden he pulled up short, he was astonished to find himself already at the gate of the churchyard, and within a few minutes of his dinner. His eyes fell on the mausoleum.

"Ah," he said, "Count Magnus, there you are. I should dearly like to see you."

"Like many solitary men," he writes, "I have a habit of talking to myself aloud; and, unlike some of the Greek and Latin particles, I do not expect an answer. Certainly, and perhaps fortunately in this case, there was neither voice nor any that regarded: only the woman who, I suppose, was cleaning up the church, dropped some metallic object on the floor, whose clang startled me. Count Magnus, I think, sleeps sound enough."

That same evening the landlord of the inn, who had heard Mr. Wraxall say that he wished to see the clerk or deacon (as he would be called in Sweden) of the parish, introduced him to that official in the inn parlour. A visit to the de la Gardie tomb-house was soon arranged for the next day, and a little general conversation ensued.

Mr. Wraxall, remembering that one function of Scandinavian deacons is to teach candidates for Confirmation, thought he would refresh his own memory on a Biblical point.

"Can you tell me," he said, "anything about Chorazin?"

The deacon seemed startled, but readily reminded him how that village had once been denounced.

"To be sure," said Mr. Wraxall; "it is, I suppose, quite a ruin now?"

"So I expect," replied the deacon. "I have heard some of our old priests say that Antichrist is to be born there; and there are tales—"

"Ah! what tales are those?" Mr. Wraxall put in.

"Tales, I was going to say, which I have forgotten," said the deacon; and soon after that he said good night.

The landlord was now alone, and at Mr. Wraxall's mercy; and that inquirer was not inclined to spare him.

"Herr Nielsen," he said, "I have found out something about the Black Pilgrimage. You may as well tell me what you know. What did the Count bring back with him?"

Swedes are habitually slow, perhaps, in answering, or perhaps the landlord was an exception. I am not sure; but Mr. Wraxall notes that the landlord spent at least one minute in looking at him before he said anything at all. Then he came close up to his guest, and with a good deal of effort he spoke:

"Mr. Wraxall, I can tell you this one little tale, and no more—not any more. You must not ask anything when I have done. In my grandfather's time—that is, ninety-two years ago—there were two men who said: 'The Count is dead; we do not care for him. We will go to-night and have a free hunt in his wood'—the long wood on the hill that you have seen behind Råbäck. Well, those that heard them say this, they said: 'No, do not go; we are sure you will meet with persons walking who should not be walking. They should be resting, not walking.' These men laughed. There were no forest-men to keep the wood, because no one wished to hunt there. The family were not here at the house. These men could do what they wished.

"Very well, they go to the wood that night. My grandfather was sitting here in this room. It was the summer, and a light night. With the window open, he could see out to the wood, and hear.

"So he sat there, and two or three men with him, and they listened. At first they hear nothing at all; then they hear someone— you know how far away it is—they hear someone scream, just as if the most inside part of his soul was twisted out of him. All of them in the room caught hold of each other, and they sat so for three-quarters of an hour. Then they hear someone else, only about three hundred ells off. They hear him laugh out loud: it was not one of those two men that laughed, and, indeed, they have all of them said that it was not any man at all. After that they hear a great door shut.

"Then, when it was just light with the sun, they all went to the priest. They said to him:

"'Father, put on your gown and your ruff, and come to bury these men, Anders Bjornsen and Hans Thorbjorn.'

"You understand that they were sure these men were dead. So they went to the wood—my grandfather never forgot this. He said they were all like so many dead men themselves. The priest, too, he was in a white fear. He said when they came to him:

"'I heard one cry in the night, and I heard one laugh afterwards. If I cannot forget that, I shall not be able to sleep again.'

"So they went to the wood, and they found these men on the edge of the wood. Hans Thorbjorn was standing with his back against a tree, and all the time he was pushing with his hands— pushing something away from him which was not there. So he was not dead. And they led him away, and took him to the house at

Nykjoping, and he died before the winter; but he went on pushing
with his hands. Also Anders Bjornsen was there; but he was dead.
And I tell you this about Anders Bjornsen, that he was once a beautiful man, but now his face was not there, because the flesh of it was
sucked away off the bones. You understand that? My grandfather did
not forget that. And they laid him on the bier which they brought,
and they put a cloth over his head, and the priest walked before; and
they began to sing the psalm for the dead as well as they could. So, as
they were singing the end of the first verse, one fell down, who was
carrying the head of the bier, and the others looked back, and they
saw that the cloth had fallen off, and the eyes of Anders Bjornsen
were looking up, because there was nothing to close over them. And
this they could not bear. Therefore the priest laid the cloth upon
him, and sent for a spade, and they buried him in that place."

The next day Mr. Wraxall records that the deacon called for him
soon after his breakfast, and took him to the church and mausoleum. He noticed that the key of the latter was hung on a nail just
by the pulpit, and it occurred to him that, as the church door seemed
to be left unlocked as a rule, it would not be difficult for him to pay
a second and more private visit to the monuments if there proved to
be more of interest among them than could be digested at first. The
building, when he entered it, he found not unimposing. The monuments, mostly large erections of the seventeenth and eighteenth
centuries, were dignified if luxuriant, and the epitaphs and heraldry
were copious. The central space of the domed room was occupied
by three copper sarcophagi, covered with finely-engraved ornament. Two of them had, as is commonly the case in Denmark and
Sweden, a large metal crucifix on the lid. The third, that of Count
Magnus, as it appeared, had, instead of that, a full-length effigy engraved upon it, and round the edge were several bands of similar
ornament representing various scenes. One was a battle, with can-
non belching out smoke, and walled towns, and troops of pikemen.
Another showed an execution. In a third, among trees, was a man
running at full speed, with flying hair and outstretched hands. After

him followed a strange form; it would be hard to say whether the artist had intended it for a man, and was unable to give the requisite similitude, or whether it was intentionally made as monstrous as it looked. In view of the skill with which the rest of the drawing was done, Mr. Wraxall felt inclined to adopt the latter idea. The figure was unduly short, and was for the most part muffled in a hooded garment which swept the ground. The only part of the form which projected from that shelter was not shaped like any hand or arm. Mr. Wraxall compares it to the tentacle of a devil-fish, and continues: "On seeing this, I said to myself, 'This, then, which is evidently an allegorical representation of some kind—a fiend pursuing a hunted soul—may be the origin of the story of Count Magnus and his mysterious companion. Let us see how the huntsman is pictured: doubtless it will be a demon blowing his horn.'" But, as it turned out, there was no such sensational figure, only the semblance of a cloaked man on a hillock, who stood leaning on a stick, and watching the hunt with an interest which the engraver had tried to express in his attitude.

Mr. Wraxall noted the finely-worked and massive steel padlocks—three in number—which secured the sarcophagus. One of them, he saw, was detached, and lay on the pavement. And then, unwilling to delay the deacon longer or to waste his own working-time, he made his way onward to the manor-house.

"It is curious," he notes, "how on retracing a familiar path one's thoughts engross one to the absolute exclusion of surrounding objects. To-night, for the second time, I had entirely failed to notice where I was going (I had planned a private visit to the tomb-house to copy the epitaphs), when I suddenly, as it were, awoke to consciousness, and found myself (as before) turning in at the churchyard gate, and, I believe, singing or chanting some such words as, 'Are you awake, Count Magnus? Are you asleep, Count Magnus?' and then something more which I have failed to recollect. It seemed to me that I must have been behaving in this nonsensical way for some time."

He found the key of the mausoleum where he had expected to find it, and copied the greater part of what he wanted; in fact, he stayed until the light began to fail him.

"I must have been wrong," he writes, "in saying that one of the padlocks of my Count's sarcophagus was unfastened; I see to-night that two are loose. I picked both up, and laid them carefully on the window-ledge, after trying unsuccessfully to close them. The remaining one is still firm, and, though I take it to be a spring lock, I cannot guess how it is opened. Had I succeeded in undoing it, I am almost afraid I should have taken the liberty of opening the sarcophagus. It is strange, the interest I feel in the personality of this, I fear, somewhat ferocious and grim old noble."

The day following was, as it turned out, the last of Mr. Wraxall's stay at Råbäck. He received letters connected with certain investments which made it desirable that he should return to England; his work among the papers was practically done, and travelling was slow. He decided, therefore, to make his farewells, put some finishing touches to his notes, and be off.

These finishing touches and farewells, as it turned out, took more time than he had expected. The hospitable family insisted on his staying to dine with them—they dined at three—and it was verging on half-past six before he was outside the iron gates of Råbäck. He dwelt on every step of his walk by the lake, determined to saturate himself, now that he trod it for the last time, in the sentiment of the place and hour. And when he reached the summit of the churchyard knoll, he lingered for many minutes, gazing at the limitless prospect of woods near and distant, all dark beneath a sky of liquid green. When at last he turned to go, the thought struck him that surely he must bid farewell to Count Magnus as well as the rest of the de la Gardies. The church was but twenty yards away, and he knew where the key of the mausoleum hung. It was not long before he was standing over the great copper coffin, and, as usual, talking to himself aloud. "You may have been a bit of a rascal in your time,

Magnus," he was saying, "but for all that I should like to see you, or, rather—"

"Just at that instant," he says, "I felt a blow on my foot. Hastily enough I drew it back, and something fell on the pavement with a clash. It was the third, the last of the three padlocks which had fastened the sarcophagus. I stooped to pick it up, and—Heaven is my witness that I am writing only the bare truth—before I had raised myself there was a sound of metal hinges creaking, and I distinctly saw the lid shifting upwards. I may have behaved like a coward, but I could not for my life stay for one moment. I was outside that dreadful building in less time than I can write—almost as quickly as I could have said—the words; and what frightens me yet more, I could not turn the key in the lock. As I sit here in my room noting these facts, I ask myself (it was not twenty minutes ago) whether that noise of creaking metal continued, and I cannot tell whether it did or not. I only know that there was something more than I have written that alarmed me, but whether it was sound or sight I am not able to remember. What is this that I have done?"

POOR MR. WRAXALL! HE set out on his journey to England on the next day, as he had planned, and he reached England in safety; and yet, as I gather from his changed hand and inconsequent jottings, a broken man. One of several small notebooks that have come to me with his papers gives, not a key to, but a kind of inkling of, his experiences. Much of his journey was made by canal-boat, and I find not less than six painful attempts to enumerate and describe his fellow-passengers. The entries are of this kind:

24. Pastor of village in Skåne. Usual black coat and soft black hat.
25. Commercial traveller from Stockholm going to Trollhättan. Black coat, brown hat.
26. Man in long black cloak, broad-leafed hat, very old-fashioned.

This entry is lined out, and a note added: "Perhaps identical with No. 13. Have not yet seen his face." On referring to No. 13, I find that he is a Roman priest in a cassock.

The net result of the reckoning is always the same. Twenty-eight people appear in the enumeration, one being always a man in a long black cloak and broad hat, and the other a "short figure in dark cloak and hood." On the other hand, it is always noted that only twenty-six passengers appear at meals, and that the man in the cloak is perhaps absent, and the short figure is certainly absent.

On reaching England, it appears that Mr. Wraxall landed at Harwich, and that he resolved at once to put himself out of the reach of some person or persons whom he never specifies, but whom he had evidently come to regard as his pursuers. Accordingly he took a vehicle—it was a closed fly—not trusting the railway, and drove across country to the village of Belchamp St. Paul. It was about nine o'clock on a moonlight August night when he neared the place. He was sitting forward, and looking out of the window at the fields and thickets—there was little else to be seen—racing past him. Suddenly he came to a cross-road. At the corner two figures were standing motionless; both were in dark cloaks; the taller one wore a hat, the shorter a hood. He had no time to see their faces, nor did they make any motion that he could discern. Yet the horse shied violently and broke into a gallop, and Mr. Wraxall sank back into his seat in something like desperation. He had seen them before.

Arrived at Belchamp St. Paul, he was fortunate enough to find a decent furnished lodging, and for the next twenty-four hours he lived, comparatively speaking, in peace. His last notes were written on this day. They are too disjointed and ejaculatory to be given here in full, but the substance of them is clear enough. He is expecting a visit from his pursuers—how or when he knows not—and his constant cry is "What has he done?" and "Is there no hope?" Doctors, he knows, would call him mad, policemen would laugh at him.

The parson is away. What can he do but lock his door and cry to God?

PEOPLE STILL REMEMBERED LAST year at Belchamp St. Paul how a strange gentleman came one evening in August years back; and how the next morning but one he was found dead, and there was an inquest; and the jury that viewed the body fainted, seven of 'em did, and none of 'em wouldn't speak to what they see, and the verdict was visitation of God; and how the people as kep' the 'ouse moved out that same week, and went away from that part. But they do not, I think, know that any glimmer of light has ever been thrown, or could be thrown, on the mystery. It so happened that last year the little house came into my hands as part of a legacy. It had stood empty since 1863, and there seemed no prospect of letting it; so I had it pulled down, and the papers of which I have given you an abstract were found in a forgotten cupboard under the window in the best bedroom.

❋

Alice and Claude Askew

(Jane de Courcy, 1874–1917, and Arthur Cary, 1866–1917)

THIS NOW FORGOTTEN HUSBAND-AND-WIFE team of collaborators wrote many novels and story cycles. Their one series about the supernatural featured an investigator of the occult named Aylmer Vance. The brisk and rather lightweight stories are narrated by Vance's admiring dogsbody and chronicler, Mr. Dexter, in a Holmes and Watson sort of way. Vance himself, in his attention to the vast gray area beyond the purview of Holmes, is reminiscent of two earlier detectives in this vein, William Hope Hodgson's Carnacki the Ghost Finder and Algernon Blackwood's John Silence. Vance is not quite up to the level of these two characters, but the stories are fun, as he investigates various apparitions and hauntings, as well as once pursuing a memorable vampire.

The series appeared in *The Weekly Tale-Teller* during 1914, with "Aylmer Vance and the Vampire" published in the August 1 issue. Later the same year, all eight Vance stories were gathered into *Aylmer Vance, Ghost Seer.* Both authors died when their ship was torpedoed by a submarine during World War I.

Aylmer Vance and the Vampire

AYLMER VANCE HAD ROOMS in Dover Street, Piccadilly, and now that I had decided to follow in his footsteps and to accept him as my instructor in matters psychic, I found it convenient to lodge in the same house. Aylmer and I quickly became close friends, and he showed me how to develop that faculty of clairvoyance which I had possessed without being aware of it. And I may say at once that this particular faculty of mine proved of service on several important occasions.

At the same time I made myself useful to Vance in other ways, not the least of which was that of acting as recorder of his many strange adventures. For himself, he never cared much about publicity, and it was some time before I could persuade him, in the interests of science, to allow me to give any detailed account of his experiences to the world.

The incidents which I will now relate occurred very soon after we had taken up our residence together, and while I was still, so to speak, a novice.

It was about ten o'clock in the morning that a visitor was announced. He sent up a card which bore upon it the name of Paul Davenant.

The name was familiar to me, and I wondered if this could be the same Mr. Davenant who was so well-known for his polo playing and for his success as an amateur rider, especially over the hurdles? He was a young man of wealth and position, and I recollected that he had married, about a year ago, a girl who was reckoned the greatest beauty of the season. All the illustrated papers had given their portraits at the time, and I remember thinking what a remarkably handsome couple they made.

Mr. Davenant was ushered in, and at first I was uncertain as to whether this could be the individual whom I had in mind, so wan and pale and ill did he appear. A finely built, upstanding man at the time of his marriage, he had now acquired a languid droop of the shoulders and a shuffling gait, while his face, especially about the lips, was bloodless to an alarming degree.

And yet it was the same man, for behind all this I could recognize the shadow of the good looks that had once distinguished Paul Davenant.

He took the chair which Aylmer offered him—after the usual preliminary civilities had been exchanged—and then glanced doubtfully in my direction. "I wish to consult you privately, Mr. Vance," he said. "The matter is of considerable importance to myself, and, if I may say so, of a somewhat delicate nature."

Of course I rose immediately to withdraw from the room, but Vance laid his hand upon my arm.

"If the matter is connected with research in my particular line, Mr. Davenant," he said, "if there is any investigation you wish me to take up on your behalf, I shall be glad if you will include Mr. Dexter in your confidence. Mr. Dexter assists me in my work. But, of course—"

"Oh, no," interrupted the other, "if that is the case, pray let Mr. Dexter remain. I think," he added, glancing at me with a friendly smile, "that you are an Oxford man, are you not, Mr. Dexter? It was before my time, but I have heard of your name in connection with the river. You rowed at Henley, unless I am very much mistaken."

I admitted the fact, with a pleasurable sensation of pride. I was very keen upon rowing in those days, and a man's prowess at school and college always remains dear to his heart.

After this we quickly became on friendly terms, and Paul Davenant proceeded to take Aylmer and myself into his confidence.

He began by calling attention to his personal appearance. "You would hardly recognise me for the same man I was a year ago," he said. "I've been losing flesh steadily for the last six months. I came up from Scotland about a week ago, to consult a London doctor. I've seen two—in fact they've held a sort of consultation over me—but the result, I may say, is far from satisfactory. They don't seem to know what is really the matter with me."

"Anaemia—heart," suggested Vance. He was scrutinising his visitor keenly, and yet without any particular appearance of doing so. "I believe it not infrequently happens that you athletes overdo yourselves—put too much strain upon the heart—"

"My heart is quite sound," responded Davenant. "Physically it is in perfect condition. The trouble seems to be that it hasn't enough blood to pump into my veins. The doctors wanted to know if I had met with an accident involving a great loss of blood—but I haven't. I've had no accident at all, and as for anaemia, well I don't seem to show the ordinary symptoms of it. The inexplicable thing is that I've lost blood without knowing it, and apparently this has been going on for some time, for I've been getting steadily worse. It was almost imperceptible at first—not a sudden collapse, you understand, but a gradual failure of health."

"I wonder," remarked Vance slowly, "what induced you to consult me? For you know, of course, the direction in which I pursue my investigations. May I ask if you have reason to consider that your state of health is due to some cause which we may describe as superphysical?"

A slight colour came to Davenant's cheeks.

"There are curious circumstances," he said, in a low and earnest tone of voice. "I've been turning them over in my mind, trying to see light through them. I daresay it's all the sheerest folly—and I must tell you that I'm not in the least a superstitious sort of man. I don't mean to say that I'm absolutely incredulous, but I've never given thought to such things—I've led too active a life. But, as I have said, there are curious circumstances about my case, and that is why I decided upon consulting you."

"Will you tell me everything without reserve?" said Vance. I could see that he was interested. He was sitting up in his chair, his feet supported on a stool, his elbows on his knees, his chin in his hands—a favourite attitude of his. "Have you," he suggested slowly, "any mark upon your body, anything that you might associate, however remotely, with your present weakness and ill-health?"

"It's a curious thing that you should ask me that question," returned Davenant, "because I have got a curious mark, a sort of scar, that I can't account for. But I showed it to the doctors, and they assured me that it could have nothing whatever to do with my condition. In any case, if it had, it was something altogether outside their experience. I think they imagined it to be nothing more than a birthmark, a sort of mole, for they asked me if I'd had it all my life. But that I can swear I haven't. I only noticed it for the first time about six months ago, when my health began to fail. But you can see for yourself."

He loosened his collar and bared his throat. Vance rose and made a careful scrutiny of the suspicious mark. It was situated a very little to the left of the central line, just above the clavicle, and, as Vance pointed out, directly over the big vessels of the throat. My friend called to me so that I might examine it, too. Whatever the opinion of the doctors may have been, Aylmer was obviously deeply interested.

And yet there was very little to show. The skin was quite intact, and there was no sign of inflammation. There were two red marks, about an inch apart, each of which was inclined to be crescent in shape. They were more visible than they might otherwise have been owing to the peculiar whiteness of Davenant's skin.

"It can't be anything of importance," said Davenant, with a

slightly uneasy laugh. "I'm inclined to think the marks are dying away."

"Have you ever noticed them more inflamed than they are at present?" inquired Vance. "If so, was it at any special time?"

Davenant reflected. "Yes," he replied slowly, "there have been times, usually, I think perhaps invariably, when I wake up in the morning, that I've noticed them larger and more angry looking. And I've felt a slight sensation of pain—a tingling—oh, very slight, and I've never worried about it. Only now you suggest it to my mind, I believe that those same mornings I have felt particularly tired and done up—a sensation of lassitude absolutely unusual to me. And once, Mr. Vance, I remember quite distinctly that there was a stain of blood close to the mark. I didn't think anything of it at the time, and just wiped it away."

"I see." Aylmer Vance resumed his seat and invited his visitor to do the same. "And now," he resumed, "you said, Mr. Davenant, that there are certain peculiar circumstances you wish to acquaint me with. Will you do so?"

And so Davenant readjusted his collar and proceeded to tell his story. I will tell it as far as I can, without any reference to the occasional interruptions of Vance and myself.

Paul Davenant, as I have said, was a man of wealth and position, and so, in every sense of the word, he was a suitable husband for Miss Jessica MacThane, the young lady who eventually became his wife. Before coming to the incidents attending his loss of health, he had a great deal to recount about Miss MacThane and her family history.

She was of Scottish descent, and although she had certain characteristic features of her race, she was not really Scotch in appearance. Hers was the beauty of the far South rather than that of the Highlands from which she had her origin. Names are not always suited to their owners, and Miss MacThane's was peculiarly inappropriate. She had, in fact, been christened Jessica in a sort of pathetic effort to counteract her obvious departure from normal type. There was a reason for this which we were soon to learn.

Miss MacThane was especially remarkable for her wonderful red hair, hair such as one hardly ever sees outside Italy—not the Celtic red—and it was so long that it reached to her feet, and it had an extraordinary gloss upon it, so that it seemed almost to have individual life of its own. Then she had just the complexion that one would expect with such hair, the purest ivory white, and not in the least marred by freckles, as is so often the case with red-haired girls. Her beauty was derived from an ancestress who had been brought to Scotland from some foreign shore—no-one knew exactly whence.

Davenant fell in love with her almost at once, and he had every reason to believe, in spite of her many admirers, that his love was returned. At this time he knew very little about her personal history. He was aware only that she was very wealthy in her own right, an orphan, and the last representative of a race that had once been famous in the annals of history—or rather infamous, for the MacThanes had distinguished themselves more by cruelty and lust of blood than by deeds of chivalry. A clan of turbulent robbers in the past, they had helped to add many a blood-stained page to the history of their country.

Jessica had lived with her father, who owned a house in London, until his death when she was about fifteen years of age. Her mother had died in Scotland when Jessica was still a tiny child. Mr. MacThane had been so affected by his wife's death that, with his little daughter, he had abandoned his Scotch estate altogether—or so it was believed—leaving it to the management of a bailiff— though, indeed, there was but little work for the bailiff to do, since there were practically no tenants left. Blackwick Castle had borne for many years a most unenviable reputation.

After the death of her father, Miss MacThane had gone to live with a certain Mrs. Meredith, who was a connection of her mother's—on her father's side she had not a single relation left. Jessica was absolutely the last of a clan once so extensive that inter-marriage had been a tradition of the family, but which for the last two hundred years had been gradually dwindling to extinction.

Mrs. Meredith took Jessica into Society—which would never have been her privilege had Mr. MacThane lived, for he was a moody, self-absorbed man, and prematurely old—one who seemed worn down by the weight of a great grief.

Well, I have said that Paul Davenant quickly fell in love with Jessica, and it was not long before he proposed for her hand. To his great surprise, for he had good reason to believe that she cared for him, he met with a refusal; nor would she give any explanation, though she burst into a flood of pitiful tears.

Bewildered and bitterly disappointed, he consulted Mrs. Mere-dith, with whom he happened to be on friendly terms, and from her he learnt that Jessica had already had several proposals, all from quite desirable men, but that one after another had been rejected.

Paul consoled himself with the reflection that perhaps Jessica did not love them, whereas he was quite sure that she cared for himself. Under these circumstances he determined to try again.

He did so, and with better result. Jessica admitted her love, but at the same time she repeated that she could not marry him. Love and marriage were not for her. Then, to his utter amaze, she de-clared that she had been born under a curse—a curse which sooner or later was bound to show itself in her, and which, moreover, must react cruelly, perhaps fatally, upon anyone with whom she linked her life. How could she allow a man she loved to take such a risk? Above all, since the evil was hereditary, there was one point upon which she had quite made up her mind: no child should ever call her mother—she must be the last of her race indeed.

Of course, Davenant was amazed, and inclined to think that Jessica had got some absurd idea into her head which a little rea-soning on his part would dispel. There was only one other possible explanation. Was it lunacy she was afraid of?

But Jessica shook her head. She did not know of any lunacy in her family. The ill was deeper, more subtle than that. And then she told him all that she knew.

The curse—she made use of that word for want of a better—was attached to the ancient race from which she had her origin. Her father had suffered from it, and his father and grandfather before him. All three had taken to themselves young wives who had died mysteriously, of some wasting disease, within a few years. Had they observed the ancient family tradition of intermarriage this might possibly not have happened, but in their case, since the family was so near extinction, this had not been possible.

For the curse—or whatever it was—did not kill those who bore the name of MacThane. It only rendered them a danger to others. It was as if they absorbed from the blood-soaked walls of their fatal castle a deadly taint which reacted terribly upon those with whom they were brought into contact, especially their nearest and dearest.

"Do you know what my father said we have it in us to become?" said Jessica with a shudder. "He used the word *vampires*. Paul, think of it—vampires—preying upon the life-blood of others."

And then, when Davenant was inclined to laugh, she checked him. "No," she cried out, "it is not impossible. Think. We are a decadent race. From the earliest times our history has been marked by bloodshed and cruelty. The walls of Blackwick Castle are impregnated with evil—every stone could tell its tale of violence, pain, lust, and murder. What can one expect of those who have spent their lifetime between its walls?"

"But you have not done so," exclaimed Paul. "You have been spared that, Jessica. You were taken away after your mother died, and you have no recollection of Blackwick Castle, none at all. And you need never set foot in it again."

"I'm afraid the evil is in my blood," she replied sadly, "although I am unconscious of it now. And as for not returning to Blackwick—I'm not sure that I can help myself. At least, that is what my father warned me of. He said that there is something there, some compelling force, that will call me to it in spite of my-self. But, oh, I don't know—I don't know, and that is what makes it so difficult. If I could only believe that all this is nothing but an idle superstition, I might be happy again, for I have it in me to en-joy life, and I'm young, very young; but my father told me these things when he was on his deathbed." She added the last words in a low, awe-stricken tone.

Paul pressed her to tell him all that she knew, and eventually she revealed another fragment of family history which seemed to have some bearing upon the case. It dealt with her own astonishing likeness to that ancestress of a couple of hundred years ago, whose existence seemed to have presaged the gradual downfall of the clan of the MacThanes.

A certain Robert MacThane, departing from the traditions of his family, which demanded that he should not marry outside his clan, brought home a wife from foreign shores, a woman of wonder-ful beauty, who was possessed of glowing masses of red hair and a complexion of ivory whiteness—such as had more or less distin-guished since then every female of the race born in the direct line.

It was not long before this woman came to be regarded in the neighbourhood as a witch. Queer stories were circulated abroad as to her doings, and the reputation of Blackwick Castle became worse than ever before.

And then one day she disappeared. Robert MacThane had been absent upon some business for twenty-four hours, and it was upon his return that he found her gone. The neighbourhood was searched, but without avail, and then Robert, who was a violent man and who had adored his foreign wife, called together certain of his ten-ants whom he suspected, rightly or wrongly, of foul play, and had them murdered in cold blood. Murder was easy in those days, yet such an outcry was raised that Robert had to take flight, leaving his two children in the care of their nurse, and for a long while Blackwick Castle was without a master.

But its evil reputation persisted. It was said that Zaida, the

witch, though dead, still made her presence felt. Many children of
the tenantry and young people of the neighbourhood sickened and
died—possibly of quite natural causes; but this did not prevent a
mantle of terror settling upon the countryside, for it was said that
Zaida had been seen—a pale woman clad in white—flitting about
the cottages at night, and where she passed sickness and death were
sure to supervene.

And from that time the fortune of the family gradually declined.
Heir succeeded heir, but no sooner was he installed at Blackwick
Castle than his nature, whatever it may previously have been,
seemed to undergo a change. It was as if he absorbed into himself
all the weight of evil that had stained his family name—as if he
did, indeed, become a vampire, bringing blight upon any not directly connected with his own house.

And so, by degrees, Blackwick was deserted of its tenantry. The
land around it was left uncultivated—the farms stood empty. This
had persisted to the present day, for the superstitious peasantry still
told their tales of the mysterious white woman who hovered about
the neighbourhood, and whose appearance betokened death—and
possibly worse than death.

And yet it seemed that the last representatives of the MacThanes
could not desert their ancestral home. Riches they had, sufficient
to live happily upon elsewhere, but, drawn by some power they
could not contend against, they had preferred to spend their lives in
the solitude of the now half-ruined castle, shunned by their neighbours, feared and execrated by the few tenants that still clung to
their soil.

So it had been with Jessica's grandfather and great-grandfather.
Each of them had married a young wife, and in each case their love
story had been all too brief. The vampire spirit was still abroad,
expressing itself—or so it seemed—through the living representatives of bygone generations of evil, and young blood had been demanded at the sacrifice.

And to them had succeeded Jessica's father. He had not profited by their example, but had followed directly in their footsteps. And the same fate had befallen the wife whom he passionately adored. She had died of pernicious anaemia—so the doctors said—but he had regarded himself as her murderer.

But, unlike his predecessors, he had torn himself away from Blackwick—and this for the sake of his child. Unknown to her, however, he had returned year after year, for there were times when the passionate longing for the gloomy, mysterious halls and corridors of the old castle, for the wild stretches of moorland, and the dark pine woods, would come upon him too strongly to be resisted. And so he knew that for his daughter, as for himself, there was no escape, and he warned her, when the relief of death was at last granted to him, of what her fate must be.

This was the tale that Jessica told the man who wished to make her his wife, and he made light of it, as such a man would, regarding it all as foolish superstition, the delusion of a mind overwrought. And at last—perhaps it was not very difficult, for she loved him with all her heart and soul—he succeeded in inducing Jessica to think as he did, to banish morbid ideas, as he called them, from her brain, and to consent to marry him at an early date.

"I'll take any risk you like," he declared. "I'll even go and live at Blackwick if you should desire it. To think of you, my lovely Jessica, a vampire! Why, I never heard such nonsense in my life."

"Father said I'm very like Zaida, the witch," she protested, but he silenced her with a kiss.

And so they were married and spent their honeymoon abroad, and in the autumn Paul accepted an invitation to a house party in Scotland for the grouse shooting, a sport to which he was absolutely devoted, and Jessica agreed with him that there was no reason why he should forego his pleasure.

Perhaps it was an unwise thing to do, to venture to Scotland, but by this time the young couple, more deeply in love with each other than ever, had got quite over their fears. Jessica was redolent with health and spirits, and more than once she declared that if they should be anywhere in the neighbourhood of Blackwick she would like to see the old castle out of curiosity, and just to show how absolutely she had got over the foolish terrors that used to assail her.

This seemed to Paul to be quite a wise plan, and so one day, since they were actually staying at no great distance, they motored over to Blackwick, and finding the bailiff, got him to show them over the castle.

It was a great castellated pile, grey with age, and in places falling into ruin. It stood on a steep hillside, with the rock of which it seemed to form part, and on one side of it there was a precipitous drop to a mountain stream a hundred feet below. The robber Mac-Thanes of the old days could not have desired a better stronghold.

At the back, climbing up the mountain side, were dark pine woods, from which, here and there, rugged crags protruded, and these were fantastically shaped, some like gigantic and misshapen human forms, which stood up as if they mounted guard over the castle and the narrow gorge, by which alone it could be approached.

This gorge was always full of weird, uncanny sound. It might have been a storehouse for the wind, which, even on calm days, rushed up and down as if seeking an escape, and it moaned among the pines and whistled in the crags and shouted derisive laughter as it was tossed from side to side of the rocky heights. It was like the plaint of lost souls—that is the expression Davenant made use of— the plaint of lost souls.

The road, little more than a track now, passed through this gorge, and then, after skirting a small but deep lake, which hardly knew the light of the sun, so shut in was it by overhanging trees, climbed the hill to the castle.

And the castle! Davenant used but a few words to describe it, yet somehow I could see the gloomy edifice in my mind's eye, and something of the lurking horror that it contained communicated itself to my brain. Perhaps my clairvoyant sense assisted me, for when he spoke of them I seemed already acquainted with the great stone halls, the long corridors, gloomy and cold even on the brightest and warmest of days; the dark, oak-panelled rooms, and the broad central staircase up which one of the early MacThanes had once led a dozen men on horseback in pursuit of a stag which had taken refuge within the precincts of the castle. There was the keep, too, its walls so thick that the ravages of time had made no impression upon them, and beneath the keep were dungeons which could tell terrible tales of ancient wrong and lingering pain.

Well, Mr. and Mrs. Davenant visited as much as the bailiff could show them of this ill-omened edifice, and Paul, for his part, thought pleasantly of his own Derbyshire home, the fine Georgian mansion, replete with every modern comfort, where he proposed to settle with his wife. And so he received something of a shock when, as they drove away, she slipped her hand into his and whispered: "Paul, you promised, didn't you, that you would refuse me nothing?"

She had been strangely silent till she spoke these words. Paul, slightly apprehensive, assured her that she only had to ask—but the speech did not come from his heart, for he guessed vaguely what she desired.

She wanted to go and live at the castle—oh, only for a little while, for she was sure she would soon tire of it. But the bailiff had told her that there were papers, documents, which she ought to examine, since the property was now hers—and, besides, she was interested in this home of her ancestors, and wanted to explore it more thoroughly. Oh, no, she wasn't in the least influenced by the old superstition—that wasn't the attraction—she had quite got over those silly ideas. Paul had cured her, and since he himself was so convinced that they were without foundation he ought not to mind granting her her whim.

This was a plausible argument, not easy to controvert. In the end Paul yielded, though it was not without a struggle. He suggested amendments. Let him at least have the place done up for her—that would take time; or let them postpone their visit till next year—in the summer—not move in just as the winter was upon them.

But Jessica did not want to delay longer than she could help, and she hated the idea of redecoration. Why, it would spoil the illusion of the old place, and, besides, it would be a waste of money since she only wished to remain there for a week or two. The Derbyshire house was not quite ready yet; they must allow time for the paper to dry on the walls.

And so, a week later, when their stay with their friends was concluded, they went to Blackwick, the bailiff having engaged a few raw servants and generally made things as comfortable for them as possible. Paul was worried and apprehensive, but he could not admit this to his wife after having so loudly proclaimed his theories on the subject of superstition.

They had been married three months at this time—nine had passed since then, and they had never left Blackwick for more than a few hours—till now Paul had come to London—alone.

"Over and over again," he declared, "my wife has begged me to go. With tears in her eyes, almost upon her knees, she has entreated me to leave her, but I have steadily refused unless she will accompany me. But that is the trouble, Mr. Vance, she cannot; there is something, some mysterious horror, that holds her there as surely as if she were bound with fetters. It holds her more strongly even than it held her father—we found out that he used to spend six months at least of every year at Blackwick—months when he pretended that he was traveling abroad. You see the spell—or whatever the accursed thing may be—never really relaxed its grip of him."

"Did you never attempt to take your wife away?" asked Vance.

"Yes, several times; but it was hopeless. She would become so ill as soon as we were beyond the limit of the estate that I invariably had to take her back. Once we got as far as Dorekirk—that is the nearest town, you know—and I thought I should be successful if only I could get through the night. But she escaped me; she climbed out of a window—she meant to go back on foot, at night, all those long miles. Then I have had doctors down; but it is I who wanted the doctors, not she. They have ordered me away, but I have refused to obey them till now."

"Is your wife changed at all—physically?" interrupted Vance.

Davenant reflected. "Changed," he said, "yes, but so subtly that I hardly know how to describe it. She is more beautiful than ever—and yet it isn't the same beauty, if you can understand me. I have spoken of her white complexion, well, one is more than ever conscious of it now, because her lips have become so red—they are almost like a splash of blood upon her face. And the upper one has a peculiar curve that I don't think it had before, and when she laughs she doesn't smile—do you know what I mean? Then her hair—it has lost its wonderful gloss. Of course, I know she is fretting about me; but that is so peculiar, too, for at times, as I have told you, she will implore me to go and leave her, and then, perhaps only a few minutes later, she will wreathe her arms round my neck and say she cannot live without me. And I feel that there is a struggle going on within her, that she is only yielding slowly to the horrible influence—whatever it is—that she is herself when she begs me to go. But when she entreats me to stay—and it is then that her fascination is most intense—oh, I can't help remembering what she told me before we were married, and that word"—he lowered his voice—"the word *vampire*—"

He passed his hand over his brow that was wet with perspiration. "But that's absurd, ridiculous," he muttered; "these fantastic beliefs have been exploded years ago. We live in the twentieth century."

A pause ensued, then Vance said quietly, "Mr. Davenant, since you have taken me into your confidence, since you have found doctors of no avail, will you let me try to help you? I think I may be of some use—if it is not already too late. Should you agree, Mr. Dexter and I will accompany you, as you have suggested, to Blackwick

Castle as early as possible—by tonight's mail North. Under ordinary circumstances, I should tell you, as you value your life, not to return—"

Davenant shook his head. "That is advice which I should never take," he declared. "I had already decided, under any circumstances, to travel North tonight. I am glad that you both will accompany me."

And so it was decided. We settled to meet at the station, and presently Paul Davenant took his departure. Any other details that remained to be told he would put us in possession of during the course of the journey.

"A curious and most interesting case," remarked Vance when we were alone. "What do you make of it, Dexter?"

"I suppose," I replied cautiously, "that there is such a thing as vampirism even in these days of advanced civilisation? I can understand the evil influence that a very old person may have upon a young one if they happen to be in constant intercourse—the worn-out tissue sapping healthy vitality for their own support. And there are certain people—I could think of several myself—who seem to depress one and undermine one's energies, quite unconsciously of course, but one feels somehow that vitality has passed from oneself to them. And in this case, when the force is centuries old, expressing itself, in some mysterious way, through Davenant's wife, is it not feasible to believe that he may be physically affected by it, even though the whole thing is sheerly mental?"

"You think, then," demanded Vance, "that it is sheerly mental? Tell me, if that is so, how do you account for the marks on Davenant's throat?"

This was a question to which I found no reply, and though I pressed him for his views, Vance would not commit himself further just then.

Of our long journey to Scotland I need say nothing. We did not reach Blackwick Castle till late in the afternoon of the following day. The place was just as I had conceived it—as I have already described it. And a sense of gloom settled upon me as our car jolted us over the rough road that led through the Gorge of the Winds—a gloom that deepened when we penetrated into the vast cold hall of the castle.

Mrs. Davenant, who had been informed by telegram of our arrival, received us cordially. She knew nothing of our actual mission, regarding us merely as friends of her husband's. She was most solicitous on his behalf, but there was something strained about her tone, and it made me feel vaguely uneasy. The impression that I got was that the woman was impelled to everything that she said or did by some force outside herself—but, of course, this was a conclusion that the circumstances I was aware of might easily have conduced to. In every other respect she was charming, and she had an extraordinary fascination of appearance and manner that made me readily understand the force of a remark made by Davenant during our journey.

"I want to live for Jessica's sake. Get her away from Blackwick, Vance, and I feel that all will be well. I'd go through hell to have her restored to me—as she was."

And now that I have seen Mrs. Davenant I realised what he meant by those last words. Her fascination was stronger than ever, but it was not a natural fascination—not that of a normal woman, such as she had been. It was the fascination of a Circe, of a witch, of an enchantress—and as such was irresistible.

We had strong proof of the evil within her soon after our arrival. It was a test that Vance had quietly prepared. Davenant had mentioned that no flowers grew at Blackwick, and Vance declared that we must take some with us as a present for the lady of the house. He purchased a bouquet of pure white roses at the little town where we left the train, for the motor-car had been sent to meet us.

Soon after our arrival he presented these to Mrs. Davenant. She took them, it seemed to me nervously, and hardly had her hand touched them before they fell to pieces, in a shower of crumpled petals, to the floor.

"We must act at once," said Vance to me when we were descending to dinner that night. "There must be no delay."

"What are you afraid of?" I whispered.

"Davenant has been absent a week," he replied grimly. "He is stronger than when he went away, but not strong enough to survive the loss of more blood. He must be protected. There is danger tonight."

"You mean from his wife?" I shuddered at the ghastliness of the suggestion.

"That is what time will show." Vance turned to me and added a few words with intense earnestness. "Mrs. Davenant, Dexter, is at present hovering between two conditions. The evil thing has not yet completely mastered her—you remember what Davenant said, how she would beg him to go away and at the next moment entreat him to stay? She has made a struggle, but she is gradually succumbing, and this last week, spent here alone, has strengthened the evil. And that is what I have got to fight, Dexter—it is to be a contest of will, a contest that will go on silently till one or the other obtains the mastery. If you watch you may see. Should a change show itself in Mrs. Davenant you will know that I have won."

Thus I knew the direction in which my friend proposed to act. It was to be a war of his will against the mysterious power that had laid its curse upon the house of MacThane. Mrs. Davenant must be released from the fatal charm that held her.

And I, knowing what was going on, was able to watch and understand. I realised that the silent contest had begun even while we sat at dinner. Mrs. Davenant ate practically nothing and seemed ill at ease; she fidgeted in her chair, talked a great deal, and laughed—it was the laugh without a smile, as Davenant had described it. And as soon as she was able she withdrew.

Later, as we sat in the drawing-room, I could still feel the clash of wills. The air in the room felt electric and heavy, charged with tremendous but invisible forces. And outside, round the castle, the wind whistled and shrieked and moaned—it was as if all the dead and gone MacThanes, a grim army, had collected to fight the battle of their race.

And all this while we four in the drawing-room were sitting and talking the ordinary commonplaces of after-dinner conversation! That was the extraordinary part of it—Paul Davenant suspected nothing, and I, who knew, had to play my part. But I hardly took my eyes from Jessica's face. When would the change come, or was it, indeed, too late?

At last Davenant rose and remarked that he was tired and would go to bed. There was no need for Jessica to hurry. He would sleep that night in his dressing-room, and did not want to be disturbed.

And it was at that moment, as his lips met hers in a good night kiss, as she wreathed her enchantress arms about him, careless of our presence, her eyes gleaming hungrily, that the change came.

It came with a fierce and threatening shriek of wind, and a rattling of the casement, as if the horde of ghosts without was about to break in upon us. A long, quivering sigh escaped from Jessica's lips, her arms fell from her husband's shoulders, and she drew back, swaying a little from side to side.

"Paul," she cried, and somehow the whole timbre of her voice was changed, "what a wretch I've been to bring you back to Blackwick, ill as you are! But we'll go away, dear; yes, I'll go, too. Oh, will you take me away—take me away tomorrow?" She spoke with an intense earnestness—unconscious all the time of what had been happening to her. Long shudders were convulsing her frame. "I don't know why I've wanted to stay here," she kept repeating. "I hate the place, really—it's evil—evil."

Having heard these words I exulted, for surely Vance's success was assured. But I was soon to learn that the danger was not yet past.

Husband and wife separated, each going to their own room. I noticed the grateful, if mystified, glance that Davenant threw at Vance, vaguely aware, as he must have been, that my friend was somehow responsible for what had happened. It was settled that plans for departure were to be discussed on the morrow.

"I have succeeded," Vance said hurriedly, when we were alone, "but the change may be transitory. I must keep watch tonight. Go you to bed, Dexter, there is nothing that you can do."

I obeyed—though I would sooner have kept watch, too—watch against a danger of which I had no understanding. I went to my room, a gloomy and sparsely furnished apartment, but I knew that it was quite impossible for me to think of sleeping. And so, dressed as I was, I went and sat by the open window, for now the wind that had raged round the castle had died down to a low moaning in the pine trees—a whimpering of time-worn agony.

And it was as I sat thus that I became aware of a white figure that stole out from the castle by a door I could not see, and, with hands clasped, ran swiftly across the terrace to the wood. I had but a momentary glance, but I felt convinced that the figure was that of Jessica Davenant.

And instinctively I knew that some great danger was imminent. It was, I think, the suggestion of despair conveyed by those clasped hands. At any rate, I did not hesitate. My window was some height from the ground, but the wall below was ivy-clad and afforded good foot-hold. The descent was quite easy. I achieved it, and was just in time to take up the pursuit in the right direction, which was into the thickness of the wood that clung to the slope of the hill.

I shall never forget that wild chase. There was just sufficient room to enable me to follow the rough path, which, luckily, since I had now lost sight of my quarry, was the only possible way that she could have taken; there were no intersecting tracks, and the wood was too thick on either side to permit of deviation.

And the wood seemed full of dreadful sound—moaning and wailing and hideous laughter. The wind, of course, and the screaming of night birds—once I felt the fluttering of wings in close proximity to my face. But I could not rid myself of the thought that I, in turn, was being pursued, that the forces of hell were combined against me.

The path came to an abrupt end on the border of the sombre

lake that I have already mentioned. And now I realised that I was indeed only just in time, for before me, plunging knee-deep in the water, I recognised the white-clad figure of the woman I had been pursuing. Hearing my footsteps, she turned her head, and then threw up her arms and screamed. Her red hair fell in heavy masses about her shoulders, and her face, as I saw it that moment, was hardly human for the agony of remorse that it depicted.

"Go!" she screamed. "For God's sake let me die!"

But I was by her side almost as she spoke. She struggled with me—sought vainly to tear herself from my clasp—implored me, with panting breath, to let her drown.

"It's the only way to save him!" she gasped. "Don't you understand that I am a thing accursed? For it is I—I—who have sapped his lifeblood! I know it now, the truth has been revealed to me tonight! I am a vampire, without hope in this world or the next, so for his sake—for the sake of his unborn child—let me die—let me die!"

Was ever so terrible an appeal made? Yet I—what could I do? Gently I overcame her resistance and drew her back to shore. By the time I reached it she was lying a dead weight upon my arm. I laid her down upon a mossy bank, and, kneeling by her side, gazed into her face.

And then I knew that I had done well. For the face I looked upon was not that of Jessica the vampire, as I had seen it that afternoon, it was the face of Jessica, the woman whom Paul Davenant had loved.

And later Aylmer Vance had his tale to tell.

"I waited," he said, "until I knew that Davenant was asleep, and then I stole into his room to watch by his bedside. And presently she came, as I guessed she would, the vampire, the accursed thing that has preyed upon the souls of her kin, making them like to herself when they too have passed into Shadowland, and gathering sustenance for her horrid task from the blood of those who are alien to her race. Paul's body and Jessica's soul—it is for one and the other, Dexter, that we have fought."

"You mean," I hesitated, "Zaida, the witch!"

"Even so," he agreed. "Here is the evil spirit that has fallen like a blight upon the house of MacThane. But now I think she may be exorcised for ever."

"Tell me."

"She came to Paul Davenant last night, as she must have done before, in the guise of his wife. You know that Jessica bears a strong resemblance to her ancestress. He opened his arms, but she was foiled of her prey, for I had taken my precautions; I had placed That upon Davenant's breast while he slept which robbed the vampire of her power of ill. She sped wailing from the room—a shadow—she who a minute before had looked at him with Jessica's eyes and spoken to him with Jessica's voice. Her red lips were Jessica's lips, and they were close to his when his eyes opened and he saw her as she was—a hideous phantom of the corruption of the ages. And so the spell was removed, and she fled away to the place whence she had come—"

He paused. "And now?" I inquired.

"Blackwick Castle must be razed to the ground," he replied. "That is the only way. Every stone of it, every brick, must be ground to powder and burnt with fire, for therein is the cause of all the evil. Davenant has consented."

"And Mrs. Davenant?"

"I think," Vance answered cautiously, "that all may be well with her. The curse will be removed with the destruction of the castle. She has not—thanks to you—perished under its influence. She was less guilty than she imagined—herself preyed upon rather than preying. But can't you understand her remorse when she realised, as she was bound to realise, the part she had played? And the knowledge of the child to come—its fatal inheritance—"

"I understand," I muttered with a shudder. And then, under my breath, I whispered, "Thank God!"

�֍

Bram Stoker

(1847–1912)

BRAM STOKER WOULD HAVE been astonished at his current fame—his books analyzed by literary critics, his name appearing in movie titles, his villain not only a household name around the world but even the unofficial tourist mascot of Romania. No author left a greater mark on the genre than the creator of Dracula, the character whose name is now synonymous with *vampire*. Stoker lacked the urbanity of Sheridan Le Fanu and the champagne wit of M. R. James, but he possessed more than his share of passion and verve.

Abraham Stoker was born in 1847 in Clontarf, a suburb of Dublin, his father a civil servant and his mother a social activist. In childhood he suffered from a mysterious illness—one whose nature was never satisfactorily diagnosed—that kept him bedridden until the age of seven. Then he experienced an almost total recovery. Later, at the University of Dublin, the former invalid was more athletic than scholarly, but he served as president of a philosophical debating society and gained renown for a paper prophetically titled "Sensationalism in Fiction and Society." The author of the shamelessly sensational *Dracula* also wrote *The Duties of Clerks of Petty Sessions in Ireland*. But he didn't stay long in such work. Dissatisfied with the civil-servant job he had let his father talk him into, he began writing theater criticism for the *Dublin Evening Mail* by the early 1870s—in which position Le Fanu was his editor—and also published his first short story. Then came three short novels in the single year of 1875, each published in the Dublin magazine the *Shamrock*.

After Stoker reviewed a production of *Hamlet*, its star, Henry Irving, became his correspondent and then close friend. In 1878 Irving offered Stoker the job of business manager of his new Lyceum Theatre in London. The same year, Stoker married the famously beautiful Florence Balcombe, who had been his childhood love but had since been courted by various men—including Oscar Wilde, of all people—and the next year she gave birth to a son. But Stoker was seldom home. He had begun the total absorption into the world of the theater and the life of Henry Irving that would occupy much of his time until Irving's death in 1905. And, yes, from early on the relationship between them was described as vampiric, in that Irving seemed to take so much more than he gave.

Stoker published *Dracula* in 1897. "Rich in sensations," said the *Daily News*, and the *Pall Mall Gazette* enthusiastically pronounced the novel "horrid and creepy to the last degree." But a San Francisco paper called the *Wave* declaimed solemnly, "If you have the bad taste, after this warning, to attempt the book, you will read on to the finish, as I did,—and go to bed, as I did, feeling furtively of your throat." The following story first appeared in the collection that Stoker's widow published two years after his death, *Dracula's Guest and Other Weird Stories*. "It was originally excised owing to the length of the book," claimed Florence Stoker in her introduction, but most scholars now argue that she must have been mistaken; what we now call "Dracula's Guest" must have been part of an earlier draft. For one thing, the narrator isn't identified as Jonathan Harker, the character who first journeys to the Balkans in *Dracula*. He also behaves quite differently in his reckless disregard for danger.

The story takes place on Walpurgisnacht. This ancient holiday occurs on the last day of April, the eve of May Day, precisely the other side of the year from Halloween. Like Halloween, it is a time of celebration by default because of what follows it. Halloween is a party for the damned before their enemies come marching in on All Saints' Day on November 1; Walpurgis Night is much the same before the feast of Saint Walburga on May 1. Just as early Christians timed Easter to coincide with the vernal equinox and established Christmas to supplant pagan carousing in honor of the winter solstice, so does the date for celebrating Walburga seem to have been prescribed as an antidote to the pagan antics on May Day, which honor the return of warmth and sunshine after the rigors of winter.

The Quatre Saisons (Four Seasons) hotel at which the narrator stays opened in 1858 under the auspices of King Maximilian and still stands in Munich under its German name, Vier Jahreszeiten, now part of the Kempinksi chain. This may be the only detail in the story that holds up under scrutiny; the rest of the plot demonstrates Stoker's usual disregard for consistency. As Leslie Klinger points out, at first the narrator can't speak German but later he can, and he has no trouble reading tombstone inscriptions that are in German and Russian. But as always, it isn't Stoker's details that we care about. It's his crazy, over-the-top atmosphere.

Dracula's Guest

W HEN WE STARTED FOR our drive the sun was shining brightly
on Munich and the air was full of the joyousness of early summer. Just as we were about to depart, Herr Delbrück (the maître
d'hôtel of the Quatre Saisons, where I was staying) came down,
bareheaded, to the carriage and, after wishing me a pleasant drive,
said to the coachman, still holding his hand on the handle of the
carriage door: "Remember you are back by nightfall. The sky
looks bright but there is a shiver in the north wind that says there
may be a sudden storm. But I am sure you will not be late." Here
he smiled and added, "For you know what night it is."

Johann answered with an emphatic, *"Ja, mein Herr,"* and, touching his hat, drove off quickly. When we had cleared the town, I said,
after signalling to him to stop: "Tell me, Johann, what is tonight?"

He crossed himself as he answered laconically: "Walpurgisnacht." Then he took out his watch, a great, old-fashioned German
silver thing as big as a turnip, and looked at it, with his eyebrows
gathered together and a little impatient shrug of his shoulders. I realized that this was his way of respectfully protesting against the unnecessary delay and sank back in the carriage, merely motioning him
to proceed. He started off rapidly, as if to make up for lost time. Every now and then the horses seemed to throw up their heads and
sniffed the air suspiciously. On such occasions I often looked round

in alarm. The road was pretty bleak, for we were traversing a sort of high, wind-swept plateau. As we drove, I saw a road that looked but little used and which seemed to dip through a little, winding valley. It looked so inviting that, even at the risk of offending him, I called Johann to stop—and when he had pulled up I told him I would like to drive down that road. He made all sorts of excuses and frequently crossed himself as he spoke. This somewhat piqued my curiosity so I asked him various questions. He answered fencingly and repeatedly looked at his watch in protest. Finally I said: "Well, Johann, I want to go down this road. I shall not ask you to come unless you like; but tell me why you do not like to go, that is all I ask." For answer he seemed to throw himself off the box, so quickly did he reach the ground. Then he stretched out his hands appealingly to me and implored me not to go. There was just enough of English mixed with the German for me to understand the drift of his talk. He seemed always just about to tell me something—the very idea of which evidently frightened him, but each time he pulled himself up, saying, as he crossed himself: "Walpurgisnacht!"

I tried to argue with him, but it was difficult to argue with a man when I did not know his language. The advantage certainly rested with him, for although he began to speak in English, of a very crude and broken kind, he always got excited and broke into his native tongue—and every time he did so he looked at his watch. Then the horses became restless and sniffed the air. At this he grew very pale and, looking around in a frightened way, he suddenly jumped forward, took them by the bridles and led them on some twenty feet. I followed and asked why he had done this. For answer he crossed himself, pointed to the spot we had left, and drew his carriage in the direction of the other road, indicating a cross, and said, first in German, then in English: "Buried him—him what killed themselves."

I remembered the old custom of burying suicides at cross-roads: "Ah! I see, a suicide. How interesting!" But for the life of me I could not make out why the horses were frightened.

Whilst we were talking we heard a sort of sound between a yelp and a bark. It was far away, but the horses got very restless and it took Johann all his time to quiet them. He was pale and said, "It sounds like a wolf—but yet there are no wolves here now."

"No?" I said, questioning him; "isn't it long since the wolves were so near the city?"

"Long, long," he answered, "in the spring and summer, but with the snow the wolves have been here not so long."

Whilst he was petting the horses and trying to quiet them, dark clouds drifted rapidly across the sky. The sunshine passed away and a breath of cold wind seemed to drift past us. It was only a breath, however, and more in the nature of a warning than a fact, for the sun came out brightly again. Johann looked under his lifted hand at the horizon and said: "The storm of snow, he comes before long time." Then he looked at his watch again and, straightway, holding his reins firmly—for the horses were still pawing the ground restlessly and shaking their heads—he climbed to his box as though the time had come for proceeding on our journey.

I felt a little obstinate and did not at once get into the carriage.

"Tell me," I said, "about this place where the road leads," and I pointed down.

Again he crossed himself and mumbled a prayer before he answered, "It is unholy."

"What is unholy?" I enquired.

"The village."

"Then there is a village?"

"No, no. No one lives there hundreds of years." My curiosity was piqued. "But you said there was a village."

"There was."

"Where is it now?"

Whereupon he burst out into a long story in German and English, so mixed up that I could not quite understand exactly what he said, but roughly I gathered that long ago, hundreds of years, men had died there and been buried in their graves; and sounds were heard under the clay and when the graves were opened, men and women were found rosy with life, and their mouths red with blood. And so, in haste to save their lives (aye, and their souls!—and here he crossed himself) those who were left fled away to other places, where the living lived and the dead were dead and not—not something. He was evidently afraid to speak the last words. As he proceeded with his narration he grew more and more excited. It seemed as if his imagination had got hold of him and he ended in a perfect paroxysm of fear—white-faced, perspiring, trembling and looking round him, as if expecting that some dreadful presence would manifest itself there in the bright sunshine on the open plain. Finally, in an agony of desperation, he cried: "Walpurgisnacht!" and pointed to the carriage for me to get in. All my English blood rose at this and, standing back, I said: "You are afraid, Johann—you are afraid. Go home, I shall return alone; the walk will do me good." The carriage door was open. I took from the seat my oak walking-stick—which I always carry on my holiday excursions—and closed the door, pointing back to Munich, and said, "Go home, Johann—Walpurgisnacht doesn't concern Englishmen."

The horses were now more restive than ever and Johann was trying to hold them in, while excitedly imploring me not to do anything so foolish. I pitied the poor fellow, he was deeply in earnest, but all the same I could not help laughing. His English was quite gone now. In his anxiety he had forgotten that his only means of making me understand was to talk my language, so he jabbered away in his native German. It began to be a little tedious. After giving the direction, "Home!" I turned to go down the cross-road into the valley.

With a despairing gesture, Johann turned his horses towards Munich. I leaned on my stick and looked after him. He went slowly along the road for a while: then there came over the crest of the hill a man tall and thin. I could see so much in the distance. When he drew near the horses, they began to jump and kick about, then to scream with terror. Johann could not hold them in; they bolted down the road, running away madly. I watched them out of sight, then looked for the stranger, but I found that he, too, was gone.

With a light heart I turned down the side road through the deepening valley to which Johann had objected. There was not the slightest reason, that I could see, for his objection, and I daresay I tramped for a couple of hours without thinking of time or distance, and certainly without seeing a person or a house. So far as the place was concerned it was desolation itself. But I did not notice this particularly till, on turning a bend in the road, I came upon a scattered fringe of wood; then I recognized that I had been impressed unconsciously by the desolation of the region through which I had passed.

I sat down to rest myself and began to look around. It struck me that it was considerably colder than it had been at the commencement of my walk—a sort of sighing sound seemed to be around me, with, now and then, high overhead, a sort of muffled roar. Looking upwards I noticed that great thick clouds were drifting rapidly across the sky from north to south at a great height. There were signs of coming storm in some lofty stratum of the air. I was a little chilly and, thinking that it was the sitting still after the exercise of walking, I resumed my journey.

The ground I passed over was now much more picturesque. There were no striking objects that the eye might single out, but in all there was a charm of beauty. I took little heed of time and it was only when the deepening twilight forced itself upon me that I began to think of how I should find my way home. The brightness of the day had gone. The air was cold and the drifting of clouds high overhead was more marked. They were accompanied by a sort of far-away rushing sound, through which seemed to come at intervals that mysterious cry which the driver had said came from a wolf. For a while I hesitated. I had said I would see the deserted village, so on I went and presently came on a wide stretch of open country, shut in by hills all around. Their sides were covered with trees which spread down to the plain, dotting, in clumps, the gentler slopes and hollows which showed here and there. I followed with my eye the winding of the road and saw that it curved close to one of the densest of these clumps and was lost behind it.

As I looked there came a cold shiver in the air and the snow began to fall. I thought of the miles and miles of bleak country I had passed and then hurried on to seek the shelter of the wood in front. Darker and darker grew the sky and faster and heavier fell the snow, till the earth before and around me was a glistening white carpet, the farther edge of which was lost in misty vagueness. The road was here but crude and when on the level its boundaries were not so marked, as when it passed through the cuttings; and in a little while I found that I must have strayed from it, for I missed underfoot the hard surface and my feet sank deeper in the grass and moss. Then the wind grew strong and blew with ever increasing force, till I was fain to run before it. The air became icy cold and in spite of my exercise I began to suffer. The snow was now falling so thickly and whirling around me in such rapid eddies that I could hardly keep my eyes open. Every now and then the heavens were torn asunder by vivid lightning, and in the flashes I could see ahead of me a great mass of trees, chiefly yew and cypress, all heavily coated with snow.

I was soon amongst the shelter of the trees, and there, in comparative silence, I could hear the rush of the wind high overhead. Presently the blackness of the storm had become merged in the darkness of the night. By and by the storm seemed to be passing away: it now only came in fierce puffs or blasts. At such moments the weird sound of the wolf appeared to be echoed by many similar sounds around me.

Now and again, through the black mass of drifting cloud, came a straggling ray of moonlight, which lit up the expanse and showed me that I was at the edge of a dense mass of cypress and yew trees. As the snow had ceased to fall, I walked out from the shelter and began to investigate more closely. It appeared to me that, amongst so many old foundations as I had passed, there might be still standing a house in which, though in ruins, I could find some sort of shelter for a while. As I skirted the edge of the copse I found that a

low wall encircled it, and following this I presently found an opening. Here the cypresses formed an alley leading up to a square mass
of some kind of building. Just as I caught sight of this, however, the
drifting clouds obscured the moon and I passed up the path in darkness. The wind must have grown colder, for I felt myself shiver as I
walked; but there was hope of shelter and I groped my way blindly
on.

I stopped, for there was a sudden stillness. The storm had passed
and, perhaps in sympathy with nature's silence, my heart seemed to
cease to beat. But this was only momentarily, for suddenly the
moonlight broke through the clouds, showing me that I was in a
graveyard and that the square object before me was a great massive
tomb of marble, as white as the snow that lay on and all around it.
With the moonlight there came a fierce sigh of the storm, which
appeared to resume its course with a long, low howl, as of many
dogs or wolves. I was awed and shocked and felt the cold perceptibly
grow upon me till it seemed to grip me by the heart. Then, while
the flood of moonlight still fell on the marble tomb, the storm gave
further evidence of renewing, as though it was returning on its
track. Impelled by some sort of fascination I approached the sepulchre to see what it was and why such a thing stood alone in such a
place. I walked around it and read, over the Doric door, in German:

COUNTESS DOLINGEN OF GRATZ

IN STYRIA

SOUGHT AND FOUND DEATH

1801

On the top of the tomb, seemingly driven through the solid
marble—for the structure was composed of a few vast blocks of
stone—was a great iron spike or stake. On going to the back I saw,
graven in great Russian letters:

THE DEAD TRAVEL FAST

There was something so weird and uncanny about the whole thing that it gave me a turn and made me feel quite faint. I began to wish, for the first time, that I had taken Johann's advice. Here a thought struck me, which came under almost mysterious circumstances and with a terrible shock. This was Walpurgis Night!

Walpurgis Night, when, according to the belief of millions of people, the devil was abroad—when the graves were opened and the dead came forth and walked. When evil things of earth and air and water held revel. This very place the driver had specially shunned. This was the depopulated village of centuries ago. This was where the suicide lay; and this was the place where I was alone—unmanned, shivering with cold in a shroud of snow with a wild storm gathering again upon me! It took all my philosophy, all the religion I had been taught, all my courage, not to collapse in a paroxysm of fright.

And now a perfect tornado burst upon me. The ground shook as though thousands of horses thundered across it, and this time the storm bore on its icy wings, not snow, but great hailstones which drove with such violence that they might have come from the thongs of Balearic slingers—hailstones that beat down leaf and branch and made the shelter of the cypresses of no more avail than though their stems were standing corn. At the first I had rushed to the nearest tree, but I was soon fain to leave it and seek the only spot that seemed to afford refuge, the deep Doric doorway of the marble tomb. There, crouching against the massive bronze door, I gained a certain amount of protection from the beating of the hailstones, for now they only drove against me as they ricocheted from the ground and the side of the marble.

As I leaned against the door it moved slightly and opened inwards. The shelter of even a tomb was welcome in that pitiless tempest and I was about to enter it when there came a flash of forked lightning that lit up the whole expanse of the heavens. In the instant, as I am a living man, I saw, as my eyes were turned into the darkness of the tomb, a beautiful woman with rounded cheeks and red lips, seemingly sleeping on a bier. As the thunder broke overhead I was grasped as by the hand of a giant and hurled out into the storm. The whole thing was so sudden that, before I could realize the shock, moral as well as physical, I found the hailstones beating me down. At the same time I had a strange, dominating feeling that I was not alone. I looked towards the tomb. Just then there came another blinding flash, which seemed to strike the iron stake that surmounted the tomb and to pour through to the earth, blasting and crumbling the marble, as in a burst of flame. The dead woman rose for a moment of agony, while she was lapped in the flame, and her bitter scream of pain was drowned in the thunder-crash. The last thing I heard was this mingling of dreadful sound, as again I was seized in the giant-grasp and dragged away, while the hailstones beat on me, and the air around seemed reverberant with the howling of wolves. The last sight that I remembered was a vague, white, moving mass, as if all the graves around me had sent out the phantoms of their sheeted-dead, and that they were closing in on me through the white cloudiness of the driving hail.

GRADUALLY THERE CAME A sort of vague beginning of conscious-ness, then a sense of weariness that was dreadful. For a time I re-membered nothing, but slowly my senses returned. My feet seemed positively racked with pain, yet I could not move them. They seemed to be numbed. There was an icy feeling at the back of my neck and all down my spine, and my ears, like my feet, were dead, yet in torment; but there was in my breast a sense of warmth which was, by comparison, delicious. It was as a nightmare—a physical nightmare, if one may use such an expression—for some heavy weight on my chest made it difficult for me to breathe.

This period of semi-lethargy seemed to remain a long time, and as it faded away I must have slept or swooned. Then came a sort of loathing, like the first stage of sea-sickness, and a wild desire to be free from something—I knew not what. A vast stillness enveloped me, as though all the world were asleep or dead—only broken by the low panting as of some animal close to me. I felt a warm rasping at my throat, then came a consciousness of the awful truth, which chilled me to the heart and sent the blood surging up through my brain. Some great animal was lying on me and now licking my throat. I feared to stir, for some instinct of prudence bade me lie still, but the brute seemed to realize that there was now some change in me, for it raised its head. Through my eyelashes I saw above me the two great flaming eyes of a gigantic wolf. Its sharp white teeth gleamed in the gaping red mouth and I could feel its hot breath fierce and acrid upon me.

For another spell of time I remembered no more. Then I became conscious of a low growl, followed by a yelp, renewed again and again. Then, seemingly very far away, I heard a "Holloa! holloa!" as of many voices calling in unison. Cautiously I raised my head and looked in the direction whence the sound came, but the cemetery blocked my view. The wolf still continued to yelp in a strange way and a red glare began to move round the grove of cypresses, as though following the sound. As the voices drew closer, the wolf yelped faster and louder. I feared to make either sound or motion. Nearer came the red glow, over the white pall which stretched into the darkness around me. Then all at once from beyond the trees there came at a trot a troop of horsemen bearing torches. The wolf rose from my breast and made for the cemetery. I saw one of the horsemen (soldiers, by their caps and their long military cloaks) raise his carbine and take aim. A companion knocked up his arm, and I heard the ball whizz over my head. He had evidently taken my body for that of the wolf. Another sighted the animal as it slunk away and a shot followed. Then, at a gallop, the troop rode forward—some towards me, others following the wolf as it disappeared amongst the snow-clad cypresses.

As they drew nearer I tried to move, but was powerless, although I could see and hear all that went on around me. Two or three of the soldiers jumped from their horses and knelt beside me. One of them raised my head and placed his hand over my heart.

"Good news, comrades!" he cried. "His heart still beats!"

Then some brandy was poured down my throat; it put vigour into me and I was able to open my eyes fully and look around. Lights and shadows were moving among the trees and I heard men call to one another. They drew together, uttering frightened exclamations, and the lights flashed as the others came pouring out of the cemetery pell-mell, like men possessed. When the farther ones came close to us, those who were around me asked them eagerly: "Well, have you found him?"

The reply rang out hurriedly: "No! no! Come away quick—quick! This is no place to stay, and on this of all nights!"

"What was it?" was the question, asked in all manner of keys. The answer came variously and all indefinitely as though the men were moved by some common impulse to speak, yet were restrained by some common fear from giving their thoughts.

"It—it—indeed!" gibbered one, whose wits had plainly given out for the moment.

"A wolf—and yet not a wolf!" another put in shudderingly.

"No use trying for him without the sacred bullet," a third remarked in a more ordinary manner.

"Serve us right for coming out on this night! Truly we have earned our thousand marks!" were the ejaculations of a fourth.

"There was blood on the broken marble," another said after a pause—"the lightning never brought that there. And for him—is he safe? Look at his throat! See, comrades, the wolf has been lying on him and keeping his blood warm."

The officer looked at my throat and replied: "He is all right, the skin is not pierced. What does it all mean? We should never have found him but for the yelping of the wolf."

"What became of it?" asked the man who was holding up my head and who seemed the least panic stricken of the party, for his hands were steady and without tremor. On his sleeve was the chevron of a petty officer.

"It went to its home," answered the man, whose long face was pallid and who actually shook with terror as he glanced around him fearfully. "There are graves enough there in which it may lie. Come, comrades—come quickly! Let us leave this cursed spot."

The officer raised me to a sitting posture, as he uttered a word of command, then several men placed me upon a horse. He sprang to the saddle behind me, took me in his arms, gave the word to advance and, turning our faces away from the cypresses, we rode away in swift, military order.

As yet my tongue refused its office and I was perforce silent. I must have fallen asleep, for the next thing I remembered was finding myself standing up, supported by a soldier on each side of me. It was almost broad daylight and to the north a red streak of sunlight was reflected, like a path of blood, over the waste of snow. The officer was telling the men to say nothing of what they had seen, except that they found an English stranger, guarded by a large dog.

"Dog! that was no dog," cut in the man who had exhibited such fear. "I think I know a wolf when I see one."

The young officer answered calmly: "I said a dog."

"Dog!" reiterated the other ironically. It was evident that his courage was rising with the sun and, pointing to me, he said, "Look at his throat. Is that the work of a dog, master?"

Instinctively I raised my hand to my throat, and as I touched it I cried out in pain. The men crowded round to look, some stooping down from their saddles, and again there came the calm voice of the young officer: "A dog, as I said. If aught else were said we should only be laughed at."

I was then mounted behind a trooper and we rode on into the suburbs of Munich. Here we came across a stray carriage, into which I was lifted, and it was driven off to the Quatre Saisons—the young officer accompanying me, whilst a trooper followed with his horse and the others rode off to their barracks.

When we arrived, Herr Delbrück rushed so quickly down the steps to meet me that it was apparent he had been watching within. Taking me by both hands he solicitously led me in. The officer saluted me and was turning to withdraw when I recognized his purpose, and insisted that he should come to my rooms. Over a glass of wine I warmly thanked him and his brave comrades for saving me. He replied simply that he was more than glad and that Herr Delbrück had at the first taken steps to make all the searching party pleased; at which ambiguous utterance the maître d'hôtel smiled, while the officer pleaded duty and withdrew.

"But Herr Delbrück," I enquired, "how and why was it that the soldiers searched for me?"

He shrugged his shoulders, as if in depreciation of his own deed, as he replied: "I was so fortunate as to obtain leave from the commander of the regiment in which I served, to ask for volunteers."

"But how did you know I was lost?" I asked.

"The driver came hither with the remains of his carriage, which had been upset when the horses ran away."

"But surely you would not send a search-party of soldiers merely on this account?"

"Oh, no!" he answered, "but even before the coachman arrived I had this telegram from the Boyar whose guest you are," and he took from his pocket a telegram which he handed to me, and I read:

BISTRITZ

Be careful of my guest—his safety is most precious to me. Should aught happen to him, or if he be missed, spare nothing to find him and ensure his safety. He is English and therefore adventurous. There are often dangers from snow and wolves and night. Lose not a moment if you suspect harm to him. I answer your zeal with my fortune—Dracula.

As I held the telegram in my hand the room seemed to whirl around me, and if the attentive maître d'hôtel had not caught me I think I should have fallen. There was something so strange in all this, something so weird and impossible to imagine, that there grew on me a sense of my being in some way the sport of opposite forces—the mere vague idea of which seemed in a way to paralyze me. I was certainly under some form of mysterious protection. From a distant country had come, in the very nick of time, a message that took me out of the danger of the snow-sleep and the jaws of the wolf.

Acknowledgments

FIRST I WANT TO thank George Gibson, publisher of Walker Books and Bloomsbury USA. On a sunny Los Angeles day on the UCLA campus, during the annual *L.A. Times* Festival of Books, George came up to me after I finished a panel discussion about Victorian crime fiction and said, "Michael, what do you think about doing an anthology of Victorian vampire stories?" The more we talked, the more excited we got. Soon my wonderful agent, Heide Lange, and I discussed the idea over lunch in New York, and she and George turned it into a book contract. My thanks also to Heide's charming and resourceful assistants, Jennifer Linnan and Tara Singh. At Walker, George was a perfect editor, both for overall conception and for line-by-line critique. My thanks also to George's assistants, Margaret Maloney, production editor Nathaniel Knaebel, book designer Jiyeon Dew, jacket designer Amy King, and assistant publicity director Michelle Blankenship. Thank you Nick Owchar, for inviting me to the L.A. book festival. On the same L.A. panel was Leslie Klinger, editor of those beautiful and essential volumes, *The New Annotated Dracula* and *The New Annotated Sherlock Holmes*; Les later suggested stories, gave general advice, critiqued my introduction, and provided contacts. Jon Erickson provided sources, computer advice, and insight, as usual. Perpetual gratitude to the staff of the Greensburg Hempfield Area Library, especially library director Cesare Muccari, as well as Cindy Dull and Linda Matey, whose interlibrary endeavors are essential. My thanks also to Maria Browning, Tom Mayer, Margaret Renkl, Michael Rose, Maria Tatar, Mark Wait, Craig and Robin Weirum (and Isa and Olivia), and Alana White. As always—for her suggestions and criticism, her intelligence and wit—I thank a talented scholar and wonderful woman, Laura Sloan Patterson, my wife.

�֍

Bibliography and Suggested Further Reading

THIS BIBLIOGRAPHY INCLUDES ALL sources cited in, or useful in the writing of, this book's introductory essay or its individual story introductions. It also includes certain biographies, general introductions to the topic of vampire literature, and other commentaries on particular authors and themes. It excludes works by those authors whose stories or excerpts appear in this anthology and thus receive attention in the biographical note that introduces their contribution.

Asma, Stephen. *On Monsters: An Unnatural History of Our Worst Fears*. Oxford: Oxford University Press, 2009.

Auerbach, Nina. *Our Vampires, Ourselves*. Chicago: University of Chicago Press, 1997.

Barber, Paul. *Vampires, Burial, and Death: Folklore and Reality*. Yale University Press, 1990.

Bartlett, Wayne, and Flavia Idriceanu, *Legends of Blood: The Vampire in History and Myth*. Westport, CT: Praeger, 2006.

Chabon, Michael. Introduction to *Casting the Runes and Other Ghost Stories*, by M. R. James. Oxford: Oxford University Press, 2002.

Frayling, Christopher. *Vampyres: Lord Byron to Count Dracula*. London: Faber and Faber, 1991.

Frayling, Christopher. *Nightmare: The Birth of Horror*. London: BBC Books, 1996.

The Ghosts & Scholars M. R. James Newsletter, online at http://www .users.globalnet.co.uk/~pardos/GS.html.

Gothic Faery Tales, online at http://gothicfaerytales.com/.

Grosskurth, Phyllis. *Byron: The Flawed Angel*. Boston: Houghton Mifflin, 1997.

Hitchcock, Susan Tyler. *Frankenstein: A Cultural History* (New York: W. W. Norton, 2008).

Huet, Marie-Hélène. "Deadly Fears: Dom Augustin Calmet's Vampires and the Rule over Death," *Eighteenth-Century Life*, 21.2 (1997)

Kendrick, Walter. *The Thrill of Fear: 250 Years of Scary Entertainment*. New York: Grove Weidenfeld, 1991.

King, Melanie. *The Dying Game: A Curious History of Death*. London: One World, 2008.

Klinger, Leslie S., editor. *The New Annotated Dracula*. New York: W. W. Norton, 2008.

The Literary Gothic, online at http://www.litgothic.com/index_fl. html.

MacDonald, D. L. *Poor Polidori*. Toronto: University of Toronto Press, 1991.

Marchand, Leslie. *Byron: A Portrait*. Reprint, Chicago: University of Chicago Press, 1979.

Moskowitz, Sam, editor. *Horrors Unknown: Newly Discovered Masterpieces by Great Names in Fantastic Terror*. New York, Walker, 1971.

Fitz-James O'Brien, *The Supernatural Tales of Fitz-James O'Brien* (New York: Doubleday, 1988), edited with an introduction and notes by Jessica Amanda Salmonson. Volume I comprises *Macabre Tales* and Volume II *Dream Tales and Fantasies*.

Schutt, Bill. *Dark Banquet: Blood and the Curious Lives of Blood-Feeding Creatures*. New York: Harmony, 2008.

Skal, David J. *Hollywood Gothic: The Tangled Web of Dracula from Novel to Stage to Screen.* Revised edition, New York: Faber & Faber, 2004.

Skal, David J. *The Monster Show: A Cultural History of Horror.* New York: W. W. Norton, 1993.

Skal, David. J. *Vampires: Encounters with the Undead.* New York: Black Dog & Leventhal, 2001.

A Thin Ghost. A site devoted to M. R. James, at http://www.thin-ghost.co.uk/.

Wolf, Leonard. *Dracula: The Connoisseur's Guide.* New York: Broadway Books, 1997.

Wolle, Francis. *Fitz-James O'Brien: A Literary Bohemian of the Eighteen-Fifties.* Boulder: University of Colorado, 1944.

A Note on the Author

MICHAEL SIMS is the author of four nonfiction books: *Darwin's Orchestra*, *Adam's Navel*, *Apollo's Fire*, and a companion book to the National Geographic Channel series *In the Womb: Animals*. His three previous literary collections include *The Annotated Archy and Mehitabel*, *The Penguin Book of Gaslight Crime*, and *Arsène Lupin, Gentleman-Thief*. His writing has appeared in many periodicals in the U.S. and abroad, including the *New Statesman*, *Washington Post*, *Orion*, *American Archaeology*, the *Chronicle of Higher Education*, and many others. He speaks often at colleges and other institutions and has appeared on many TV and radio programs, from CBS's *The Early Show* and *Inside Edition* to a BBC Radio series about the human body. His Web site is www.michaelsimsbooks.com.